WAYNE D. OVERHOLSER

**Twice Winner of the Golden Spur Award
and Winner of the Western Writers of America
Lifetime Achievement Award!**

THE LONG WIND

The women screamed. Miles turned to them, saying, "I don't like the idea of getting my head blowed off." He must have heard the rattle of the buggy then, for he turned and stood waiting while Jess and Farrar came up. The settler slowly got to his feet, one hand rubbing his face where Miles had struck him.

"Howdy, Farrar," Miles said. "Ain't you off your reservation?"

Miles was a tall man, Jess saw, with a bronze, fine-featured face. He was handsome in a way that would appeal to most women, Jess thought, and in this first glance he saw nothing in the man's appearance that indicated he was as tough as Farrar considered him. A slow rage began building in Jess as he stared at Miles, who was fifty pounds heavier than the man he had knocked down and half his age....

THE SNAKE STOMPER

Kim pulled Delaney into the hall, his left arm still hard against the man's throat, then let go. Delaney, with nothing to support him, went down, his head rapping against the floor. He lay on his back, half-stunned. Kim dropped on him, knees slamming into the man's hard-muscled belly and driving the breath out of him. He swung his right fist to Delaney's jaw. When he rose, Delaney lay still.

Wheeling, Kim plunged through the doorway. Rocky and Della were on the ground at the base of the steps, Rocky saying softly, "This way, Kim...."

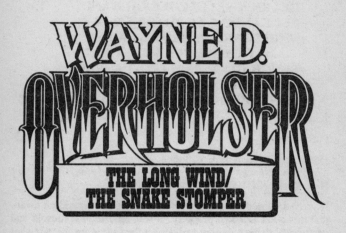

WAYNE D. OVERHOLSER

THE LONG WIND/ THE SNAKE STOMPER

LEISURE BOOKS   **NEW YORK CITY**

A LEISURE BOOK®

June 1996

Published by

Dorchester Publishing Co., Inc.
276 Fifth Avenue
New York, NY 10001

THE LONG WIND Copyright © 1953 by Joseph Wayne

THE SNAKE STOMPER Copyright © 1951 by Joseph Wayne

Printed in the United States of America.

For
DAVID and ROSA LEE
whose long lives along the Frenchman represent
the best of American pioneer tradition...
and
WAYNE and PEARL LEE
who carry on that tradition.

WAYNE D. OVERHOLSER

THE LONG WIND

FOREWORD

There was the land, prairie land that swept away on all sides of a man as far as he could see. It ran in long swells, tipping up out there to meet the downward thrust of the sky; it dropped off into the narrow meandering valley that had been carved out of the face of the prairie by the sluggish Frenchman River; it lay to the south in the lumpy barrier that was the sand hills.

There was the sky, so blue at times that it made other skies pale by comparison. It was a changing sky that held a pale sun giving light but little heat, or a sun that was a fiery ball making a dry earth still drier, or a gentle sun that stirred life in the grass roots until the brown of winter became the soft green of spring. At night it held the stars and perhaps a sterile moon that gave light only by the grace of an absent sun. It was a gigantic saucer overturned upon the earth. It was infinity.

And there was the wind. It could be bitter, dry, and cold, stealing the breath from a man's lungs. Or a blizzard blinding a man and leaving him dying within ten feet of his soddy door. It could be a scorching blast sucking life from the crops until corn stood yellow in the fields while the hopes in a man's heart withered and died. Or great gusts carrying the red devil of a prairie fire across the land. And at times it could be a welcome breeze as soft as a baby's kiss. It was nature's sword that with one thrust could destroy everything a man had built; it was man's ally bringing rain to soak a parched earth, an answer to his prayer. It was the long wind.

This was western Nebraska on the Frenchman where the strong survived and the weak retreated or were destroyed, where many gambled their sweat and labor and hopes against a hostile land.

And there were some who won.

Chapter One

MAN ON A HORSE

SHEER accident brought Jess Dawson to the man, an accident that gave shape to his future. He was not sure when he had crossed the line from Colorado into Nebraska. There were no markers, no roads, no fences; just sky and wind and the land that lay in long rolls all around him and reached out to meet the horizon.

Somewhere to the west Jess had crossed the South Platte. Since then he had ridden steadily eastward, putting miles behind him, lost in a land without people, and liking it that way. He had nothing to do; he had nowhere to go. He had been satisfied, but now a vague unrest was in him.

He dismounted beside a lagoon and loosening the cinches, stood patiently while his black gelding drank. He was a slender, long-boned man with sun-bleached blue eyes and brown hair; his hands were big, his fingers long. Wind and sun had darkened his face until it was the color of old mahogany, a young face marked by a sober, unbending mouth. Jess Dawson had almost lost the gift of laughter.

This was late April. The sun, far to the west now, was still nursing the buffalo grass with its warmth. The grass was like a low-piled green carpet with here and there a brown reminder of the winter that was gone, as crinkly as the buffalo hair from which it received its name.

When the gelding had satisfied its thirst, Jess tightened the cinches and mounting, rode east again. He topped a ridge and reined up, surprised. Below him a man was unhitching a team from a buggy. One of the horses raised his head and whinnied. The man looked up, saw Jess, and lifted a hand in friendly greeting.

Jess rode down the slope, wondering about the man's presence in this empty country. He had not met anyone for three days, and as far as he knew, there was no town within fifty miles. He had seen cattle, so there would be ranches, but when he reached the buggy, he saw that this fellow was no rancher.

"Evening, son," the man said.

"Howdy." Jess nodded, remaining in the saddle.

For a moment the man's eyes were fixed on Jess in a wary appraisal, and Jess used the same moment to make a cool study of the other. He was big, but he ran more to fat than muscles, and his face held a network of fine veins that gave him a florid appearance. He wore a wide-brimmed black hat, string tie, and frock coat. A well-fed preacher, Jess guessed, and thought irritably that in a few minutes the man would be inquiring into the condition of his soul.

"Been a damned fine day, now hasn't it?" The fat man threw back his shoulders, drawing a great breath into his bellows-like lungs. "Yes sir, makes you feel young and skittish as a colt."

The man was no preacher. Jess said, "Hadn't noticed."

"Light and cool your saddle, son," the man said. "I was just making camp. Heading into the sand hills to Long Tom Ansell's ranch, but I got lost. You one of Ansell's hands?"

"No."

The fat man shrugged. "You look like a cowboy, and most of the cowboys hereabouts ride for Ansell. Been aiming to drop in on him, but I've been too busy." He shook his head as if regretting his lack of leisure. "You wouldn't believe it, looking at me, but I've lost ten pounds in the last month. Been scratching like a hen in a rock pile. Country's sure filling up."

Jess swung down, his second guess pegging the man as a promoter. He had seen his kind in the mining camps. They all ran to a pattern, glib of tongue and filled with false heartiness, men with soft hands who possessed a talent for painting pretty word pictures for prospective suckers who might be carrying a fat money belt.

The fat man held out his hand. "Coe Farrar, at your service, sir. I have little in the way of food to offer, but what I have is yours."

"Jess Dawson," Jess said, gripping the man's hand and finding it as soft and moist as he expected.

Farrar frowned thoughtfully, eyes turning to the black gelding and swinging again to Jess. He asked, "Stranger in these parts?"

"That's right."

Farrar stood motionless, the thoughtful frown still creasing his forehead. His gaze ran down Jess' stringy figure from his sweat-stained Stetson to the scuffed boots, and lifted to rest briefly on the walnut-handled .44 in the tied-down holster. He glanced at the horse and the Winchester in the scabbard, his thoughts as easy to read as words on a printed page. He was tabbing Jess as a tough, a man on the dodge.

"I'll take care of my team," Farrar said briskly. "Then I'll see about supper."

"Where's the state line?" Jess asked.

Farrar smiled. "Twenty miles behind you, son. In case you're worried about sheriffs, you can put your mind to ease, although to tell the truth, I wish we had a little more law and order in these parts. Farmers are coming in now, and they're in the habit of looking to someone to settle their troubles."

Jess stripped his black and rubbed him down, an almost forgotten bitterness in him again, the bitterness of a man who had bet too much on a single wager and lost. But he had been luckier than most, for he carried two thousand dollars in his money belt, a fact which partially sweetened the sourness in his mind.

Slowly Jess walked back to where the fat man was building a fire of buffalo chips. Color had spread across the western sky and the wind had died as it often did at this time of day. Jess was thankful for the stillness. The constant prairie wind had honed his temper thin.

Farrar dribbled Arbuckle's coffee into his fire-blackened pot. He returned the sack to his grub box and brought bacon and a frying pan to the fire. "Reckon you're from Colorado," Farrar said in the offhand way of one who seeks information without asking for it.

Jess nodded. "Leadville."

Farrar glanced up. "Leadville, eh? They tell me that's quite a camp. Still on the boom?"

"For the lucky ones."

"I take it you weren't lucky."

Jess shrugged. "I ain't complaining."

"Well sir, you sure got into a different kind of country. Leadville's on top of the mountains, I hear. Trees all around, aren't there?"

"Stumps," Jess said. "And mine dumps. Miners play hell with a country."

"Well now, this is different. I haven't seen a real tree for quite a spell. There's one hackberry tree on the Frenchman in a ten-mile stretch. Six feet tall and as big around at the butt as your wrist. You wouldn't call that a tree, now would you?"

"No."

Jess rustled more buffalo chips as Farrar started the bacon frying. When Jess returned to the fire, Farrar had set out a sack of dry biscuits and tin cups and plates.

"Prairie coal is a wonderful thing," Farrar said. "Handy, I mean. Down south of Dodge City the settlers used to pay the Texas Drivers to lay over a night on their land so they'd have fuel for the winter. Back home the women wouldn't have dreamed of burning anything like that. Just goes to show how folks adapt themselves to a new country."

"You don't last if you don't adapt yourself," Jess said.

"That's right," Farrar agreed. "Take the American farmer. Uncle Sam gives him a quarter section of unplowed land and he'll make a living on it. Take right here. Won't be three years till this grass is plowed up and there'll be corn all around us." He pulled the frying pan off the fire. "Help yourself, Dawson."

While they ate, Farrar rattled on, "You haven't said what you're looking for. Isn't mining, that's sure. In case you've got your eyes open for a big opportunity to get ahead, this is as good a country as you'll find. I own the Lariat townsite." He jerked a hand toward the northeast. "Yonder a piece."

"Never heard of it," Jess said.

Farrar laughed. "No sir, I don't suppose you have, but there'll come a day when everybody has heard of Lariat. It's not a year old, but it's quite a burg already. Farmers coming in by the hundreds. That's what'll make my town, Dawson. Farmers and farmer trade. Inside of a year we'll have five hundred people. We'll get a railroad and then we'll have thousands. Those who invest their money in Lariat will be living on milk and honey while the doubters and the unbelievers will go on scraping for their next meal."

Jess ate, saying nothing. He had pegged the fat man all right. A glib tongue given to making easy promises. A promoter was the same anywhere you found him whether he had mining stock or a townsite to sell.

The farmers would come, sucked into the baited web of Farrar's promises. They would take land and the money they had brought with them would flow into Farrar's town to fatten his purse. If they starved out and grass grew again in Lariat's street, Coe Farrar would be somewhere else, looking for a new crop of suckers.

Jess had another cup of coffee, still saying nothing. He had made his own way since he was twelve, taking the hardest knocks life could give him and returning them when occasion demanded. Freighter, stage driver, farmer, cowboy, lawman: he had been all of those and more. He had always been able to take care of himself until he had started his own business and learned that money power was one force he could not lick by gun or fist.

It was dark now, the last trace of the sunset gone from the western horizon. The stars were out, glittering with cool, distant brilliance. Farrar had disappeared into the darkness. Jess lay with his head on his saddle, staring at the star patterns. The wind was up again, dry and chill, and Jess shivered. He threw more chips on the fire and settled back, a cigarette in the corner of his mouth.

Farrar, Jess thought, had gone into his spiel on the off chance that he might be talking to a man who had a few dollars in his pocket and would gamble on a quick profit by buying a town lot. It was all right for Farrar to go on thinking he had hooked a sucker, but he was wrong. On the other hand, there was a possibility that Jess might turn this situation to his own profit. Perhaps Farrar needed a man who was handy with his gun and his fists.

Farrar returned to the fire, whistling tunelessly, and dropped down on the other side of the smouldering chips from Jess. "A mite chilly tonight." He took a cigar from his coat pocket and lighting it, blew out a plume of smoke that was soon lost in the wind. "Coyotes are tuning up. I kind of like to hear 'em sing. I figure they're giving the farmers a welcome. In a year from now there'll be young chickens and turkeys for 'em."

"Paradise for coyotes," Jess said.

"Paradise for settlers, too," Farrar said quickly. "For those that have the guts to tame the land, I mean. That's what it takes, taming. It's a great sullen beast now, but once it's tamed and made to produce, this will be a land flowing with milk and honey."

You damned faker, Jess thought. *You damned, slick-tongued faker*. But he didn't say it. There was no use to antagonize the man.

"I am not a farmer," Farrar went on, "but I believe in this country so much that I've sunk every nickel I have into the townsite and the businesses I've started." He took off his hat and laid it beside him, his long, dark hair carefully brushed. "The farmers gamble their labor; I gamble my money. If we lose, we lose together and we both go broke."

Jess sat up. "Farrar, I never saw a promoter who didn't have his troubles. If you're smart, you'll take out some insurance against them troubles."

Farrar took his cigar out of his mouth, surprised eyes on Jess. "Now what are you getting at, friend?"

"I might take a job." Jess tapped his gun. "If the pay was good."

Farrar laughed and put the cigar back into his mouth.

"You've got gall, friend. I don't know anything about you. I don't even know what you were doing in Leadville."

"I owned a stage line."

"You gave it up?"

"You might say I gave it away, but I didn't do so bad at that. I got out with a little money."

Farrar smiled genially. "Then you're the kind of man I'm looking for. We don't need a stage line, but there are countless opportunities in Lariat. Ride into town with me tomorrow. Be my guest at the hotel. Look around. If you don't like what you see, ride on. You'll be under no obligation."

"You didn't savvy what I said. I'm looking for a job."

Farrar waved his words aside with a sweeping gesture of a fat hand. "Dawson, you're not the kind of man who works for wages. You want an opportunity to get ahead on your own, and I tell you this country is full of such opportunities. I've always been proud of my judgment of men, and you strike me as a fellow who'll stick if you like the country. Of course if you're the sort who has to look at a mountain now and then, you won't fit in the flatlands. You'd better head back for the Rockies."

"I like it where it ain't crowded," Jess said, "but that ain't the point. I thought I made it plain. I ain't looking for an investment. I'm looking for a job. Now quit trying to sell me something I don't want."

Farrar chewed on his cigar for a moment, studying Jess' dark face in the smoky light of the fire. "I see," he said. "Perhaps we might combine the two, although I'm still wondering if you'll like this country."

"The only thing I don't like is the wind."

"Ever find a place where it don't blow?"

"This is different. It don't let up."

Farrar rose and tossed his cigar stub into the fire. "I like to think of the wind as the breath of the Lord, stirring a man's thoughts and feelings which is something we need to have done for us. Be pretty damned stagnant if it didn't blow, now wouldn't it?"

Irritated by the man's talk, Jess said, "Save your gab for the farmers, Farrar. If you don't have a job for me, say so."

"Let me think it over. At least you can ride into Lariat with me tomorrow and take your look. You might change your mind about investing. Lots are cheap now." Farrar yawned. "Think I'll roll in."

For a time Jess lay awake, thinking of Leadville and the broken dreams that were behind him. He'd had a few months when the future glittered with promise, and he had put everything he had saved into his stage business. Once a day he had driven his coach from Leadville to a new camp on up the mountain and back to Leadville. Icy roads and bad weather had never stopped him, but the powers in Leadville had.

You played on the side of the big boys or you didn't play. That was the way it had worked in Leadville, and now Jess had no illusions. It worked the same everywhere. They were all tied up together, the bankers, the mine owners, the barons of transportation. You belonged or you didn't. It was as simple as that.

You could be as independent as hell. You told yourself that in this country the little man had as much chance as the big one. All you had to do was to fight and hang on. So he'd fought and he'd hung on and he'd nearly starved.

Delays. Red tape. Opposition at every turn. Then the mail contract that would have saved him had been given to the biggest stage line operating out of Leadville. He had been warned when he'd started, and his enemies had made good their warning.

It was sell or go broke, so he'd sold, getting out with something when he could have walked out flat broke. The big company had made him an offer, a better offer than he had expected, evidently considering money a cheaper commodity than lives.

Now, looking back, he knew he had never really liked Leadville with its lawlessness and its greed, the eternal hammering of the big stamp mills, the taking without the slightest thought of giving back. But he had learned one thing. Get on the side of the big boys. Around here Farrar was the big one. Getting a job with him was the first step. The opportunity Farrar had talked about might come later, the kind of opportunity that would come only to those who were on the right side.

When Jess woke, it was dawn, and Farrar was building a fire. The wind was still running in across the grass from the northwest, cold and dry and piercing. Jess shivered as he threw back his saddle blanket and ran a hand through tousled brown hair. Farrar, he saw, was as immaculate as he had been the evening before, black hat on his head, frock coat buttoned, string tie neatly knotted.

"Good morning," Farrar said cheerfully. "Feel that cool, invigorating wind. Sometimes I wonder why this country has gone unsettled for so long."

"You thought about that job?"

Farrar smiled. "I'm still thinking, Dawson. Just ride along."

Looking at Farrar's fat, affable face, Jess felt a faint prickle of apprehension run down his spine. Then it was gone. There was no sound reason for it. All he had to do was to keep his eyes open while he earned his pay.

Chapter Two

LADDER

BY the time Farrar's team was hooked up and Jess' gelding saddled, the sun was two hours high in a clear sky. The wind still came from the northwest, cutting with a chill edge remindful of the winter that had passed. Jess untied his sheepskin from behind his saddle and put it on.

"A mite cold," Farrar observed as he pulled a buffalo robe over his knees, "but spring is at hand. Listen to those meadow larks caroling like the Lord's own creatures. They don't have to look at a calendar to know that it's spring.''

Farrar lifted the lines from the whipstock and spoke to the team. He took a southwest course across the grass, Jess riding beside him and wondering what the fat man's intentions were. Lariat was not in this direction.

They had gone a mile or more when Farrar said, ''We're taking a roundabout way to Lariat, but I don't suppose you're in a hurry.''

''No,'' Jess said. ''Time's one thing I've got.''

''I told you last night I got lost looking for Long Tom Ansell's ranch,'' Farrar said casually. ''The truth of the matter is I'm not a very good plainsman, but I believe I can find it today.''

They were in the sand hills now, low rolling ridges, each looking exactly like the others. When they topped one, there was another directly ahead. It gave Jess the weird feeling that he was moving steadily but getting nowhere. He could see how a man who was unable to take his directions from the sun would be lost here, and he wondered why Farrar, who seemed so completely out of place away from his town, was insisting on seeing this man Ansell.

There was little buffalo grass here. The sand hills were covered by a shaggy growth of vegetation that gave them an unkempt look as if needing a pruning shears. There were scattered clumps of sagebrush as high as the bed of the buggy, innumerable soapweed plants, stiff leaves jutting upward like sharp-pointed, unsheathed blades, and rank bunchgrass that Jess judged would be poor graze at best.

Life was all around them. Jess caught the white blur of a cottontail's rear as it darted ahead of them and disappeared. Blackbirds took wing in front of the horses and finding other grass stems at a safe distance, resumed their singing as they bobbed up and down. And lizards darted away in front of the horse's hoofs. A kangaroo rat leaped into the haven of the nearby sagebrush clump, while a sand turtle, escaping a buggy wheel by inches, continued his leisurely journey toward some secret destination, unperturbed by the invasion of these foreign giants.

It was a useless, low-growing jungle, Jess thought, harboring life that was peculiar to it. He burst out, "Farrar, is this damned country good for anything?"

Farrar laughed softly. "Why, it's good for them that live there, but I'd never encourage a farmer to settle in these hills. I reckon it's one place where the homesteaders won't bother the cowmen." He threw a big hand out in a wide gesture. "Lot of critters out yonder you don't see and they're doing right well, most of 'em. Half a dozen coyotes are watching us from that ridge top over there, likely. Might even be a gray wolf sneaking around. Badgers, too, and a whole passel of skunks and civet cats."

Farrar glanced at Jess, frowning, "I kind of like these sand hills just to ride through 'em, but I'm damned if I could live here like Long Tom Ansell does. Reminds me of a fundamental law of nature. Something's eternally after something else. A skunk is fixed up by nature so he gets along all right, but you take a cottontail now. He's got nothing but trouble. Always some coyote hanging around looking for a quick meal."

"Humans ain't no different," Jess said.

"I was just going to say that. Take this Ansell fellow. Got maybe five thousand head of range stock under his Ladder iron, although nobody seems to know where he got 'em. Anyhow, his critters are grazing as far north as the Frenchman. He used to be just a little man. Now he allows he's big. To my mind, there's nothing more bothersome than a little man who outgrows his britches."

"Ain't there any big outfits in the good grass?"

Farrar shook his head. "Used to be. Big spreads all along the Frenchman. Hancock's Rafter H and Vestry's Skull and some others, but they were all claiming land along the river they didn't own. They tell me Uncle Sam caught 'em at getting their land patented by fraud. Along the river, you know, so they'd control the water. Well, Uncle Sam moved 'em out, lock, stock and barrel, and they're over in Colorado and Wyoming now.''

Farrar reached for a cigar and bit off the end. "A vacuum's a dangerous condition, Dawson. When Vestry and Hancock pulled out, it left nothing. Takes time for the settlers to fill the country up. That's how Ansell got the notion he'd spread out. Got his patents legal enough, but he's claiming too much range. Some of the land south of the Frenchman is good. It'll be plowed up before fall, and Ansell will be so mad he'll have a mess of kittens.''

They rode in silence for a time, Farrar pulling on his cigar, Jess wondering what the fat man expected to do with Ansell. It was a familiar situation to Jess. Before he had gone to Leadville he had spent most of his life in the cow country, and he had learned to expect a fight when men came with plows.

"Ansell's a queer duck," Farrar said after a time. "He's got a ramrod who's downright ornery. Fellow named Lane Miles. They never come to Lariat. Only way to see 'em is to go to 'em.''

"Figure you'll do any good?"

"I've got to try," Farrar said somberly. "I can reason with most men. I'm hoping I can with Ansell. It'd save a pile of trouble if I can talk him into pulling his cattle back from the Frenchman.''

"If he's like most cowmen, you'll be wasting your wind.''

"He's not like anybody else. I'm a peaceful man, Dawson, but there are times when violence seems to be the only answer. If Lane Miles was dead, Ansell would find out he was a little man again.''

They moved deeper into the sand hills until Jess lost count of the number of times they climbed a ridge and went down the opposite side only to find themselves repeating the process. It was like being lost at sea with only the sun to give a clue to the direction they were traveling.

Near the middle of the morning they reached twin wagon

ruts that ran directly north and south. Farrar heaved a great sigh of relief, fat cheeks quivering as he shook his head. "Now what do you know about that? I've always been lucky, Dawson. This is proof that my luck is still good."

"What are you talking about?"

Farrar turned his team south to follow the ruts. "I'm not lost now. Ansell's place isn't far from here. Damned country swallows a man. Don't see how anybody gets around."

"I don't, neither. It's different in the mountains where you've got something to go by."

Farrar was staring ahead, frowning. He said suddenly, "A tough lot, these cowmen. They don't give a damn about developing the country. Drive their stock to Julesburg or Ogallala to the railroad. Do their trading there. Ansell or Miles or none of 'em have ever spent a dollar in Lariat."

"Ansell's outfit the only one around here?"

"You might say that. Oh, there's a few one-bull outfits scattered through the sand hills, but they don't amount to much."

Within the hour they reached Ladder's headquarters. It was a surprising ranch to Jess. The buildings were of sod, low and ugly and seeming to sprout out of the land itself. The main house was the biggest soddy Jess had ever seen, with deep-set windows and door. Smoke rose from the stove-pipe chimney to be immediately swept into oblivion by the wind.

The corrals were constructed of wire, the posts the only wood in sight with the exception of the doors and the window frames set in the sod walls of the buildings. There was a single horse in sight, a bay gelding in one of the smaller corrals. Jess could not hear any sound of human activity, and aside from the horse and the smoke, there was no sign of life anywhere about the place.

Farrar looped the lines around the whipstock. "My stomach says it's dinner time. Hope Ansell's got something on the stove."

Jess said softly, "Don't get down, Farrar," and easing his .44 from its holster, held it across the saddle horn.

A man strode out of the house, a Winchester cradled in his left arm, the thumb of his right hand on the hammer. Queer, Jess thought. Most cowmen would depend on a six-gun if they expected trouble, but this man did not even have a gun belt strapped around his lean middle.

"Howdy, Ansell," Farrar said affably. "How are things on Ladder?"

Ansell made no pretense of greeting his visitors or answering Farrar's question. He crossed the trodden earth of the yard, eyes flicking uneasily from Farrar to Jess and back to Farrar. He moved with quick, springy steps, Winchester held on the ready.

A tall man, this Long Tom Ansell, with thick-muscled arms and shoulders, and legs that were inordinately long and skinny. His eyes were jet black and smaller than average; his hair, worn so short that it stood prickly straight to the back of his head, was as black as his eyes and shiny under the noon-high sun.

"You ain't welcome, Farrar," Ansell said, his voice as grating as the squeal of a rusty gate hinge.

"Why, we just dropped in for a visit." Farrar seemed surprised by the cowman's words. "I've been aiming to get down to see you all spring, but I've been right busy."

"You mean your slick tongue's been busy making purty talk to the plow pushers. Well, I ain't listening to none of it."

"Don't cost nothing to listen," Farrar said. "A lot to be done. Country's settling up."

Ansell's black eyes were pinned on Jess. "Who's this?"

"Now I'm right sorry I forgot you boys hadn't met," Farrar said contritely. "Jess, this here is Long Tom Ansell. He owns Ladder and is one of the outstanding citizens of what is going to be Blake County. Tom, meet Jess Dawson."

"Howdy, Ansell," Jess said, his tone civil.

Ansell ran a big hand over his short hair, glowered at

Jess, then swung his gaze again to Farrar. "A hardcase if I ever saw one. What's he doing here?"

"I brought him along for company. Might be he is a hardcase. Leastwise it's my guess he's salty enough to take care of himself. Maybe you'd better put that Winchester down."

"I guess not," Ansell said. "Now I'll give you some advice. Leave your toughs on the other side of the Frenchman."

Farrar reached into his pocket for cigars and offered one to Ansell. "Have a smoke, Tom," he said, his voice still affable.

"Get your gabbing done and drift." Ansell ignored the proffered cigar. "I've got work to do if you ain't."

"We've all got work to do." Shrugging, Farrar replaced the cigars. "It's the kind of work that has been done in every new country and will be done here. We're building a town, Tom. A year from now you won't have to drive your beef to Ogallala or go there for supplies. We'll have a railroad. We'll have an organized county and appointed officials. Being an important man, you'll want to have a hand in these activities."

"You got the wrong coon," Ansell flung at him. "A county won't do nothing but increase my taxes. I don't need no railroad as long as my cows can walk to Ogallala or Julesburg. As for your town, take it and go to hell. I don't need it, neither."

The man was too proddy, Jess thought. He understood what Farrar had meant by saying he had outgrown his britches. He was scared. It was there in the way his eyes flicked from one of them to the other, in the nervous twitching of his mouth. Yet Ansell had nothing to be afraid of unless he forced a fight. His fear might have other causes, roots that went back to the days when he had been a small cowman, living alone here in the sand hills.

"We're here to talk," Jess said. "What are you afraid of, Ansell?"

"I ain't afraid of nothing," Ansell said in his grating

voice. "All the hardcases Farrar can buy don't scare me."

Farrar took a long breath. "Tom, we came here in a friendly spirit. If we reach an understanding now, we won't have bloodshed later."

"If there's bloodshed, it'll be of your making." Ansell's lips flattened against yellow teeth. "I started here with ten cows and a bull. Injuns was around." He motioned to a low-roofed dugout back of the house. "I fought 'em from right there. Lived in that damned hole for three years. There was buffler around then. Outlaws. I fought them, too. I never took nothing that wasn't mine. Vestry and Hancock got run out. Why? Because they were crooks trying to swindle the government. I'm still here. Why? Because I didn't steal nothing from nobody."

"I know, Tom," Farrar said. "But times are changing. Nothing can keep the farmers out. You've got two choices. Either you live with them peaceably, or you'll have 'em fighting you and eating your beef. I'm talking as a friend now."

"Friend!" Ansell said the word as if it were an oath. "You make my belly ache. You ain't a friend to nobody but Coe Farrar. I can smell your kind a mile off. Now dust before I put a window in your skull."

"You're wasting your wind, Farrar," Jess said testily. "Let's mosey."

But still Farrar held his eyes on Ansell who had worked himself into a fury. He might explode any minute like the faulty mainspring of a watch that had been too tightly wound. Jess felt a growing admiration for Farrar. There was a hard core of courage in him, and a patience that was beyond Jess' understanding.

"Just a minute, Dawson," Farrar said. "I'll make this plain, Tom. Keep your cattle off the grass along the Frenchman. Nobody will bother you if you stay in the sand hills, but there's some good land south of the river that will be settled. Don't try to run those people off."

"Keep your plow pushers north of the Frenchman and

there won't be no trouble," Ansell shouted, his voice made thin by his anger. "Now I won't tell you again to dust."

Ansell had thumbed back the hammer of his rifle, the barrel lined on Farrar's bulging middle. Jess said, "Mister, if you pull that trigger, you're a dead man."

Ansell's eyes remained on Farrar. "Tell your tough hand to get off Ladder range. If he comes around here again, he'll wind up with one of Lane Miles' slugs in his guts. That's a promise."

Farrar did not try again. He removed the lines from the whipstock, and speaking to his team, turned sharply and drove back over the twin ruts he had followed a short time before. Jess rode beside the buggy, half turned in the saddle so he could watch Ansell. The cowman, he thought, would not be above shooting a man in the back.

Ansell remained there until they were fifty yards away. He stood motionless, Winchester still held on the ready, a tall figure filled with the violence of his fury. Suddenly he wheeled and strode back into the house. Only then did Jess ease around in the saddle and glance at Farrar.

"I'd as soon crawl into bed with a rattlesnake as to trust that hombre," Jess said.

Farrar glanced up, licking dry lips. Tiny globules of sweat had broken through the skin of his face. He said, "So would I. I thought he'd be civil enough to give us dinner and be willing to listen."

"You're lucky I was along."

Farrar glanced at Jess. "I know. I should have warned you it might turn out this way, but damn it, I didn't think Ansell would be so unreasonable."

They were silent a moment, then Jess said, "Now what about that job?"

Farrar's eyes came to him again, this time giving him a searching look. "I can use a man like you. I thought I could last night, but I wanted to wait until after we'd seen Ansell. After watching you just now, I don't have the slightest doubt about you filling the bill. It's only temporary, but it'll pay you good while you look around for a business that suits you. I don't take you for a man who would work for wages indefinitely."

"No, I wouldn't," Jess agreed. "What sort of a job have you got in mind?"

"I need a man who knows what to do in a fight. Not a lawman, you understand. Someone who doesn't have his hands tied by a star. We might call you a trouble shooter."

"What's the pay?"

"One hundred dollars a month. I'll throw in a hotel room and your meals."

"You've hired yourself a hand," Jess said. "Just one string. I'll do my own thinking."

"I wouldn't want a man who couldn't think, Dawson," Farrar said quickly as if that would never be an issue between them.

So it was settled. Jess, looking ahead at the long rise before them, thought that this was what he wanted. For a time at least he would settle down here on the Frenchman. He wouldn't be alone beating his brains out fighting the big boys; he'd be on their side. Sure, it was what he wanted. Still, he failed to find the satisfaction in this arrangement that he should have. He wondered ruefully if a man who possessed a spirit as turbulent as his ever found exactly the thing he wanted.

Chapter Three

THE TULLYS

FOR WEEKS it had seemed to Sam Tully that half the farmers in the Middle West were moving with him to western Nebraska. He and his family had camped with other emigrants beside rivers and lagoons, at the edge of sprawling towns that had sprung up along the new railroads. Always the talk was the same, the kind of talk he had heard since he was a boy, and he was fifty now.

Too crowded back in Missouri and Iowa, they said. In Illinois and Indiana. Good enough in their fathers' and grandfathers' days when that country had been new, but hell, it had got so the bankers could pinch the fat right off a man's ribs. Wall Street was getting too big. Time Congress was whittling it down. If Congress didn't, they'd do it themselves.

Their great great grandfathers had known what to do with the red-coats back in Washington's day. Their own fathers had taken care of the Johnny Rebs in Lincoln's day. Some of them had had a hand in it themselves. Now, by all that was holy, they'd handle the bloated millionaires who sat on their rumps behind mahogany desks and squeezed the blood out of the little fellows. More silver dollars was what everybody needed, not less. Just let those big bankers try taking away the silver, and by grab, they'd get showed a thing or two.

Sam listened, but he contributed little to the talk. Most of his fellow travelers had callouses on their palms from years of battle with bucking plow handles. Some had enough money to buy seeds and supplies for the first year. But those who did the loudest talking were men who had failed before and would fail again. For them western Nebraska would be no different from Indiana and Illinois and Missouri.

So Sam listened to their talk, feeling superior to the windy ones. He had gone out to western Nebraska the fall before; he had picked his homestead and filed on it. He knew what he was getting. Most of them didn't. More than that, he believed in his destiny in a new land. He told himself he was the kind who could help build a civilization where there was none. He would be there when the failures had gone back home.

Regardless of what happened that first year, prairie fires or grass-hopper invasions or drought, Sam would make out. He had saved some money. Not enough to buy a

Missouri farm, but enough to get a start in a homestead country. He had been a renter, a fact that had filled him with discontent all his life. To Sam Tully the desperate hunger for land was the only thing that was more important than the welfare of his family. Now, in a few days, he'd be breaking sod that was his own.

He'd had a sale the fall before and had done well. He had hidden his money in a feather tick in the covered wagon, good hard money that would see them through the first year. After that they'd make out. He had bought a team of Percherons in Omaha where they had outfitted, three saddle horses, and a milk cow.

The wagon was tightly packed with field and garden seeds, food, clothing, cooking utensils, home remedies, and a small cook·stove. A grasshopper breaking plow was tied outside the wagon, a crate of Plymouth Rocks behind, and still he had some money left.

They'd make out fine. A man couldn't be licked who wouldn't be licked. He said it over and over in his mind from the day he had made the great decision until it had become a refrain, and he had bolstered his confidence with it. The only sour note was his wife's opposition to the move, her certainty of ultimate failure.

Now they were near the end of the journey. Josephine, his seventeen-year-old daughter, pointed ahead, crying out, "That it, Daddy? Is that Lariat?"

He raised himself in the stirrups, staring ahead at the bulge of the prairie, and nodded. Josephine's eyes were better than his, but he could make out the collection of houses huddled together as if seeking mutual protection in this lonely sweep of an otherwise empty land.

"That's it, Joe," he said. "That's Lariat. Our place ain't another day's travel on the other side." He swung around in the saddle, motioning to his wife on the wagon seat. "See it, Ruth? That's Lariat."

She nodded, her face gravely sober. She had driven the Percherons most of the way from Omaha, partly because she didn't like to ride a horse, but mostly because·it gave her something to do, and she was a good hand with horses.

Sam had been willing to let her do the driving. Nineteen years of married life had taught him that there were times when he could be firm, and times when he couldn't. Ruth had come with him. That was all he could ask now. Her acceptance of the new life would come later.

Time. That was what Ruth needed. Time to get her roses started. A garden in. A hatching of chicks to care for. All the work of starting over. She would be with him in spirit then as well as body. He could not bring himself to think of it any other way.

Staring ahead at the town, Sam reminded himself that he was a lucky man to have Ruth for his wife. She was thirty-five, her dark brown hair showing only a trace of gray. In spite of the hard years on a rented farm, she was a round-bodied attractive woman with dark eyes that held a zest for living, a woman who could still command admiring stares from other men.

Her beauty was something else that added to Sam's feeling of superiority. Ruth was not like the other women he had seen along the trail since they had left Omaha, dowdy, flat-chested women who had been broken by constant moving and hard work, broken until their eyes were dead lamps set in sterile faces.

Sam threw a glance at Paula, his older girl not yet nineteen who rode beside him. She had her mother's dark hair and eyes, but in no other way were they alike. She was quiet and reserved, her thoughts often secrets that she seldom shared with anyone else in her family.

Paula had not voiced the slightest discontent over this move, but Sam felt she had not been happy about it. She was engaged to a boy back home, and although he had promised to come out in the fall, Sam was certain he wouldn't, a certainty that might have stemmed from the hope that he wouldn't come. Paula deserved the best and she had made a poor choice. That was one point on which Ruth and Sam agreed.

Paula had a boyishly slim body; she could ride a horse

better than Sam, and he had assured himself that she would like it out here where she could see for countless miles across the prairie to a far horizon. Now Sam found himself worrying about Paula more than Ruth. If Paula was unhappy, there would be no happiness for him. He was not sure why he loved her the way he did unless it was because she was his first born.

Josephine was the problem. She had been a worry to both Ruth and Sam from the time she had been a toddler. At seventeen she was physically mature. She had Sam's chestnut hair and gray eyes that held laughter as naturally as a clear swift stream reflected the glint of a bright sun, and she possessed a talent for attracting a man's admiration with one quick glance. That admiration, Sam knew, was essential to her, and when she discovered there were few men out here, she would be lonely and she would become sullen.

They reached Lariat in late afternoon. The wind that had been beating at them all day was lifting a gray haze from the rutted, wheel-marked street. Sam straightened in the saddle, his eyes brightening as he noted the changes that had come to the new town.

He had seen Lariat as a tent city the previous fall. Now bold false fronts crowded the street, the new lumber still yellow. Tall letters on a two-story building stated, LARIAT HOTEL, COE FARRAR, PROP. Across from it other letters read, LARIAT GENERAL STORE, COE FARRAR, PROP. On down the street a small building held the sign, LARIAT TOWNSITE COMPANY, COE FARRAR, PRES.

"This Coe Farrar must be a big man," Josephine said.

Sam smiled, thinking of Farrar's bulky body. "He's a big man, all right," he said, "a real big man."

There were a few rigs flanking the street, a half dozen saddle horses racked at the hitch poles, and some covered wagons. Knots of men stood on the boardwalk, blinking red-veined eyes as the wind whipped past them. A few raised hands in greeting and Sam nodded back, noticing that

Josephine was smiling brightly as she always did when she had an audience of men.

It was too late to reach the quarter section Sam had picked. It lay miles to the southwest on the Frenchman, the best piece of land in the country, or so the locator had told Sam. He had taken it because of the three-headed spring that bubbled out of the ground a short distance south of the river. He would build his soddy above the spring. Water would not be the problem it was on so many places out here. Ruth would like that.

They camped just east of the last sod house, each tending to the chores Sam had assigned them when they had left Omaha. It had always been a bitter disappointment to Sam that he did not have a son, but the years had taught him to accept his girls.

Paula milked the Jersey cow. The horses were cared for. The chickens in the crate lashed to the back of the wagon were fed, and water was placed in the pan. Chips were gathered for the fire. Coffee boiled. Sow belly and potatoes fried.

Sam never had reason to be dissatisfied over the way his women folks took their responsibilities. Even Josephine, too often given to day dreaming, was not afraid of work. It was something else Sam had to be thankful for. He hated a nagging note in a woman's voice, and he had heard many such tones at camping time along the trail. When Ruth grew so dissatisfied over something that she had to talk, she gave it to him in one direct volley, but she was not a nagger.

While they were eating, Paula asked, "Who is this Coe Farrar who had his name scattered all over Main Street?"

"The town father," Sam answered. "Owns most of Lariat. He's the one who ran advertisements in eastern newspapers about this country being ready for settlement."

"A promoter," Ruth said with some asperity.

"You could call him that," Sam admitted.

"What I don't understand is why this country has opened

up just now," Paula said. "The land's been here all the time."

"It's been here all right," Sam agreed, "but there were some big cattle outfits that made it hard on the settlers. Farrar told me they got their patents by fraud and the government moved them out."

Ruth rose to lift the coffeepot from the grate and filled their cups. "I can tell you another reason," she said. "The good land's gone. This is all that's left."

Sam patted the buffalo grass beside him. "Now don't say this ain't good land, Ruth. Dirt that will grow grass will grow other things."

There was an uneasy silence then, Sam glancing often at his wife's face. She hadn't said much for several days and it always worried him when she was in one of her silent moods. She was like a tea kettle gathering steam on a hot stove. Sooner or later she had to get it out of her system, and he had a growing fear that he was in for one of her verbal bombardments.

He finished his meal and laid his plate down. "I'm going into town to find the locator."

"Thought you knew where the place was," Ruth challenged.

"I do, but I figured it might save some time if he went with us tomorrow."

Sam saddled his horse and rode away, troubled now by growing doubts. Tomorrow Ruth would see the land that belonged to them. Not rented land. One hundred sixty acres that belonged to Sam and Ruth Tully. He had enough to pay the government and there would still be some left over. They would not wait the full five years to prove up on their homestead.

Now, with the chill wind driving in from the northwest, he pulled his coat up and around his neck, groping for the pleasure of anticipation that had been in him through the long weeks of travel that had brought them from Omaha out here to the very western end of Nebraska. But he found no pleasure, no satisfaction. He was too worried about

Ruth. He didn't know what she would say tomorrow when they reached their place.

He tried to put the doubts out of his mind, but suddenly his years lay heavily upon him. He was too old a man for Ruth. He should have thought what the future would be when they were married. And he was too old to start over. He wasn't even sure he was a pioneer, and a man had to be if he survived out here. The women, too.

There had been no future back home. He found some assurance in that thought. Renting year after year. Never really respected in the way a land owner was respected. Working from sunup to dark and past, but always improving some other man's land.

Well, he had done the right thing. He had to hold to that thought. Whatever a man did was the right thing, for it could not be undone. Moving westward had been the pattern of success in this country for generations. The danger from Indians was past. This took work and faith; he had never been afraid of work, and he had faith or he would not have started.

Reaching Lariat, he tied his horse in front of the townsite office. It was dusk now, lamps in the buildings along Main Street laying yellow spots against the gray dust. He turned into the office, seeing at once that the lanky man behind the desk was a stranger to him.

"Howdy," The lanky one rose and offered an inkstained hand. "I'm Jim Brennan, willing and able to do anything I can. Like selling you a year's subscription to the *Lariat Eagle*."

Sam shook hands. "Right now I'm looking for the locator."

"Bill Hays? Why, I haven't seen him today. Don't think he's in town."

"Farrar?"

"He's out of town, too. I'm holding down his desk till he gets back."

Sam hesitated, chewing on his thin lower lip. Brennan was watching him, a small smile curling his mouth as if he were amused by the prospect of this man forcing a living from the reluctant prairie.

Brennan was fifty or more, Sam judged, somewhat stooped with white hair that was closely cropped. He was not clean, and he smelled of whiskey and chewing tobacco. Sam's lips tightened as irritation stirred in him. He was tempted to tell Brennan that if either was superior, he was the one, but he knew no good would come of it.

"Anything I can tell Hays or Farrar for you?" Brennan asked.

"No. Just say that Sam Tully got here with his family. Hays located me south of the river. I thought I could get him to ride out there with me."

The small smile lingered on Brennan's lips. "Sorry he isn't around, Tully. I'm just the newspaper man, the voice of Lariat telling folks about the fine country we've got here. Our sawbones almost starves to death because the wind blows the germs plumb back to Missouri. That's why we have such a salubrious climate."

"I had purty good luck selling out last fall. I figure I'll pay out on my homestead after six months."

Brennan nodded. "Sooner you get title to your land the better. If a prairie fire burns you out, or the hoppers move in, you can borrow on your place from the bank."

"I'll never borrow," Sam said stiffly. "I've paid enough interest to Missouri bankers."

Sam turned toward the door, and swung back when Brennan asked, "Got a gun, Tully?"

"A shotgun. Why?"

Brennan shrugged skinny shoulders. "Prairie chickens make good eating, but you'll need a rifle for antelopes." He scratched the tip of his nose. "You say Hays located you south of the river?"

Sam nodded. "Why do you ask?"

"Just thinking, friend. You'll need a Winchester damned bad. I don't reckon any new country was tamed with just a plow."

Sam stared at Brennan, breathing hard. There was

something in the newspaper man's manner that sent a warning trickle down Sam's spine. He wanted to ask Brennan what he meant, but he sensed that the man would not say anything more definite than he had.

"I'll get along," Sam said, and walked out.

For a time Sam stood on the walk, listening to the banging of the piano from the saloon down the street. He could find talk there, and companionship to warm him along with the whiskey. For some reason a coldness he had not felt before began working along his spine. He decided against the drink. Ruth wouldn't like it if she knew.

Mounting, Sam rode back to the wagon. The fire had burned down until it made only a faint glow in the blackness. He made his bed under the wagon. Ruth and Paula slept inside, but Josephine usually slept between the front wheels. Sam pulled off his boots, being careful not to disturb Josephine, and lay back, drawing the quilts over him, but he did not sleep for a time.

Brennan's vague warning haunted him. He could not think of any danger. The Indians were gone. So were the cattlemen. There weren't many dangerous animals around. Farrar had said a few gray wolves were left. Perhaps that was what Brennan meant. Then gradually his uneasiness left him. He thought, *Tomorrow we'll be home.*

Habit got them up early, but they all knew they had little more than half a day's journey ahead of them, and they dawdled. Sam ate breakfast because he knew he needed food, not because he was hungry. His hat lay on the ground beside him, his bald head with the scraggly fringe of chestnut hair shiny bright in the morning sun.

In a way Sam was sorry this day had come. The pleasure of these past weeks of anticipation was gone. This was the end of the journey. Tomorrow work would start, turning the stubborn buffalo grass, sod that had lain undisturbed through the centuries. Planting a garden. Getting the camp set up so they could eat and sleep with some comfort. The past week had been dry, but the spring rains would come.

They would have to live in the wagon for awhile. Or if he

found that he needed it, he could remove the over-jet from the wagon and live under the canvas. Ruth would be after him to build a house, but the sod must be broken first and a crop planted. When he had time later in the summer, he would build a dugout.

Ruth wouldn't like it. She hated dirt worse than she hated sin, and when you lived in a dugout, you lived with dirt. It was overhead and underfoot and on all sides of you. Ruth would throw up her hands and cry, "I won't put my good rugs down in a place like this." Somehow he had to make her see that a frame house must wait at least until another summer. Luck and a good crop might make a real house possible later on. Now they must watch every nickel, hoarding their money against the hard days which lay ahead.

Sam finished his second cup of coffee and filled his pipe. The wind blew his first match out and he had to use a second. He rose, suddenly feeling very tired. It was because he hadn't slept well the night before, and knew at once it wasn't that. He was too old to start from scratch, just too old. Funny he hadn't thought of that when he had dreamed his dreams in Missouri.

"Hook up, Sam," Ruth said. "Let's get rolling. I want to see this heaven on earth you picked out for us, though a body wonders where you'd find any heaven in an ironed-out piece of . . ."

"It won't be so bad, Mother," Paula said. "There's a river, you know, and a spring."

Sam thanked her with a glance. Paula wouldn't use half the words in a day that Josephine would, but she had a talent for saying the right thing at the right time.

"You'll like it, Ruth," Sam said. "We won't have to worry about a well. That spring's good water. Not many springs out here, you know."

"Any trees?" Josephine asked.

"I can't remember seeing any," Sam admitted, "but we'll plant some."

"That will be nice," Ruth said sarcastically. "I always wanted some shade on my grave."

Sam turned away, pulling on his pipe. Ruth was building up, all right. He harnessed the Percherons and hooked up while Josephine threw gear on the saddle horses. Paula fed and watered the chickens, then brought the cow to the wagon and tied her behind it. Ruth packed up, the gathering storm showing on her face.

A wagon creaked by, the driver calling, "Where you from, Neighbor?"

"Missouri."

"We're from Illinois. On the Wabash. Where you bound?"

"I've got a place south of the Frenchman."

"Purty sandy down there, I hear. I like the hard ground myself."

The wagon rolled on. Ruth climbed to the seat and pushed her sunbonnet farther back on her head. As she took the lines, she asked, "Ever hear of sand in heaven, Mr. Tully?"

It was a bad sign when she called him *Mr. Tully*. "I've never been there," he said, "but it wouldn't surprise me if there was."

Sam mounted and pointed his horse southwest, wishing he had bought a Winchester in town. Well, he'd get one the next time he was in Lariat. Maybe Brennan meant there were outlaws around. The sand hills would be a good hiding place, at least until the country was organized.

They angled over one long roll of the prairie after another, Sam a little uncertain just where the river was and hoping Ruth wouldn't ask. They made noon camp, and went on, the wind beating at them with irritating constancy. Then, quite suddenly, they were dipping toward the river and the country seemed to grow smaller. The sand hills to the south and the uplands to the north cut down their view.

It was midafternoon when they reached the Frenchman, Sam plagued by the knowledge that they had wandered from their course and had traveled more miles than they should. The river was a meandering little stream with an occasional deep hole. A turtle's head appeared above the surface, and as Sam rode along the north bank, a flock of mallards took sudden flight and returned to the river farther downstream, skidding into the water feet foremost in their headlong way of breaking to a stop.

"You can put duck on the table any day you want to, Paula," Sam said. "In this country you can shoot our Thanksgiving dinner."

"Sam," Ruth called, "have you got the gall to say that this slough is a river?"

He nodded. "It's the Frenchman. Lot of fish in it, Hays said. Turtles as big as a dishpan, too. Hays told me they make good soup."

"Sam Tully, I don't care if there's alligators and lobsters. I wouldn't eat anything that came out of such a stinking mess."

He shrugged, wanting no argument today. "We'll go upstream a piece," he said. "Ought to be a ford along here somewhere."

Sam rode on. They'd follow. They'd have to now. Given a little time, Paula would talk her mother into accepting this new life. He wondered what he would have done without Paula. He realized now with a sudden rush of emotion that no son could have done as much for him as Paula had.

Josephine rode up beside him, her cheeks bright with excitement. "It's going to be fun," she said. "I'll catch fish and Paula can shoot ducks."

He nodded, not wanting at that moment to talk. The wind tugged at Josephine's hair, a loose strand fluttering above her eyes. Her round breasts rose and fell with her breathing. She wasn't one to look ahead. She never had been, but for this day at least she was happy. He glanced at her, thinking how much she looked like Ruth when they were married.

Half an hour later they reached wagon tracks that crossed the river and ran up the opposite bank and went on toward the sand hills to the south. Sam felt a sudden relaxation that came from relief. He remembered this ford. His spring wasn't far up the river.

He rode into the water. The water was deep, but they could cross. Reaching the south bank, he turned to wait for the wagon, motioning for Ruth to come on. He knew she could handle the crossing as well as he could.

Ruth made a wide swing and came directly at the stream, whipping up the horses so they lunged into their collars. Chain traces tight, they hit the river in a rush, the water sprewing out from hoofs and wheels. The ponderous wagon swayed perilously and almost stopped, wheels gripped by the mud, then they broke free, and the team labored up the south bank, great muscles knotted.

"Good," Sam called. "You could cross the plains with that outfit," and turned his horse upstream not waiting to hear what Ruth had to say.

Within a matter of minutes Sam reached the spring. Dismounting he knelt beside it, and cupping his hands in the cool water, raised them to his lips and drank. He rose and turned to wait for the girls and Ruth.

"This is it." He motioned to the flat above them. "Forty acres of good bottom land. That'll raise dandy hay. All we've got to do is to let the grass grow. Here's the spring. I figured we'd build yonder just above it so the water would be handy."

Ruth pulled up and wrapping the lines around the brake handle, stepped down. Before she could say anything, Sam swung a hand to the higher land south of the river. "That's where I'll break the first sod. Get in some corn right away. Some sorghum, too. Have to experiment a little. See what does the best. Think of it, Ruth, a quarter section that belongs to us. No stumps to grub out. No rocks to move. Just good deep soil."

Ruth looked at him, the kind of look that pushed him away from her. She said, "What fools we are, Sam, what fools to leave a settled country and come to a place like this."

Paula and Josephine had ridden up in time to hear what she said. They dismounted, Josephine saying, "I don't think we're fools."

And Paula, "Neither do I: It makes me feel kind of small, so much country around us, but I think we'll like it."

"You think we will, do you?" Ruth asked tartly. "We'll wait till the wind addles your brain for awhile and then we'll see what you say."

Paula was staring upstream, standing motionless as if she were frozen. Now she gripped Sam's arm. "Daddy, have you seen that?"

He turned quickly, alarmed by her tone. Breath sawed out of him as if he had been clubbed in the stomach. West of the spring there was the low sod wall of a dugout, and a roof with a projecting stove pipe for a chimney. Someone had jumped his claim. So that was what Brennan had meant when he'd said Sam would need a Winchester.

"Somebody beat us to it," Ruth cried. "What are you going to do, Mr. Tully?"

"I don't know," he said heavily. "I'll have to see."

This was the place. He couldn't be mistaken. The spring just above the ford. The bottom land along the river. No, this was the right place, the one he had filed on. Whoever was here had no right to this quarter section. If he couldn't drive the man off, he'd appeal to the law. There must be some kind of law out here, law that would protect a man's rights.

"So you brought us all this way for this," Ruth screamed. "I never wanted to come. I tried to talk some sense into you, but no, you knew it all. We'd own our land, you said. You hear me, Sam? You said we'd own it."

She stopped for breath. This was the explosion he had known was coming, but she never finished. A man shouted, "Look at that, Lane. A granger outfit."

Sam wheeled, frantically wishing he had taken the shotgun out of the wagon. It was probably the man who had jumped his claim. Then he saw there were three of them. He was wrong. They weren't settlers.

"Cowboys," Ruth whispered, shrinking back against a wagon wheel.

Sam glanced at her. She was afraid, terribly afraid. He brought his gaze back to the riders who were coming at a brisk pace along the river. Cowboys, all right. Stetsons, bandannas, chaps, guns in holsters. But Hays had said the big outfits had moved out. These men must be outlaws, coming out of the sand hills. Sam's thoughts turned to the money in the feather tick. They'd be killed. The wagons burned. No, they'd kill him and abuse his women folks.

At that moment Sam Tully felt the kind of fear he had never known before in his life, the same fear that gripped Ruth. It crept through his belly and up into his heart so that it beat at irregular intervals; it took the middle out of him and left him old and stooped and gray of face. He stood there, staring at the men who were riding up, the power of movement gone from him.

He had expected too much out here. He had never been able to give Ruth and the girls the things they had a right to expect from a husband and a father. He'd tried, but his trying hadn't been good enough.

The cowboys were there then. They reined up, the one in the middle touching his hat brim. He pinned his eyes on Josephine, frank speculation in them, and finally turned his head and nodded at Sam. He said in a courteous tone, "I'm sorry, friend. You're trespassing on our graze. You'll have to settle on the other side of the river."

Then something broke in Sam. He'd never fail again. It would be better to die than go back. He started toward the wagon in a desperate run, his mind fixed on one thing. He had to get the shotgun from the wagon.

Chapter Four

FIRST BLOOD

JESS and Farrar made a short noon stop to fry bacon and boil coffee. Farrar's frayed temper lay close to the surface. He had kept his calm front until he had left Ansell. Now there was no calmness in him.

"I wish I knew what Ansell was up to," Farrar said. "He's got quite a crew, five or six men. With Lane Miles leading 'em, they could raise Cain with the settlers south of the Frenchman."

"Keep your farmers north of the river."

"Can't do it. There's a dozen families located on this side already. Besides, the good land on the north side has been taken. That is, unless they go a long ways from Lariat."

"Then you'd have another town started."

"Which is one thing we can't allow." Farrar carried the grub box to the buggy. "I'd stand to lose everything if it did. The business would be split. We'd have a fight over the county seat. Might even have trouble getting the railroad into Lariat."

Jess kicked out the fire and swung into the saddle. They followed the wheel tracks, riding north, Farrar grumbling about prairie fare being all right for a meal or two, but it got mighty monotonous after awhile. Jess paid little attention, for his thoughts were on what Farrar had said about another town.

Townsite! New county! Railroad! It made a familiar pattern, and behind it there was always the scheming of men like Coe Farrar. Jess shrugged, thinking it made little difference to him, not if Farrar was paying a hundred dollars a month and was throwing in a hotel room and meals.

By midafternoon they were out of the sand hills and dropping down the slope toward the river. Farrar said, "I sure missed those tracks yesterday . . ." He paused and pulling his team to a stop, motioned upstream. "Take a look, Dawson."

Jess had already seen the covered wagon. Three women were beside it. A man stood some distance from them, his back held stiffly straight, eyes on the three riders who were motionless in their saddles. It was trouble, the kind of trouble any family could expect that attempted to settle south of the river.

"That's Lane Miles on the middle horse," Farrar said in a jerky voice. "The settlers must be some new family. They haven't got any business here. Dake Ennis owns this quarter section. He's a bachelor who used to live with the Indians and rode for Iliff . . ."

"Come on," Jess said.

"This isn't our put in . . ."

"We'll make it ours."

"No sense kicking Ansell in the teeth till we have to," Farrar said worriedly. "We'll go on to town . . ."

"Look, Farrar. You've been talking about what a tough hand this Lane Miles is. Well, if you want to show him he ain't running this country, you'll never find a better time than right now."

Jess touched up his gelding, Farrar following in the buggy. Apparently the people at the wagon were not aware that anyone else was around. The man who had been facing the three riders started toward the wagon, but Miles spurred his horse forward in a savage lunge that made the settler jump back to keep from being ridden down.

Jess heard the settler's frantic scream, "You trying to kill me?"

Miles swung down. "Climb into your wagon, mister. Roll back across the river and stay there. You hear?"

Again the settler started toward the wagon, shouting, "I ain't going nowhere. I'll get my shotgun and blow your damned head off."

Lane caught him by a shoulder and whirled him around; he hit the man in the face, a vicious blow that knocked the settler flat on his back in the grass. The women screamed. Miles turned to them, saying, "I don't like the idea of getting my head blowed off." He must have heard the rattle of the buggy then, for he turned and stood waiting while Jess and Farrar came up. The settler slowly got to his feet, one hand rubbing his face where Miles had struck him.

"Howdy, Farrar," Miles said. "Ain't you off your reservation?"

Miles was a tall man, Jess saw, with a bronze, fine-featured face. He was handsome in a way that would appeal to most women, Jess thought, and in this first glance he saw nothing in the man's appearance that indicated he was as tough as Farrar considered him. A slow rage began building in Jess as he stared at Miles who was fifty pounds heavier than the man he had knocked down and half his age.

"No," Farrar was saying, "I'm not off my reservation. We've been visiting your boss."

Miles jerked a hand toward Jess. "Who's that?"

"Jess Dawson. He's working for me."

The settler burst out. "Talk to this man, Mr. Farrar. You remember me, Sam Tully."

"Of course. You were in Lariat last fall."

"That's right. Hays located me here. Now this fellow says I can't stay and knocks me down."

"No excuse for that," Farrar said severely. "I'm sorry about it, but Miles is right when he says you can't stay here. You must be mistaken about where Hays located you. This quarter section was pre-empted some time ago. A man named Dake Ennis bought it last winter."

"I ain't mistaken," Tully cried. "I remember how it was, the spring and all."

Miles made a cool study of Jess and now ignored him. He stood between Tully and the wagon, an amused smile on his lips. Jess remained on his horse, holding his anger under a tight rein, and he took this moment to make his estimate of the women.

A handsome woman, older than the other two and probably their mother, stood with her back to a wagon wheel. The girls were young, seventeen or eighteen, Jess judged, one quite slender, the other roundly molded. Both were pretty, unexpectedly pretty for a homesteader's daughters, with the clean, washed appearance of decency about them that set them apart from the girls Jess had known in Leadville.

"You are mistaken," Farrar was saying patiently. "Come into town with me and we'll talk to Hays."

"Good idea," Miles said, "and don't give no more of these grangers the notion they can settle on this side of the river."

Jess had waited until he was sure Miles had pinned his attention on Farrar, then he swung down, drawing gun the instant his horse was between him and Miles. He stepped forward, saying, "Reach, all three of you."

Miles was caught flat-footed. It was, Jess thought, an indication of the man's supreme self-confidence. He had not expected trouble, assuming that Jess would make no move unless Farrar ordered it.

"What's this?" Miles demanded, bristling.

"It's like Farrar said. There wasn't no excuse for you piling into this man," Jess motioned to the mounted men. "I said reach. Make a try for your guns and Miles gets it in the brisket."

There was no hint of a smile now on Miles' handsome face. Jess, watching him closely, sensed an inner toughness in the man that had been missing in Long Tom Ansell. Ansell, as Farrar had said, was a little man who had suddenly become big. Miles was cut from a different bolt. Whatever strength Ladder possessed would come from him, not Ansell.

For a moment Miles hesitated, eyes searching Jess' dark face. He was trapped, Jess knew, with the devil's own choice. If he surrendered he would lose prestige, but he must have known that if he resisted, he'd get the bullet Jess promised. Slowly his hands lifted shoulder high.

"You're making a mistake, friend," Miles said.

"You made a bigger mistake getting tough with Tully."
Jess nodded at the other Ladder men. "I said to get 'em
up." They raised their hands, one starting to curse in a
flat, bitter voice. Jess said, "Shut up," and the man
became silent.

Tully moved forward eagerly. "I'll get their guns."

"Stay back," Jess said curtly. "Miles, drop your gun
belt." He motioned again to the other two. "Drop yours."

Tully stopped, puzzled. Miles unbuckled his gun belt
and let it go, asking, "What's this going to buy you,
friend?"

Jess waited until the mounted men had dropped their
gun belts into the grass. Then he said, "I don't know
anything about who owns this land, but I saw the play as I
rode up. What was he gonna do to you, Tully?"

"I . . . I don't know. Said we had to get back across the
river, but I wasn't gonna do no such thing. This is my
land."

"I'm new hereabouts," Jess said, "so I want to get one
thing clear. There used to be some big outfits on the river,
but they had to get off the range. When they were here,
Ladder stayed in the sand hills. That right, Farrar?"

"That's the way I heard it," Farrar said.

"Well then, Miles is out of line telling folks they can't
settle south of the river. That's right, too, ain't it?"

"Right as rain," Farrar said.

Now Jess had the answer to the question that had been
in his mind. Farrar would back him. Jess asked, "Got a
gun, Tully?"

"A shotgun."

"Get it."

"I'll get it," the slender girl said, and whirled toward the
wagon. A moment later she returned with the shotgun.
"What do you want me to do?"

"If these two boys make a move," Jess motioned toward
the men on the horses, "blow 'em out of their saddles.
Maybe you never killed a man before, but chances are you
will if you stay out here."

The girl's mouth was a taut line across her face. She said as if it were a cold statement of fact, "They won't move."

Jess wasn't sure about the older woman or the other girl, but this one would do. He handed his gun to Farrar. "Give her a hand if she needs it. Miles, in my book a man who'd pull this off in front of three women and scare 'em to death ain't got good manners. I aim to teach you some."

Miles let out a whoop. "You won't teach me nothing, mister," and drove at Jess.

The Ladder foreman was a bigger man than Jess, and at another time he might have been a smarter fighter, but now, stung with humiliation, he charged blindly, intent only on smashing this man he had so completely misjudged.

Jess stepped aside, slashing Miles' cheek with a rapier-like blow. Miles wheeled back and rushed again, this time running squarely into a driving right that slammed him half around. Jess moved in, giving Miles no chance to recover, and battered him with rights and lefts.

There was no sound but the panting of the two men, the solid crack of fists on bone and muscle. Miles clubbed at Jess, a futile rage growing in him as he missed, or connected only with an elbow or a shoulder. Jess was fast on his feet and he made himself as difficult to hit as a dust devil.

Goaded by constant failure to land a damaging blow, Miles changed tactics. He dived at Jess' legs, bringing him down in a jarring fall. Jess broke loose and rolled. Miles jumped at him, half blinded by blood dripping from a cut above his eyes; he got his hands on Jess but it was not a good hold and Jess jerked free. He regained his feet and stepped back, waiting for Miles to get up.

"Get on him," Farrar bawled. "Boot him."

But Jess stood motionless while Miles struggled to his hands and knees. He raised his head, eyes searching for Jess; he wiped a hand across his blood-smeared face and lunged at Jess again, his arms extended. Jess took one step forward, and before Miles' arms could close around him, he drove a knee upward into the man's face. The sound of the blow was as sharp as the crack of a butcher's ax on the skull of a beef. Miles' head snapped back and he fell belly-flat on the grass and lay still.

Jess wiped sweat from his face with a swipe of his arm and turning to Farrar, took his gun. He motioned to the mounted men. "Load him and git." They were run-of-the-mill cowhands, Jess judged. Without Miles' leadership, they would give no trouble. They obeyed sullenly, picking Miles up and lashing him face down across his saddle as if he were a dead man. As they stepped back into leather, Jess said. "Tell Ansell he don't make big enough tracks to close this country to settlement. He'll keep his beef on Ladder range."

They rode away, not giving Jess a backward glance. Tully came to Jess, hand extended. "Thank you, Mr. Dawson, I wish I had been young enough to have done the job myself."

Jess gripped Tully's calloused hand, thinking that here was a man typical of all the settlers, filled with hopes and dreams and the hunger to own his land, but still uncertain in his mind whether he was strong enough to defeat the forces that were against him.

"You ain't out of the woods yet," Jess said.

"Next time I'll have a gun," Tully said bitterly.

"It ain't just having a gun," Jess told him. "It's using it first and using it good."

Mrs. Tully had not moved from the wagon wheel. Now she asked, her voice trembling, "What kind of a country is this?"

"A wild one, ma'am," Farrar answered. "Even the wind gets wild at times, but the land's free and it's rich."

"Free," she cried. "Free, you say, when we have to fight men like that Miles?"

The round-bodied girl moved to Jess, her full lips smiling. She said, "Thank you, Mr. Dawson." She put her hands on his arms, her face up-turned, her gray eyes bright. For a moment she stood with her face quite close to his, then she kissed him on the lips, casually as if she always thanked a strange man that way for doing her a favor.

"I'm Josephine," the girl said. "This is my mother." She motioned to Mrs. Tully and then to the slender girl who still held the shotgun. "And my sister Paula."

Jess stared blankly at the girl, shocked by surprise and not knowing what was expected of him. Then he touched his hat brim, blue eyes locked with Paula's dark ones. He said, "I'm beholden to you for coming up with that scattergun, ma'am."

"Oh no, we're beholden to you." Paula glanced briefly at her father and brought her gaze to Jess again. "We're beholden more than you'll ever know."

"Mr. Farrar, in all this excitement I forgot I hadn't introduced my family," Tully said. "I told you last fall I'd fetch them out this spring."

Farrar stepped down from the buggy, wide-brimmed hat in hand. He bowed to the women, a graceful gesture for a fat man. "It's a lucky day for all of us on the Frenchman when you brought your women folks along, Mr. Tully. Never has the prairie bloomed with such beauty as now."

Josephine gave him her smile. "It's wonderful to hear you say that, Mr. Farrar. Daddy said you were a big man, but he didn't tell us you were polite and charming, too."

Farrar slapped his leg, loud laugh booming out. "I don't know just what he meant when he said I was a big man, but I sure fill up a buggy seat." He turned to Mrs. Tully. "I assure you, ma'am, that Lane Miles and his men do not represent the people you will meet out here."

"But they'll come back, won't they?" she asked dully. "They'll murder us in our sleep, won't they?"

"You just quit worrying," Farrar said in a comforting tone. "They may be a mite rough, but out here men have a high respect for good women."

Irritation stirred in Jess as he saw Farrar's gaze linger on Mrs. Tully's face. He said, "Let's get to town, Farrar."

"No hurry, Dawson," Farrar said. "I want to say, Tully, that I regret this mixup in your location, but things like that do happen. You folks camp here by the spring. Tomorrow you come back to town and we'll straighten things up."

Tully's mouth lightened. "We're staying. I tell you I know this is my place."

"You've got your women folks to think of," Farrar said as if reasoning with a stubborn child. "Regardless of the fact that Dake Ennis owns this quarter section, anyone settling south of the river will have trouble with the Ladder crew. You can't afford to endanger your family."

"It's this spring," Tully said doggedly. "I wouldn't have come here if I hadn't thought it was mine. I'm going to hold it."

Farrar scratched his cheek thoughtfully. "You haven't seen Dake Ennis?"

"We haven't seen anyone but them cowboys."

"I'll look in the dugout," Jess said.

"I'll go with you," Farrar said.

They walked toward the dugout, the Tullys remaining at the wagon. Farrar said, "Miles has a good memory."

"I handled him, didn't I?" Jess saw that Farrar was not entirely satisfied. He said, "You savvy the grangers, I reckon. Well, I've handled men like Miles before and I savvy them. You said it would be a good thing if he died. All right. He'll come gunning for me and I'll kill him."

Farrar smiled. "It would be a better country if it goes that way. I have no doubt you will take care of him."

They reached the dugout and Jess pulled the door open. It was gloomy inside, and for a moment Jess could distinguish nothing. He was out of the wind; he smelled the stale used-up air of a place that needed the door and windows open. There was another smell, too, the repellent stench of sickness. Then he made out a bunk in a back corner, and he heard a faint, rasping breathing.

"He's here," Jess said, and strode to the bunk.

Jess knelt beside the unconscious man. He had been shot high in the left side of the chest. Now he was hot with fever; his face was flushed and he stirred uneasily. Jess unbuttoned his shirt. It was stuck to his undershirt, stiff with dried blood.

Suddenly the man seemed aware that someone was there. He struck out weakly with his right hand, muttering, "I ain't getting out, Miles. You ain't running me off my place."

Jess rose. "This Ennis?"

"It's Dake, all right," Farrar said, troubled. "Miles must have shot him and left him here."

"Got a sawbones in Lariat?"

"Yeah. Ben Ives. Go after him. If Dake dies, I'll get the sheriff in here if I have to fetch him myself."

"How do I find your town?"

"Keep riding northeast. You can't miss it."

Jess wheeled out of the dugout. As he ran to his horse, Tully called, "What is it?"

"Ennis. He's been shot." Jess swung into the saddle. "I'm going after the medico."

"I hope you'll come back and see us," Josephine shouted.

"I'll be back tonight," Jess said, and rode away.

He had the impression that Mrs. Tully was frozen to the wagon wheel, that Josephine was unconcerned about all of this. He looked around. Josephine waved to him and he lifted a hand to her, remembering the quick, warm touch of her lips when she had kissed him.

He splashed across the river, scaring a pair of squawking teals into flight, and coming up out of the water, pointed his horse northeast. Paula had not waved good-bye. For some reason that was not clear to him, he was impressed by her more than Josephine. Slender, dark-eyed, quick to react, she was the one who had given him support when he needed it against Miles and his men.

Thinking about the two girls, it seemed to him that he had never seen sisters who were more different. Paula was the kind who would last but Josephine would grow weary of homestead life and find some way to drift on.

The upland to the north stretched away before Jess.

Killdeers rose from the grass and flew toward the river, their melancholy cries stirring some deep unexpressed feeling in Jess. He looked up at the sky with its lacy white clouds that were being swept along by the wind as if hurrying to get out of the country.

Let them go, he thought. He'd stay. He considered what had happened since he had met Coe Farrar; he thought of the man and his ambition. If the country beat the homesteaders, Farrar would lose and that meant Jess would lose, for he had tied his string to the fat man's kite.

Still, it might not work that way in the long run. At the moment he had a job; he'd save his money and watch for the kind of opening he wanted. If cattle returned to the grass, he'd go into cattle. If the farmers stayed, there would be something, perhaps a freighting business.

It was good country. It would be tough at times, but it challenged a man, and Jess would accept that challenge just as Sam Tully was accepting it. He thought of the man's weather-beaten face that was so much like the face of other men he had known who had tried the same thing Tully was trying here. Some succeeded and some failed, but in the end the prairie would be settled by men like Tully, standing hard against the wind and drouth and blizzards.

Then Jess' mind turned to Paula, and he wondered what she had thought of him.

Chapter Five

CAMPFIRE

JESS reached Lariat with the sun a full, red ball above the western horizon, the wind a steady force laid against him. He rode along the dusty street, eyes scanning the false fronts. Farrar was a bigger man than he had supposed, bigger any way Jess considered him.

Jess' eyes searched for the doctor's office. He passed a saloon, noticing the man who stood beside the batwings with a shiny, gold-plated star on his brown and white calfskin vest. Two guns on his hips. Hawk-like head tipped back. A sweeping black mustache and a sharp nose. Dark eyes that were pinned questioningly on Jess.

The doctor's office was at the end of the block. Jess dismounted and tied his horse, thinking that the fellow with the star must be the town marshal. He would be Farrar's man, too, Jess thought as he stepped into the doctor's office. Still, Farrar needed someone else, someone who, as the fat man had frankly said, did not have his hands tied by a star.

The office was empty, but as Jess opened and closed the door, a bell hanging beside the knob gave out a metallic tingle and a short, paunchy man came out of the back room, still chewing on a bite of supper. He wore a beard, and although the line-carved face indicated he was sixty or more, there was no trace of gray in either the beard or his dark hair.

"I'm looking for Doc Ives," Jess said.

"You found him." Ives swallowed, bird-like eyes on Jess. "You look healthy enough."

"It ain't me that's needing you. A gent named Dake Ennis has got a slug in his brisket and he's in bad shape."

"Who shot him?"

"Lane Miles, I reckon."

"Where is he?"

"In his dugout."

"It's a long ride." Ives sighed wearily. "I just had a baby. Be a lot of babies around here. Always that way when there's homesteads. It's different in a ranch country. You treat broken bones and you dig lead out of a man, but when you get plows in the country, babies come just as naturally as the sunrise." Ives picked up his black bag from an ancient desk. "So Dake got himself plugged, did he? I told him he'd get it, told him myself not more'n a couple of weeks ago."

"I'll go back with you," Jess said.

Ives started to turn, then stopped. "Who are you?"

"Jess Dawson. I'm working for Farrar."

"Are you now," Ives murmured. "So he decided that dude of a Duke Morgan wasn't man enough. Well, I'll saddle up and be with you in a minute."

Jess stepped back into the street. The man with the gold-plated star had moved along the boardwalk to the doctor's office. Now he shoved his expensive Stetson to the back of his head with a quick, upward thrust of his thumb, asking, "Riding through, friend?"

A dude, Ives had called him. Probably Ives was right. The gold-plated star. Pearl-handled guns. Long hair that reached to his shoulders. A fake Buffalo Bill. Jess knew the kind.

"Riding through today," Jess said, "but I'll be back. I like it here."

"Why now," the lawman said, "maybe you won't like it. Hell of a mean climate."

"I'll see as to that," Jess said, and reined away from the hitch rail.

Jess rode down the street at a walk, the marshal staring after him. A moment later Ives caught up with Jess, and they left town at a brisk pace.

"Who's the star toter?" Jess asked.

"Gent by name of Duke Morgan." Ives made no effort to hide his contempt. "Claims he's a bad man. Had to leave Virginia City because he killed a couple of men who had friends. You can take it or leave it, but that's the way Morgan tells it."

Ives would leave it, Jess thought, and felt an instinctive liking for the blunt medico. He had never met a doctor he didn't like except a few in Leadville who catered to the bonanza kings and refused to make a call unless they knew they would be paid. Ives, Jess thought, would not be that kind. He wouldn't be in the homestead country if he was.

They rode in silence, the wind dying down and the twilight deepening until the doctor's face became an expressionless blob. The clink of chain traces sounded ahead, and presently Farrar's buggy appeared, wheeling up out of a dip in the prairie.

"That you, Doc?" Farrar called as he stopped.

"It's me right enough." Ives swung to the buggy and reined up beside it. "How'd you leave Dake?"

"I think he's dying," Farrar said. "Damn that Miles."

"We need a sheriff," Ives said.

"We'll have one." Farrar leaned forward, peering at Jess. "Doc don't have any more use for a guide, Dawson."

"Didn't figure he did," Jess said, "but I thought I'd stay with the Tullys tonight."

"Lane won't be back."

"I'll stay anyhow."

Farrar was silent for a moment, and Jess had the feeling the fat man was going to order him back to Lariat. Instead he said, "I'll see you in town in the morning."

"I'll be there," Jess promised.

Farrar drove on, Ives saying softly, "Your boss is a smart man, Dawson, and he's ambitious. He likes men he can handle."

"You know, Doc," Jess said, "I get the notion you don't cotton to the way things are shaping up out here."

"You get the right notion," Ives said. "I'm an old man, Dawson. Started practicing when I was a young fellow in eastern Kansas before the Civil War. Got my share of patching up men with bullet holes in them. I prefer bringing babies into the world because they've got their life ahead of them and I keep hoping they'll make this a better world, but they never do."

He didn't say anything for a time as if thinking about this. Then he went on, talking more to himself than to Jess, "It ain't the babies' fault when you figure it out. They're rasied to act like the old folks. Sometimes I think the Lord ought to give us another flood and drown everybody but the babies so they could get a head start on the cussedness that's just naturally in 'em."

"You'd drown, too."

"That'd be all right. I ain't changed much of the misery that's in the world. Too many men like Coe Farrar, and Bill Hays who calls himself a locator. Biggest crook north of the Frenchman, Bill is. And Duke Morgan's nothing but a showcase. Or take Jim Brennan. Traded his soul to Farrar for a few fonts of type and a Washington hand press."

Ives sighed. "I'm trying to make you out, Dawson. You see, I've got a lot of respect for homesteaders. A raggle-taggle lot, some of 'em drifting around looking for free land because they couldn't make the grade farther east, but I know 'em. They've got guts to even tackle this country. It can be hell sometimes. Blizzards and drouth and prairie fires. But some of 'em will stick and the others will go back, and the ones who make a go of it will produce something."

"You're trying to say I won't produce anything. That it?"

"That's it. I mean, if you work for Farrar. Neither will he. A damned parasite, Farrar is. Skims off the cream because he's got some money to start on. He'll work every deal he can, his town and the county and the railroad, work for his profit and to hell with the homesteaders."

Jess sensed truth in what the doctor was saying, and he felt a quick burst of irritation. "I'll live my life the way I see it, Doc. That's the way you live yours, ain't it?"

"I aim to. Well, you never change a man by talking, I guess, but I keep trying. I'm a prophet as well as a doctor. Now I'll prophesy. Farrar will pay you well, so he'll expect you to do the chores he won't and can't do. I'll be pulling your bullets out of men who get in Farrar's way, providing you don't do a neat job."

"I always do a neat job," Jess said. "They won't be needing you."

"They'll still need me," Ives murmured. "I'm the undertaker, too, you know. Dead or alive, they'll need me."

They reached the Frenchman and splashed across, the

Tully campfire a small red point ahead of them. "If Dake's dying, what's he got a fire going for?" Ives asked.

"There's a homesteader family here. Name of Tully. A man and his wife and two girls. He claims this is the place Hays showed him and he won't budge."

"He's probably right," Ives said grimly. "Proves what I said. Hays is a crook."

They reined up beside the wagon and dismounted. Tully was squatting beside the fire. Josephine and Paula were with him. Jess introduced them, then Tully said, "My wife is with Ennis, Doc. She's a good nurse."

"Never saw a homesteader's wife who wasn't." Ives took his black bag down from behind his saddle. "Water my horse, Dawson, and lariat him out on the grass."

Ives stalked toward the dugout, Tully beside him. Paula asked, "Have you had supper, Mr. Dawson?"

"No."

"I'll fix something while you take care of the horses."

When Jess returned to the wagon, Paula had thrown more chips on the fire, and the smell of coffee and frying bacon was strong in the air. As Jess hunkered beside the fire, Josephine asked, "Didn't you tell Miles you were new here?"

"That's right," he said.

Paula broke an egg into a frying pan and poured coffee into a tin cup. She glanced at him. "You seemed to know what was going on."

"It ain't hard to savvy. I heard Farrar's side of it and I saw Miles' boss. Fellow named Ansell who owns Ladder. I just added it up. Your dad's gonna have trouble any way you figure."

"That's what Mamma says," Josephine said scornfully, "but this prairie country scares her. I don't think we'll have any trouble. You know, I thought Miles was kind of handsome till you got done with him."

Paula handed a plate to Jess, her face grave, and again Jess was struck by the difference between the two girls. Josephine would be as changeable as the wind, but Paula was like a rock. He wondered what the next months would do to them. This was spring, the weather was good, and it was their first night. The testing would come later.

"Do you think Daddy is wrong about this being the place he filed on?" Paula asked.

He hesitated, not wanting to give her an honest answer. Josephine laughed, an easy laugh that seemed to bubble out of her. She said, "You're afraid to tell us what you think."

"I don't know," he said, "but it's a common enough trick for a locator to show a good quarter section and then give the wrong figures. Doc claims that's what happened. He says Hays is a crook."

"It'll kill Daddy," Paula said in a low tone. "He wanted the spring. He isn't usually stubborn, but he's awfully stubborn about this."

"We'll probably wind up with a dry quarter section ten miles from a neighbor," Josephine said. "We'll have to dig a well, or haul water in a barrel so we won't have more than a cupful to wash dishes."

Jess went on eating, thinking that what she had said was true. Bill Hays had pocketed his fee and nothing could be done. Farrar would be very sorry about it and offer to show Sam the land he had actually filed on. Again the sense of irritation stirred in Jess. Doc Ives had been right, but there was nothing he could do, nothing as long as he worked for Farrar.

Josephine rose and moved to the fire, her hips swaying slightly in the insinuating manner which was natural with her. She filled Jess' cup and replaced the coffee on the grate, asking, "Do you like the country?"

"I will," he said. "Trouble is I've lived in the mountains most of my life. It's kind of like moving into another world."

"No trees," Josephine said. "No real hills. Just grass and a little river and all this sky and land that seems to go on forever. Mamma hates it."

"She'll like it," Paula said fiercely. "She'll have to."

"But you won't," Josephine said. "You'll go back to

Missouri and marry Neil Comer. She's engaged, Mr. Dawson, but she made a mistake. She'd do better out here where she's got a choice of men."

Jess saw resentment flow across Paula's face. She opened her mouth to say something and closed it, turning her head to stare at the smoldering fire. Jess drank his coffee, regretting that Josephine had told him about Neil Comer. If Paula went back, Sam Tully would fail. She was the balance wheel, the solid one, and her father needed her.

"I won't go back," Paula said finally. "Not right away. I like it here. I like it awfully well. If Neil wants me he'll have to come out here."

"You won't catch him getting that far from home," Josephine taunted. "He'll rent and you'll marry him and have a lot of kids and be poor all your life." She smiled at Jess. "A renter never gets ahead, you know. That's why Daddy insisted on coming out here. He isn't as poor as most of the settlers. I mean, he's got enough to start."

Paula glanced at her sister, resentment growing in her, then she turned her head away. There was something between them, Jess saw, something that probably went back to their childhood. That something, whatever it was, would grow with time. The struggle against a new, raw country like this stripped the veneer from people. Jess had seen it happen many times. It would happen with the Tullys.

Ives and Sam Tully and his wife left the dugout and came to the fire. Paula rose and filled a cup of coffee for Ives. He took it, measuring the girls with sober eyes, then he said, "Dake Ennis will live or die according to the care he receives. You folks owe him nothing, but I can't move him to town."

"He'll get good care," Paula said quietly.

Ives nodded. "I thought so. When you've been tending folks as long as I have, you get so you can judge them pretty well. I figured you folks would be that kind."

"That dugout," Mrs. Tully said bitterly. "Just a cave. How can anyone live in a place like that?"

"It's the kind of place you'll live in," Ives said pointedly.

"Everybody starts out here in a dugout. The land comes first. You break the sod and you plant, and maybe later if there's time, you build a soddy. If you've got a little extra money, you might even have glass in your windows. If you don't, you leave them open, and when the weather's bad, you put little doors in 'em to keep the cold out."

"I won't live like a gopher," Mrs. Tully cried. "I tell you I won't."

Ives shrugged, glancing at Tully who was fidgeting on the other side of the fire. Then Ives asked, "You riding back to town with me, Dawson, or you still figuring on staying here?"

"I'll stay the night," Jess said, and saw the quick relief on Paula's face.

"Thank you," Paula said impulsively.

"Fetch my horse in, will you, Dawson," Ives said.

Jess turned away. When he led the doctor's horse to the wagon, Ives picked up his bag and tied it behind the saddle. "I'll be out in a couple of days. I've done all I can for Dake now." He stepped into the saddle, eyes pinned on Tully's face as if there was something he was reluctant to say but was still compelled to say it. "You go ahead, Tully. Start breaking sod if that's what you're bound to do, but don't count on this being your land. I know Dake Ennis bought this quarter section from the man who preempted it."

Nodding, Ives rode away. For a moment the Tullys stood by the fire until the darkness had swallowed the doctor, then Mrs. Tully said, "I'm going to bed," and turned toward the wagon.

"I'll sit with him tonight," Paula said, and taking the lantern, walked to the dugout.

"Might as well go to bed." Tully shifted uncertainly, hands deep in his pockets. "I'm thankful you're with us tonight, Mr. Dawson. We'll all sleep better because of it."

Jess nodded, not knowing what to say. Later, lying beside the dying fire and listening to Tully's snoring, he regretted that there was so little he could do. In the end it depended on the Tullys, but Sam did not have the support from his wife that he deserved.

Jess understood how it was with the man. He could not go back. His stubbornness was the one quality which might give him strength; his dogged determination to stay might be enough to bring him success in the last stand against the economic current of his time.

Again as on the night before, Jess found it hard to go to sleep. Ives' needling had had its effect, but Jess was not one to break his word. Still, there was something that a man owed himself. In that way Jess was no different from Sam Tully. Everyone lived by his own standards. If a man was false to them, he made his own hell. Now, staring upward at the tall sky, Jess could feel the hell already beginning to pinch his soul.

Chapter Six

CHAINS THAT BIND

Long Tom Ansell was a prisoner. He was bound to Lane Miles as a slave was bound to his master. Worse than that, he was a prisoner to his own fear, to an ambition that was somehow related to that fear. He had never really admitted this to himself; he had always been able to rationalize, to find excuses, to tell himself that he deserved more than life had given him. Now he did admit it, and he cursed himself for making the mistake that tied him so closely to Lane Miles.

After Farrar and Jess Dawson had disappeared, he stood by the window, staring at the empty slope to the north where they had been, and he shouted oaths at them that echoed through the house, finding in his burst of anger an escape from his own self-condemnation.

He hated Farrar because the townsite man represented a

way of life that was foreign to everything he wanted; he cursed Dawson because he was a stranger, but shrewd enough to recognize the fear that had been inside Ansell when he had faced them, a fear that he thought he was hiding from everyone but Miles.

For a time Ansell wandered aimlessly through the house, thinking sourly that it had been foolish to spend money building a place like this in the middle of the sand hills where no one would see it and realize that after all these years Long Tom Ansell had become an important man. Even Coe Farrar had said that.

Because he was lonely, he left the house and saddled his sorrel gelding. Miles and the crew were somewhere to the north patrolling the Frenchman when they should be working. It was almost time for spring roundup, and Miles was so intent on holding the grass south of the river that he had forgotten that the first job of a cowman was to look after his cattle.

Ansell rode south, the wind to his back. The hills were steeper and higher here, and he rode slowly, his mind turning to his first meeting with Lane Miles. It seemed a long time ago, the big cattlemen, Hancock and Vestry, were on the Frenchman and riding high. Ansell as a matter of survival saw to it that his stock did not work north onto the good graze along the river.

In those days there had not been a homesteader within a hundred miles. There were still a few small herds of buffalo in the country, and now and then a band of Cheyennes drifted through the sand hills. Miles was trail boss of a Texas herd bound for Ogallala. They had camped some distance west of Ansell's place, and Ansell had ridden over to see them, largely because he was lonesome. He was tolerated but never welcomed when he visited the big ranches to the north.

He had liked Miles. That in itself had been unusual, for he liked few people. It was the reason he had settled in the sand hills. No one bothered him, he made a living of sorts, and he was slowly building a herd that might one day make him rich. Still, he had found little satisfaction in his way of life, and there were times when his loneliness beat at him so that it was almost unbearable.

Now, thinking back, he was not sure what had drawn him to Miles except that the man had been friendly and welcomed him. Miles had asked about the country north of the river, and about the possibility of crossing Vestry's range without trouble. On impulse Ansell had volunteered to go with Miles for a couple of days.

They had made a wide swing to the west, crossing the Frenchman where it was a dry creek bed that was filled with water only at flood time; they had avoided Vestry and his hands, and there had been no trouble. Vestry considered himself a cattle baron, sharing the valley of the Frenchman with Hancock whose ranch lay downriver from Vestry's, and neither wanted Texas herds crossing their grass.

Miles had seemed grateful because there had been no trouble. When Ansell was ready to turn back, Miles produced a bottle and they'd had a drink. Even at that time Miles might have sensed the inherent weakness that was in Ansell, but he had treated him as if he were an equal and that had pleased him. Then Miles had asked how many head could be run in the sand hills, and Ansell had said several thousand.

It had been a mistake, the biggest Ansell had ever made. Miles had asked him how he'd like to have a partner if the partner had a herd of cattle. It would be an even split, Miles had said, with Miles offering a half ownership in the herd for a range to throw it on.

Ansell had the range. More than that, he held title to half a section that had water, the small lakes that were common in the sand hills, for here water was close to the surface. If the lakes dried up, it was no great task to dig wells. Too, there were fertile valleys scattered through the hills that were rich with grass so that putting up enough hay for the horses was a simple matter.

Ansell had welcomed the proposition; he had shaken

hands with Miles who promised he'd be here next summer with a herd. Ansell hadn't understood. He had been a sucker, not realizing when he was well off. Miles had come just as he had promised, but the cow-and-calf herd was stolen. Then it was too late to back out. At least Ansell had lacked the courage to say he wanted no part of it.

They had spent weeks changing the "II" brand into the Ladder. At that time there was little travel through the sand hills, and the brand altering had been completed without question. Ansell found himself changed from the owner of a small herd that was honestly his to half owner of a stolen herd that was larger than anything he had ever dreamed of running under the Ladder iron.

Trouble had come as Ansell had been afraid it would. It was late fall with the sand hills turned to drab brown and the sky an ominous lead-gray that promised a blizzard. Two men rode into the ranch late one afternoon, their horses carrying the "II" brand. One was old with a white patriarchal beard; the other was a kid, the old man's grandson, or so Ansell gathered from their talk. They were looking for Miles and the herd he had stolen.

Ansell never knew what brought them here. Luck, perhaps, or they might have run across somebody to the south who remembered a herd which had been driven north. Possibly that somebody had remembered the brand. In any case, the old man and the kid had found some of the cattle, they had killed a cow and cut out the brand, and they had known what had happened.

As long as Ansell lived, he would not forget the next hour. The old man had asked Ansell if he owned the Ladder outfit. When he said yes, the man had pulled his gun and said he was taking Ansell to the nearest sheriff. Ansell was alone at the time. There was nothing to do but go outside and saddle a horse, although he told the white-bearded man that the nearest sheriff was at McCook and a blizzard was on the way.

They were still wrangling when Miles rode up with the crew. Ansell did not know what sort of a deal Miles had made with his men. He didn't know yet, but whatever it was, it had been good enough make them stay. Perhaps they had worked for the old man in Texas and were wanted by the law, and this was a good place to hide out. Or it may have been that Miles was the kind of leader who could hold a tough bunch together. But regardless of how it was, the crew stayed out of the trouble, idly watching and ignoring the old man's pleading to help regain his cattle.

There were tears in the old man's eyes when he saw that he would get no help here. The crew regarded him with stony indifference while they waited for Miles to handle this. The bearded man turned to Miles, his gun still in his hand, and cursed him for a double-crossing cow thief.

Miles sat in his saddle, a mocking grin on his handsome face, and then for no apparent reason he swung down. The old man's attention was fixed on him, fixed so closely that he forgot about Ansell who had his chance and jumping him from behind, knocked him down.

Without a word Miles drew and shot the old man while he was still on the ground. The kid yelled, "No, no," but Miles killed him as coolly as he'd shoot a beef he was planning to butcher. Then he told two of his men to take the bodies away from the ranch and bury them.

When they were in the house Ansell told Miles that if he'd known what he was getting into, he'd never have been a part of a steal. Then Miles said coldly, "You are a part of it, Ansell, and you'll stay a part of it. I'm just supposed to be your foreman. Now don't mention it again."

He never had. The two men who had buried the bodies came in at dusk with the first snow beginning to fall, and to this day Ansell did not know where the bodies were buried. He didn't want to know, but the knowledge that he'd had a part in the robbery and murder was never fully out of his consciousness.

Now, with the memories flooding his mind, Ansell hated himself for his cowardice and he hated Miles, and still he saw now way to change anything. Ladder had made money. If there were those who wondered about it, they did not ask questions.

Every fall a drive was made to Julesburg. Ansell took

half the profits and banked the money, and all the time the certainty that someday he would die before Miles' gun was in his mind. He would wake up at night, cold sweat breaking through his skin, the thunder of a gun in his ears; he could feel a bullet tearing into his body, and he seemed to be falling into endless space.

He reached a band of cattle and rode around them, finding some comfort in looking at them and forgetting at the moment that Lane Miles had brought them here. He thought of the money in a Julesburg bank. He had often considered taking it and getting out of the country, but he never had. He was trapped, afraid to stay and more afraid to run.

Slowly Ansell rode back to the ranch. He started a fire and began to get supper, knowing they would be here soon. Cooking had been his job from the first, another injury which he mentally stored against Miles. He was supposed to be the owner, but he took Miles' orders in this as he did in everything else.

For one thing Ansell could be thankful. Miles was honest in dividing the profits. When anyone was around, Miles treated him with the respect that a foreman owed his boss. When they were alone, he made no secret of his contempt. A breakup was sure to come and then Ansell would die. Probably Miles would gather the cattle, sell all of them, and drift on. Perhaps that was the understanding he had with his men.

Ansell was closing the oven door on a pan of biscuits when he heard someone ride in. He glanced out of the window. Miles and two of the crew. The others would be in soon. He set the table and was frying steak when Miles came into the kitchen through the back door. Ansell looked at him, startled. Miles' face was a mass of cuts and bruises, and one eye was closed.

"What fell on you?" Ansell asked.

"A gent by name of Dawson," Miles sat down at the table. "Farrar said him and Dawson had been here."

"Yeah, they was here, Farrar wanted to sweet talk me

into keeping our beef off the grass along the Frenchman. I ran 'em off with my Winchester.''

Miles felt of his bruised jaw. "If my face didn't hurt like a boil, I'd laugh. You couldn't run that Dawson anywhere.''

"They left, didn't they?" Ansell demanded angrily. "I had my Winchester all right.''

"If they left, it was because Dawson was ready to leave, not on account of your Winchester. He's the first real tough hand who's hit this country since I've been here. That Duke Morgan in town ain't even a good shadow to Dawson.''

Ansell stood at the stove, eyes on the frying meat. He picked up a fork and turned each piece. Without looking at Miles, he said, "Farrar claims we can't keep the settlers out and I reckon he's right. They won't come into the sand hills, though, and we don't really need the grass along the river . . .''

"Shut that up," Miles said testily. "There's a family on Dake Ennis' place we ain't bothering. They've got a couple of girls. I like one of 'em. We're pushing everyone else across the river but they're staying. Savvy?"

"Hell, Lane, I ain't augering," Ansell said quickly.

Miles had made a fool of himself over more than one woman in Julesburg and now he'd make a fool of himself over a homesteader's girl. Ansell stood with his back to Miles, wondering if he could use the girl to get at Miles. He gave up the idea at once. He didn't understand women. Whenever he was around them, he just couldn't talk.

"Turn around," Miles ordered.

Ansell made a slow turn. "Now what?"

"I can read you like a book," Miles said. "You're yellow. That ain't news to either one of us, but I'll tell you something that is. Me and the boys have got what we want here. With the good grass along the river, we'll have a better deal than we have now. We ain't quitting. Savvy?"

"No," Ansell said. "I sure don't."

"I'll make it plain. Texas Rangers never forget. Maybe

me and the boys will light out for Argentina if and when we get enough money. I dunno about that. Anyway, we ain't got it yet. You just be damned sure you don't do nothing to spoil our setup."

Ansell turned back to the stove. He had never associated fear with Lane Miles, but now he sensed that the man was afraid and the knowledge brought comfort to him. He had no idea what sort of a past Miles had, but a man who could kill as easily as he had killed the white-haired man and the kid might have the kind of record that would never be forgotten. As long as Miles and the crew were making money and thought they were safe, they would stay.

"Farrar said we'd have a county and a railroad," Ansell said. "There's bound to be a lot of people in here, and they'll have a sheriff in Lariat."

Miles snorted. "Nebraska law don't worry me. And if anybody in Texas hears about us, you'll be the one to hang. You're a good front, Ansell. That's the only reason I've put up with you as long as I have."

Ansell took the biscuits from the oven and set the pan on the back of the stove. His head was throbbing as it often did these days, throbbing so that he could not think coherently. At times he wondered if he was going crazy.

He forked the meat into a platter. It didn't make sense, Miles insisting on holding the grass along the river. There must be something back of it that Ansell didn't know. Mechanically he stepped through the door and rang the gong, one thought gripping his consciousness. His life wasn't going on much longer like this. He had to do something. Then the old familiar weakness of fear was in him again. He thought, *There's nothing I can do. Not a damned thing.*

Chapter Seven

BARGAIN DEFINED

THE Tullys rose at dawn. Jess got up, too, and washed in the spring. He picked up a gunny sack and walked to the bench that lay south of the river. When he had filled the sack with chips, he returned to the fire to find that Paula was there, shivering in the chill air. Clouds were building up along the western horizon, and the wind, heavy with dampness, was running in from the southeast.

Jess dropped the sack beside the fire. "How's Ennis?"

"He's conscious," she said. "He couldn't understand who I was. He seemed to think he'd died and I was an angel."

Josephine, lifting the coffeepot from the grate, heard what Paula said. She laughed, winking at Jess. "An angel! He must be out of his head."

"I guess he is," Paula said.

Tully came to the fire, rubbing his hands. "Mighty cold this morning. Feels like we're in for a rain."

"It's been dry," Jess said. "You could use a rain if you're going to break any sod this spring."

Tully nodded. "That's right. I got here a little later than I figured I would. If I'm going to turn any grass, I've got to do it."

Mrs. Tully said, "Breakfast."

Her eyes were heavy as if she had not slept well, and there was a sullen set to her mouth. A rain would not improve her disposition, Jess thought. He wondered why she had come. She was not a docile woman who would follow her man anywhere he went, willingly sharing his hardships and his dreams, but neither was she a nagging woman who used her tongue to continually flay her husband as so many homesteader wives did.

While they ate, Jess asked, "Why did you bring three saddle horses out here, Tully? Figuring on buying cattle?"

"I would if I could afford to," Tully answered. "No, I thought I could sell them at a profit. Last fall Farrar said there weren't many good riding horses in the country."

"Besides," Josephine said, "Paula and me like to ride. I won't let Daddy sell them unless we just have to have the money."

"Which will be soon," Mrs. Tully said. "What we have won't last. You know what it is to start over, Mr. Dawson, to throw away everything you had and just start all over?"

He nodded. "Yeah, I know."

"But you're working for Farrar," Mrs. Tully said. "If you have a job, you have money coming in all the time. Besides, you don't have three women to support."

"I'm not that lucky." Jess grinned, hoping to divert her. "But I did have a business in Leadville that turned bad on me, and I figure on finding something around here."

"What sort of a man is Mr. Farrar?" Mrs. Tully asked.

"I don't know. I guess that's something we'll find out."

"We've got to know whether we can trust him or not. It seems to me that if this Hays is a crook and he's in with Farrar, then Farrar must be a crook. If that's true, we don't have any business staying here."

Tully glanced up from his plate. "It don't make no difference about Farrar, Ruth. He ain't big enough to change the country."

"I know," she murmured. "You're going to start breaking sod. This may not be your quarter section, but you'll stay and work it no matter who owns it."

Tully lowered his gaze, saying nothing. Paula rose, yawning. "I'm going to bed. Joe, you sit up with Mr. Ennis. I think he could eat something. You might beat up an egg for him."

Jess put down his plate. "I've got to get to town. If you folks need me for anything, get word to me."

"I'll remember that," Tully said gratefully.

"What do folks do out here for fun?" Josephine asked. "Dances, maybe?"

Her smile was a frank invitation. Paula opened her mouth to say something and closed it as she turned toward the wagon. Jess said, "We'll find out."

He walked to where he had lariated his gelding, Tully beside him, and when they were far enough from the wagon so the women could not hear him, Tully asked, "What do you think, Dawson, about Farrar and the doctor saying the place belongs to Ennis?"

Jess was silent until he had saddled his horse and wound up his rope, then he said, "I'm afraid they're right."

Tully stood there, his weathered face working with emotion. Suddenly he burst out, "I've got to do something. You're a man. You can understand. Ruth can't. There's got to be something I can do."

"Maybe there will be." Jess stepped into the saddle. "I'll have a talk with Hays. Don't do anything for a few days. Wait till Ennis is better. Maybe Ennis will sell."

"Don't reckon he will. Not with a spring on the place." Tully looked south at the bench, hands knotted at his sides. "All this time I've been so sure everything would be all right. Coming out here was my idea, just mine, and now it looks like I was as wrong as a man could be."

Looking at him, Jess thought that his own disappointment when he had sold out in Leadville had been nothing compared to the tragedy that Sam Tully faced now. He said, "It's a little early to say that." He nodded and touched his hat brim to the women at the fire. Josephine waved, but Mrs. Tully remained motionless, staring at him. Paula had disappeared.

Jess rode away. After he had crossed the river, he heard the humming of a prairie cock from somewhere out in the grass. It was mating time, he thought, and wondered if that was the cause of his growing turbulence of spirit. When he had been in Leadville, he had been too busy to think about women, and the ones he had met were not the kind he would marry.

The Tully girls were different, as different as the high Rockies were different from the prairie. As he pointed his horse toward Lariat, he knew he would be returning soon, but it might not be any use. Paula was spoken for, and Josephine would be courted by every single man who lived within twenty miles of the Tullys. He'd take her to a dance, and as soon as the single men saw her, she'd be the most popular girl on the Frenchman.

It was midmorning when he reached Lariat and rode into the livery stable. Clouds had spread across the sky, low and sullen gray, and the biting wind was heavy with the promise of rain.

"Storm coming," the stableman said. "Guess the home-steaders will be glad to see it. Been awful dry."

"I want this horse treated right," Jess said. "I'll be around town for awhile."

The man pinned questioning eyes on Jess. "You Dawson?"

"That's right. Why?"

"I've got my orders. I'm supposed to treat this here animal like he was a thoroughbred. Mr. Farrar pays the bill."

Shrugging, Jess picked up his war bag and stepped into the street. It was all right if Farrar wanted to pay the bill. He found the hotel and asked for a room. After he had signed his name, the clerk spun the register, glanced at it, and nodded.

"Been expecting you, Mr. Dawson." The clerk picked a key off the rack behind the desk and handed it to Jess. "Room 25, the best in the house. Mr. Farrar's paying for it. He's also paying for your meals. You can eat at the drummers' table. They get the best, you know."

"I don't like drummers," Jess said shortly, and picking up his bag, climbed the stairs to his room.

If Room 25 was the best in the house, the others weren't much, Jess thought. There was a bed, a rough pine bureau that held the scars of years of hard usage, a cracked mirror, a white bowl and pitcher, and a single cane-bottomed chair. Probably Farrar had bought the furniture from some hotel farther east and had freighted it out here.

Jess dropped his war bag in a corner, poured water into the bowl and washed. He had the world by the tail and a downhill pull, or at least that was what Farrar wanted him to think. He dried on the coarse towel and emptied the bowl into the slop jar, the familiar sense of irritation working through him again.

He wondered what a man's soul was worth. A hundred dollars a month? Well, he was getting more than that. Stable care for his horse and free board and room. Sure, a lot more. It was a good bargain.

Jess stared at his face in the mirror, thoughtfully fingering a stubble-covered cheek. Buying a man's gun was one thing, buying his soul was something else. A bargain that looked good on the face of it was not always good in the long run. He'd get a shave and see Farrar. There were some things that had to be made clear now.

The barber shop was next to the hotel. Jess dropped into the empty chair as the barber came out of a back room, tossing a battered copy of the Police Gazette on a bench. He said, "Good morning, friend. Shave and a hair cut?"

"Shave," Jess said, wondering idly why so many barbers were bald.

The barber shook out an apron and briskly covered Jess and fastened it at the back of his neck. "You Jess Dawson?"

"I'm Dawson. I suppose this is on the house."

"Why now, it ain't exactly that way, Mr. Dawson." The barber picked up a shaving mug and began stirring up a lather. "Mr. Farrar says you're working for him and the best is none too good for you. He'll pay, Mr. Farrar will. His word's good. I don't do no work on the cuff for nobody but him, and he don't pay for nobody else. If you're a friend of his, you're a friend of Fred Ash. That's me."

The barber droned on while he worked, and when he was done, he rubbed bay rum on Jess' face with quick, deft strokes. "Now how about a hair cut, Mr. Dawson?"

"Not today." Jess got out of the chair and slipped into his coat. "You say Farrar don't pay for nobody else?"

"No sir. I guess you're real special. Come in any time, Mr. Dawson. It'll put us both ahead."

Jess nodded and stepped outside, wondering if the way he had whipped Lane Miles had made him something special in Coe Farrar's eyes. He angled across the street to the townsite office, and found Farrar at his desk, immaculate and cheerful and smelling of bay rum.

"Sit down." Farrar shoved a ledger back on his desk and reached for a cigar. "I've been looking for you."

Jess took a chair, thinking that Farrar had a way about him. The barber had said you couldn't listen to Farrar and believe that Lariat would fail. It was the secret of his success, and every settler who had come to Lariat and talked to him as Sam Tully had must have felt the same way.

"I just found out something," Jess said. "My money's no good in this town."

Farrar laughed and fired his cigar. "Jess, I'll tell you something. The more I think of the way you whittled Lane

Miles down, the more I'm convinced you're the man I need. Frankly, I was worried about him. Now he'll walk easy."

"So you aim to make me happy in case Miles don't walk easy."

"If I can." Farrar reached for his bill fold. "I said I'd pay you a hundred dollars a month. I'll make it in advance."

Jess shook his head. "I'll earn my pay before I collect."

"Why now," Farrar said, pleased, "I like that."

"You paying for my drinks, too?"

Farrar's big laugh boomed out. "Not by a damned sight." He tilted his chair back, a creaking protest coming from it. "Your drinking is your problem. Likewise your gambling and your women. Well, how'd you leave Ennis?"

"Conscious. Paula Tully sat up all night with him. Said he thought he'd died and she was an angel."

"She looks like one and no mistake. I've seen lots of homesteader women, but I never laid eyes on three of 'em like the Tully women before. Funny thing, Mrs. Tully being married to an old goat like her husband. Why, he must be fifteen years older than she is."

Jess reached for the makings, catching the note of envy in the fat man's voice. He said, "You're giving me a good deal. Too good, so I figured I'd make one thing clear. There's a few things I won't do even for the deal you're offering."

Frowning, Farrar took the cigar out of his mouth. "Jess, I'll make something clear, too. I told you you're the man I need. I may not have anything for you to do this month. Perhaps not in six months, but the day will come when I do. You're my insurance against that day, but I'm going to make you a promise. I shall not ask you to do anything that will involve you with the law."

It was fair enough, Jess thought as he fired his cigarette. He remembered his resolve that he would never buck the big boys again. He'd play on their side. That's what he was doing now. Coe Farrar was a very big boy as far as this country was concerned.

"I've got a good deal here," Farrar went on. "This is my town. I've picked every business man in Lariat except Doc Ives. He just moved in on me. Got some crazy ideas, but ideas won't hurt us if they remain nothing more than ideas. We need a sawbones and Ives will do. I'm just asking one thing. Don't let his talk turn you against the biggest opportunity that ever knocked on your door."

Jess grinned at him. "I reckon I won't do that."

"Good. Go get your dinner. Be here at one. Now and then I call the boys together for a palaver. I'm having one today. I want you to meet them and I want them to meet you. They're good boys, Jess. Each one fits his job like a glove."

Jess rose. "I'll be here." He moved to the door and paused there, looking back at Farrar. "When I left the Tullys, Josephine asked if there was any fun around here."

"A dance every Saturday night in the room over the store. We keep it decent so even the pious folks don't kick." He grinned knowingly. "You thinking of fetching the girls in?"

"That's exactly what I was thinking about," Jess said, and left the office.

Chapter Eight

THE BIG BOYS

JESS waited in the hotel lobby with a hungry, impatient crowd of drummers, townsmen and homesteaders who had not yet found land that they wanted. A blonde woman rang a big auctioneer's bell that hung near the door, and the lobby was emptied at once, Duke Morgan leading the way into the dining room.

Jess saw that there was one long table for the townsmen and homesteaders, another smaller one set near the windows for the drummers. They would pay a higher rate, Jess knew, and get the choice food, but it would have been a mistake to eat with them, for it would have separated him from the people who were gambling on this country, the people who would make Farrar a success or a failure.

Jess took a chair near the foot of the long table and shook hands with his neighbors, Will Rollins who ran the bank, and Sandy McBain, the storekeeper. The blonde woman brought a platter with a roast on it and set it before Morgan. Jess, watching the marshal, thought that the way he picked up a long knife with a grand flourish and began to carve was typical of him. His gold-plated star was bright even in the thin light that came in through the curtained windows. A showcase exactly as Ives had said.

Neither Rollins nor McBain seemed inclined to talk. Jess was thankful for that because he wanted to listen to the conversation at Morgan's end of the table. Actually it was a monologue as the food was passed, Morgan's voice rising over the clatter of knives and forks and the chomping of ravenous men, the optimistic talk of one who saw nothing but prosperity for folks who lived on the Frenchman.

The county would soon be organized, Morgan said. The railroad was already being built up the river. The spring rains were at hand that would soon soak the ground and make sod breaking easy. A lot of good land left, Morgan kept saying as if he wanted to impress that fact upon his listeners. He advised the settlers to stay north of the Frenchman on the uplands where there was hard land. It held moisture better than the sandy soil on the other side of the river.

Jess wondered about the white-haired man with the ink-stained fingers who sat at Morgan's left and kept nodding agreement to everything he said. Later, when the pies were being passed, Jess identified the land locator, Bill Hays. He sat halfway down the table between two settlers, a small man with pale blue eyes and light brown hair. His long sharp nose gave his chin a receding appearance; he wore a mustard-yellow mustache that made a repellent splotch of color under his nose.

Suddenly, as if it had been rehearsed, Hays took up the

talk, telling the homesteaders to look around and pick out the quarter section they wanted. He would take care of the details for them. It was fortunate they were here now, he told them. By next fall the good land would be filed on as far west as the Colorado line. The late comers would have to take what was left, or they would have to buy outright from someone who had pre-empted, paying as much as five hundred dollars for land that was free now.

Jess saw with some amusement that the settlers were impressed. To them five hundred dollars represented a small fortune. Jess could guess what some of them were thinking. They'd spend the summer here, taking land that they could sell to the tardy ones, then they could go home with hard money jingling in their pockets.

One of the men at the long table rose and drifted back into the lobby, the drummers lingering over their coffee. Duke Morgan pushed past Jess, ignoring him, but the banker, Will Rollins, fell into step with Jess.

"Going over to Coe's office?" Rollins asked.

Jess nodded. "That was my order."

Rollins smiled. He was a middle-aged man who wore a plain brown suit. His mouth was thin-lipped; his hazel eyes gave no hint to what he was thinking. A good poker player, Jess thought, and wondered how much faith the banker actually had in the country. He had taken no part in the table talk.

"For the time being we all accept Coe's orders," Rollins said. "Coe tells me you're working for him while you look for an opening."

"That's right."

"Drop into the bank sometime," Rollins said. "I may be able to help you. I take it you're not an innocent who believes all you hear."

"No. At least I'm not a farmer."

They left the hotel together. It had begun to rain, big drops that stirred the street dust, and the wind, stronger now, made a shrill cry around eaves and corners as it swept in from the grass.

"We'll sink or swim with the farmers," Rollins said. "I've watched them come and a few of them go, and my respect for Coe Farrar increases every day. He's an honest-to-God gambler if I ever saw one."

"You own the bank?" Jess asked. "Or is it Farrar's?"

"It's mine, which makes me a gambler, too, but I'm a small one compared to Coe. He's sunk a fortune here, and if the railroad misses Lariat, he's broke."

"He don't look like a plunger."

Rollins shrugged. "He has influence if that makes him anything less than a plunger."

Jess and Rollins were the last to enter the townsite office. Farrar was standing beside his desk. When he saw Jess, he nodded affably, saying, "I see you've met Mr. Rollins." He motioned to McBain. "My store manager . . ."

"We've met," McBain said shortly.

"Fine, fine. How about Jim Brennan, our editor. Jim, meet Jess Dawson."

Jess shook hands with the white-haired man, liking the hard grip and the way Brennan's eyes met his despite the smell of whiskey and chewing tobacco that flowed from the editor.

"I'd like to sell you a year's subscription to the *Lariat Eagle*," Brennan said. "You'll want to read about yourself."

"I never make news," Jess said.

Brennan grinned. "I've got another guess on that. You'll be on my front page in a week."

"Met the marshal, Jess?" Farrar asked.

Morgan stood by the door, hands shoved inside the waistband of his pants, his handsome face barren of expression. He gave Jess a half-inch nod, saying curtly, "We've met."

Farrar hesitated, eyes appraising Morgan as if wondering whether he should let his discourtesy go without reprimand. He said, his voice quite soft, "Duke, you need a drink."

"Not me," Morgan said harshly. "We're supposed to

have a rule about gun toting in Lariat. What's Dawson going to do about it?"

"Jess is above any rules," Farrar said, "but if he needs an excuse, we'll pin a star on him. I'd rather not do that unless you need help keeping folks in line."

Morgan lowered his gaze, his face as red as a kid's who has been disciplined. Farrar swung to Hays. "How about you, Bill? Did you meet Jess?"

"No sir, I haven't." Hays held out a plump hand. "Glad to have you with us, Dawson."

"How are you, Hays," Jess said, giving his hand a quick grip and dropping it.

Jess felt an instant dislike for the man. He wasn't sure whether his feelings for Hays stemmed from the fellow's ferret-like personality, or whether it was because he knew what had happened to the Tullys. Then, remembering Doc Ives, he wondered why the medico was not here.

"Sit down, boys." Farrar dropped into his swivel chair that creaked ominously under his weight. "We'll make this brief. Jim, I want your paper to tell the folks that Blake County will soon be organized and Lariat will be the county seat."

Brennan drew a plug of tobacco from his pocket. "Heard about this gent Knoll who took a quarter section at the falls?"

"I knew he'd settled there," Farrar said, frowning.

"He might make trouble for us," Hays broke in. "Used a Soldier's Additional and holds a fee simple title. Might get the notion to start a town."

"He's got power to talk about." Brennan cut a corner from his plug and slipped it into his mouth. "I hear he's figuring on putting in a grist mill."

"And the railroad's been coming up the river," Hays added worriedly. "Looks like it'll hit Knoll's place and miss Lariat."

Farrar tapped the desk top impatiently. "We won't let that happen. When the time's right, we'll take steps. Meanwhile we won't worry about the railroad. It will come to Lariat and go on to Sterling. Our farmers will have a direct line to Denver which is the only big market that's reasonably close. Miners have money. They have to eat. All right, we'll feed them. Work that into your next issue, Jim."

Brennan nodded. "Just thought you ought to know about this other business."

"That's what these meetings are for," Farrar said, affable again. "Now the big headline news is that I'm going to deed one block north of Main Street to the new county. No cost, you understand, and I'll put up a building for county offices. No rent for a year, so Blake County will get a good start free of debt."

"That's mighty generous of you, Coe," Hays cried enthusiastically.

Farrar seemed a little irritated by what the locator had said. Jess suppressed a smile, thinking it was like Hays to bring an apple to the teacher.

"It'll be on the front page," Brennan said.

"Good. Now I want to tell you boys about Jess." Farrar briefly related what had happened at Ansell's ranch and at the Tully wagon, then added, "Jess is looking for a business opening, and I'm sure something will turn up by fall that he likes. Meanwhile, he's what I call my trouble shooter. He takes orders from me and no one else, but we all have one goal which we're striving for. Whatever Jess does will be for the common good."

"I don't like it, Coe," Morgan said harshly.

"You don't like what?"

"Jumping Lane Miles. I say the smart thing to do is to get along with Ladder, and knocking Miles around ain't no way to get along."

"Takes a good man to handle Miles," Farrar murmured.

"Maybe, but they've got quite an outfit, Miles and Ansell have. Suppose they ride into town and shoot things up?"

"Suppose they do?"

"Why hell, they'll scare the pants off the settlers. I know what they're like. They came to farm, not to fight a bunch of proddy cowhands."

Jess leaned forward. "It strikes me, Morgan, that a man rigged up like you are with a fancy star and a brace of pearl-handled guns ought to be able to handle Ladder."

"If you can't," Farrar said, "we'll accept your resignation."

Morgan pinned truculent eyes on Jess, then turned his gaze to Farrar. He said sullenly, "I'll handle 'em."

Farrar laughed softly. "That's better. All right, boys, that's it for today."

They rose and filed out into the rain, Morgan the first to leave the office. Jess remained until they were gone, then got up and walked to Farrar's desk. He said, "You told me you hand-picked these men. Looks to me like you made a mistake with Morgan."

Farrar shook his head. "I don't like Doc Ives very well, Jess, but he's smart. I'll say that for him. He calls Duke a showcase. He's right. That's why I hired Duke."

"I don't savvy."

"You would if you understood the homesteaders. They come from a settled country and they know this is wild and new. They feel safer when they see we've got a man upholding the law who looks like he could do it. Duke does. You heard him at dinner, didn't you?"

"Yeah, but . . ."

"Look, Jess. You called Duke and he wilted. I'm not fooling myself about what will happen if something comes up that calls for tough treatment. That's where you come in."

Jess shrugged, thinking that Doc Ives had been right. He'd have the nasty jobs to do, the jobs Farrar couldn't and wouldn't do, the jobs Duke Morgan wasn't man enough to do. He turned toward the door, remembering that his pay was good. He'd have to keep reminding himself of that.

"What do you think of the rest of them?" Farrar asked.

Jess turned back. "They'll do. All but Hays. What about the Tullys?"

"I'm sorry about that mistake," Farrar said. "Tully will have to come to town and let us show him the place he really filed on."

"Where is it?"

"Eight miles west of town on the upland. It's good soil."

"Dry?"

Farrar nodded. "He'll have to put a well down."

"Then he won't budge."

"In that case we can't do a damned thing for him. Hays made a mistake. That's all. Of course Dake may die. If he does, we can fix it."

"We can't count on that," Jess said, and stepped out into the rain.

He stood there for a moment, looking along the deserted street, and for some reason he thought of Jim Brennan. Ives said the man had sold his soul for a few fonts of type and a Washington hand press. But Jess wasn't sure. He had liked Brennan, liked his grip and the way he looked at a man.

Jess went on toward the hotel, grinning ruefully. Ives would say the same thing about him, that he had sold his soul for a hundred dollars a month. Well, Farrar had sweetened the kitty better than that. To hell with Ives. He could say and think what he damned pleased.

Chapter Nine

A CROOK AND A LIAR

THE wind switched to the northwest again after the rains; it was cool and clear for more than a week, and growing patches of turned sod marred the prairie like freckles on a green face. Still the settlers came, their wagon wheels beating the road and Lariat's street to dust again.

Jess was haunted by the feeling that time was standing still, that he was living the same day over and over. The wind was a steady, monotonous power striving to uproot Lariat and sweep it off the prairie, but the buildings held. The sun made its daily swing across the sky with now and then a vagrant cloud veiling its bright face and throwing a patch of shadow upon the grass. And the land was constant, too, changed only by the puny attacks of men and teams and breaking plows, men who were hurrying now while the earth was still soft from the rain.

But it was mostly the people who gave Jess his weird sense of time standing still. Settlers and wagons and stock, each outfit looking much like the one that had gone before it. Every face was different and yet somehow the same, these people "who heard the sunset call and just had to go."

Jess' first meal in the hotel dining room was identical to those that followed. Duke Morgan took his place at the head of the table, his talk following the familiar line. Each day the group of settlers changed, but the questions were the same, and Bill Hays showed a fine talent for picking up the conversation at just the right point so that his promises seemed to fit naturally into the talk.

To Jess it was the same as hearing the first act of a play, given over and over so that the repetitious weight of it tightened his nerves until he couldn't stand it. He realized that it was the tedium of idleness more than anything else which was bothering him. Farrar had hired him as insurance against the day when he would be needed. That day might come this month, Farrar had said, or in six months, but this first week proved to Jess he could not stay here and do nothing while he waited for the undefined explosion that Farrar expected.

Sheer monotony of living forced Jess to find ways to spend his time. He would sit on the bench under the wooden awning in front of the saloon and count the kids as settler outfits wheeled in from the east. Or he'd go inside and play a few hands of solitaire until it palled on him and he'd throw the cards down in disgust. Or he'd drop around to the newspaper office and visit with Jim Brennan, the one man in town besides Doc Ives whom he genuinely liked. And all the time the restlessness in him grew.

He was tempted to ride out to the Tully place on Saturday night, but he couldn't bring himself to ask Paula to go with him. She was the kind, he thought, who would take her engagement seriously, and she'd turn him down. He instinctively shrank from asking Josephine because Paula was the one he wanted to take. So he solved the problem by spending the evening in the saloon and losing twenty dollars in a poker game.

Then, on Wednesday of the following week, he saw the Tully wagon come into town from the west. The over-jet had been removed so there was just the wagon bed with Sam and Paula on the spring seat. Jess, sitting in front of the saloon, recognized the Percherons long before he could identify Sam or Paula. None of the other outfits on the Frenchman had a team like Sam Tully's, and Jess judged it was a point of vanity with the man.

Jess crossed the street to the store as Sam drew up at the hitch rack, and when he touched the brim of his hat to Paula, her quick smile and "Good morning" raised his spirits and momentarily drove the restlessness from him.

"Howdy," Jess said as Sam nodded. "How's Ennis?"

"He's coming around," Sam answered. "Kind o' puny yet, but he's eating and he can walk a little if he takes it easy."

"You all settled now?"

Sam stepped down and tied the team. He made a slow turn to face Jess, gray eyes filled with misery. Paula remained on the wagon seat, her hands folded on her lap, and Jess saw at once he had asked the wrong question. The pleasure at seeing him had fled from her face.

"We're settled as much as we can be," Sam said bitterly. "I mean, living on land that belongs to another man."

"Mr. Ennis showed us his deed," Paula said.

"You haven't tried to find the quarter section Hays actually settled you on?" Jess asked.

"No and I won't." Sam rubbed his face, glancing at Paula and bringing his gaze back to Jess. "If I hadn't found that piece of land I liked, I wouldn't be here today. Go ahead, Dawson. Tell me I'm a fool. I ain't heard nothing else since Ennis dug up his deed. Tell me I'm a fool because I'm working to improve another man's land."

"Daddy. . . ." Paula began.

Sam silenced her with a sudden, violent gesture. "And I'm a fool because I was sucked in on Hays' and Farrar's crooked game and believed what I was told. I dunno, Dawson. I guess I won't ever believe nobody else as long as I live."

"Maybe you oughtta take a look at the right place," Jess said. "You might like it."

"No," Sam said stubbornly. "I've broken some sod and I came in today to buy posts and wire. I'll put a fence up and I'll stay. I aim to be buried on Ennis' land and then my women can go back to Missouri."

Sam swung around the hitch rack and walked into the store. For a moment Paula remained on the wagon seat, looking at Jess, then impulsively she got down, taking the hand that Jess raised to her.

"It sounds stupid for Daddy to put work and money into a place that isn't his," Paula said. "I don't understand it. He isn't really stupid, you know, and I never saw him act so pig-headed about anything else. He just says it'll work out and he goes right on."

"Has he tried to buy the place from Ennis?"

"No. Ennis hasn't felt like talking, but I don't think he'd sell. He says good springs are hard to find."

She was wearing a blue sunbonnet and a linen duster over her dress; her dark eyes were fixed on him as if she had no doubt he could help them if he would. He glanced away, kicking at a wagon wheel, embarrassed because he knew nothing could be done for them.

"Looks like your dad's hunting for trouble," Jess said.

"You've been awfully good to us," she said in a low tone. "I'm ashamed to ask you for anything else, but I can't help it. Isn't there something you can do?"

He brought his eyes to her pale, tense face. "You got a notion about it?"

"No. I just thought that since you're working for Farrar, maybe you could make him help us."

"I'll see if Hays is in town. You'll be here in the store?"

She nodded. "For a few minutes." She hesitated, coloring, and added, "I didn't have to come today except to keep Daddy company, but I did want to see you."

He grinned. "I wanted to see you, too, but for a different reason." Nodding, he turned away.

Farrar was alone in the townsite company office. He glanced up from the desk when Jess came in, frowning, and Jess guessed he had seen the Tully wagon go past.

"Morning," Farrar said.

Jess had not seen much of Farrar since the meeting in his office. The townsite man cooked his meals in his back room, content to let others run Lariat's business, although he was always friendly to settlers who came to see him. Now he was on guard, hiding his thoughts behind a bland, round face.

"Howdy." Jess dropped into a chair and stretched his legs out in front of him. "How's business?"

Farrar snorted. "You ought to know. Won't be no better till the railroad gets here and we have the county seat for sure. Things will pop then."

"I was looking for Hays," Jess said.

"He ain't in town. Went out at sunup to locate a family north of here."

"He oughtta be back by now."

Farrar nodded. "Reckon he will before long." He drummed his finger tips on the desk top. "Worrying about the Tullys?"

"Sort of. Ennis is gonna make it. He showed 'em his deed, but Sam allows he'll hang and rattle."

"Damn fool, that Tully," Farrar snapped. "Too bad. He'll wind up going back to Missouri. We need women folks like his out here." He scratched a droopy cheek. "Stay out of it, Jess. Hays can't do nothing now."

"Maybe. Maybe not." Jess rose. "He's a liar and a crook. He won't do your business no good, operating like he does. I don't savvy why you let him stay."

"It ain't easy to find a locator. Anyhow, it's none of your put in."

Jess grinned. "I'm looking out for your interest, Coe."

Farrar shrugged, and changed the subject with, "Thought you were fetching the Tully girls to the dance."

"Never got around to it," Jess said, and left the office.

When he returned to the store he saw that Sam and Sandy McBain were loading cedar posts and spools of Marshalltown barb wire into the wagon. There was a roll of chicken wire in the bed, and Sam, looking up, pointed to it.

"I'm gonna fix up a chicken pen," Sam said. "Got a couple of hens that want to set, and Ennis says there's a lot of skunks around."

"Wouldn't be surprised," Jess said, and turned into the store.

Paula was standing at the counter on the dry goods side of the store. She did not know he had come in until he stood beside her. She gave a start, frowning, and then smiled. "You gave me a turn," she said. "Didn't hear you come in."

"Next time I'll holler."

"I was day dreaming," she said. "Just looking at the dress goods."

"Gonna blow yourself for a new dress?"

She shook her head. "Just being a woman and wondering which one I'd pick." She pointed to a bolt of Silver Lake batiste that was on sale at seven cents a yard. "I'd take that, I guess. I mean, if I could afford it. Maybe I can this fall. Ennis says I can get a job teaching school, but it won't pay much. Nobody has any money."

"Nobody ever does in a homestead country." He hesitated, then added, "Hays ain't in town. He's locating a family north of here."

"They'll probably wind up in the sand hills," she said bitterly.

"Seen anything more of Lane Miles?"

"He's been to see us, but he didn't come to make trouble."

No, Jess thought, Miles wouldn't make trouble with two girls in the Tully family. He said, "I'll fetch Hays out when he gets to town, but don't count on it doing any good."

"Don't bother," Paula said. "I shouldn't have said anything to you."

"I'll fetch him if I have to put a rope on his neck," Jess said.

He turned away, leaving her standing there at the counter, and when he left the store, he saw that Sam and McBain had come back in and that Sam was dickering for a Winchester. He was asking for trouble, Jess thought, more trouble than he'd ever found in Missouri.

Hays did not return to town until the middle of the afternoon. He reined into the livery stable and stepped down, the weariness of a long ride stamped upon him. He saw Jess standing inside the archway and gave him a short nod.

"Good land around here about gone," Hays said. "Damn long ways from town for the new pilgrims."

"Don't pull your saddle off," Jess said. "We're calling on Sam Tully."

The locator froze. "I've got no business with him, Dawson. Not unless he wants me to show 'em the right piece of land. If he does, he can come to me."

"You're going to him," Jess said. "Now."

"Damn it, you can't buffalo me . . ." Hays stopped, his gaze touching Jess' holstered gun and lifting again to Jess' face. "Look, Dawson. You'd better save your cussedness for them that's bucking Coe."

"My cussedness ain't a patch alongside yours," Jess said. "You're coming with me."

"Coe will fire you," Hays shouted angrily. "He'll kick the seat of your pants plumb across the Frenchman."

"Nobody kicks me," Jess said. "Let's ride."

Hays stood motionless, breathing hard, hating Jess with his eyes, then defiance drained out of him. He said, "All right, but it won't change nothing."

There was no talk on the way to the Ennis place. The wind quartered in from the northwest, so strong that conversation would have been difficult even if Jess and Hays had been inclined to talk. It was not until they forded the Frenchman and turned toward the Tully camp that Hays shouted, "I don't savvy why you're taking up this ruckus. The damned settlers ain't worth it. Just a raggle-taggle bunch of drifters who'll be on their way by fall."

"I take it you don't believe in the country like Farrar does," Jess shouted back.

Hays snorted in derision. "Put it the other way, Dawson. Coe believes in the country as much as I do."

"There's nothing raggle-taggle about the Tullys," Jess said. "They deserve a better deal than you gave 'em."

"Maybe it's the girls you're interested in," Hays taunted.

"Maybe it is," Jess said.

It was late afternoon now, Jess' and Hays' long shadows following them. The wind was beginning to taper off. It would die down within the next hour or so. As they rode up to the Tully camp, Jess saw that Sam was working on his chicken pen, his new Winchester leaning against a corner post.

Paula and Josephine were helping him, but Mrs. Tully was evidently inside the over-jet that had been placed on the ground not far from Ennis' dugout, the stove pipe poking through the wagon sheet. Apparently they had set up their stove inside so they would not have to cook in the rain.

Sam put down his post hole digger when he recognized his visitors. He grabbed up his Winchester and wheeled to face Hays, calling, "Get down off that horse, you damned, lying crook. I've been wanting to see you ever since I got here."

Josephine looked at her father, bright-eyed as if anticipating what was coming, but Paula leaped toward him and frantically batted the rifle barrel down. She cried, "Don't make trouble, Daddy. I asked Jess to bring Hays out here."

Hays licked dry lips, gaze whipping to Jess. "Trying to get me shot, Dawson?"

"I ain't particular," Jess said, "except that I'd hate to see 'em hang Sam. Paula's right, Sam. Let's hear what this hairpin has got to say."

For a moment Sam fought his temper, bitter eyes on Hays, then he set the rifle back where it had been. He said, "Make your spiel, Hays."

Jess dismounted. "Just a minute, Sam. Can Ennis walk this far?"

"I think so," Paula said, "but he's taking a nap. I'll see if he's awake."

They waited while Paula ran to the dugout. Josephine moved to stand beside Jess. She asked, "Didn't they have a dance last Saturday?"

"I reckon so," Jess answered. "I got into a poker game and didn't go."

She pouted. "I thought you were going to take me."

It was like her, he thought. As bold as brass. Well, why not? He looked at her, chestnut hair loosened by the wind, a stray lock fluttering above her eyes. Her calico dress, shapeless and faded to a dingy, blue-gray, was molded against her body by the wind so that it made no secret of the seductive curve of her hips and breasts.

"I'll take you next Saturday," he said, "if you want to go."

"I'd like to go," she said eagerly.

"I'll fetch a buggy," he said. "About sundown."

A quick, warm smile touched her full lips. "I'll be ready."

He looked past her at Paula and Ennis who were walking slowly toward them, and again he was struck by the difference between the two girls. They were not far apart in age, but Paula possessed a serious, mature mind, while Josephine was still a girl, squeezing all the pleasure she could from each immediate moment. More than that, she was a pusher, and he found himself considering Saturday night with some uneasiness.

"This is Dake Ennis," Paula said. "Mr. Ennis, meet Jess Dawson. You've heard us mention him."

Ennis held out a bony hand. "Howdy, Dawson," he said in a voice that was as soft as the wind. "They tell me you handled Lane Miles. Wish I could have seen it."

Jess gripped his hand, thinking he had never seen a man who was as nearly a walking skeleton as Dake Ennis. He had bushy iron-gray hair that had long needed trimming; the yellow skin of his face was pulled tightly across cheek bones, and his blue eyes had been bleached by the sun until they were very pale. He did not look like the kind of man who would want to farm the land, and Jess wondered about it.

"It was fun for awhile," Jess said. "I hear you had a close call."

"Close enough." Ennis eased himself to the ground and leaned against a post. "I had one foot inside the pearly gate and I was listening to Gabriel blow his horn when Paula yanked me back into this veil of tears."

Hays shifted uneasily, wary eyes on Sam. He said, "No sense in me being here, damn it. There ain't nothing I can do for these folks."

"One thing we can do," Ennis said in his soft voice. "We can shoot you like we'd shoot any varmint, and the country would be better off." He glanced at Jess. "They tell me you're working for Farrar."

"That's right."

"Funny what a man will do for a few dollars," Ennis said. "Or maybe you ain't got him sized up right."

Irritated, Jess said, "The country needs a town and Farrar made one. What's wrong with that?"

"Nothing except that he fetched Hays with him, and Hays done the same trick with half a dozen settlers that he done with Tully. Showed this quarter section before I bought it, and all the time he knowed it had been pre-empted."

Sam reached for the Winchester, his anger hot again. "I don't reckon nobody would string me up for shooting a varmint. Jess, I don't know what you had in mind bringing him out here . . ."

"I asked him for help." Paula grabbed his arm. "Put that rifle back."

Sam hesitated, his eyes the sick eyes of a man who had been driven close to insanity. "What was your idea, Jess?"

"I was hoping you'd go look at the quarter section you filed on," Jess said. "I don't see no other way out of this."

"I'll show it to you, Tully," Hays cried eagerly. "I made a mistake. That's all, I just made a mistake."

"On purpose," Ennis said in his soft voice. "Well, Tully, what's done is done. You might as well make the best of it."

"I ain't budging from here," Sam shouted. "I keep telling you that. Before I'm done with Hays . . ."

Suddenly panicky, Hays dug a handful of gold coins out of his pocket and threw them at Sam's feet. "There's your locator's fee, Tully," he screamed. "I'm giving it back to make up for my mistake. I can't do nothing else for you."

Hays wheeled his horse and cracked steel to him. Once more Sam raised his rifle, and from the wild look on his face, Jess realized he was capable of shooting Hays in the back. He took two more steps and jerked the Winchester from Sam's grip.

"It's no good," he said. "Let him go."

Sam wiped his face, shaking now. He turned and picking up his post hole digger, jammed it into the hole. Ennis said, "First time I ever saw Hays scared. Nobody goes around bucking Farrar, and when you tangle with Hays, you're tangling with Farrar. I don't savvy, Dawson."

Jess swung around and mounted. "I just don't cotton to a crooked deal, Ennis."

Ennis grinned at that. "You ain't been here long, friend. You'll find out a lot of things you don't cotton to if you stick."

"I'll stick." Jess motioned to the gold on the ground. "Pick up your dinero, Sam. It's all you could expect."

Sam kept on digging. Paula said, "Thanks for bringing him out. I didn't know what . . . I mean, I just hoped we could work something out."

It was up to Ennis and Sam now, Jess thought. He nodded at Josephine. "Saturday night."

"I'll curl my hair," she said, laughing. "And I'll put on my best dress. You won't know me."

"Stay for supper, Jess," Paula said.

He shook his head. "I'd best slope along. Farrar might have something to tell me."

He swung his horse around and left, Hays a small, fast-moving dot on the prairie ahead of him. Jess rode slowly, and presently Hays was lost to sight beyond a swell in the land. The wind had lot its vitality so that now it was only a breeze, and the velvet softness of the twilight was all around him.

Jess saw that Sam had broken an acre or more of sod on the bench. It was only a beginning. A new feeling was in Jess as he rode away, a deep respect for any man who was willing to pit himself against a land as vast as this.

Behind him the sky was aflame with the sunset, but it went unnoticed by Jess. He was thinking of Mrs. Tully who had not bothered to come out of the over-jet to see what the trouble was about, of Sam Tully who was doggedly waging his lonely, hopeless fight, of Josephine who was so anxious to go to the dance, and Paula who was spoken for. But Paula was the one he wanted, not Josephine, and he realized he was as foolish as Sam Tully who refused to look at the face of reality.

Chapter Ten

THE SUNRISE

FOR Sam Tully each day was a sort of walking sleep. He could not destroy the thought in his mind that if they had let Dake Ennis die, he might have secured title to this quarter section. He was ashamed of the thought, for he was not a greedy man by nature, or a cruel one. He wondered if the country had changed him into a different person, a small-souled person who would rather see a man die than lose a piece of land to which he had no legal claim.

Physical work was the only way Sam could hold to his sanity. He finished the chicken pen and even Dake Ennis admitted it was skunk proof. Paula pulled some of the tall dry grass along the creek and filling several boxes for nests, started the setting hens on their three-weeks' vigil.

Each day Sam felt a growing thankfulness that he had Paula. Back in Missouri Ruth had always taken the responsibility of the yard chores. Now she maintained a sullen, tight-lipped silence, remaining inside the over-jet most of the time and showing a cool indifference toward the work that was begging to be done.

Paula and Josephine put in the garden Sam had plowed below the spring, Paula working with the hoe until her hands were calloused as a man's and it was Paula who brought sack after sack of chips to the pile beside the over-jet until it was as tall as she was. This was one thing Josephine refused to do, saying indignantly, "I won't touch those nasty things. Whoever heard of burning cow manure?"

For Sam there was the daily job of breaking the sod. "Get the corn in this month," Dake Ennis told him. "Plant White Mexican and it'll mature come fall." So with the exception of finishing the chicken pen and plowing the garden, Sam held doggedly to his job, ignoring the other things that needed doing. Now it was a respectable three-acre patch of brown soil on the bench. If the good weather held, he would have ten acres turned by the end of May.

Sam was up at dawn each day. He slept in the dugout on a mattress he had laid on an oil cloth that had been spread upon the dirt floor. He would slip from the dugout without waking Ennis who was still too weak to work; he would build a fire under the grate and take care of the stock. When he returned Ruth would have breakfast ready. It was one obligation which she did not shirk.

Every morning it seemed to Sam he could not get up. He felt as if his joints had ceased to function; his body was one great solid ache. But he would limber up by the time he harnessed the Percherons, and he was always on the bench holding to the bucking handles of the breaking plow when the sun showed in the east. Then the wind would come up, and it seemed to Sam that it sucked every bit of moisture out of his body until he was like Dake Ennis, a pile of bones rattling inside the dry sack of his skin.

Sam turned out at dusk on Saturday night the same as he had been doing every night, thinking of the meeting on Sunday at the Brown soddy across the river. The Tullys would go. Mrs. Brown had come over Friday to invite them. The preacher, she said, came to their place the second Sunday of every month and all the neighbors were welcome. There would be time to visit after they'd heard some good gospel preaching.

Sam watered and fed the horses and walked stiffly to the fire, bone-weary, thankful that Sunday came once a week and he could rest. It was nearly dark now, and he noticed that there was a lighted lantern inside the over-jet. When he reached the fire, he saw Jess Dawson standing there, a team and buggy behind him. Then Sam remembered the dance in Lariat and that Jess had promised to take Josephine.

"Howdy, Jess," Sam said, and dropped into the grass beside the fire.

Paula brought his meal on a tin plate; bread, salt side, and thin white gravy made of milk and flour. Typical homesteader fare, one of the things Ruth complained about when she said anything. No fruit and no vegetables, she'd say, and then ask, "What'll we look like five years from now, eating this stuff?"

Sam wanted to say that the Browns who had settled across the river had been eating the same things since they had come a year ago and they were healthy enough. But he never did. An argument was the last thing he wanted.

"How's the breaking going?" Jess asked.

"Slow." Sam began to eat, wondering what Ruth was doing in the over-jet. "What did Farrar say about the way you handled Hays?"

"Didn't like it," Jess said.

Sam could guess how it had gone with Farrar. Then he felt a sharp stab of envy. Jess had youth and strength and the kind of tough courage that a man needed in this country. They were qualities Sam did not have.

He thought of Neil Comer back home, a boy who should have been a man by now and wasn't, and he regretted Paula's engagement to him. Jess would make a better son-in-law. In time he might get around to asking Josephine, but Sam doubted that she would take him. Lane Miles was her kind. The thought was another source of worry to him.

Josephine came out of the over-jet, her chestnut hair freshly curled. She was wearing the one good dress she had, a flowered organdie lawn that went well with her coloring, and as Sam looked at her, he felt a sudden burst of pride. Feather-brained or not, she was the prettiest girl he had ever seen.

Josephine pirouetted in front of Jess, eyes begging for his approval. Jess murmured, "Mighty pretty. You'll be the most popular girl there."

"I aim to be," she said in a matter-of-fact voice.

"Just don't forget I've got some dances coming."

Josephine laughed. "How could I?" The laughter faded from her eyes and she lowered her voice. "Jess, you wouldn't mind if Mamma goes with us, would you?"

Jess glanced at Sam, hesitating. Then he said, "Of course not. Lots of room in the buggy."

"I'll tell her." Josephine whirled to the over-jet, calling, "It's all right, Mamma."

"Better get a coat," Jess said. "The nights get kind o' cool."

"Bring my coat, Mamma," Josephine said.

Sam put down his plate. He was not surprised about Ruth wanting to go to the dance, and he tried to rationalize about it. She was lonely. She had always liked to dance. She hadn't had a good time since they'd left Missouri. But it didn't quite do. She hadn't asked him if he wanted to go or if he'd mind if she went. She'd just got ready.

"Aren't you going, Paula?" Sam asked.

Paula was sitting on the other side of the fire, her arms clasped around her legs. She said, "No."

Ruth came out of the over-jet, carrying Josephine's coat. In that moment, with the murky firelight on her face, it seemed to Sam that he could not let her go. There would be men at the dance, a lot of them, lonely men who would admire Ruth. She would stand out among the homesteader women almost as much as Josephine would. He remembered the way Coe Farrar had looked at her that first day. Cold sweat broke through his skin as he thought, *She might not come back.*

Ruth did not look at Sam. She handed Josephine's coat to her, saying to Jess, "I know that three's a crowd and this is an imposition . . ."

"It's all right, Mrs. Tully," Jess said quickly. "It's just all right."

Jess helped Josephine and Ruth into the buggy and then stepped up. Ruth had not even glanced at Sam. As they wheeled away, Josephine called, "Don't wait up for us."

Sam sat motionless, his half-filled plate on the ground beside him, and presently the clatter of the buggy was lost across the grass.

Paula said gently, "Don't worry, Daddy. Jess is a good man."

"The best," Sam said thickly. "Paula, I was just thinking about him. Why don't you break it off with Neil? Alongside Jess he just ain't no man at all."

"Don't say that," she cried. "Don't even think it."

"Why not?"

She lifted the coffeepot from the grate and filled his cup. "I gave Neil my word. That's why." She replaced the coffeepot, adding, "Besides, Jess doesn't have any time for me."

Sam finished his supper, realizing that she thought more of Jess than she would admit, but he knew how highly she valued her word, so he didn't press the matter. He heard a man splash across the creek. He got up and started toward the over-jet for his Winchester when he heard the man call, "You there, Mr. Tully?"

It was Matt Brown, their neighbor north of the creek. Sam sat down, weak with relief. He called, "Come on in, Matt. The coffee's hot. Get him a cup, Paula."

Brown lumbered up to the fire, a massive, square-built man who had measured himself against this land and had hung on. He squatted beside Sam, taking the cup Paula handed him.

"Thank you kindly, ma'am," Brown said. "I reckon you folks are rich. We ain't had no coffee since we got here." He gulped half the cup and smacked his lips. "You don't know how much you miss coffee till you do without it for awhile. We brew some slop from roasted grain. That's what it is, just slop."

"We ain't exactly rich," Sam said. "By fall we'll be as broke as anybody. I bought a Walter A. Wood mower from McBain the last time I was in town. Cost me two prices, but I figured I could pay for it by cutting bluestem hay on the bottom. Best horse feed in the world. Ought to be able to sell it somewhere."

"Sure, you can sell it." Brown finished his coffee and held his cup out when Paula offered the pot again, making no pretense of hiding his eagerness. "I came over to ask for a job, Mr. Tully."

"I don't need a man."

"Mighty good quarter section you've got here. Buy it from Ennis?"

"No."

Brown stared at the coffee, his weather-blackened face

thoughtful. "Ennis won't be working for awhile. Reckon you two made a deal. I'll work for fifty cents a day, Mr. Tully."

There was no use to tell the fellow that he hadn't made a deal with Ennis, Sam thought. Brown would think he was crazy, too. He said, "Sorry. I can't afford to hire anybody."

"I'm a good hand," Brown urged. "You could buy some sows in Lariat and make enough off the pigs by fall to pay my wages and then some."

"Can't afford to build pig pens," Sam said irritably.

"Don't need to cost you much. In this country you don't build sheds like you're used to. You just make some wall trenches, two feet wide and two feet deep. Hogs can't jump 'em. Pork is one thing folks eat. You can sell every pig you raise." Brown finished his coffee, smacking his lips loudly. "And there's your breaking. You ain't got much time left to plant this spring. I've got a team and a grasshopper plow."

Sam held his answer until he had his temper under control. Brown was a good man. No use making an enemy out of him. He just couldn't possibly understand how it was.

"No," Sam said, not trusting himself to say anything else.

Brown sighed. "Well, I was hoping. Purty hard country, but if a man can pull through the first two-three years, he'll make it. I hit the Frenchman with a dollar and a four bit piece in my pocket."

"I should have thought you'd starve," Paula said.

"No ma'am, we haven't. I've got four boys and none of 'em had shoes last winter, but they got through without nary a cold. But I've got to make a little cash money somewhere. Maybe I can get a job on the railroad. I hear they're building into Lariat this fall."

"They'll be needing men," Sam said.

Brown rose. "Well, if you change you mind, just holler. I'm a good hand." He nodded at Paula. "Thank you kindly for the coffee."

He disappeared into the darkness. Sam heard the water splash as Brown waded back across the creek. Paula said, "Daddy, can't you see? It just isn't good sense, working yourself to death on another man's land."

"No," Sam said dully. "It ain't no sense."

"Maybe it is," Ennis came into the firelight, footsteps silent on the grass. "I heard what Brown said. Hire him, Sam."

For a moment Sam said nothing. He couldn't. Again the thought gripped his mind it would have been better if Dake Ennis had died. Now the man was telling him to hire Brown, to pay him hard money to work on land that Sam would never own. Anger rose in him, wiping out his restraint.

"Damn you!" Sam shouted. "Damn you! Ain't it enough for me to work your place for nothing?"

"No, not enough." Ennis dropped down beside Paula, the fire throwing a smoky light across his gaunt face. "I've been in hell, Sam. I've wanted this place for a long time and now I've got to sell it to you. Know why?"

Sam stared at Ennis, not believing he could have heard right, yet he knew he had, and he could not stifle the wild burst of hope that Ennis' words raised in him. "No, I don't know why."

"I'll tell you. It's because you're the gol-dangedest, mule-headedest human I ever met up with. I never allowed I was a good man, but damn it, I must be. Anyhow, I'd be dead if it wasn't for Paula. Only way I can pay off my debt is to sell to you."

Now another fear gripped Sam. Ennis would want too much, and the money in the feather bed had been dwindling fast. He said, "I can't afford to buy it. I reckon I'm licked, Dake."

"A man's licked when he says he is, and you ain't saying what you mean." Ennis picked up a chip and tossed it on the fire. "Took me a long time to see how it is in this country. I've lived here-abouts for years. Back to when the Injuns and the buffler had it. Before Ansell's day. Hell, back before Vestry and Hancock drove their herds to the Frenchman.''

Sam leaned forward, finding it hard to breathe. He had waited a long time to hear what Ennis was saying. Now the man was punishing him, taunting him, holding back on the price he'd ask. The seconds dragged out. Sam watched Ennis pull a plug of tobacco from his pocket and bite off a chew, and he could stand it no longer.

"What's your price?" Sam asked, and was surprised at the sound of his voice, so low it could not have been heard by Ennis.

"I was trapping in them days," Ennis went on. "Living with the Cheyennes and knowing all the time I was too late for my day. Jim Bridger and his breed was before me. I was born too damned late for their kind of living, but I kept thinking about this country and this here piece of land in particular, and even then I was figuring there'd be folks here someday. I done some riding for Iliff, saving my money, and then damned if another fellow didn't beat me to this quarter section and I had to buy it from him."

"How much do you want?" This time the words came out of Sam's throat in a shout. "You keep dangling me along. How much?"

"I've been thinking," Ennis went on in his soft tone. "There's a lot to figure on. Take Farrar. I'd like to whittle him down to size and maybe this Jess Dawson will do it, given time. Anyhow, we've got to work together and vote together so Farrar can't rob us by loading bonds on us which same I'm guessing is what he's up to. Railroad bonds, I mean. I'll take up some land above you. I've thought it over. You're the kind of gent this country needs, you and your women folks."

Sam rose. Sweat ran down his face. He wiped a hand across his mouth, tasting the sweat. He was shaking as if he had the ague. Now he threw out a trembling hand. "Dake, name your figure."

Suddenly Ennis seemed to be aware of Sam's feelings. He said, "Five hundred dollars which is what I paid, and the only reason I'm doing it is because of what Paula done. Just one string. I'd like to stay here till I can handle myself. I'm as weak as a dad-gummed pup with his eyes closed."

"Five hundred." Sam sat down, his knees breaking under him. He wouldn't have been surprised if Ennis had said five thousand. "You mean that?"

"Sure I mean it. I said I still aimed to be a neighbor. I won't have the spring, but the land upstream is good enough, and it ain't been taken on account of Ansell and Miles, but I'll take it and I'll fight 'em to hellangone."

"You've made a deal." Sam wiped his face again, eyes turning to Paula. He felt like shouting. He wished that Ruth was here to know about this. "You sure have."

"I'll get the papers fixed up soon as I get to town." Ennis took a long breath as if the talking had tired him. "But it ain't gonna be all roses. You know why Miles ain't been shoving at you?"

"No."

"Josephine, that's why. I know that huckleberry. No good, just no damned good. If you ain't careful, she'll run off with him and he won't bring her nothing but trouble."

"I'll talk to her," Paula said.

But her words brought no assurance to Sam. He knew how stubborn Josephine was, and he doubted if Ruth could stop her if she made up her mind she wanted Miles. He stared at the fire, the satisfaction that had been in him a moment before dying.

Even a strong man could stand only so much trouble, and now Sam felt his weakness and his age. He was tired in every bone and muscle of his body. An hour of rest did not revive him as it had when he was younger, and he could not blot out a sense of guilt for having brought his family out here. Even the knowledge that he could own this land was not enough.

Ennis rose, reeling a moment from dizziness. Then he said, "Remember one thing, Sam. Miles shot me and figured I'd cash in. If it hadn't been for you folks he'd have been right. Now if you kick his rump off the place and keep him from seeing Josephine, he'll be after your hide.''

Ennis walked back to the dugout. When he was gone, Paula said, ''It's going to be all right, Daddy.''

Sam didn't say anything. He couldn't. He was trapped, for he knew it wasn't going to be all right. Josephine was too big a price to pay for peace, and he wasn't man enough to fight Miles and his crew. But he would take Ennis' offer. He had no choice, for he could not go back to Missouri and start over on a rented farm.

''I'm going to bed,'' Paula said. ''You won't stay up all night will you?''

''No. I'm just not sleepy yet.''

But he did stay up, occasionally feeding the low-burning fire with another chip. He slept now and then, and waking, felt the loneliness of the prairie night press against him. Occasionally he heard the call of some night bird from along the creek, or the bark of a coyote from a sand hill to the south.

His mind seemed to be freed from the aching confines of his body; he felt the wildness of the prairie that was in the night breeze and the sky and the haunting coyote chorus. He shivered, trying to think of what this country would be in five years with fences and grain fields and a railroad, but he could not project his thoughts into the future. They kept returning to Ruth.

She was his wife; he loved her, and she was the mother of his girls. She had never been forced to live as Matt Brown's wife lived, an existence so meager that her children did not have shoes for the Nebraska winter.

The bitterness in Sam grew as he brooded over the unfairness of Ruth's attitude. All of his troubles were rooted in that attitude. A man could do anything when a wife had faith in him, but Ruth had no faith. Now she had brought him to the place where he had no real faith in himself.

The morning star showed and then the eastern sky was brightened by the pale promise of dawn, and he heard a buggy coming up the creek. He rose, wanting to tell Ruth that the land was theirs, and yet afraid of what she would say. He could not throw off the depressing feeling that she wanted him to fail so he would have to go back to Missouri.

Sam moved away from the fire to the covering shadow of the over-jet and stood there while the buggy stopped and Jess stepped down. He gave Josephine a hand and she swung down lightly, laughing. Sam saw her kiss Jess in her careless way; he heard her say, "I had a wonderful time, Jess."

Sam strained his eyes, but he was too far from the buggy to see it clearly. Jess said something to Josephine, his voice so low that the words did not reach Sam's ears, then Jess got into the buggy and drove away. Sam's hands were clenched, nails biting into the calluses of his palms, and pressure grew in his chest until each breath was torture. Ruth had not come back!

Josephine walked toward the over-jet, yawning. She saw Sam and stopped, startled. "Why aren't you in bed, Daddy? It's almost daylight."

"Where's Mamma?" Sam asked, his voice strange to his own ears.

"Oh, Farrar's bringing her. They're right behind us. I had such a good time, Daddy. I danced with a lot of men." She hummed a little and sang softly, "First lady to the right, swing the man who stole the sheep, now the one who hauled it home, now the one that ate the meat, and now the one that gnawed the bones."

"Why didn't Mamma come with you and Jess?"

"Our buggy was kind of crowded," Josephine said carelessly. "You should have seen Jess, Daddy. Lane Miles was there and Jess had another fight with him. I didn't see it. They went outside and Lane never came back. Jess got a black eye. He's wonderful. Maybe he'll propose."

It took a moment for Sam's mind to focus on that. He asked, "You going to take him?"

"Oh, I don't know. I'm not ready to get married yet. I'm going to bed. I'm tired. I didn't miss a dance."

She climbed into the over-jet. Still Sam stood there, hearing the other buggy, and at that moment he hated Ruth and he hated Farrar. He moved past the fire, and when the buggy appeared out of the opalescent light of dawn, he called out, "Farrar." Then it occurred to him he had not thought to get his Winchester from the over-jet.

"Yes sir," Farrar said in his hearty voice. "I brought your wife home safe and sound. She's a fine dancer and she was very popular tonight, just mighty popular."

The buggy stopped and Ruth got out at once without waiting for Farrar to help her. Sam said, "Farrar, if you ever touch her again, I'll kill you."

"Whoa there, Mr. Tully," Farrar said, surprised. "I just fetched her home so the young folks could be alone. No harm done, no harm at all."

"You heard what I said."

"Good night, Mrs. Tully," Farrar said, and turning his team sharply, drove away.

Ruth stood motionless, staring at him. There was a moment of silence, then she breathed, "Sam. I — I didn't know."

He looked at her and it seemed to him she was a stranger who had grown farther apart from him each day since they had left Missouri. He didn't want it that way. He didn't hate her. He was cursed by his love for her and he always would be.

Then, because he wanted her to share this with him, he said, "Ennis is selling the quarter section to us. It'll be our land, Ruth. Our land." When she turned away, he raised his voice at her, "Don't that mean nothing to you, Ruth? Don't it mean nothing?"

She ran past him and disappeared into the over-jet. He stood there, staring at the weathered canvas pulled tightly across the bows, the sense of loss making him sick. He walked toward the bench and climbing the slope, stopped at the edge of the sod he had turned.

The sun was almost up now, the eastern sky rosy. Here he had worked and sweated; he had strained with his hands on the handles of the breaking plow, the small patch of brown earth almost lost in the great sweep of grass, a pale-green carpet. He heard the sweet morning song of a meadow lark, and yet he didn't hear it. The sound reached his ears, but it made no real impression on his consciousness.

He knelt on his knees and scooped up a handful of earth that had broken free from the grass roots. He let it trickle through his fingers. Good soil, good rich soil. No stumps. No rocks. Just good soil that belonged to him.

He had not been a fool. It had worked out as he had said it would. This was what he had hungered for all his life. Now he had it, but the hunger was not satisfied. More than anything else, he wanted to share his moment with Ruth.

Sam Tully had never felt as lonely as he did now, kneeling here in the clean, prairie earth.

Chapter Eleven

STRAW BOSS

BY then end of May the settler tide had almost stopped running. "They'll be coming again in the fall," Doc Ives told Jess. "Too late now to plant anything, but there's still free land, and this railroad talk will fetch another crop for Farrar and Hays to harvest."

Restlessness still prodded Jess, although not as sharply as it had. The country had grown on him. Even the wind was not as irritating as it had been. He couldn't explain it. He didn't try. He just knew that he would stay on the Frenchman.

He didn't know what had changed his attitude or what had brought him to this decision. Perhaps it was Paula Tully who lingered in his mind like the memory of a flaming sunset, the perfection of beauty that is remembered through the leaden winter days when the sun is swallowed by a gray bank of clouds. Or perhaps it was Josephine with her warm soft body that was hungry for a man. Or Sam Tully whose dogged, seemingly stupid stubbornness had been rewarded by Dake Ennis.

Jess often stayed awake after he had gone to bed in his hotel room, thinking of his months in Leadville when he had been pilloried on an altar of silver. Now, with so much time to consider it, he understood something he had not fully understood the night he had met Coe Farrar on the prairie.

He had been crushed by the powerful; Farrar represented that same power. Jess would take what he could when he could with no pangs of conscience about it. But the Tullys and Doc Ives had made a difference. They had their way of looking at a new country; Coe Farrar and Bill Hays had theirs, and Jess was caught with a foot in both camps.

Jim Brennan never actually admitted it, but Jess had a feeling that the newspaper man was snared in the same trap. "Hang on till fall," Brennan said one morning when Jess dropped into the print-shop. "You haven't got anything to lose."

"Hang on for what?"

"The railroad. Coe will fetch it in as sure as you're a foot high. In a new country like this a railroad is the same as an artery in your body. I don't know what kind of business you're looking for, but whatever it is, you'll get a chance at it when the railroad comes."

"I don't know what I'm looking for," Jess admitted. "That's the trouble."

Brennan laughed dryly. "I know what's wrong with you. When a man lives in a mining camp, he gets the feeling that everything is temporary. Bonanza talk, and all the time every mother's son in camp knows that maybe tomorrow the vein will pinch out and they'll be helling over the next ridge."

Jess nodded, knowing exactly what Brennan was talking

about. "Some ways I'm glad I'm out of it, but there's one thing I can't get over. The bankers gave me the dirty end of the stick."

"They always do," Brennan said. "They like sure things, bankers do. You can bet your bottom dollar that Will Rollins wouldn't be here if Coe hadn't made the first gamble. Will won't lose."

"I ain't sure I can hang on till fall. I'm not built like Rollins and Duke Morgan and Bill Hays."

"Hell, you've got your chips bet on Coe. Let 'em lie. He'll see you get a crack at what he calls opportunity."

"You're fooling yourself and you know it. There's only one opportunity Coe's looking for. That's for Coe Farrar."

Brennan eyed him for a moment, chewing rhythmically, then he wiped a hand across his mouth and shook his head. "I'm not fooling myself, Jess. I aim to ride on Coe's shirt tail, and when the time's right, I'll get a cut out of his pie. Maybe just a little piece, but it'll do for me."

"But when you get it, you won't be proud of yourself," Jess said. "Not like it was your own pie."

Brennan shrugged. "I don't give a damn whose pie it is as long as I get a hunk of it."

Someone came in. Jess swung toward the door and saw that it was Duke Morgan, the gold-plated star winking in a vagrant gleam of sunlight. Morgan never made any effort to hide his dislike for Jess, and he didn't now.

"Coe wants you," Morgan said, and wheeled and walked out.

"You're going to kill that bastard someday," Brennan said. "I think he knows it."

"If he was real sure," Jess said, "he'd be sloping out of here."

"He's not sure enough to give up his piece of pie," Brennan conceded.

"I'll see what Coe's got on his mind," Jess said, and left the print shop.

Farrar was alone in his office. He motioned to a letter on his desk. "The mail just got in. I've got bad news."

Jess sat down. He rolled a smoke, waiting for Farrar to go on. It was the first time since he had met the man that he had seen Farrar's complete self-confidence shaken, but now there was no question about the worry that gripped Farrar. His fat face was pale; his long dark hair that he usually kept slicked down was ruffled as if he had been running a hand through it repeatedly.

"I thought I had all the backing I needed when I started this townsite," Farrar said as if not quite sure how much to explain, "but now it looks like I need more, so I've got to go to St. Louis. Either I keep my fences mended or we all go down together."

Jess fired his cigarette and remained silent. He had never been given the slightest hint how much Farrar had invested or how much he had in reserve, but he had never pegged Farrar as a shoestring man.

Farrar shoved a cigar between his teeth and chewed on it, blue eyes pinned on Jess. "I've got to catch the morning stage, and I don't have the slightest idea how long I'll be gone. I want you to take my place here. Just keep the office open. There may be some important decisions to make, but I know I can trust your judgment."

"About the money," Jess said. "Why can't you get it from Will Rollins?"

Farrar laughed. "Will is a penny ante man and he plays his cards close to his vest. We're all in this together. We'll make it big or we won't make it, and that goes for Will. Besides, I've got to pull all the political wires I can get my hands on."

Jess drew on his cigarette, thinking of his talk with Brennan. If he turned this job down, he was finished with Farrar, and he wasn't ready to step out yet. Now, honest with himself, he mentally admitted that he wanted his piece of pie along with the others.

"Suppose I can't make a decision," he said. "Who do I go to?"

"Brennan." Farrar chewed on his cigar, frowning. "Or I'll put it another way. Don't go to Doc Ives."

Jess nodded. "I'll be here when you get back."

"The main thing is to talk to anybody who comes in. You know what to say. There won't be many settlers, but you may have a chance to sell some lots. Lariat needs more business. Don't pass anything up."

"Women? Or another saloon?"

"You know better than that. These settlers are a bunch of damned Puritans. The one thing we've got to do is to keep a clean town."

"Do the other boys know you're tapping me on the shoulder?"

"They will before I leave."

Jess rose. "Duke won't like it."

"Didn't figure he would. If he needs sweetening, pass him the sugar bowl. Never trap a fly with vinegar."

"I never was much of a hand with sugar," Jess said and wheeled out of the office.

When the stage left town, Farrar was on it. They had shaken hands with him, these men who belonged to what Doc Ives called the "Farrar clique." While the dust that the coach had stirred was still settling, Duke Morgan said, "He made a hell of a poor choice when he picked you, Dawson."

Brennan said, "Shut up, Duke. We've gone along with Coe this far. We've got to keep on going."

Bill Hays turned and walked toward the saloon. Will Rollins and Sandy McBain nodded agreement to Brennan's words. Morgan glared at the three of them, his face stormy, then he wheeled to follow Hays, the usual swagger gone from his stride.

"You aiming to clean house, Jess?" Brennan asked.

"Looks like I'll have to."

"You know what Coe will do then?"

"Maybe nothing. He said he trusted my judgment." Jess nodded and moved away, leaving the three men standing in the middle of the street.

It took only a moment for Jess to discover that Farrar had cleaned out his desk. The safe was locked and Farrar had not given him the combination. Here was proof of what Jess suspected. Farrar did not fully trust him. Probably he trusted no one.

Jess stepped into the back room where Farrar cooked his meals and slept. The bed was made, the dishes washed and put away, the top of the stove wiped clean. Except for a few clothes hanging in the closet and some shirts folded neatly in the top drawer of the bureau, the room had the appearance of belonging to a man who had no intentions of returning.

Farrar was a fastidious man who could not leave anything in disorder. Looking around the room, it occurred to Jess that Coe Farrar never intended to step foot in Lariat again, a possibility that gave the lie to all of his talk about believing in the country.

Late that afternoon Dake Ennis rode into town on one of Sam Tully's saddle horses. He was still thin, and weariness was stamped on his bony face as he reined up in front of the townsite office and went in.

Jess was sitting behind Farrar's desk. When Ennis saw him, he stopped in the doorway, a gaunt shoulder against the jamb. He said in his soft voice, "Well sir, a man runs into the damnedest things. That's the last thing I ever expected to see, you sitting in Farrar's chair."

"You'll see it more'n once if you stay in town," Jess said. "Coe took the stage to St. Louis and left me to run things."

Ennis sat down. "I don't savvy. I just don't savvy."

"You don't savvy what?"

"I was thinking about the old saying that birds of a feather flock together. Well, Farrar and Morgan and the rest of 'em have got the same feathers, but looks to me like you walked into the wrong coop."

"Maybe not," Jess said, irritated. "You buy one of Sam's horses?"

Ennis nodded. "Miles took my horse when he shot me. I dunno where he is." He took off his hat and ran a hand through his iron-gray hair. "You ain't getting me off the subject that easy. I seen you handle Hays. Likewise I've heard talk that you and Morgan are building up to a run-in. That proves what I said about being in the wrong coop. Now why in hell did Farrar leave you to run things?"

"I don't ask questions about Farrar's business," Jess said. "I just take orders."

"Maybe it ain't so hard to figure it out at that," Ennis said thoughtfully. "Farrar knows the settlers are uneasy about some of the dirty tricks Hays has pulled, so he decided he needed somebody who looks honest. You do, but now I'm wondering whether it's just looks."

A hot flash of anger burned through Jess. He put his hands palm down on the desk, fighting the desire to get up and throw Ennis out. Then he remembered that folks like Doc Ives who knew Ennis trusted him, and the thing Ennis had done for Sam Tully was proof enough of his inherent integrity.

"Coe could use you, too," Jess said. "I heard about you selling out to Tully."

Ennis lowered his gaze. "When you owe folks your life, you've got to pay 'em back any way you can." He looked up. "Where's Hays?"

"In the saloon."

Ennis rose. "I want to see him."

He was wearing a gun, and Jess knew that Hays was armed. This had the smell of trouble, trouble that could be avoided, but Morgan wouldn't have sense enough to stop it. He might not even want to.

"I'll go along." Jess rose. "Time to lock up anyhow."

"I don't need a nurse maid. . . ."

"Who said you did? I'm just going along to watch the fun."

Ennis stalked out. Jess followed, locking the door and dropping the key into his pocket. Ennis did not wait. He moved down the board walk, Jess running to catch up. When they reached the store, he asked, "What have you got up your sleeve?"

"My business," Ennis said, and crossed the street to the saloon.

Jess kept with him, their boots stirring the deep, gray dust. He glanced at Ennis' white, set face, wondering about him. He did not know the man well enough to make an intelligent guess about what he planned to do.

They pushed the swing doors apart and went in, Jess a step behind Ennis. The light was thin, and it took a moment for Jess' eyes to become accustomed to the gloom. The air was cool inside, and heavy with the smell of whiskey and tobacco smoke.

The talk stopped as suddenly as if someone had given an order. Hays and Morgan were at the bar, a half-filled bottle before them. Rollins stood five feet from them, Jim Brennan beside him. Brennan had started to reach for a plug of tobacco when the batwings opened. Now his hand dropped to his side, his face showing a distaste for what he sensed was coming.

Ennis walked directly to Hays, a board squealing under foot. The locator faced him, gaze flicking uncertainly to Jess and returning to Ennis, the pale blue pupils of his eyes becoming pin points so that they seemed to disappear. Fear was in him. He began to tremble, the corners of his mouth quivering. No man, Jess thought, no man at all. The only question was what Morgan would do.

"Take your belt off and give it to the bartender," Morgan said. "We've got a rule about packing a cutter."

"Make your rule work both ways," Ennis said.

"Hays has got need of one," Morgan said. "That makes a difference."

"It does for a fact," Ennis agreed. "I can think of ten men who have got reason to plug him." He fixed his gaze on Hays' face. "I sold out to Sam Tully for five hundred dollars. I reckon you heard that."

"Yeah, I heard it. You're a damned fool."

"I may be," Ennis said, "but I ain't a cheap thief. I owe the Tullys my life, and I don't like to see 'em robbed of five hundred dollars. I'm going to take it back to 'em. Dig up."

So that was it! Jess moved forward to stand at Hays'

side. Morgan was behind the locator, and again Jess felt a moment of uncertainty. The marshal might stay out of the play, but Jess could not be sure.

Hays regained control of himself. Color flowed back into his cheeks and he stopped trembling. He threw out his voice in a burst of defiance, "You can pay 'em, Ennis. I ain't."

"Then I'll kill you," Ennis said, his voice softer than usual. "I'll take that money to Sam and it's coming out of your pocket or I'll kill you."

Hays' hand slid under the skirt of his coat and gripped the butt of his gun. He jerked the Colt upward in a frenzied motion; the barrel caught in the leather and it took him a second to free it. Ennis drew, but he was pathetically slow. At another time it would have been different, but he was still weak from his wound and the ride into town had sapped his strength.

Jess caught Hays' wrist before he could fire. Ennis' .45 was still moving into line. "Put it back, Ennis," Jess said, watching Morgan. "A killing won't do us no good."

"I'll handle . . ." Morgan began.

"You wasn't handling nothing." Jess gave Hays' wrist a twist, making him drop his gun. "Dig that five hundred up, Hays."

For a moment there was absolute silence. Brennan's hands were knotted at his sides, his gaze fixed on Jess' face. Rollins took one step and stopped, staring at Morgan who was standing motionless, an empty showcase now, bravado drained out of him.

Hays jerked free from Jess' grip. "You standing for this, Duke?"

"It's Dawson's play," Morgan answered sullenly. "Coe gave him the reins."

"Pay up and get out of town," Jess said. "You've located your last man in this country."

"Now hold on . . ." Rollins began.

"Will," Jess said, "you stick with your banking. If there's one thing that's been wrong with the set up you boys rigged, it's Bill Hays and his stealing just like he tried to do with Sam Tully. Now he's paying the five hundred and he's getting out of town. I'll give him ten minutes and then I'm coming after him if he ain't gone.''

For a time Hays stood there, his spirit beaten by the conflict between his fear and his pride, and in the end the fear won. He said sullenly, ''When Coe Farrar is fool enough to leave you in charge of his business, it's time I was getting out.''

He drew a wallet from his pocket and took five hundred dollars from it; he handed the money to Ennis and started toward the swing doors. By the time he reached them he was running. He pushed through them and went out. Morgan gave Jess a glance, his handsome face masked against the sting that his bruised pride brought him, then he left the saloon, his back held stiffly straight.

Rollins turned to the bar and took a drink. He wiped his mouth, gaze shuttling to Jess' face. ''You didn't do yourself any good just now, Dawson.''

Jess laughed, a deep, belly laugh. In that moment he felt better than he had for months. ''I don't care much, Will. Fact is, I just don't give a damn.''

''I don't get it,'' Rollins said. ''You haven't pulled your gun on a man since you've been here, but Morgan stands there like a fool and lets you beat Hays down.''

''You know what Doc Ives calls Morgan?'' When Rollins nodded, Jess added, ''That's the answer. With some men you don't have to pull a gun.''

Brennan reached for his plug of tobacco and chewed off a mouthful. ''You're missing one thing, Jess.'' He slid the plug back into his pocket. ''We need a locator. Now we ain't got one.''

''We've got one.'' Jess nodded at Ennis. ''An honest one.''

''Coe won't stand for it,'' Rollins said. ''He'll kick the seat of your pants clear across the Colorado line.''

''You know, Will, I've got a hunch he knew I'd get rid of Hays. He just didn't have the guts to do it himself.''

Ennis was leaning against the bar, body slack with the sheer weariness that was in him. "Dawson, if you think I'll throw in with . . ."

"You bet I think you will. You'd have been dead five minutes ago if I hadn't horned in. I'm remembering what you said about owing the Tullys for your life."

"But I never done no locating."

"You know the country. You can find corners, can't you?" When Ennis nodded, Jess said, "It don't make no difference what you think of me or Farrar or anybody else. Just do an honest job."

"All right, I'm a locator." Ennis turned to the bartender who had been silently watching. "Give me a drink. I never needed one so bad in my life."

"You think Hays will leave town?" Rollins asked.

"I know he will," Jess said.

He moved to the swing doors and waited there until he saw Hays ride out of town, heading east. Morgan was nowhere in sight along the street.

Chapter Twelve

ENNIS' PROPOSITION

LARIAT changed after Farrar left. Jess was conscious of it at once, although the change was an intangible thing and Jess could not explain it. For one thing, the meals in the hotel dining room were strained.

Morgan still took his place at the head of the table. When there was a roast to be carved, he performed the rite with neatness and dispatch as he had always done, but it was apparent that he took no pride in it. He got up and left the instant he finished eating. He never spoke to Jess. If they met on the street, neither gave any sign of recognition.

"He's waiting for Farrar to get back," Ennis said.

"We all are," Jess said, "but sometimes I wonder if he ever will."

"He'll be back. He'll talk them St. Louis money bags right out of their shirts." Ennis shrugged. "Well, I'm waiting, too, I reckon. I'm done locating the minute he shows up."

Jess was not sure whether the change was due to Farrar's absence as much as it was to the incident in the saloon. McBain was more reticent than ever. Rollins spoke to Jess only when he had to, usually about townsite business. Brennan was so coldly reserved that Jess stopped dropping into the print shop. Even the barber, garrulous by nature, maintained a stony silence when he cut Jess' hair.

But Dake Ennis' friendship was compensation for anything Jess had lost. Ennis regained his strength, color returned to his face, and he ate with a voracious appetite that brought his weight back to normal. He made it a habit to step into Jess' hotel room after supper where they sat talking for hours. Actually Ennis did the talking, Jess listening with interest to his experiences with the Cheyennes, as a buffalo hunter, and as a cowhand riding for Iliff in Colorado.

Occasionally they took walks in the June twilight circling the town, their footsteps silent in the buffalo grass. Darkness would move in on them and lights would come to life, and while they walked, human sounds flowed out across the prairie from Lariat's street. But Dake Ennis had a way of being in this world of people, and still living apart from it.

At times Ennis would stop and stand motionless, his head cocked as if listening for something that escaped Jess. "The wind will talk to you if you've got an ear for it," he told Jess one evening. "Most folks cuss it, but I like it. Anyhow, you can't stop it from blowing, so you might as well learn to live with it."

"It don't talk to me," Jess said.

"Then you ain't got the ear for it. Or maybe you never took time to listen. When a man lives alone, he learns to take company wherever he finds it."

"Maybe you can tell me what the wind's saying," Jess said skeptically.

Ennis nodded. "It'll rain tomorrow."

Jess glanced up at the sky. It was not yet fully dark, the first stars just beginning to appear. He could see a few ominous looking clouds along the western horizon, but they were no different from the clouds he had seen for weeks when there had been no rain.

"I'll bet on that," Jess said.

Ennis laughed softly. "Wouldn't be fair to bet with you, ignorant like you are. You'll learn if you live here for thirty year like I have." He swung back to town. "What are you gonna do when Farrar gets back?"

"Keep sitting. I've got a good deal."

"You ain't got no such thing. What have you done since you started keeping Farrar's chair warm besides booting Hays out of the country and keeping him from plugging me?"

"Sold a lot today. Fellow from Omaha is gonna build a drugstore beside the townsite's office. Last week I sold a lot to a gent who's aiming to start a lumber yard."

"Real proud of your work, ain't you?"

"Why not?"

"A man's got just one life. That's why. He lives it right or he lives it wrong, and you're wrong if you stick with Farrar."

"You sound like Doc Ives."

"I sound like him because I think like him. You ain't satisfied. Don't try to make me think you are. Something's eating on you but I ain't figured it out."

Jess knew what it was. He had never been free from the humbling his pride had taken in Leadville. The preachers were wrong when they said the world belonged to the meek. It belonged to men like the Leadville bankers and mine owners, to men like Coe Farrar, so Jess was on Farrar's side.

By fall Jess would be several hundred dollars ahead. If he found a business he liked, he'd take it. If he didn't, he'd drift on. Either way he won. That was the way he reasoned it out, but there was something wrong with the reasoning. Sooner or later his thoughts got around to Paula Tully and he knew he would not be drifting on.

"All right, something's eating on me," Jess said. "Let it go."

"Get out while you can," Ennis urged. "If you stay with Farrar, you'll wind up doing something you'll hate yourself for the rest of your life."

"There's preaching at the Brown place Sunday," Jess said. "Let's go out and get our souls saved."

"Go to hell," Ennis said.

"Maybe the wind's been talking to you 'bout me."

"Now maybe it has. The Lord's in the wind and the sky and the earth. There's some of Him in all of us. Likewise there's some of the devil."

"Now you sound like a preacher."

"No more'n Doc Ives does. Jess, I wouldn't have taken this locating job if it hadn't been for you. I ain't sorry, but I won't keep on. I'm going into cattle. I'll take some land above the Tully place and get some good shorthorn stuff. I'd like to have you for a partner."

Jess stared at him in the thin light, finding it difficult to say anything. This was the biggest compliment that anyone had ever given him in his life.

"Thanks, Dake," he said after a moment's silence. "I don't know. I'd like to think it over."

"Sure, but don't wait till Christmas. You've got to bust it off with Farrar, and that means coming over to the side of folks like me and Doc Ives and the Tullys who are here to stay."

"Yeah, I know. What about Ansell and Miles? Last I heard Miles had run everybody across the Frenchman but the Tullys."

"They won't last," Ennis said. "They're like the buffler and the Injuns. The day of the big cattleman was gone when Vestry and Hancock were moved out."

"Miles and Ansell don't know that."

"Then we'll show 'em. We've got to thank 'em for one thing. If it wasn't for them, there wouldn't be no good land left south of the river."

They reached Lariat's street and moved along the walk to the hotel. As they climbed the stairs to their rooms, Ennis said, "Let's take a ride out there Sunday. I'll show you the piece of land I had in mind and we'll drop in on the Tullys. Ain't seen 'em since I left."

"Sounds good," Jess said.

It did rain the next day, a hard downpour that turned Lariat's street to mud again, then the wind switched back to the northwest and the sky cleared. Sunday was hot. The wind was steady, sucking up the moisture that had fallen, and again dust rose from the street, a constant gray haze that worked through doors and windows and left a thin trace on sills and furniture.

"I ain't sure I like this sod being turned," Ennis said as they left town. "I've seen a whole damned summer go by without enough rain to wet your neck. Nobody'll raise corn in a year like that."

"And we'll be eating dust."

Ennis nodded. "That's why I aim to keep the grass. You'n me together could take up a big piece of it. When Ansell's gone, there'll be all the range we need in the sand hills."

They rode west, then angled toward the river, passing soddy after soddy, patches of broken ground beside them. Children waved, and Jess and Ennis waved back. Occasionally a dog barked, and at one place they heard a guinea hen's angry potrack.

By noon they reached the Frenchman, found a shallow place, and forded the stream, horses' hoofs stirring mud that roiled the clear water. They put their horses up the steep south bank, crossed a stretch of bottom land, rich green with bluestem, and rode on to the bench beyond it.

Ennis reined up. "This is it. Not as good as what Tully got, and there ain't no spring, but it'll do. The river water's all right. We can raise enough wild hay on the bottom for horse feed." He motioned toward the low sand hills to the south. "Ladder range now, but it won't be in six months or a year."

Jess said nothing, but he could not understand why Ennis was so sure that Ansell and Miles would be gone in that time. Ennis gave him a quick glance as if appraising his interest, then pointed to a spot above them.

"I'll put my dugout yonder so it'd be above any flood water we get. Won't be no trouble getting good sod from the bottom, and I'll build my walls so thick Miles will need a cannon to get a slug through 'em."

"You'll be meeting Miles one of these days."

"And I'll kill him," Ennis said quietly. "Next time he won't get the drop on me." He scratched his nose, eyes seeking Jess' face again. "What do you think about throwing in with me?"

"Dake, I never met a man I'd rather be partners with than you, but there's some things I ain't sure about. Maybe I'll run into something I'd like better than the cattle business."

"Like what?"

"I've figured some on starting a freight line. Of course if Farrar gets his railroad, it might not be a good notion. Depends on whether there's other towns around that need freighting done."

"Farrar won't stand for no other towns."

"There's some things even Farrar can't stop."

"Glad to hear you say that," Ennis said. "Sometimes I get a feeling you think Farrar's God."

"He's a little short of that."

Ennis swung his horse downstream, his face showing disappointment. "Let's go see the Tullys."

"Don't shut the door, Dake. It's just that I've got to be sure."

"You'll be the one to shut the door. Not me."

They rode in silence, the sun swinging westward. An uneasiness worked into Jess. He knew, and he realized Ennis knew, that a great deal depended on what happened when Farrar returned, if he returned. The cattle business might be the answer.

Jess thought of what Brennan had said about getting a piece of Farrar's pie. Well, that was a part of the trouble. His piece might be handed to him soon and it might be big. He'd be a fool, he told himself, to walk out before he knew.

As they rode into the Tully place, Jess could see no change except that the garden was fenced, the long rows of vegetables green and lush. They were irrigating from the spring, he saw, and there was not a weed in sight.

Smoke was pouring from the chimney of the dugout. Ennis called, "Sam."

It was Paula who came out. Her quick smile warmed Jess, and he thought for a moment that her eyes lingered on him, then he decided it was his imagination. He was that hungry for some sign from her.

"Come in," Paula said. "It's so nice to see both of you again. We thought you'd forgotten us."

"We'd never do that." Ennis dismounted. "You alone?"

"I am right now, but the folks will be back any time. They went to the meeting at Brown's. I stayed home to cook dinner."

"Thought everybody ate over there when they had a meeting," Ennis said.

Most of them do, but Daddy wanted to rest this afternoon. Put your horses up."

Ennis and Jess watered their mounts and turned them into a wire corral that Sam had built upstream from the dugout. "They've done a lot," Ennis said. "Makes me ashamed of myself. I didn't have much time, though. Miles plugged me right after I moved out here."

As they walked through the tall grass to the dugout, Jess asked, "Why don't you go take a look at Sam's corn?"

Ennis grinned. "I should have thought of that myself." Then his face turned grave, and he gave Jess a close, studying look. "Hell, I've been blind. I should have known how you felt about her."

"Dunno why you would. Paula don't know."

"I ain't so sure. But damn it, she's engaged to some kid back home that Sam don't like. You knew that, didn't you?"

"Didn't know what Sam thought of him."

"He figures the kid ain't good enough for her."

"No man is," Jess said, and went into the dugout.

Paula was standing at the stove, a red-checked apron tied around her slim waist. She glanced at him, raising a hand to her moist forehead. "Where's Dake?"

"He went up to take a look at Sam's corn."

"Oh." She swung to the stove, and picking up a fork, began turning pieces of frying meat. "Lane Miles brought in a hind quarter of antelope yesterday. It's the first we've had."

Jess sat down near the door and looked around. The Tully women had worked miracles with the dugout in the short time they had been here. A print curtain had been hung across the middle of the room, separating the bed in the back from the front. Sam had built a crude cupboard, somehow contriving to anchor it against the wall. The shelves were crammed with dishes and cans and sacks of food. A table stood in the middle of the room, two benches beside it, and beyond the table were two rocking chairs with bright anti-macassars covering their backs. A rag carpet lay on the dirt floor. Lace curtains hung at the glassless windows.

"Looks good in here," Jess said, wondering what Ruth Tully thought about it.

"We've done the best we could," Paula said. "Daddy says we can't have a real house till next year."

"You can get along."

"Of course we can, only it's kind of hard on Mamma. She hates dirt, but you can't get rid of it when your house is made of dirt."

Paula began setting the table, moving quickly from the cupboard to the table and back. Jess asked, "How do you like it by now?"

"Fine." She paused, smiling, and turned to the table

again, her hands filled with silverware. "I don't know why I like it. I'm not a violent person, and this is a violent country, but I do like it, even the storms." She shook her head. "But when it rains the roof leaks. The other day we had every pot and pan we own on the floor."

She opened the oven door, glanced in, and closed it. Jess said, "So Lane Miles is still friendly?"

She gave him a questioning look. "You know why?"

"Josephine."

Paula nodded. "It worries us, especially Daddy. Miles has been taking Josephine to the dances. You probably know about it."

He nodded. He hadn't gone to a dance since the time he had taken Josephine and her mother, but he had heard the gossip, and he knew Ruth Tully had not been back.

"You're the only family left on this side of the river," he said.

"That's what worries Daddy. He knows what Miles will do if he quits going with Josephine. But he's no good for her, Jess."

He was silent, thinking of other gossip he had heard, about Josephine and an Omaha drummer who had danced with her too many times. Lane had fought him and knocked him out, but the talk was that Josephine liked him better than Miles.

"I don't know why I talk to you about our troubles," Paula said apologetically. "I guess it's just that you have a way of settling things. Like making Hays give the five hundred dollars back to Dake."

"I can't do nothing about Miles and Josephine. She's old enough to know what she wants."

"I didn't expect you to do anything," Paula said quickly. "I just had to talk to somebody. I know Josephine doesn't really like Miles. She has to have men admire her. That's all. Daddy would do anything to break it up. The real reason they aren't staying at the Browns is because Miles will be there."

"Must be something new for Miles to be going to meetings," Jess said.

Paula whirled to the stove and set the coffeepot on the back. "Why don't you take Josephine to a dance again, Jess?"

He heard the rattle of chain traces. They would be here in a minute or two, and he had said none of the things he wanted to say. He rose and walked to the stove.

"It's not Josephine I want," he said. "Are you still engaged?"

"Yes."

She stood with her back to him, her slim body tense. He put his hands on her shoulders and made her turn to face him. He said, "You can't marry that fellow. I don't know anything about him, but I know you can't marry him."

She threw her head back, her chin thrust defiantly at him. "Why can't I?"

"Because if he loved you, he'd be here. You'll never go back to Missouri, and he won't come to you."

"I don't know. I mean, I think he'll come when Daddy has work for him."

"But you won't marry him. I won't let you. I never told a woman I loved her, but I'm telling you. I ain't much, but I'd do my damnedest to make you a good husband."

Her face was pale. She could not meet his eyes, and it was a moment before she could say, "I'm sorry, but I've given Neil my word. You wouldn't break a promise, would you?"

"You bet I would. For anything as important as this."

He put his arms around her and brought her to him in a sudden, violent motion. She braced herself against him, her fists beating at his chest. She cried, "No, Jess, no . . ."

He smothered her lips. She went slack in his arms, helpless against him and then her hands came up around his neck and he felt the pressure of her firm round breasts. The will to resist had left her and she became a fire in his arms; her lips were sweet and hungry.

The sound of voices reached them, Sam calling, "How are you, Dake?" and Ennis answering, "I'm fine except that I just can't get enough to eat, seems like." And Ruth said, "We'll fill you up on home cooking. Paula's the best cook in the world."

Paula drew her head back, slowly as if reluctant to lose this moment. She said softly, "I am sorry, Jess. I'm sorry for anything I've said or done that made you think I loved you."

"You do love me. Don't try telling me anything else. The only thing I'm sorry about is that you think your word is more important than your love."

She whirled away from him and picked up the fork. "It's got to be that way, Jess. It's got to be that way."

"I ain't one to give up," Jess said. "Not when I know you love me."

He turned to the door; he spoke to Ruth who was smiling at him, her face showing none of the bitterness that had been there the last time he had seen her, and he nodded at Josephine who looked at him sullenly. He heard Ruth ask, "What's the matter, Paula?" And Paula said, "Nothing, Mamma. We were just talking."

He crossed the yard to where Sam was unhitching the Percherons from the buggy. Sam said, "Mighty glad to see you, Jess. Ain't had a chance to thank you for getting the money back . . ."

"No need to thank me," Jess said brusquely. "Just gave me a good chance to get rid of Hays."

Ruth called, "Dinner's ready. Wash up."

"Just a minute till I yank the harness off," Sam shouted. "We'll be right in."

Jess met Ennis' questioning gaze and shook his head. He wished he could get his hands on Neil Comer. He'd break the fellow's neck.

Chapter Thirteen

FARRAR'S RETURN

JULY turned hot, the wind running in from the southwest. Not a hard wind, but it was steady and dry and hot, a death wind that would burn out the crops if it continued. Corn, a foot high in the rows, begged for rain, its leaves rolled up to preserve the scanty moisture that its searching roots found in the parched earth.

Lariat was an island in the prairie sea, its only communication with the outside world the tri-weekly stage that came in from McCook. For weeks Jess did not see a stranger except the few drummers who drifted in, filled with optimism when they came, emptied of it when they left. No new settlers, no business men seeking lots. Life in Lariat stood still while human hope was fried by the wind and sun like an egg in a hot skillet.

Jess met each stage that came in, hoping Farrar would be on it. But he didn't come, and as far as Jess knew, no one had heard from him. Each time he turned back toward the townsite office, Jess grew sicker of his bargain. He was surrounded by people, yet he lived alone.

Paula never came to town and Jess could not bring himself to ride out to the Tully place. Dake Ennis moved to the quarter section he had showed Jess, promising he would come back to town if he was needed. The wall between Jess and the others in Farrar's organization grew higher each day. The only friend Jess had was Doc Ives, and Ives was usually out on the prairie somewhere, black bag tied behind his saddle, treating everything from colic to broken bones.

Saturday was Lariat's one busy day. The settlers had found too much to do during the spring and early summer to come to town. Now their soddies were built, a few acres of sod broken, corn and sorghum planted, so on Saturday they flocked to Lariat. They gathered in the saloon to talk, or under the wooden awnings of the store and hotel; they stared at the brassy sky and cursed the weather.

To these people Jess had become a hero. They had fastened their hate on Bill Hays, and the way of his leaving town had been passed from neighbor to neighbor until every settler as far as the Colorado line knew what had happened. So Jess was accepted as Farrar had never been, but on his part the relation was impersonal. No one could be as close to him as Dake Ennis.

Every Saturday Jess moved along the street, talking to the settlers and trying to bolster their courage with his assurance that it would rain, that the long pull was the thing which counted, and one dry summer was not enough to condemn a country. He paid for drinks; he insisted on Sandy McBain giving credit although the storekeeper contended that it was past time to cut it off, and when it was noon, he picked up the hungriest children he could find and took them to the hotel dining room for dinner.

Rain fell along the Platte to the north; another storm soaked the sand hills to the south. The settlers, staring across the prairie at the sullen edge of the sky, would shake their heads and say somebody was getting rain, but all they had was the hole in the doughnut. And Jim Brennan, drinking more than ever, was prompted by a perverse sense of humor to write an editorial about the valley of the Frenchman being in the rain belt. That Saturday Jess had all he could do to keep the settlers from lynching Brennan.

"Next time you get a fool notion like that, I'll let 'em string you up," Jess told Brennan after the town had quieted down.

Brennan grinned and chewed off a mouthful of tobacco from a tattered plug. "Coe's got to have something out of backing me."

"That piece of pie you're counting on will have damned tough crust and nothing in the middle," Jess said. "I'm doubting that you'll ever see Coe again."

"He'll be along." Brennan said with quiet certainty.

"Heard from him?"

"No, but he'll be along. You'll see."

Brennan was right. That Wednesday Coe Farrar stepped down from the stage, immaculate except for the dust and carrying no trace of the worry that had gripped him when he'd left. They gathered in the street to shake hands: Morgan, McBain, Rollins, Brennan, and Jess.

"Hell of a dry ride," Farrar said. "Let's cut the dust out of our throats." He looked along the dusty street, smiling. "Boys, this is a damned fine town. I must have traveled a million miles since I left here, but I never saw another place I like as well as Lariat."

They went into the saloon and had a drink. Then Rollins asked, "What's the news?"

Farrar filled a glass and raised it. "Boys, we're drinking to Blake County. I don't reckon you've heard, but the job's done. What's more, you'll be hearing a locomotive whistling right here in Lariat by spring." He winked at Morgan. "Here's mud in your eye, Sheriff."

They drank again, Morgan as pleased as a boy with a new pup. Brennan said, "I knew you'd do it, Coe." He glanced briefly at Jess. "We had some doubting Thomases, but I wasn't among them."

Farrar laid his wide-brimmed hat on the bar and ran a hand over his long, glossy hair. "Well sir, I talked till I had callouses on my tongue, but we're set now. The first thing I've got to do is to deed that block to Blake County and get the courthouse started. Then we've got to win the county seat election. Start tooting the horn for Lariat, Jim."

"It'll be all over the front page," Brennan said.

"Who's your doubting Thomas?" Farrar asked.

Brennan jabbed a finger at Jess. "Dawson."

Morgan's face turned ugly. He said, "He sold you out while you were gone, Coe. Couldn't wait till you left town to move Bill Hays out. Now you ain't got no land locator."

"That ain't all," McBain added. "He wouldn't let me cut down on credit. That damned store will bust you, Coe."

Rollins nodded agreement. "I've quit making loans, Coe. I won't break my bank just to keep a bunch of farmers going."

Farrar looked at Jess, his fat face bland. "You seem to stand alone."

"I like it alone," Jess said.

"Give me the word, Coe." Morgan dropped a hand to gun butt. "Just give me the word and I'll throw him into the jug. The biggest mistake you ever made was leaving him to run things."

"You don't need the word," Jess said. "Start your gun smoking, Showcase."

It was the first time Morgan had been called that to his face. His lips sprang apart; his black eyes were filled with sullen rage. He stood motionless, the saloon silent except for the suddenly loud ticking of a clock on the wall, then his hand fell away from the gun butt and he turned mechanically to the bar; he poured a drink and gulped it.

"What have you got to say, Jess?" Farrar asked.

Jess thought of the parched corn, of the hungry, bare-footed kids he'd fed; he thought of Dake Ennis' words, "If you stay with Farrar, you'll wind up doing something you'll hate yourself for the rest of your life." Farrar's return had not changed anything.

"I've got one thing to say." Jess threw out a hand toward Brennan and the others. "There's your doubting Thomases. It ain't me. Either we're a bunch of damn, lying hypocrites or we ain't. We believe in the country or we don't. Which is it?"

Anger raised a bright stain in Brennan's cheeks. "I don't like that talk, Coe. There never was a day I didn't back this country."

"This takes more'n talk," Jess said. "It means believing we'll get rain. Next year maybe, but we'll get it and the farmers will raise a crop. It means backing 'em up and keeping 'em here till they do, and that means credit at the store and the bank. Otherwise you'll have folks coming in this fall to look at a bunch of empty soddies. What'll you tell 'em, Coe? Will you tell 'em the truth that your storekeeper and your banker didn't believe in the country enough to pull the first batch of settlers through a tough year?''

"Damn you." Rollins shook his fist in Jess' face. "You think I'm the kind of businessman who'd break my bank just to keep a bunch of raggle-taggle homesteaders eating?''

"No, you ain't that kind of businessman, Will, and get your fist out from under my nose. I reckon it's natural for a banker to get scared the first and run the fastest when times get tough.''

"I'm not a missionary," Rollins muttered. "Maybe Doc Ives is, starving while every man and his dog owes him money. Well, I'm not built that way.''

"You ain't for a fact," Jess agreed. "Let's tell 'em it's a desert that ain't fit for farming. Tell 'em Jim Brennan lied about this country being in the rain belt. Tell 'em they're a bunch of damned fools for believing us and they'd best go home.''

"You see?" Morgan said bitterly. "You see what you done, Coe, leaving Dawson to run things?''

Farrar had been listening, his big head cocked, a smile working at the corners of his mouth. "You know, Duke, the smartest thing I ever did was to leave Jess in charge. He's the only one in the bunch with brains enough to understand the position we're in. Keep giving credit, Sandy. Don't turn down no more loans to a bona fide homesteader, Will. Jim, tell folks that I'm back and we're working together. Tell them that the railroad's coming and it'll run right on through to Denver and give them the biggest market in the country. Paint it pretty, Jim. Colorado miners will be eating Blake County beef and grain.. Savvy?''

Brennan grinned. "You bet I do.''

"But Hays . . ." Morgan began.

"Duke, I told Jess I trusted his judgment," Farrar said. "I still do." He jerked his head at Jess. "Come over to the office."

Farrar walked out of the saloon. Jess winked at the bleak-faced Morgan. "Keep trying, Sheriff," he said, and followed Farrar.

Farrar was already across the street. Jess picked up his heavy valises and carried them to the townsite office. Farrar was behind his desk. He said, "You did a job."

Jess dropped into a chair and rolled a smoke. He said, "I wonder."

"Tell me what happened."

Jess fired his cigarette, then he told Farrar about Hays and Dake Ennis, about the lot sales he had made, and added, "There's one more thing I done that's hard to put your finger on, but it's big if I'm seeing this right. Folks cotton to me because I stood behind 'em and ran Hays out of the country. They cuss Hays and they don't like Rollins, but I ain't heard a man kick you or the townsite company."

"Good will is something you can't measure, but it's a big asset," Farrar said. "Yes sir, a good job. I haven't got a thing to complain about." He drew a cigar from the pocket of his black coat. "I thought I could hear Doc Ives talking when I listened to you while ago, only you're on the right side and Doc isn't."

Jess ground out his cigarette stub. "No, I'm not Doc Ives, Coe." He brought his eyes to the fat man's face. "Brennan says that if we play along with you, we get a slice of your pie. What's my slice gonna look like?"

Farrar laughed expansively. "It'll be thick and juicy. But there is one more thing I didn't mention to the other boys. We've got to swing some railroad bonds this fall. After the county seat election. In November, I think. Some folks like Doc Ives will kick, but it's being done in all the new counties. It's fair enough. We need a railroad and it's the only way to get it in the immediate future. That's where your good will is going to pay off."

Jess was silent. Both Doc Ives and Dake Ennis had foreseen this move. They'd kick, all right, but maybe they were wrong and Farrar was right. Now, looking at the promoter's round, bland face, Jess was reminded of his doubts about the man, even though Farrar had backed him against the others.

Farrar drew his checkbook out of his pocket and wrote Jess a check for his June wages. He shoved it across the desk, saying, "Keep on the good side of folks, Jess. We'll need everything we've got to carry two elections."

He sat back, his chair creaking under his great weight. "When I left, I told you we'd make it big or we'd go down together. Well, we'll make it big. I've got all the financial backing I need and I've mended my political fences. We've got the county organized. That worried me when I left. Funny about some men. When the weather's good, they like to go for a boat ride, but if a squall comes up, they start diving overboard."

Jess picked up the check and rose. He said, "You'd better curry Morgan down, or I will."

"We need him," Farrar said. "Don't forget that."

The wind switched to the southeast during the night. The rain started before morning, long silver lances splashing against the window of Jess' hotel room. When he woke, he looked out upon a wet world and the street was mud again.

Chapter Fourteen

DEATH MISSION

THE weeks that Dake Ennis had spent in town became a pleasant island of time in Jess' memory. July wore out and August came, and Jess was still gripped by the strange feeling that he lived alone. Farrar's return had brought no real change. The man had little capacity for friendship. He was pleasant and courteous, but it was a veneer. Nothing more.

The courthouse was started. Railroad surveyors reached Lariat, their stakes running out across the prairie like a line of immobile soldiers. Everyone in Blake County was waiting, Jess thought. Waiting! Time could not be hurried. Here, on the Frenchman, men did not live by the clock. They lived by weather; by the sun and the wind. It was a pattern. The wind brought rain and the sun gave life; roots spread out into the deep, fertile soil and the corn shot upward.

It seemed years instead of months that Jess had been here. Leadville with the defeats and bitterness that had warped Jess' soul faded into the background of the unimportant past. His thoughts focused on the present, on Paula who, without conscious intention on her part, held his future in her small hands. On Dake Ennis who had a talent for listening to the wind. On Sam Tully who had grown in stature because he had been too stubborn to be smart.

The days slid by like the silent passage of the wind. Sandy McBain was generous with store credit. Will Rollins reluctantly accepted notes and passed gold coins through the teller's window. Jim Brennan wrote flowery editorials about the valley of the Frenchman being in the rain belt and no one took exception, for the wind brought three soaking rains during the first half of August. The despair of the month before gave way to confidence.

"A damned good country," the settlers said. "Sure, it ain't no paradise, but where's a man going to find paradise?"

A pattern, the wind and the sun and the land, and you could not separate one from the other. The roads and Lariat's street were muddy more times than dusty, and no one objected. The black sky and vivid lighting that often struck too close to be comfortable and thunder that hammered across the roof tops of Lariat's buildings. But it was all right. The corn crop was made.

The county seat election was set in September. Jim Brennan gave no publicity to Lariat's rivals: a tiny settlement called Halsey near the Colorado line and the collection of tents on the falls of the Frenchman known as Knollsburg. As far as Brennan was concerned, Lariat had already won, and Farrar glowed with the high flown songs of praise that Brennan sang in each issue of the *Eagle*.

A generous man, this Coe Farrar, giving an entire block to the new county and donating the courthouse. Brennan said it over and over, but failed to point out that the deed had not been given to the county; that before it was, the county would reimburse Farrar for the cost of constructing the courthouse. So far there were no permanent offices for the county officials. The jail and three rooms in the hotel served as temporary quarters.

A week before the county seat election Farrar called Jess into his office. He said in a casual way, "Looks like we won't have much trouble winning. What do you think?"

"All you've got to do is to read the *Eagle*," Jess answered.

Farrar laughed. "Only Jim's throwing loaded dice. I want to know what you think."

"Lariat'll win. Giving store credit made you a lot of votes."

Farrar rolled a cigar between fat fingers. "The grangers say you're responsible, Jess. Looks to me like you can't do nothing wrong. They'll be running you for governor next."

"I reckon not," Jess said. "Politics ain't my meat. Coe, I've been thinking about throwing in with Ennis. We'll buy a few cows. Starting is gonna be slow, but in the long run it'll be a good business."

"Penny ante stuff," Farrar said disparagingly. "I've been thinking about you, boy. After the railroad gets to Lariat, we'll have more people and some little towns. They'll need fast transportation. It would be a good business to put in a line of hacks to hook Lariat up with the other towns. Carry mail and passengers and some small freight. Sort of an express service."

Jess rolled a smoke, considering that. It wouldn't go like

the Leadville business had, not with Farrar backing him.
He said, "Sounds good, Coe."

"I'll put up the money and be a silent partner," Farrar
went on. "You manage the business for an even split. How
about it?"

Here it was, the juicy piece of pie that Farrar had promised. Two months ago Jess would have jumped at it. Now
he hesitated, studying Farrar's face. There was a sort of
bland gall in the fat man's eyes that bothered him. Some
like Dake Ennis showed their thoughts and feelings on
their faces. Farrar never did.

"Sounds good," Jess said again, "but I've kind of run
out of patience. We won't have the railroad for a year."

"It'll be awhile," Farrar admitted. "I know how you
feel. A man gets so he wants to give time a kick." He fished
in his coat pocket for a match. "We need a business like
that now, Jess. We'll run your line between here and
Julesburg. It's a small start, but it'll keep you busy."

"I'll think about it."

Farrar struck a match and fired his cigar. "About this
election. We can discount Halsey. It's too far to one side
of the county. If we have any trouble, it'll come from
Knollsburg. They're talking about a grist mill on the falls
and they've got a good argument. This fellow Knoll is
tolerable smart."

Jess nodded, waiting. Farrar often worked up to something this way, and there was no hurrying him.

"I'm not as sure about this election as you and Brennan
are," Farrar said. "I want you to get Knoll and fetch him
to Lariat. Maybe we can make a deal of some kind. If we
can get him to pull his town out of the election, we'd have
a cinch."

"Why don't you go down there?"

Farrar shook his head. "I want him to see Lariat and the
courthouse. Maybe he'll figure out he's licked before he
starts."

It was a waste of time, Jess thought. He didn't know
Knoll; he had never even seen the man, but the chance of

his backing down now that he had gone this far seemed a slim one. Still, Jess had received an order in Farrar's round-about way, and he could see no reason to disregard it.

"I'll go after dinner," Jess said.

Farrar nodded as if there was no hurry. "It's about a two hours' ride, I'd say."

The day was cool for late August, the sky filled with fat clouds that drifted south with the wind. Jess had never been to Knollsburg, but he knew its general location. He passed a few farms, stopping to talk briefly with men he had met in Lariat. The county seat election was in their minds, and he was surprised that they were still undecided.

"Sure, a lot of railroad talk," a farmer said, "and Lariat's in the center of the county, but it's up there on the hard land. I kind of cotton to the notion of having our county seat on the river. Knoll is starting work on his grist mill. A fellow could take wheat in to be ground, buy supplies, tend to any county business he had, and it'd be just one trip."

All of them said the same thing in their own way, and it made sense to Jess. He had not thought of it before. Now it occurred to him that Farrar had had his ear to the wind. Someone, Knoll or Doc Ives or both, had been canvassing the county, and they had met with a better reception than Jess had thought possible.

He rode through a prairie dog town, the animals darting into their holes at this intrusion upon their private lives. Jess reached the river, crossing a slough that lay north of the stream, his horse's hoofs making a sucking sound in the soft mud.

A chalk rock bluff rose to the south, and from somewhere up there Jess heard quails whistling. He reined up, looking at the water that was deep and clear at this point, and decided Knollsburg would be down-stream. He had not angled far enough to the east.

He followed the bank to the end of the slough, year-old cattails rattling against his stirrups, and put his horse up the steep bank to a bench. Fifteen minutes later he saw Knollsburg, and he found it hard to believe that this poor excuse for a town would furnish any real opposition to Lariat.

Jess counted three tents, two covered wagons, and the gaunt, half-finished frame of Knoll's grist mill. He could hear the rumble of the falls. It was, he knew, the only power for miles along the Frenchman. In a country without coal, it formed an important factor in the thinking of the farmers.

Apparently Knoll had no financial backing, and he was putting what money he had into the grist mill. If he could have interested someone with capital and developed a going town as Farrar had done, it would be a different story.

Jess reined up beside the grist mill and dismounted. Someone was sawing a board on the other side; another man was pounding with a hammer. The tents and covered wagons were deserted. At least there was no indication of human life anywhere except here at the grist mill.

Several horses were staked out on the other side of the tents. Two milk cows were grazing on the bench north of the river, and somewhere near one of the tents a rooster crowed. As Jess stepped around a pile of lumber, it struck him that if every voter in the county could have a look at Knollsburg and another at Lariat, the election would be a landslide for Lariat.

The racket of saw and hammer stopped. Jess called, "Hello." No answer, no sound at all except the steady racket of the falls. Then he saw a man and a boy, sixteen or so, standing inside the frame of the grist mill. Both were staring at him with brittle intensity.

The man was around fifty, medium tall and bearded, his face barren of expression. Only his eyes seemed alive as they locked with Jess' who was quite close to him now. The kid began edging away, furtively as if he wanted no part of this.

Jess asked the man, "Are you Knoll?"

"I'm Knoll," the man said. "Stand still, Hank."

The kid paused, uneasy gaze shuttling from Jess to Knoll and back to Jess, then he started moving away again. The man repeated, "Stand still, Hank." The boy stopped, sweat making a shiny film on his face.

Knoll remained motionless, waiting, right hand held behind him. Jess stopped at the end of a lumber pile. Something was wrong! He had lived with danger most of his life, and he had developed a sixth sense that warned him. Now he felt it prickle like a faint chill along his spine. Actually there was nothing definite that he could put his hands on except the way Knoll stood there, his hand behind his back, shoulders hunched forward, gaze pinned unwaveringly on Jess' face.

"I'm not here to make trouble," Jess said.

"Who are you?" the boy screamed. "Tell us who you are before Mr. Knoll kills you."

"Shut up, Hank, damn you," Knoll breathed. "Shut up now."

"I'm Jess Dawson from Lariat. Coe Farrar sent me . . ."

Apparently Knoll had been waiting for that. He jumped forward whipping a double-barreled shotgun from behind him and throwing it to his shoulder. Jess had no time to draw. He dived behind the pile of lumber just as Knoll fired; he lay there belly flat while the echoes of the blast died, and smoke drifted with the wind. Fear lay like a cold iron against his spine as he thought, *If I hadn't moved, he'd have blowed my head off.*

"I'll kill you," Knoll shouted. "Damn you and Coe Farrar and Lariat. I'll kill every gunslinging bastard he sends after me."

"Let him go, Mr. Knoll," the boy cried. "He didn't do nothing."

"He was going to." Knoll's voice held the wild, frantic tone of a man who had been driven close to insanity. "He was going to kill me, but I'll kill him. Before I'm done I'll kill Farrar. Get that .44 yonder and go around on the other side of the lumber. Run him out."

Jess had his gun in his hand. Words would be wasted. It

was kill or be killed, for Knoll was past talking. Then Jess felt anger boil up in him. He had done nothing to provoke this, but whatever happened, he couldn't shoot the boy.

"I won't take your gun," the boy whimpered. "I won't let him kill me because you've gone loco."

"Take it or I'll kill you," Knoll screamed.

"This is between you and me," Jess called. "Don't drag the kid into it."

He ripped a long splinter from a board above him and yanked his hat from his head. He put it on the end of the stick, shouting, "I'm coming after you, Knoll," and shoved the hat forward so that Knoll could see it. He had judged the man accurately. Jittery, Knoll let go with the second barrel, the buckshot blowing the crown out of Jess' hat.

Gun in hand, Jess lunged to his feet, smoke from the shotgun blast swirling between them. Knoll let out an unintelligible howl as he grabbed his .44 from a saw horse and whirled. "Put it down," Jess shouted, but Knoll was beyond reason. He swung the long-barreled gun into line, the hammer back.

Jess fired. The kid screamed and started to run. Knoll had been spun half around by the impact of the slug that had caught him in the shoulder; he shouted an obscene name at Jess and threw a wild shot that missed by three feet. Jess fired again, the bullet hitting him in the chest and knocking him off his feet. He fell across the saw horse and dangled there for a moment like a piece of limp wash on a clothesline, then he slid off and lay motionless, his face in the saw dust.

Jess called, "Come here, Hank. Come back here."

The kid had reached the first tent. He paused, looking back, his face white. Jess said, "Come here, Hank. I won't hurt you. I didn't come here to hurt anybody."

Jess held his gun at his side. Still the boy stood there, squeezed between the urge to hide and the fear that if he didn't obey, he'd be shot. Slowly he walked back, his chin trembling. He saw Knoll's body and he turned and was sick. Jess waited, and when the kid straightened up, Jess asked, "What's your name?"

"Hank Bolton."

"Your folks here?"

"They live yonder." Hank jabbed a trembling finger at the nearest tent. "But my folks and the Crews, they're the other family that's staying here, are working for some folks down the river. They're putting up hay and the women folks are cooking."

Jess picked up his hat and ran a hand through the gaping hole in the crown. "See what would have happened if my head had been there?"

The boy nodded, swallowing. "Mr. Knoll, he was awful bullheaded. Nothing could stop him when he got his mind made up."

"Why did he try to kill me?"

"He thought you aimed to kill him. He'd been warned to get out of the country. A fellow came here last week and told him to be gone by today."

"What fellow?"

"Dunno his name. Tall and kind of stooped. Chewed tobacco."

Jess reloaded his gun, Dake Ennis' words hammering against his mind, "If you stay with Farrar, you'll wind up doing something you'll hate yourself for the rest of your life." Now he had. But he had done the only thing he could have done.

"I'll take the body into town," Jess said. "The sheriff may want to talk to you about it."

"You had to do it, mister," the boy said quickly. "I'll tell the sheriff. But you can't blame Mr. Knoll. They'd been pestering him till they drove him crazy."

"Help me get a horse that'll tote his body," Jess said, and holstering his gun, walked toward his black gelding.

Chapter Fifteen

THE BREAKING POINT

THE sun had swung far down toward the western rim of the sky when Jess rode into Lariat, leading the horse with Knoll's body tied belly-down across the saddle. He was unaware of the hard wind running in from the northwest; he was unaware of the rigs along the street and the farmers who stared at him, shocked by what they saw. When he had left Knollsburg, it had been hard to think coherently, but he was thinking clearly now, and he knew there were several things he had to do before he left Lariat.

Reining up in front of the saloon, Jess tied the horses and went in. Duke Morgan stood at the bar with Will Rollins. Jess said, "Come here, Duke."

Morgan put his glass down, scowling. He polished his shiny star with his coat sleeve, glancing briefly at Rollins. Then he said, "Maybe you'd better come here, Dawson."

"I killed a man," Jess said. "I thought you'd want to see him."

Eagerness flowed across Morgan's handsome face. This, Jess thought with cool detachment, was exactly what Morgan had been waiting for. He crossed the room to the swing doors, saying, "You're under arrest, Dawson. Don't make no fast moves."

Jess backed through the batwings. When Morgan reached the boardwalk, Jess said, "It's Knoll. Coe sent me to fetch him to Lariat. When I got there he tried to kill me."

Morgan stopped, his gaze on the dead man. "So you're claiming self-defense?"

Jess nodded. "A kid named Hank Bolton saw it. Go out and see if you don't want to take my word."

"Coe will have your scalp if you arrest Dawson for killing Knoll," Rollins said as if he regretted it.

Morgan stroked his mustache, disappointment in him. "All right, Dawson. Justifiable homicide, I'd say."

So they knew it had been rigged. Jess said, "I'll take the body to Doc's place. Is he in town?"

"In his office," Morgan said, and turned back into the saloon.

Wheeling, Jess led Knoll's horse along the street to Doc Ives' office. He tied the animal and went in, the bell on the door announcing his arrival with its bright, metallic jingle. Jess called, "Doc?"

The door leading into the back room was open. Ives shouted, "I'm eating supper."

Jess crossed the office and stood in the doorway. Ives sat at the table, his bearded face looking old and tired. He lifted his coffee cup and drank, and put it down. "If you haven't had supper, I'll fix you something. Come in and sit down."

"I ain't hungry," Jess said.

Ives shrugged. "I saw Dake Ennis this afternoon. He was at the Tully place helping Sam build a sod shed. He asked about you."

"I shot Knoll today," Jess said. "Got his body outside."

Ives started to reach for a biscuit. He drew his hand back, bird-like eyes blinking as the full significance of this stuck him. He rose, his lips tightening against his teeth. He said in a low tone, "Luke Knoll was my friend."

"It was him or me, Doc. He'd been warned to get out of the country. When I said I came from Lariat, he tried to kill me with a shotgun."

Ives sat down, suddenly as if he had lost control of his legs. "Didn't you know Farrar had been trying to bluff him into leaving?"

Jess shook his head. "Coe just told me to fetch him to town."

Ives ran a hand across his face. "I should have told you." He got up again. "I remember you saying you always did a neat job. Looks like you did today."

"Want me to stand there and let him blow my head off?" Jess asked.

"No. I wouldn't expect any man to do that."

Jess carried the body into a small room next to the office

and laid it on the table. He turned and walked out. For a moment Ives stood staring at the dead man, then he backed out of the room and shut the door.

"He was a good man, Jess," Ives said. "Just a little fellow believing in what he was doing. You aren't little, Jess. You're big like Coe Farrar, big as all hell. You've got it soft and easy. You don't know what it is to go hungry and work from sunup to dark while you're hoping you can lick a man like Coe Farrar."

"You're wrong, Doc," Jess said quietly. "I've been so hungry my belly was just dangling inside of me, but it didn't get me nothing. Well, this hasn't either. Remember what you said that night we rode out to see Dake after Miles had shot him? You prophesied. Remember?"

Ives shook his head. "I'm always prophesying."

"You said I'd do the chores Farrar wouldn't and couldn't do. That's what I done and I'm quitting."

"What's done is done," Ives said. "I don't think Knoll had any kin. Kind of visionary and maybe a little crazy, but it seemed to me his town was the best for the county seat. Well, Lariat'll win now, and that's what Farrar's been scheming for." He sat down behind his desk, staring at Jess, the bitterness gone from his eyes. "So you're quitting. I've got to see that. The dollar's still talking to you."

"I'm throwing in with Dake. The dollar ain't talking loud enough to keep me in Lariat."

"You think that today. Tomorrow you'll talk yourself into believing you did right. You won't quit, Jess."

"Damn it, I am quitting," Jess said bitterly. "I'll beat hell out of Coe and leave town."

Ives pulled at his beard, leaning back in his swivel chair. "I almost believe you, Jess. Almost. I reckon I would if you used your head. You know who warned Knoll?"

"Brennan."

Ives nodded. "Fetch him over here. Don't see Farrar till you do."

Jess hesitated. He had not blamed Brennan. It was Coe

Farrar who had killed Knoll. It had been a cheap, dirty scheme, the kind of thing he had seen worked in Leadville many times. Perhaps it was the way the big boys built their fortunes, but he had been on the other side then. He was on their side now, and he still didn't like the way it worked. At least he knew he was wrong. Knoll's death had made him see that.

"Go get Brennan," Ives said. "He's drinking like a fish, but he's not so drunk he won't know a dead man when he sees one. He's the only man in town besides Farrar who knows what they're up to, and I aim to make him talk."

Jess swung out of the doctor's office and walked to the print shop. He had expected Ives to curry him down, to blame him, to call him a paid killer. The fact that Ives had not did nothing to lighten the weight of guilt that Jess carried.

When he stepped into the print shop, Jess caught the usual smells of ink and paper and whiskey. Brennan was seated on a stool near the type stand, a half-filled bottle at his elbow, his back to Jess. The wall lamp had been lighted, its yellow glow falling across Brennan's stooped body.

"Git off that stool, Jim," Jess said. "There's something in Doc's place I want you to see."

Brennan did not turn. Jess came on across the room and rammed his gun into the man's back. "Your type setting can wait, Jim. Git off that stool."

Brennan put down the stick of type he had been holding and looked at Jess. He said, his voice thick, "I'm composing an editorial about Lariat being the best damned town in Blake County. I ain't got time to go sashaying around."

He was very drunk, drunker than Jess had ever seen him before. Jess said, "Jim, I ain't sure you'll finish that editorial unless you do it in hell. I won't tell you again to get off that stool."

Brennan shrugged. "The pen may be mightier than the sword, but I figure a gun is mightier than a pen." He lifted the bottle and took a long drink; he replaced the bottle and ran a hand across his mouth. "I'll go, but Coe's going to know about this."

He slid off the stool and reeled to the door. Jess dropped his gun into holster and followed. Brennan paused outside, his eyes on the long scarlet banners that swept across the western sky.

"Remind me to write an editorial about our sunsets," Brennan said. "They're about the prettiest sunsets a man can look at, I guess."

"Doc's place, Jim," Jess said.

"Sure, sure," Brennan agreed, and went on toward the doctor's office.

Ives had lighted a lamp. When Brennan came in, Ives picked up the lamp and opened the door of the room that held Knoll's body. He said, "In here, Jim. See if you can identify this fellow."

Brennan hesitated, wiping his gaunt face with a trembling hand. He said, "I need a drink, Doc. Got anything?"

"Come here, Jim," Ives said.

"I'm getting orders I don't like," Brennan said complainingly. "Coe won't stand for it when I tell him."

"Come here, Jim," Ives repeated.

Brennan staggered to the door leading into the side room; he gripped the jamb to steady himself. Ives held the lamp high, the light falling on the dead man's face.

"Know him?" the doctor asked.

"He's dead," Brennan said. "You're not fooling me. I'm alive, but he's dead. I'm drunk, but I'm not so drunk I think I'm dead."

"Did you ever see him before?"

Brennan peered at the dead man. "Looks a little like that fellow Knoll."

"He was alive when you saw him last week," Jess said. "Remember?"

"Yeah, sure. He was building a grist mill at the falls. Ran me off with a shotgun."

Ives came out of the room and shut the door. He said quietly, "You killed him, Jim."

Brennan sat down, the doctor's accusation beating at his whiskey-soaked mind. "I didn't kill anybody. I need a drink, Doc. Got anything?"

Ives opened a drawer and took out a quart bottle. "You'll get a drink in a minute, Jim. I'm telling you again. You killed Knoll. Listen close now. Farrar sent you out there to tell Knoll he had a week to leave the country or somebody would come out and kill him. Jess had to kill him in self-defense."

Brennan blinked. "I've got to get back to the shop and finish . . ."

"Not yet," Ives said. "What's Farrar after?"

Brennan scratched his chin, his face turning sullen. "How do I know? I just do what he tells me."

"Look at your hands." Ives held up the bottle. "Look at your hands and then look at this whiskey. You know why you're drinking?"

Brennan stared at his hands. "Nothing but ink on 'em. I always have ink on my hands."

"It's blood, Jim," Ives said harshly. "Luke Knoll's blood. You threatened him, but Jess didn't know that. Jess had to shoot him to save his own life. That makes you the killer, Jim."

"Isn't blood," Brennan said sulkily. "Just ink. That's all. Just ink."

"No, it's blood. You'll dream about it till one of these days you'll shoot yourself." He tapped the bottle. "When you tell us what Farrar's up to, you get a drink."

Brennan got up and put his hands against the back of the chair. "Aims to make Lariat the county seat. Now I'm going back and get my own bottle."

Jess jerked the chair out of his grip and sliding it behind Brennan, forced him to sit down. "What else, Jim?"

"Damn you, you can't . . . ." Brennan began.

"Kill him, Jess," Ives said coldly. "The law in this county won't touch him, so we'll have to kill him. Shoot him in the belly. It's an execution, not a murder."

Jess stepped around the chair to face Brennan and drew his gun. Brennan's eyes were fixed on the Colt as it was lifted from holster, the hammer back. "You can't do it, Jess," he croaked. "You're not that kind."

"I didn't want to kill Knoll," Jess said. "But I did."

Brennan's bleary eyes swept to Ives who still held the bottle and came back to Jess. "All right," he muttered. "Gimme a drink, Doc. I've got to have it."

Ives handed the bottle to him. He pulled the cork and took a long drink. He sat back, his eyes closed, and for a moment Jess thought he was unconscious.

"Get some hot coffee, Doc," Jess said. "We'll get it down his gullet and scald his damned belly till he comes out with it."

"I don't need no coffee," Brennan said. "It's no skin off my nose. Hell, there won't be no slice of pie for me or you, neither, Jess. Coe's pulling out soon as he sells the townsite to a land development company in St. Louis. He'll fill his pockets, Coe will."

"He believes in the country," Jess said. "We're all working together. Remember, Jim?"

Slack-lipped, Brennan said, "He's a liar, just a damned liar. They'll lay steel to Lariat, but it stops here. Won't go through. The land development company won't buy unless Coe gets the county to vote the bonds. Then they're going to make Lariat the end of steel. If the railroad goes on to Sterling, Lariat won't be no big town. This way it will."

Ives looked at Jess. "His promises never meant a thing. I didn't figure they did."

"See that Knoll's horse is taken back, Doc," Jess said.

"I'll tend to it." Ives laid a hand on Jess' shoulder. "Don't beat Farrar up. Just tell him you're going in with Ennis."

"Why?"

"He'll do anything to put over them railroad bonds."

"What's that got to do . . ."

"Folks will vote for 'em thinking they'll get a through line to Denver. We've got to stop it, Jess, and you can help. If Farrar thinks you're dead set against him, you'll get a slug in the guts. We can't keep Lariat from being the county seat, but we can lick the bonds."

"I don't like . . ."

"It doesn't make any difference what you like," Ives snapped. "Farrar is counting on you pulling votes his way. Let him think it for awhile. When the time comes, we'll hold meetings in every school house in Blake County."

Jess nodded, seeing the logic in what the doctor said. "All right," he said, and left Ives' office.

There was a lighted lamp in the townsite office, and when Jess went in, Farrar looked up from his desk, smiling affably. "You fetch Knoll in?"

He'd heard from Morgan what had happened, Jess thought, although there was no hint of it on his moon-like face. Jess said, "Yeah, I brought him in."

"Well, where is he? I want to talk to him."

"He's lying on a table in Doc's place. I shot him."

"The hell." Farrar appeared surprised. "That's too bad. I mean, it would have been better if we could have settled our differences."

It wasn't good enough, Jess thought, not nearly good enough. He said, "It's what you wanted."

"No." Farrar leaned back, his chair squealing its protest. "I never like killings, Jess, but I know you wouldn't have shot Knoll if you could have avoided it. There won't be any trouble with Duke being sheriff, so we'll just mark it off. Now about that express business . . ."

"I don't want it. I'm throwing in with Dake Ennis like I said."

Genuine surprise was in Farrar now. "Why, with things set up the way they are . . ."

"I've made up my mind. You don't need me any more."

Farrar's meaty lips held a smile, smothering any expression of annoyance that was in him. "Why, we'll get along, but I'm sorry you've decided this way. Now there is this matter of the railroad bonds. Even if you're in the cattle business, you can swing some votes our way. I'll make it worth your while, Jess."

"I'll remember that," Jess said, and making a quick turnabout, walked out into the twilight.

Farrar should be satisfied with the investment he'd made, Jess thought. Knoll's death was a good return for all that Farrar had paid him.

Chapter Sixteen

PARTNERSHIP

IT was fully dark when Jess left Lariat. He took a southwest course, the night breeze cutting him with its cold bite. He shivered, the result of an inward chill rather than the penetrating wind.

The prairie was pinpointed by lamps set in the windows of the soddies. Dogs barked. Once Jess heard the faint, distant crying of a child. For some reason he thought of his first talk with Farrar. It had been only months ago, but it seemed a long time. Farrar, for all of his devious scheming, had been right. People had come to the Frenchman and they had brought changes.

Some of the settlers would go back and new ones would replace them. The valley of the Frenchman would never again be the same as it was when Dake Ennis had seen it in his youth. Yet it was still a wild and primitive land; the wildness was in the night wind and the lonely sweep of the prairie and the coyote chorus sounding from the sand hills south of the river. Some of that wildness would always be here, resisting time and change.

Then Jess' thoughts turned inward. The old bitterness was gone; a real passion for taking root here had replaced it. Now he could balance evil against evil and good against good, and he knew that evil was never completely evil and good never completely good. It was a thought which would never have occurred to him last April. Life had seemed very simple then. He had been driven by one ambition that now seemed unimportant.

Paula was in his mind as she always was when he had time to think. More than anyone else she had changed him without being aware of it. He could not give her up; he would not admit defeat until she was married to another man. He was unable to bring himself to think what he would do if she did. Somehow he had to keep it from happening, and he maintained a stubborn faith that it wouldn't happen, that time would bring the right answer to both of them.

Near midnight he crossed the river above the Tully place and turned upstream to Dake Ennis' quarter section. He was sure that Ennis had avoided trouble with Ansell and Miles or he would have heard about it, but he was equally sure that Ennis would not be caught off guard. He would have a gun at his side and he was a light sleeper.

Jess reached the bench Ennis had showed him the time they had ridden out here. He saw the vague shape of the dugout ahead of him; he heard a horse whinny from a wire corral a short distance to the west. Jess reined up, calling, "Dake."

There was silence for a moment, then Jess called again. A door squeaked as it was flung open, and Ennis shouted, "Who is it?"

"Jess Dawson."

Ennis let out a whoop. "I thought I recognized your voice. Come on in, boy."

Jess rode to the dugout and dismounted. "I was afraid you'd think I was Lane Miles and start throwing lead."

"Good thing you hollered," Ennis admitted. "I've been expecting that coyote to call. Put your horse up and come in."

Jess stripped his black and turned him into the corral. Ennis had lighted a lamp and built a fire, and when Jess came in, Ennis said, "I'll fix up a bait of grub."

"I could use it," Jess said, "I'm as lank as a week-old calf that's lost his mamma."

"Sit down." Ennis motioned to the bunk. "I'll fill you up."

Jess dropped down on the bunk and rolled a smoke. The dugout was obviously a man's place, sparsely furnished with only a stove, table, two benches, and a crude bunk. Ennis started bacon frying and made coffee; he sliced potatoes into the skillet and got out some cold biscuits. Without turning, he said, "Them Tully women sure had a garden. I've been buying garden sass from 'em and paying 'em back by helping Sam build a sod barn. That's one thing he can't do."

Jess smoked in silence, not knowing how to approach Ennis. It had seemed simple while he was riding, but now it wasn't simple at all. His pride was in his way. He had to humble himself, something he had never done willingly as he had to do now.

"Paula's gonna teach in the school north of here," Ennis said. "Sam'll draw her pay next spring when the kids' pa's do some sod breaking for him, which same leaves Paula holding the short end of the stick. Funny how troubles pile up on you and then they just disappear, sudden-like. Take Sam. You know how his wife gave him hell at first, but she's getting to like it here. Put folks through enough trouble and they come out one way or other. Ruth's got good stuff in her. She just let it get covered up on account of she was so damned mad at Sam for coming. They're getting along now."

Ennis stirred the potatoes. "But they've still got some worries. It's that rabbit-brained Josephine. She's engaged to Miles. He rode up to Julesburg to get her a ring. Plumb loco 'bout her, I guess. Maybe that's why he's let me alone. Anyhow, Josephine's gonna work in the Lariat hotel. Can't stand it out here, she claims. Well, she won't like it on Ladder, neither. She'll leave Miles sitting on the church step when the wedding day comes, or I'm mistook.''

"Dake."

Ennis turned. "Yeah?"

Jess dropped his cigarette on the dirt floor and ground it out. "When you asked me to come in with you, you said you'd never slam the door. How about it?"

"You're damned right I'd never slam it." Ennis' faded blue eyes were filled with expectancy. "You talking serious?"

"I'm serious enough, but before you say anything, I've got to tell you I shot and killed Luke Knoll today."

Ennis said nothing for a moment, his eyes on Jess' set face. Then he asked, "Farrar?"

"I quit him, and I reckon that changes everything. Doc Ives says we can lick the railroad bonds, so I figured we'd help him do the job."

Ennis strode to the bunk, holding out his hand. "If you shot Knoll, you must have had a reason. All I want is for you to come in with me."

Jess rose and gripped Ennis' hand; he met Ennis' gaze, humbled as he had never been humbled in his life before. "It ain't easy to say I've been wrong, Dake, but I'm saying it now."

"It ain't what's behind a man that counts," Ennis said. "It's what's ahead. Come over here and eat."

Jess sat down at the table while Ennis dished up the food. While he ate, Jess told Ennis what had happened. Ennis listened closely, nodding.

"No man would be fool enough to stand there and let Knoll blow his head off," Ennis said. "He must have gone loco, worrying about what Farrar was gonna do."

"Sure he was loco, but that don't make me think any better of myself for doing it."

"If your pet dog goes to foaming at the mouth, you have to shoot him, don't you?" Ennis scratched his chin, frowning thoughtfully. "Doc Ives smelled this bond business right from the first. He'd seen it happen more'n once when some slick-tongue like Farrar gets to promoting a piece of country. Raises hell, folks loading a debt onto themselves to build a railroad, then they pay through the nose when they go to ship their stuff."

"Farrar claims it's the only quick way to get a railroad."

"Sure, sure," Ennis said derisively, "but you can bet your bottom dollar that when enough people move into a new country, the railroad will come. Meanwhile we'll get along."

Jess leaned back and rolled a smoke. "Dake, I've still got two thousand dollars that I saved out of my Leadville deal. We'll use it to buy them shorthorns you were talking about."

"You're a rich man alongside me," Ennis said with some bitterness. "You'd best start your own outfit. I can't match your dinero, boy."

"I don't want it matched. It'll be even Stephen, your savvy and my money. I'll take another quarter section on the river and we'll own our herd together. We'll call it the DE for Dawson and Ennis."

Ennis walked to the stove. "I can't do it."

"It's gonna be my way or not at all," Jess said hotly. "Damn it, I've been counting on this."

"Don't be so damned stubborn."

"Who's stubborn?" Jess shouted. "Look, you mule-headed maverick. I don't know this country like you do. I'd lose every head I had the first winter. The trouble with you is you've let pride build up so high you can't see over it."

Ennis gave him his back, standing there by the stove for a long moment, his great shoulders slack. Then he turned, grinning a little. "All right, boy. Pride's a purty small thing at that, I reckon."

"If you know where to get them shorthorns, we'll start out tomorrow."

Ennis shook his head. "No hurry, Jess. If Farrar pulls off his bond election, I ain't staying here and paying them kind of taxes. Let's wait till it's over. Might even wait till spring. Meanwhile we've got work to do, building you a dugout and picking up chips to get you through the winter and cutting hay. Sam's got a mower and a rake. We'll get him to help." He yawned. "Well, let's roll in."

Ennis was right about the work. They cut and stacked hay on the bottom land between the river and Ennis' dugout; they helped Sam Tully with his hay in return. Josephine had gone to town. Jess could not tell whether Sam and Ruth approved of it or not, but apparently it was not a question of approval. Josephine had simply left.

Paula was quietly aloof when she was with Jess. She treated him with cool courtesy, seeing to it that she was never alone with him. Once, early in October, Jess asked Sam about Neil Comer.

"I don't know," Sam said heavily. "He ain't much man, not enough man to come here and buck this country."

"Paula won't go back," Jess said.

"No, she won't." Sam spread his hands. "She's downright stubborn, Paula is. I don't know what will come of it." He looked closely at Jess. "You like her?"

"I love her." Jess clenched his fists. "But I don't know what to do. If it was something I could fight with my hands . . ."

"I know," Sam said. "It was that way with Ruth when we got out here and I'd been married to her for nigh onto twenty years. I doubt that a man ever knows what to do with a woman when she gets her neck bowed. Nothing to do but wait."

"I ain't one to wait when there ain't no need for it," Jess said. "Maybe I'd be waiting for nothing. I'd like to know."

Sam shrugged, and changed the subject with, "Dake and me was talking about timber claims. There's a fellow down the river who's got a thousand maple trees to sell for two dollars."

"Cheap enough," Jess said.

Sam was watching him closely. "We'll do real well with our hay, Jess. They'll be grading for the railroad now that Lariat's got the county seat. I hear native hay's gonna be worth five dollars a ton."

"Won't be no grading if we lick the bond election," Jess said, and walked away.

To Jess there was no sense in fighting the country or Farrar or anything else if his relationship with Paula remained unchanged. He had never seen Neil Comer. The man was a shadow. Then, late in the month with the wind holding the bite of early fall, Jess had his first hint that Neil Comer was not the real trouble between him and Paula.

They had started work on Jess' dugout, but the north wind had dried the ground so that it was impossible to turn the sod for the dugout walls. The wind changed to the southeast, still cold and heavy with moisture. That night it rained, and Ennis said they had better get to work on the dugout. It was early for snow, but a man never knew.

"You can listen to the wind, can't you?" Jess asked, winking at his partner.

"I don't always know what it's trying to tell me," Ennis said.

Sam brought his team of Percherons and they spent the morning breaking the tough bottom-land sod along the river, two and one half inches thick and twelve inches wide. Jess had the job of cutting the sod into two-foot lengths with a sharp spade. Ennis laid the wall, setting the door and window frames and building around them.

Paula brought them their noon lunch, dismounting in front of the partly finished dugout and admiring Ennis' craftsmanship. Jess dropped his spade and walked up the slope to the bench, touching the brim of his Stetson to Paula. She gave him a smile, coolly impersonal as she had been from the time he had moved in with Ennis.

"You'll have a nice home, Jess," Paula said. "You're lucky to have Dake build it for you."

"A man's luck runs funny sometimes," Jess said. "I was hoping it would be more'n my home."

She looked away, color working into her cheeks. "I brought your dinner. Mamma thought you wouldn't want to take time to cook."

"Now that's real luck," Ennis said in his soft voice. "Say, have you heard if they've set a date for the bond election?"

"The fifteenth of next month," she answered. "Doc Ives stopped with us this morning. He'd been out to see the Brown children. They've got whooping cough."

"Looks like we'll be right busy for a spell," Ennis said. "Doc's got it all figured out. We'll be riding from one end of the county to the other, holding meetings and talking some sense into the voters."

"Coe will be talking, too," Jess said, "and Brennan will spread their side of it all over the front page of the *Eagle*."

"I don't know," Paula said. "Doc told me Brennan was drinking a lot."

"I'll go down and help Sam unhook," Ennis said abruptly, and strode around the corner of the partly-finished dugout.

"I've got to get back," Paula said, and turned to her horse.

Jess caught her arm. "You ain't given me a chance to talk to you since I moved out here. If I'm poison, just say so and I sure won't bother you."

"Jess, you know better." She jerked her arm free and brushed at a stray lock of hair that had fallen across her forehead. "We owe you so much. Everything you've done has put us into debt to you."

"You ain't in debt to me," he said roughly. "I'm just hoping you love me, or maybe give yourself a chance to love me. That's why I moved out here. One reason, anyhow."

She stepped back toward her horse, refusing to look at him. "Let's not go over it again, Jess. We won't do anything but hurt ourselves."

"What about Comer?" he demanded. "Are you going back, or is he coming out here?"

"Neither one," she said in a low voice. "I mean, not now."

"But you can't go on like this. You love him or you don't. You're gonna marry him or you ain't. If you are, I'll quit asking you."

Her head tipped back slowly, her dark eyes on his weather-burned face. She said, "I guess I'm afraid, Jess. Sometimes I get to thinking about this country and you and how it was back home where there was never any real trouble. People just lived and got married and raised their crops. And died. Sounds kind of dull, doesn't it?"

"I never thought of you being afraid," he said slowly. "You mean you're afraid of me on account of my killing Knoll?"

"Oh no, Jess. Doc told me about that. You couldn't help it." She turned away, looking southward to the sand hills that bulged against the sky like low waves of a vast sea. "Maybe I'm afraid of Ansell and Miles. Josephine won't marry Miles. I know her too well. But that isn't all of it." She took another step toward her horse. "Jess, I've just got to go."

He gripped her shoulders and made her turn to face him; he put a hand under her chin and forced her to look at him. He said, "Paula, I want it plain, one way or the other."

She was pale now, her lips trembling, and for a moment she was unable to say anything. He asked, "What is it you're afraid of?"

"I'm not sure I know," she breathed. "But it isn't because of Neil. He's . . . married. He wouldn't come here and he wouldn't wait."

Shocked, Jess dropped his hand to his side. "Then it's something else. If I hear you say you don't love me, I'll never bother you again."

"I guess I'm not sure how I feel," she said. "It's just that you belong to this country. I mean, well, marriage ought to last a long time. I want mine to last a lifetime, Jess."

Still he did not understand. "You told me you like the

country. So do I. Ennis has taught me how to understand it, partly anyhow. I don't see that . . ."

Then he remembered she had said it was a violent country. She was thinking of him as a violent man. She had seen him fight Lane Miles. She knew how he had handled Bill Hays. He had killed Luke Knoll. Then he understood and there was nothing for him to say. This time he let her go when she turned again to her horse.

She mounted and holding her reins in one hand, smoothed her tan riding skirt with the other, hesitating as if there was something she wanted to say and could not find the words.

"School starts next week," she said. "I think I'll like it."

"Sure," he said. "You'll like it."

She smiled uncertainly as if not wanting to break it off this way but not knowing what to say or do. She said, "So long, Jess," and rode away.

He stood there, eyes on her straight, slender back watching until she disappeared into a dip in the prairie. A sense of utter failure gripped him. She liked a violent country. He remembered her saying that. But living with a violent man was something else. *She was afraid of him.*

Still he could not give up. He turned toward the river, calling, "Come on up and eat. We've got a hell of a lot of work to do." When Ennis and Sam walked up the slope to the bench, they questioned him with their eyes, but he told them nothing.

Chapter Seventeen

BLIZZARD

THE day before the bond election Paula left the dugout with the early morning light still thin around her. A faint mist was rising from the river. She passed the big pile of buffalo chips that represented countless hours of labor, glancing toward the bench where Sam was shucking corn. She could not see him, but she knew he was there. He had gone to work before sunup.

"I aim to get that job done before snow flies if I can," he had said. "We'll have some cobs to burn along with the chips. I don't aim for us to freeze this winter."

Paula went into the sod barn, and lifting the side saddle from the hook, carried it to her horse. She could not help thinking how much life had changed for all of them since they had left Missouri. She understood better than anyone else how her mother had moved through the shadows of doubt and fear, but now the shadows were behind her and Ruth Tully was a better and stronger woman for it.

In some ways the same thing was true with her father. He had been plagued by self-condemnation and doubts, yet those weaknesses had been balanced by the dogged faith that everything would work out. And it had. Now Sam Tully was proud of himself and of Ruth; he was proud of Paula for taking the teaching job. But most of all he was proud because a life-long ambition had been realized. He owned a quarter section of land.

Set against this was her folks' worry about Josephine. She had played with Lane Miles, a more dangerous thing than she realized. Doc Ives had mentioned the gossip about the drummer from Omaha. Paula knew that her folks were afraid Josephine would marry the man and leave the country. She would not be happy if she did, Paula thought, for Josephine was never happy except when she was doing something different or being admired by a man. Nobody could change her.

Paula cinched the saddle and led her horse out of the barn. Mounting, she glanced at the sky, thinking how often this Nebraska weather surprised her. The frost had nipped her nose and fingers every morning while she was riding to school, but now the air was balmy, the sun hidden by an overcast, and the mild breeze running in from the east held a hint of moisture. The children could play out-side at noon and recess, she thought.

She rode leisurely, for she had plenty of time and she en-joyed the softness of the morning. Before she forded the river, she saw a rider coming downstream. Recognizing Dake Ennis, she stopped to wait for him.

He reined up when he reached her and tipped his hat, an awkward gesture. He often seemed ill at ease when he was around her. She wasn't sure whether he was that way with all women because he had spent so much of his time alone, or whether he could not forget he owed his life to her and didn't know how to repay so great a debt.

"Howdy, Paula," Ennis said.

"Good morning, Dake."

She smiled, liking him and thinking how perfectly this country fitted him and how well he got along with Jess. Then the smile faded when she thought of Jess. She tried to keep him out of her mind, to regard him with cool indif-ference, but she never could. He stirred her as no other man had ever stirred her before, and she was honest enough with herself to admit it.

Ennis cocked his head in the peculiar way he had as if listening to the message of the wind. "Don't look like it's a good morning to me. You keep your eyes open."

"Why, it feels like spring, Dake."

"Ain't spring in November. Weather can change mighty fast around here. I thought I'd borrow your dad's team and wagon and fetch a load of supplies from town. Me and Jess are both low. I don't hanker to be caught short if a blizzard hits us."

"We couldn't have one this early, could we?" she asked, alarmed.

He nodded. "Sure we could. You pay attention to the wind. If it switches to the northeast and starts raining, get your kids started home. You light out, pronto."

"I'll watch it," she promised, and reined her horse toward the river.

Dake was more worried than he let on, she thought. A premonition of disaster gripped her. She had never faced this kind of danger before. A Nebraska blizzard! She had heard Dake talk about them, how the wind carried the snow, laying a white, thick curtain across the prairie so a person could not see more than a few feet ahead. She shook her head, telling herself Dake was imagining things. It was too early in the season. This was fall, not winter.

For no reason that she could identify, Jess crept back into her thoughts. He repelled her and still attracted her. She could not understand it, but that was the way it had been from the time he had kissed her that Sunday afternoon.

She had never felt that way about Neil Comer, although she had tried to make herself believe she had. It had been a simple matter of knowing she must have a husband so that she would not continue to be a burden to her folks, and Neil had been the only eligible boy in their community. She thought with a feeling of guilt that actually she had been enormously relieved when she'd read his letter saying he was married.

She had used Neil to hold Jess at arm's length, but the trouble was in herself, the contrary feelings that he aroused in her. Even more than Dake Ennis, Jess fitted his environment. He had become a leader without intending to. He had a talent for shaping circumstances; he was respected. Killing Luke Knoll had not changed that.

She remembered the meeting at the schoolhouse when every settler for five miles around had come to listen to Jess and Dake and Doc Ives. When the meeting broke up, the settlers were convinced that the bonds would break them if Farrar had his way. Jess had been responsible more than the other two.

The three of them had covered the county so effectively that Coe Farrar was wild with worry. She had no idea what the townsite man would do, but Ives hinted that Farrar was not above having Jess murdered just to keep him out of town the day of the election.

Paula reached the schoolhouse a few minutes after eight and put her horse in the sod barn. On her way from the barn she stopped at the little wooden leanto on the north end of the schoolhouse and gathered an armful of sagebrush that had been put there before school started for winter fuel.

She carried the sagebrush inside and breaking off the tops, put them in the stove which stood in the center of the room. Lighting a piece of paper under the brush, she watched the flame lick up around the dry twigs until the fire was roaring. Then she dropped several of the brush roots into the stove. She had already discovered that they would burn like coal for hours.

The children came, most of them on horses, the Moran brood in a buggy. An even dozen today. The Browns hadn't come, and she was thankful for that. They lived almost as far from the schoolhouse as she did. The others were closer, and she felt certain they would have no trouble reaching their homes if a blizzard struck.

Paula called the children to their places, then stuffed more sagebrush roots into the stove. For a moment she stood beside the desk, taking the roll, eyes on their expectant faces. They were good children, hungry for the meager schooling she could give them, and she was thankful that she didn't have a single troublemaker in the lot.

The boys wore old overalls, faded from sun and hot wash water and strong soap; the girls were in cheap gingham or calico dresses, their hair hanging down their backs in braids. Strong, earnest faces, darkened by prairie wind and sun. Patched clothes, but clean. They would stay on the Frenchman, she thought with a sudden burst of anger. They would stay and break the sod and grow up, meeting the challenge of this new raw land in spite of the debt Coe Farrar was trying to load upon them and their fathers and their own children.

Her pupils sat on two long benches that faced the walls. In front of them and braced against the sides of the building were wide boards that served as writing desks. Paula smiled at them and sitting down, opened her arithmetic book for the first lesson.

Although school had started only a few days before, Paula had each class organized and the daily routine established. She felt a little guilty because she assigned long lessons, but she remembered from her own school days that the teachers who demanded hard work kept an orderly school and obtained results. It would be a short term, and probably the biggest boys would not be back next year, so this was their only chance to secure a little learning that would have to last a lifetime.

Paula called the first arithmetic class of small children and three large boys whose parents had drifted so much that their children had never been in school before. They came forward to stand before her, the girls giggling a little, the big boys overly conscious of their lack of learning and being forced to stand here with others half their size.

The morning passed with provoking slowness, for Paula's mind was on the weather, and she could not help glancing through a window every few minutes. She went through the usual routine of arithmetic, geography and spelling classes, and found herself irritated because big, overgrown Jerry Colter couldn't remember the capital of Delaware. He had missed it the day before, and he was still mixed up on his multiplication tables.

The morning brought no change in the weather and Paula began to relax. Dake Ennis had probably been unduly excited this morning. She remembered that he had been worried about her taking the school in the first place.

"She's still a greenhorn about this country," Ennis had told her father. "You'd never forgive yourself if she freezes to death coming home some evening."

When Sam had told her about it, he'd added, "Dake's right, but I'm counting on you using your head."

She had patted her father's hand, smiling. "It's just three miles, Daddy, and I don't consider myself a greenhorn even if Dake Ennis does."

Now she wasn't sure. She felt relieved about the weather, but still she could not shake off the feeling that Dake Ennis knew what he was talking about. She realized that she was trying to bolster her courage when she told herself Ennis had been excited over nothing.

She called up the reading class for the small children after dinner. Then, quite suddenly, she heard the low moan of the wind as it struck the sod building. She rushed outside. The wind had changed, switching to the northeast, and it was growing stronger by the second.

Jerry Colter came to stand beside her. He cleared his throat and said apologetically, "We're in for a storm, ma'am, a bad one. Last year we had almost two feet of snow about this early."

The wind was driving a heavy mist before it, and she could see a few scattered snowflakes flying in front of her. The balmy air had cooled until now the wind held a vicious bite.

Paula ran inside, thinking that fifteen-year-old Jerry with the peach fuzz sprouting on his face might not be able to remember the capital of Delaware, but he knew the things that counted in this country.

"Storm coming, children," Paula said crisply. "School dismissed. You'll have to hurry home."

They sensed the alarm that was in her. Books were slammed shut and put away. Coats vanished from the nails beside the door and there was a rush to the barn to get horses. Paula helped the smaller ones into their wraps, urging them to greater speed. She waited in front of the schoolhouse until they had started, telling them not to loiter on their way home.

Jerry Colter was the last to go. He had helped the others saddle up; he had even waited until the Morans harnessed their team and hooked up. Now he rode around the schoolhouse and stopped. He said anxiously, "Don't you wait around, ma'am. This here blow is going to be a woolly-whipper."

"I'm going right away, Jerry. You hurry, too."

"I sure will, ma'am," he said, and dug his heels into his mare's flanks.

Paula smiled as she watched one horse trotting off across the prairie. It carried four children, the smallest one hanging desperately at the end of the line where seating space was at a premium. Jerry caught up with them and said something and galloped on.

They'd be all right, she thought as she went inside. She put on her coat and ran out to the sod barn. It took only a moment to throw gear on her horse, tighten the cinch, and step up. She rode south, her nerves relaxing with the thought that she had only three miles to go.

Within a matter of minutes she realized that the storm was moving faster than she was. The mist was gone and snow was all around her, the white flakes running with the wind that had swung farther to the north. She shivered, for already the cold was working into her.

At least she didn't have to face the wind, she thought, and turned a little more to the southeast. The wind slashed at the side of her face as she urged her horse to a faster pace. Suddenly panic gripped her. She should have gone back to the dugout before she'd left home and put on warmer clothes. She just hadn't taken Dake Ennis' warning seriously enough. The balmly morning had fooled her. She was a greenhorn all right, a greenhorn in a violent country.

Her hands and feet were numb. The snow raced past her along the prairie, running ahead of her horse and then whirling in little eddies while it laid a white carpet upon the buffalo grass. The storm was playing with her, she thought, taunting her, laughing at her because she couldn't keep up, boasting because she was in its power.

She covered one mile, then two, and with each passing moment the wind grew stronger. Gusts beat at her, whirling the snow around her and the horse until she could not see beyond her mount's ears. When the blasts became unbearable, she had to duck her chin into the top of her coat to breathe. She wanted to scream, to cry out against this monster that had seized her. It was more than a violent country now; it had become a vicious, killing beast, and she wondered why she had ever thought she liked it.

She couldn't fight the reins to keep her horse going straight. Numb hands refused to obey her commands. Her legs had lost their feeling. Then she realized she had no idea where she was. She was lost, her sense of direction completely gone, and she remembered the stories she had heard about people being caught by storms like this and freezing to death within ten feet of their soddy door.

The horse plodded on, head down, moving with snail-like slowness. The rocking motion became a torment to her. It would go on forever because there was no place to go in this swirling, white wilderness. Then she was touched by regret. She should have told Jess she loved him. Now, with her mind focused on him, she could think only of his strength, of his talent for shaping life, his ability to defeat any enemy that faced him. He could whip a storm, even a terrible storm like this.

Vaguely she was aware that the wind was not cutting into her face. Perhaps it had moved on around to the northwest, or her horse had veered direction to get his tail to the wind. It didn't matter. Nothing mattered now but getting out of this white eternity which covered her and the horse and the prairie.

Later, and she had lost all sense of time, she was faintly aware that her horse was splashing across some water. Water in this world of white nothingness? Crazy! She wanted to laugh, to cry out, to shout and beat at this curtain that smothered her. It wanted her life, and it would have it. Maybe she was freezing. It didn't make any difference. Her hands and feet were warm. Soon she would be warm all over. She wanted to go to sleep.

Chapter Eighteen

QUIET INTERLUDE

DAKE ENNIS stopped at Jess' dugout on his way to town. "I smell a storm coming," he said, "but don't worry if I don't get back tonight. I won't leave Lariat if it looks bad." He grinned. "I aim to vote tomorrow, come hell or high water."

"I'll be there if the snow's ten feet deep," Jess promised.

"Don't do nothing foolish. Farrar ain't got more'n fifteen votes, and there's more'n that many farmers who live close enough to town to get in unless a real blizzard blows up."

"I know Coe better'n you do," Jess said. "He ain't gonna sit on his hands while he loses a fortune."

Ennis shrugged. "I ain't worried. He was licked the day you left him and throwed in with me."

"He's got an ace up his sleeve," Jess said doggedly. "It's been too damned quiet to suit me."

"The only ace he's got is Duke Morgan, and you got his number a long time ago."

Nodding, Ennis rode downstream, filled with the cool confidence of a man who considers the fight already won. Doc Ives held the same attitude, but it was a confidence Jess could not feel. He had expected trouble, and trouble hadn't come.

Farrar had kept to himself, making no effort to strike back at the anti-bond meetings except through the columns of the *Eagle*, but he was not one to discount the effective campaign that had been waged against him. To Jess it could mean only one thing. Farrar was counting on some trick, a trick that he'd produce the day of the election.

Jess saddled his black gelding, and taking some sacks, rode southward. He spent the morning gathering buffalo chips. He didn't have enough to get through the winter, so he'd probably have to bunk with Ennis before spring. Now and then he glanced at the sky, finding it hard to believe that a storm was coming. It would be a strange trick of nature if a blizzard prevented the settlers from getting to Lariat in time to vote.

The day was still warm when Jess returned at noon. He cooked dinner, leaving his door open and occasionally glancing outside, thankful that Sam Tully had worked with him and Ennis until the dugout and sod shed had been finished. When he went outside, it had begun to rain and the wind had swung into the northeast. He decided against another trip. Even if a blizzard came today, there would be more good weather later on when he could build up his chip pile.

He brought hay from the stack at the end of the shed and filled the manger, stopping a moment to pat his black. When he stepped outside, snow was a smothering mass that almost hid the dugout even at this short distance. Ennis would stay in town, but Paula might be out in this. He crossed the yard to the dugout and went in, reasoning with his worry. She would have started home in plenty of time. Ennis had warned the Tullys about blizzards, and Paula was not one to take such a warning lightly.

He dropped more buffalo chips into the fire and topped them with a twisted sagebrush root. He made several trips outside and carried chips into the dugout, building a pile in one corner by the stove. He shivered as he slapped snow from his clothes. For a time he stood by the range, his hands over it, listening to the roar of the fire as the wind sucked it up the stove pipe that served as a chimney.

More than once he had tooled his stage coach over mountain roads with snow whipping around him, but somehow this was different, treacherous and sudden and violent, and he could not get Paula out of his thoughts. He walked to one of the half windows that reached from the ground level to the roof of the dugout and looked out, but he could see nothing except the white curtain that was drawn over the prairie, pressing down against the low walls of the dugout.

For a time he paced the dirt floor from the crude double bed in one end of the room, past the pots and pans hanging on nails between the stove and the table and on to the coats hanging beside the door. There was little furniture to hinder his pacing, just two chairs, a bureau, a small table, and a washstand with a filled water bucket.

It occurred to Jess that in this country the wind controlled all life. Ennis had expressed the same idea in his own way. Ennis understood the wind. You had to, Jess thought, if you survived. You used it when it was a friend, and you stayed under cover when it was an enemy, and the trick was to recognize which it was in time.

The light grew thin in the dugout. Jess lighted his lamp on the bureau and filled the stove again, thinking of Paula who was probably safely home a long time ago. To go out and look for her would be nothing less than suicide. More than that, it would be stupid because he could pass within a few feet of her and not see her.

A sound came to him, a strange sound that was different from the howl of the wind or the roar of the fire. It might have been the whinny of a horse. His gelding, he thought, and decided against it. Probably a queer shriek of the wind. Just his taut nerves playing tricks with him.

He heard it again. This time he could not be mistaken. A horse was out there in the storm, a horse whose instinct had brought him through the storm to shelter. He wasn't far away because no animal or human sound would carry more than a few feet in this wind.

He put on his heavy coat and cap, pulling the ear flaps down, and took a rope from a nail. He opened the door and went outside, quickly closing the door behind him to husband the heat, and tied the rope to the knob. Holding the other end, he started up the steps, wondering if it was some stray animal that had drifted in, perhaps one of Ansell's Ladder mounts.

The wind whipped down the stairway and sucked breath out of him. He struggled for a moment, fighting to get air back into his lungs, and went on up the steps, feeling the full force of the gale. For a moment he stood, one hand in front of his face, realizing that a stray horse would probably have found shelter before this.

He saw it presently, a dim outline in a sudden break in the shifting white curtain. The horse had stopped, sensing that he had found protection from the storm, and now stood waiting for his rider to dismount.

Holding to the rope, Jess moved forward before the snow closed in again, and caught the horse's bridle. He raised a hand and pulled the rider out of the saddle, and it was not until she was in his arms that he recognized Paula. She was conscious, but strength had washed out of her so that she was a limp burden in his arms.

He was within a few feet of the shed. He jerked the door open and let the horse go in, then closed the door. The rope fell out of his hand. He stooped, feeling for it, and when he failed to find it at once, panic rushed through him. The soddy might as well be a thousand miles away if he didn't find the rope, and Ennis' terrifying tales crowded into his mind of men lost and freezing to death when they were even closer to home than he was.

Paula stirred against him. He was afraid to move. The rope had to be here, somewhere, for this was where he had been standing when he had dropped it. He thought of going into the shed, and then knew it wouldn't do. The storm might blow itself out, or it might last for days. He had to get to the dugout. Food and warmth were there, and Paula needed both.

It seemed an eternity before he found the rope and he was sick with relief when his fingers closed over it. He felt like a man who had been condemned to death and then unexpectedly pardoned. He straightened up, and holding Paula's slender body with his left arm, got his fingers free, and worked his way back along the rope. The wind struck at him, a mighty blast that almost knocked him off his feet and drained air out of his lungs again.

He struggled against the impact of the wind, stubbornly refusing to give up the rope, somehow holding to Paula and feeling thankful that she was no heavier that she was. Then the gale eased up; he got his breath and moved on. The dugout loomed dimly ahead of him; he reached the steps and went down into the warm room. He got the door closed, fighting it for an instant as another perverse blast whipped at the dugout, then when it was securely fastened, he carried Paula across the room to the bed.

She peered at him, whispering, "Jess?"

"It's Jess," he said. "You're all right. Just be still."

It was hard for her to talk; the words were almost incoherent because the muscles of her face were half frozen. She mumbled, "I didn't think I'd make it."

"You're fine," he said. "Now don't worry."

He unlaced her high top shoes, then crossed the room and took a big pan down from a nail. He went back up the steps, and finding a small drift of snow, scooped the pan full and went back into the dugout. Setting the pan on the stove, he returned to Paula and gently pulled off her shoes and stockings. Her toes were as white as the snow in the pan. Frostbitten! Both thumbs and the ends of two fingers on each hand showed the same whiteness. So did one side of her face and her nose.

He went back to the stove. The snow in the bottom of the pan was beginning to melt. He took a handful from the top and carrying it to the bed, held it out to her.

"Hold this over your nose and the left side of your face," he said.

"But I'm freezing now . . ."

"You've got to. We can't let the frosted parts warm up too fast."

She obeyed, holding the snow over her face. Jess returned to the stove. He saw that there was water in the bottom of the pan. He brought another empty pan to the stove, poured the water into it, and took it to the bed.

"Put your feet in this," he said, and brought the other pan from the stove. He pressed snow around the fingers of her hand that was holding the melting snow over her face.

"Keep the fingers and thumb of your other hand in the snow."

"It hurts," she whispered.

"I know. It hurts like blazes, but not as bad as it would if we didn't use snow and ice water."

He kept her well wrapped except for the frosted parts. When the snow began to melt away from her face, he took over the job of keeping it in place and told Paula to put her hand in the pan of cold water. Gradually the water in the pans became warmer and white flesh started to redden until it was rosy.

In time the pain of the frostbite left and Jess dried Paula's hands and feet and put her in bed. She went to sleep at once, her slender body motionless between the blankets, her dark hair spilling across her face. For a time he stood looking down at her, choked by an intensity of emotion that was new to him. He would not bring himself to consider what would have happened if she had been out in the blizzard for another hour.

He went back into the wind and worked his way along the rope to the barn. He unsaddled and fed Paula's horse, and when he came back to the dugout, she was still asleep. He kept the fire going, fighting the chill that crept into the thick-walled room. Hours later she woke up and he cooked supper. She lay watching him, her dark eyes following as he moved from the stove to the table and back.

He brought a plate of food and cup of coffee to her. She shook her head. "I'm not hungry, Jess," she said.

"Try to eat," he said.

She drank the coffee and pushed the plate away. "I can't. I just want to sleep." She swallowed. "Jess, will you be here when I wake up?"

"I'll be here."

He took the plate to the table and finished his meal, then he saw that she had gone to sleep again. That night he stayed by the stove, keeping the fire going, sleeping now and then sprawled out on the dirt floor. When the first trace of dawn worked into the sullen sky, he stepped outside. The wind held a slack, weary note and he knew the blizzard had run its course.

When he went back to the dugout, he saw that Paula was sitting up. He asked, "How do you feel?"

"Awfully good," she said, "considering."

"I'll get breakfast. You'll be able to eat now."

"Jess."

He came to her, puzzled by her tone. Her dark hair hung down her back and her face was pale, but she was smiling, and he sensed that she was concerned about something more important than her appearance.

"Your folks will be worried," he said. "Looks like another hour ought to take the steam out of the storm and then we can ride."

She rose, standing motionless until a wave of dizziness passed, then she walked to a window. It was banked with snow so that she could see nothing. She moved on around the room to the window in the northwest corner, the only one that was clear. For a moment she stood there, watching the wind whip the snow over the prairie in stinging white waves.

"Funny how important some things are in a country like this. Like having glass in your windows." She paused, eyes on the snow. "It would be pretty if I could forget what it was like yesterday. Look at it, Jess. The snow's skimming over the drifts like a million fairies on tiny sleds."

"I reckon there's something pretty in everything for them that can see it," he said gravely.

"That's right. I always have been able to see something pretty in this country, but Mamma couldn't until just the last few weeks. The prairie scared her, so it was ugly, but the other day she called me out to look at the sunset and then I knew she was getting over being scared."

Jess waited, sensing that she had still not said what she wanted to say then. Then she asked, "How long will it last?"

"Dunno. Sometimes the ground blizzards last a day or two after it quits snowing. That's what Dake says."

"This is election day."

He nodded. "I ain't forgot it. I've got to get to town."

She whirled to face him, anxiety in her. "Not if it stays like this. Jess, I've got to say something. It's not easy, but I want you to know." She bit her lower lip, frowning. "I thought I was going to die yesterday. I didn't suppose I'd ever see you again, and I wished I'd told you that I love you."

Something began singing in him then, and he had a sudden affection for the storm. "Say it again," he said. "Real slow."

"Oh Jess, you heard what I said. I ought to explain, but I can't. I guess I loved you from the moment you rode in that time with Farrar and you fought with Miles. But I was afraid of you, too. When you kissed me, it was, well, it was like being held by a volcano."

He stood with his arms at his sides, wanting to hold her, to tell her again that he loved her and that his love for her had made him a different man than he had been six months before, but he wasn't sure it was the right thing to do and he couldn't make a mistake now.

"I know," he said. "I'm a violent man."

She nodded. "I knew that a man has to be violent to make a living here, but I wanted to find some gentleness in you, too, and I couldn't until you brought me in out of the storm. Then everything you did and said was gentle."

He looked at the floor, scraping a toe across the dirt. "I had my sights on the wrong thing when I came here. It took you and Dake and Doc Ives to set me right."

"Dake told me that you kept thinking wrong and doing right. He said all you needed was time." She reached out and gripped his arms. "I know how I feel now, Jess. I mean, I'm sure."

He felt her tug at his arms, her face upturned, and he knew he would not make a mistake now. He kissed her, letting his lips tell her how much he loved her and needed her, and when he let her go, she still clung to him, reluctant to lose the magic of this moment.

"We'll eat breakfast," he said. "You stay here. I'll get to your place and tell your folks."

"I'll go with you," she said. "Don't make me stay here alone."

When they finished eating, he pulled on his heavy coat and cap and overshoes. When he opened the door he found himself facing a solid wall of snow. It had drifted into the doorway and molded itself against the panels of the door, completely shutting off the sunshine. But it appeared light in the middle, so he knew the stairway wasn't packed full. If it had been a three-day blizzard, he'd have been blocked inside until somebody dug him out.

"Shut the door behind me," he called.

Closing his eyes, he plunged into the snow and fought his way through it. He reached the top of the steps, snow in his eyes and mouth. He shook his head, digging at his face with a hand until he could see. The clouds had drifted out of the sky and the sun was above the eastern horizon, its bright light glaring on the white earth.

The wind was still up, whipping snow against him as he fought through the drifts to the sod shed. He saddled both horses and led them back to the dugout, and when he tramped through the snow in the stairway and opened the door, he saw Paula had her coat on and was ready to go.

They had a cold ride downriver, the wind knifing at them. Jess broke trail, telling Paula to keep close to him. He took a zigzag course between the drifts, trying to follow the lanes where the wind had swept the grass clean, but there were times when they had to put their horses through belly-deep drifts that slowed their progress.

Jess looked back often to see that Paula did not lose him. The air was filled with snow that the wind was lifting from the ground. Landmarks were blotted out, but Jess could see several yards in all directions. By keeping reasonably close to the river, he would not miss the Tully place, but he was worried about Paula. He was chilled, and he knew that her frostbite would be hurting her.

Suddenly he caught the vague bulk of the Tully barn to his right, and he swung away from the river, calling, "Sam." The dugout door was flung open and Sam peered out, then he shouted, "Ruth, come a running. It's Jess and he's got Paula."

Sam waded into the snow, Ruth floundering behind him. Paula swung out of the saddle and both Sam and Ruth were hugging her and crying, and Ruth kept saying over and over, "We thought we'd lost you, honey, we thought we'd lost you."

Jess, watching, knew that there had only been one finer moment in his life than this. That had been an hour or so before when he'd heard Paula say she loved him.

Chapter Nineteen

COWARD'S COURAGE

LANE MILES and the Ladder crew had left the ranch the day before the blizzard, returning just as the first snowflakes were swept past the house. Long Tom Ansell, watching from the front window, saw the men put their horses away and disappear into the bunkhouse.

He would not see anything of them until supper time, he thought. They'd sit around the oilcloth-covered table in the bunkhouse playing poker, not giving a damn whether every Ladder cow in the sand hills froze to death or not, but they'd be in the kitchen by six, and if he didn't have supper on the table, he'd be in trouble.

The storm became worse so that Ansell could not even see the bunkhouse. He paced around the living room, stuffing the potbellied stove with sagebrush roots, but still the cold swept in around him. It was not altogether the storm. He had been cold all summer, a strange inner chill that had clung to him.

These last months had not changed anything except to make his situation worse. On some nights he had slept very little, and when he did, he would awaken suddenly, sitting bolt upright in bed, sweat breaking through his skin. He would know then he had been dreaming, the old familiar nightmare. He had faced Miles and tried for his gun and failed. Even when he lay back, fully awake, he could feel the paralyzing pain in his chest where he had dreamed Miles had shot him.

Ansell had lost weight. Usually he missed at least one meal a day simply because he had no appetite. Many times he had tried to muster enough courage to face Miles and draw against him, knowing he could not go on like this, but he could not bring himself to do it.

Now, with the blizzard gathering its fury, Ansell paced back and forth from stove to window, his thoughts tormenting him. He had not been out of the sand hills all summer. The Ladder crew had not even made their annual drive to Julesburg. When he mentioned it to Miles, he was always cut off with a curt, "We'll tend to it when we get around to it."

Ansell had studied the south bank of the Frenchman through his glasses from the northern fringe of the sand hills. He knew that all the settlers had been driven across the river except the Tullys, then Ennis and Dawson had come, and for some reason Miles and his men had left them alone. It must have been because of the younger Tully girl, Ansell thought. Miles had made a fool of himself over her just as Ansell had known he would.

Now, pausing at the stove with his hands spread over it, Ansell tried to put some of the things together he had learned from the idle talk around the table. Miles went to dances in Lariat on Saturday nights, at times alone, at other times with some of the crew. He planned to marry

Josephine Tully; he had even gone to Julesburg and bought her a diamond ring. He had been joshed by the crew about it, obscene jests that had brought equally obscene responses from Miles.

What Miles would do after he was married was a question in Ansell's mind, for he had never indicated he was planning to bring Josephine here. Perhaps Miles didn't know himself. Ansell gathered from the talk that she was a feather-headed girl and Miles was not real sure she'd marry him. Apparently she liked someone else. That, Ansell discovered, was a sore point with Miles.

At one time Miles had said something about going to Argentina. If that was what he had in mind now, it would mean he had all the money he wanted and Ansell doubted that he had. The Ladder crew could have gathered the cattle and driven them north to Julesburg, but it meant some risk. Blake County had a sheriff. Duke Morgan wasn't much of a lawman, but he carried a star, and Miles had been careful not to antagonize him.

Ansell glanced at his watch. It was five and almost dark, the wind howling with terrifying screams, the house trembling under the heaviest gusts. He turned into the kitchen and lighted a lamp; he built a fire in the kitchen stove. When the crew came in, knocking snow off their clothes and cursing the cold, Ansell had supper on the table.

"It won't last long," Ansell said, "coming this early. We'll have to get out in the morning and see what happened to our cows."

"To hell with the cows," Miles snapped.

Ansell held his silence then. Miles was in an ugly mood. He had been drinking. His curly, blond hair lay in a turbulent mass on his head and he had not shaved for three days. It was not like him, for he was usually a fastidious man, overly proud of his appearance.

One of the men winked at Ansell. "Lane's a mite proddy.

His girl ran off with an Omaha drummer. I told him he should've plugged that gent last summer. You just can't trust a drummer."

Miles rose, a hand dropping to his gun butt. "Butch, if you open your mug . . ."

"All right, all right," Butch said quickly. "I didn't mean nothing."

They ate in silence, the tension building. In all the years they had been together, Ansell had never known of any trouble between Miles and his men. But trouble was at hand, ready to explode. After they had put on their heavy coats and caps and followed the rope back to the bunkhouse, Ansell sat down and drank a cup of coffee, considering what he had learned.

He could not tell what lay ahead, but they might be leaving if Miles had run into something that would give him the big money he wanted. A wild hope, but a possibility. If Ansell was rid of them, he could hire a crew that would be loyal to him. He had money in the Julesburg bank; he had a herd. He would be a big cowman like Vestry and Hancock had been. An hour slipped by, Ansell letting his dream build before he rose and washed the dishes.

Ansell did not sleep that night. Finally he got out of bed, and stirring the coals in the potbellied stove, stoked it with sagebrush roots. The blizzard had not tapered off. He wiped frost from the window, but he could see nothing in the pit-black night.

Something would happen in the morning. The sense of futility that had been in Ansell so long now gave way to the hope that he could still salvage something out of this. Perhaps he would be repaid for the humiliation he had suffered.

Ansell knew the great pride that was in Miles. Losing his girl to a drummer was one thing he could not stand. He had been beaten twice by Jess Dawson, but he had stayed, swearing he'd even the score when the sign was right. But woman trouble was something else.

Suddenly Ansell laughed, the first time he had laughed

in months. He saw both humor and justice in this. Miles was licked. He couldn't get square with a girl who had taken his ring and left with another man; he couldn't get square with the drummer unless he went to Omaha and he wouldn't take that risk. No, he was licked. The thought warmed Ansell. Miles couldn't stay here and face it. He'd pull out and take his crew.

The blizzard had lost its strength by the time morning light replaced the darkness. Ansell built a fire in the kitchen range. He'd cook breakfast as usual; he wouldn't let on that in a few hours he'd be free. Then it occurred to him that he'd have to see about the cattle by himself.

He had not carried a gun for years. Impelled by a sudden burst of courage, he went into his room and taking his gun out of a bureau drawer, slid it inside his shirt. Then he pulled on a heavy coat and cap and went outside into the storm. No snow was falling now, but the wind was still blowing, lifting the snow and hurling it along in a white haze. He made his way to the barn, chin pressed against his chest; he saddled his sorrel and started to lead him outside.

Then caution replaced the rashness that had brought him here. He would stay in the house until they were gone, pretending he had not guessed they were leaving the ranch. Besides, the wind might die down later in the day if he waited. Probably the cattle were all right anyhow.

He returned to the house, thinking that even during these few minutes the wind had slacked off. He hung his coat and cap on a nail beside the door, thankful that no one had come in. Half an hour passed before they did come, and he had breakfast ready.

Miles was still in his ugly mood. His men glanced at him occasionally, saying nothing, and Ansell found some comfort in the fact that they were afraid of Miles too. He thought of Jess Dawson who had demonstrated twice that Miles could be handled and he found himself wishing that Dawson was here. No, he didn't really wish anything of the kind. He didn't need Dawson. He wouldn't need anyone once that Miles and his men were gone.

Miles finished and rose, kicking his chair back against the wall. "Where's your checkbook, Ansell?"

Ansell felt the old, familiar fear crowding him. He had hoped they'd just ride out. Now he stared at Miles' bleak face, sensing the evil that was in the man, and he lowered his gaze, unable to meet Miles' eyes.

"I don't need my checkbook," he said.

Miles moved toward him. "You need it worse than you ever needed it in your life. We're pulling out for Argentina and we're taking all the dinero we can get our hands on. You wasn't fool enough to think we'd let you keep the money you've got in Julesburg, was you?"

Ansell backed against the wall, his fists clenched. "It's my money, damn it. I ain't stopping you from sloping out of here, but that's my money."

"You're writing out a check for all you've got," Miles said tonelessly. "Hurry it up. We'll be late getting to Lariat now."

"I won't do it . . ."

Miles hit him, a driving right to the side of his head. It jarred him and hurt him, and suddenly the caution that had controlled everything he had done for so long went out of him. He drove at Miles, both fists swinging, but he never landed a blow.

The men at the table swarmed over him; they knocked him down and Butch hauled him off the floor by his coat collar. Two of them held his arms while Butch brutally kneed him in the crotch. He sagged in their grip, sick at his stomach, paralyzed by waves of pain. Miles hit him in the belly and drove another fist into his face, swivelling his head half around on his shoulders.

"Go look in his room, Butch," Miles said. "He's got his checkbook in there. Fetch a pen and a bottle of ink along."

They slammed him into a chair, someone clearing a place on the table. He couldn't think now. The room whirled in front of him. Blood dribbled down his face to his mouth, he licked his lips and tasted it, then Butch was there with the checkbook.

"Write it out," Miles said. "What you got was just a beginning if you don't do what you're told."

He made the check out, his hand trembling. Miles jerked it out of Ansell's grip, glanced at it and snorted derisively. "Hell of a signature, but I reckon they'll honor it. Let's ride."

They started toward the door. In that moment Ansell lost his sanity. It seemed to him in this crazy moment that he'd rather die than let them go. They were taking his money, money he needed to make Ladder the ranch he wanted it to be. He got up and lurched toward them, clawing at his shirt; he gripped the butt of his gun, but before he could get his Colt clear, Miles turned and drew and shot him.

Ansell fell beside the table. He didn't lose consciousness. His mind seemed strangely clear as the thought struck him that this was the moment he had known was coming. He had lived through this time after time in his dreams and during his waking hours; his chest hurt with the numb pain he had experienced so many times.

"I'm glad he tried it." Miles' voice came across a great distance to Ansell. "Makes it legal, though I didn't give a damn one way or the other."

"Hell, you were gonna drill him anyway," Butch said.

Another man said, "With that five thousand from Farrar, we'll be setting real good. They tell me some of them Argentina senoritas are really pretty."

They tramped out, leaving the door open. Then Ansell was aware that blood was oozing across his chest. He got a bandanna out of his pocket and wadding it up, placed it over the wound. It was in his shoulder. Not bad, he thought, if he could get to Doc Ives, but if he followed Miles and the others, they'd shoot him again. He wondered vaguely why they hadn't finished him, and then he knew. He'd die slowly, and that would be the way Miles wanted it.

He got to his feet, one hand pressing the bandanna against the shoulder, and lurched to the door. He gripped the lamp, not feeling the cold that flowed in around him.

The wind had slacked off now so that there was little snow in the air. While he stood there, he saw Miles and the crew ride off, headed north, and Ansell could do nothing but curse them. If he stayed here, he'd die. If he rode for the doctor, he'd die. Then he thought of Jess Dawson.

Ansell got into his heavy coat and putting on his cap, pulled the flaps down over his ears. If he had to die, he had to die, and that would be the end of it, but he might live long enough to finish Miles. Dawson would know that Miles would not leave the country until he had settled for the beatings he had taken. Dawson would go after Miles. He wasn't a man to wait until Miles came for him.

Somehow Ansell struggled through the snow to the barn. He leaned against the wall until his head cleared, then he backed his sorrel out of the stall, and gripping the horn, pulled himself into the saddle and rode north.

The next two hours were worse than any nightmare he'd ever had. He rode with his head down, swaying in leather, one hand gripping the horn. He wasn't cold. He had no feeling at all except the dull, constant pain in his chest. His dream of a great ranch was gone. Nothing seemed important except Lane Miles' death. He couldn't kill Miles, but Jess Dawson could.

He followed the tracks that Miles and his men had made, occasionally forcing his sorrel through drifts that the wind had built since the others had gone. Sunlight glared upon the snow. He shut his eyes against it, then opened them to see that his horse was keeping the right direction.

It occurred to Ansell that he would not live long enough to reach Dawson's dugout. He was dying. He had no doubt of that. The rocking motion hurt him, but it helped to fight the overpowering desire to sleep. It would be easier to stop and lie down in the snow, but his passionate desire to punish Miles kept him in the saddle.

He was aware that the river was ahead of him. He shook his head, fighting his weakness, and saw where Miles and his men had crossed. At this point the snow had not drifted enough to blot out the tracks. Dawson's dugout was upstream and Ansell turned his horse that way.

He remembered the Tully place. Tully would carry his message to Dawson. They would do that much for a dying man, even for Long Tom Ansell. He saw smoke rising from the Tully dugout that was whipped into oblivion by the wind. He tried to shout, but his voice was only a whisper. He went on, still clinging to the saddle horn, and he tried to call again, but no sound came. Then he heard a man call to him. He spilled out of the saddle into a snow drift, and he did not feel the cold on his face.

"It's Ansell," someone said. "Now what in hell is he doing here?"

He had heard the voice before. He stared at the man who was lifting him out of the snow. Someone else said, "He's been shot." He was carried into the dugout; he strained to focus his eyes on the man who held him, then he was inside and warm air flowed around him. It didn't make any difference. He'd reached the end of his twine with nothing but failure behind him.

"Who shot you?" a man asked.

Two men were bending over him, and he saw two women behind the men. "I want to see Dawson," he whispered. "Dawson."

"I'm Dawson," one of the men said.

It was Dawson who had carried him inside. Funny how things worked out. He hadn't expected to find Dawson here. He wanted to go back to sleep again.

A woman said, "Get his boots off. He's been frostbitten. You can save him like you did me, Jess."

"No use. He's about gone."

That was right. Well, it didn't matter. Nothing mattered but Miles. He breathed, "Miles shot me. His girl ran off with a drummer. Miles and his men have gone to Lariat."

A woman cried out, and the other woman put an arm around her. Ansell vaguely wondered what was the matter with them. Dawson was asking, "What's he going to do?"

"Leave the country. Farrar's paying him five thousand.

"You've got to get him, Dawson, or he'll dry gulch you before he slopes out. You've got to get him."

"So that's what Farrar had up his sleeve," Dawson said. "Five thousand dollars for their guns. There won't be any settlers voting today if we don't get to town, Sam."

Ansell didn't know what he meant. But Dawson would go after Miles. He wasn't the kind who'd wait to be dry gulched. Ansell had one clear flash of memory of Jess Dawson on his horse beside Farrar who was in his buggy, and he remembered Miles coming in with his face bruised by Dawson's fists. A tough hand, Miles had called Dawson, the first tough hand to hit this country since Miles had come. Sure, Dawson would go after him. Dawson was that kind of man.

"He's gone," Sam Tully said.

But Long Tom Ansell did not hear.

Chapter Twenty

THE REAPING

It was after noon when Jess and Sam Tully saw Lariat ahead of them, snow drifted on the south side of the buildings as high as the eaves. The wind had slacked off, but the air was cold, and Jess knew he'd have to get warm before he faced Lane Miles.

The ride had been a silent one. Occasionally Jess had glanced at Sam, wondering what was in his mind and if he realized that death might be waiting for him in Lariat's windswept street. Sam rode with his head down, face almost covered by a muffler, and if the thought was in his mind that everything he had done this summer might be blotted out now by a violent death, he gave no indication of it.

During the long, bitter ride, Jess' mind had been on

Paula. She was not like her mother who had become almost hysterical when Sam had said he was going to Lariat with Jess. Ruth had clung to him with a sudden sense of impending loss, crying that she could not live without him, now that they had gone through so much together.

In a way it had pleased Sam, and Jess had sensed that it had been his moment of triumph, that the barrier between him and his wife was broken down once and for all. Sam had kissed her, saying he'd be back. The dogged stubbornness that had grown in him through the months still controlled him. A man had to do what he had to do, he'd told Ruth, and she had let him go, apparently realizing the futility of arguing with him.

Paula had been entirely different. She had kissed Jess unabashedly before her parents, a soft lingering kiss given as if she knew it might have to last her a lifetime. She had not protested about his going, and that was the way Jess wanted it. He could not stand a crying woman. It was, as far as he was concerned, the final test of Paula's character, and he was reminded again of the first impression he'd had of her, that she was like a rock in the wind.

He had given some thought, too, about Long Tom Ansell, but he had come to no conclusion about the man. Ansell had been concerned only about Jess going after Lane Miles. He must have known that the ride would kill him, but he had probably known that if he'd stayed on Ladder, wounded and alone, he would die. No lofty motive had impelled him to bring the warning. He had simply wanted Jess to go after Miles.

The reason for it was not clear to Jess; it probably never would be, but there must have been something about Ansell's relationship with Miles that no one understood except those who had lived together on Ladder. Then Jess put it out of his mind. It was enough that Ansell had brought the message. Otherwise Jess and Sam would have waited until later in the day and that would have been too late.

They made a half circle of the town, coming in from the

north and reining up behind Doc Ives' office. The wind carried little snow now, so there had been no way to hide their approach. But perhaps Farrar had not recognized them. Jess had expected a greeting of rifle fire, but the silence was broken only by the faint moaning of the wind as it rushed by across the white prairie.

Someone had cleared a path through the drift behind the doctor's office. As Jess and Sam dismounted, the back door was flung open and Ives called, "Come in. We've been looking for you."

"We can't leave our horses out here . . ." Jess began.

"Henkle will put them in my barn," Ives said. "Come in."

A farmer stepped past Ives. "Go in and warm up," he said. "I'll take care of 'em."

He was a big, ruddy-faced man wearing a heavy sheepskin coat and overshoes. Jess knew Henkle well enough to consider him a good man, better than average. Jess had no illusions about most of the settlers who had come to vote, but there were a few like Henkle who could be counted on.

"Any trouble?" Jess asked.

"No, but there will be, now that you're here," Henkle said, and led the horses toward the barn behind the office.

Ives had closed the back door against the cold. Now he opened it and Jess and Sam went in, kicking snow from their feet. Dake Ennis said, "Glad to see you, Jess. You just made me ten dollars."

Jess took off his coat and cap, and stood with his hands over the stove, stomping circulation back into numb feet. "How could I make ten dollars for you on a day like this?"

"We made up a pool," Ives said, "betting on when you'd get here. Dake said it'd be before two."

Another man came in from the office, nodding at Jess and Sam as he leaned a Winchester against the wall. "Quiet as a tomb," he said. "Ain't even a dog on the street."

He was Barney Oram, a slender homesteader who had

settled two miles west of Lariat. Like Henkle, Jess thought he could be counted on. With Doc Ives, there would be six of them. He stood by the fire, warmth working into him as he considered this. Not enough.

"Any others?" Jess asked. "Or do we do the job?"

"The saloon's full," Ennis said. "They've been drifting in since noon, but there ain't been a vote cast on our side. Won't be, neither, if we don't bust Lane Miles and his bunch loose from the townsite office."

"That where we're voting?" Jess asked.

Ives nodded. "You can bet your bottom dollar they've voted. Twelve, I figure, but we've got thirty votes if our men don't get scared and ride out of town."

Jess told them about Ansell, adding, "We left the body in Sam's barn, Doc."

"I'll send for it tomorrow," Ives said. "What do you suppose made him fetch you the news?"

"Dunno," Jess answered. "He sure wanted me to go after Miles." He glanced at Ives. "Anybody tried to vote our side?"

"I did," Ennis said. "I got halfway across the street when Miles came out. He said he'd plug me if I kept coming. You know, Jess, a man gets to thinking he's as tough as all hell till he runs up against a deal like that." He shrugged. "I just came back here."

"Thirty men's enough to rush 'em," Jess said.

Henkle came in, stomping snow from his overshoes. "I heard that, Dawson. You're talking foolish and you know it. They don't want to vote bad enough to die. Neither do I."

"There's been some dying already," Doc Ives said. "Jess, had you heard Jim Brennan shot himself two days ago?"

Jess stared at him, shocked by this news. "No, I hadn't heard. Why did he do it?"

"I'm guessing," Ives answered, "but I think I know. When it got down to cases, Jim couldn't go on printing the lies Farrar wanted him to. He told me he was going to tell the truth just like we've been doing at our meetings, but I reckon he couldn't do that, either."

"Sure he done it himself?" Jess asked.

Ives shrugged. "He was dead when I got there. The gun was on the floor beside him, so Morgan called it suicide."

Jess rubbed his wrists and worked his hands, the stiffness leaving them. He had liked Jim Brennan, feeling something in common with him he had not felt with any of the others who took Farrar's orders. Perhaps his part in Knoll's death had preyed upon his conscience. In any case, whiskey had not given him the courage to face the final issue. "Farrar's at the end of his twine," Ennis said. "He lost Hays, then you, and now Brennan."

"But he's got Miles," Ives said tartly, "and if he wins the election, he'll be out of town by morning. He'll make his deal with the St. Louis land development company and he won't be cutting the pie Brennan used to talk about. He'll eat it all himself."

Impatient with the waiting, Henkle demanded, "We gonna stand here gabbing all day?"

"No," Jess said.

He took his gun out of holster, checked it, and dropped it back into leather. Somehow he had become a leader without intending to. This was not like Leadville. He was not alone now, yet in one way he was alone. He had to break it open, and he wondered briefly how he had worked himself into this position. He could not back out with so many looking to him; he could not face Paula if he did.

"It's a hell of a note when a man can't vote," Jess said.

They nodded, watching him expectantly as he took off his belt and laid it on the table. He was doing this for himself, he thought, and for Paula. But not entirely for himself. Then he felt a sudden burst of pride that comes from knowing that other men had confidence in him. They didn't know how he would do the job, but they were certain he'd do it.

Henkle, the impatient one, said, "Well?"

"How many guns have we got?" Jess asked.

"Nobody in the saloon is armed," Henkle said.

"I can't do this alone."

"We know that." Henkle jammed his fists into his pockets. "Hell, don't look to me like there's much anybody can do."

"A man gets what he fights for," Jess said. "If he don't fight, he don't deserve nothing."

"But unarmed men . . ." Oram began.

Jess motioned him into silence. "Listen. I'm cutting across the street and I'll hit Farrar's back door. When I start the ball, you boys open up from the saloon with all the artillery you've got."

"Miles and his bunch won't scare," Oram said uneasily.

"Anybody will scare, and they know how many are in the saloon." Jess put his sheepskin and buckled his gun belt around it. "I asked you how many guns we've got?"

"I fetched my Winchester," Sam Tully said. "I'll go with you, Jess."

"No, you're going with the others. Dake, you run the show. We've got your cutter and Oram's got a rifle. Doc, how are you fixed?"

"A Winchester and a Greener."

"Fetch 'em. Where's Morgan?"

"In the saloon," Ennis said. "Walks around saying he's keeping order regardless."

"We'll have a new sheriff when this is over," Jess said. "Can you take his guns and star away from him, Dake?"

Ennis laughed. "It'd be like taking candy from a baby."

"Get over to the saloon," Jess said. "Wait till you hear my first shot."

They put on their coats, Henkle taking the shotgun Ives handed him. Ennis said, "We'll have a couple more irons when I get done with Morgan, real fancy ones."

"You need some men behind 'em," Jess said, and went into the office.

He waited behind a window, watching the wind whip snow down the street; he heard Ennis and the others go out through the back and knew he had to allow them time.

Five minutes, then ten, the seconds dragged by as he considered the element of time. Once that he was out in the cold he'd have to keep moving.

You look at death and you're afraid. You've got a lot to live for now, a lot to fight for, and the others share your courage if you have it, and your fear if you have it. You balance your courage against your fears: you balance good against evil as you understand them now, not as you did six months ago, and the tumult is stilled in your mind. You know what you have to do, and there is no desire to turn back.

Jess waited until a great gust of wind picked up a burden of snow and channeled it down the street in a thick, covering blanket, then he opened the door and ploughed through a drift. He crossed the street in a run, not sure how well he was hidden from the townsite office. Still the silence gripped the town. He reached the side of the store and stopping, pulled air into his lungs.

He went on around the store, the wind slacking off again. He ran past the back of the building, and kept on, his hands deep in the pockets of his coat; he raced along the rear of the new drugstore that had been built since he'd left town, thankful that there were no drifts behind the buildings on this side of the street.

Now he hesitated, breathing hard, sheltered by the back wall of the townsite office. He mentally pictured the interior of the building, judging that Miles and his men would be in the front where the ballot box was probably setting on Farrar's desk. Farrar might be in the back room. Knowing the man as long as he had, Jess still could not be sure what Farrar would do in this final moment when every hope and dream he'd cherished was about to be brought tumbling down upon him.

He pulled his gun and pronged back the hammer; he bent low to keep under a window and lunged toward the back door. Turning the knob, he slammed the door open and went in. Farrar was shoving sagebrush roots into the stove. He wheeled as Jess crossed the room in long strides, calling out in a frantic voice, "Miles."

Jess was past the line of vision from the front office. Farrar jumped back, pulling a gun from his coat pocket, but he was shocked by surprise and scared, and he was slow. Jess struck him across the head with his gun barrel. Farrar's legs gave under him and he fell heavily and lay still.

Jess whirled toward the office door as Miles appeared, his gun palmed. Jess got in the first shot, the impact of the bullet spinning Miles half around; he fired again as Miles frantically threw a shot at him, then Miles spilled forward on his face, his body half in the office and half in the back room.

Jess yelled, "Throw down your guns." Then the firing broke out from the saloon, and Jess jumped back toward the stove and waited there, uncertain what the men in front would do. The air was hideous with gunfire, bullets smashing through the street windows of the townsite office and hammering into the wall.

Two of Miles' men plunged through the door into the back room, their guns working. A bullet hit the stove and screamed as it ricocheted across the room. Jess knocked the first man down with a bullet through the middle, the second laced a shot at Jess. He felt the white heat of the bullet along his ribs. The fellow had been moving too fast to make his shot good. Jess pulled trigger twice, missing with the first and scoring with the second. The man stumbled and fell headlong, his gun dropping from his slack fingers.

Jess dived back behind the stove, his gun empty. He reloaded, and in an unexpected lull in the firing, someone yelled, "They're coming," and Will Rollins, his voice a high scream, cried, "No, no." Then the firing came again, wiping out the sound of the banker's voice.

Jess waited, gun in hand. Farrar was stirring. Smoke rolled across the room in blue waves to be swept into oblivion by the cold wind that rushed in through the back door. Jess could not tell what was happening in the office, but he hoped that sheer numbers would panic the rest of Miles' men. He was right. Three of them crowded into the back room, their hands up, the desire to fight gone out of them.

Dake Ennis shouted from the office, "Jess?"

"All right, Dake," Jess called. "We've got 'em."

Ennis appeared in the doorway, looking at the men who stood with their hands high. Farrar sat up, blinking and rubbing his head, unable at the moment to comprehend what had happened.

Ennis said, "Now don't they look tough?"

Jess was watching Farrar. He asked, "What do you think, Coe?"

Slowly Farrar got to his feet, still holding his head. From the office Sam Tully called, "You ought to see this, Jess. You wouldn't think two men could get under Farrar's desk, but that's where Rollins and McBain are."

"Lock these boys up in the jail Coe built," Jess said to Ennis. "Take him along, too."

Farrar looked coldly at Jess. He said, "You're a fool, Dawson. You had everything and you threw it away. I took you for a smarter man."

"That was your mistake, Coe," Jess said.

Farrar drew a cigar from his pocket and bit off the end. Ennis hesitated, Oram and Henkle crowding into the back room behind him. With quiet dignity Farrar struck a match and fired his cigar. He drew on it, eyes still fixed on Jess.

"The mistake I made," Farrar said, "was fetching you here in the first place. It was the first time I was ever wrong on a man. But maybe I wasn't wrong. You can handle this bunch. Know what it would be worth to me?"

"More'n you could pay," Jess said. "He's busted, Dake. He built a town and it busted him."

"I've been busted before," Farrar said. "I'll start again."

"Not for awhile," Jess said. "I don't know much about law, but using force to keep men from voting ought to send you up for a long stretch."

"We'll see." Farrar turned to the door, his great shape erect as he stepped over Miles' body. "We'll see."

Ennis and Henkle took them to the jail. When Jess stepped into the office, he saw that Sam Tully and Oram were holding their guns on Rollins and McBain who were backed against the wall as thoroughly scared as two men could be.

"Had to pry 'em out from under the desk," Sam said.

Jess motioned to Rollins, "You boys running this here election?" Rollins nodded. "Then get back on the job. We aim to vote." He turned to the door. The settlers had formed a solid knot on the walk, grim-faced and a little frightened by this sudden death. "Form a line, boys. Don't look like nobody's gonna kick about our voting now."

A moment later Jess left the townsite office with Sam Tully. Ennis was coming back from the jail. Jess said, "Stay in town, Dake. Might be a little lynch talk if our boys get to drinking."

Ennis nodded. "I'll take care of it. You know, that damned Farrar don't even look scared and he ought to."

"He won't do no more promoting for awhile," Jess said. "What about Morgan?"

Ennis laughed softly. "I saw him riding out of town while ago, heading east. Might be he'll catch up with Bill Hays."

"A good team," Jess said, and went on across the street with Sam.

When they left town, the sun had swung westward, the wind still sweeping in across the prairie. Sam said in the thoughtful way of a man who is surprised at himself, "Queer what a country does to a man. When I left Missouri, I'd have tucked my tail and run before I'd have bit off a piece of that kind of trouble."

"You don't know what you'll do till you have to," Jess said. "Anybody get hit?"

"Three of 'em got nicked. Doc's taking care of 'em." Sam rubbed a hand across his face. "Jess! I'm gonna be real proud, having you for a son-in-law."

"It goes both ways," Jess said. "Find out about Josephine?"

"She's married. Doc Ives told me." He rubbed his face again, eyes on Jess. "You know, I've been happier the last month or so than I ever was in my life before. I didn't know it at the time, but I started getting Ruth back the morning Farrar brought her home from the dance. I told him I'd kill him if he ever touched her again." He paused, and added, "I would have, too."

They rode in silence, the wind carrying the snow in front of them. Not everything was settled, Jess thought. The country would never be fully tamed, for violence was an inherent part of it and it took violent men to live here. Paula understood that now. He was as sure of her love for him as he was sure of his love for her, a love that was as big as this land in which they lived. They would fit, Jess told himself, here in the valley of the Frenchman.

WAYNE D. OVERHOLSER

THE SNAKE STOMPER

CHAPTER 1
THE STRANGER

Kim Logan followed the pass road to the top, paused for a moment until he saw the coach and six climbing far below him, and went on. No hurry. Plenty of time. This might be a wild goose chase, but still the job had to be thought out. That was a rule of the profession. Think it right down to the finish. The odds weren't so important if you have the edge and hold it. Never pull a gun until you have to, and not then unless you're willing to kill the man you're drawing it on. Never let the idea that the other man might be faster enter your mind.

Professor Kim Logan, M.G. Master of Guncraft. Kim laughed softly as he jogged down the east slope. Why, he could write a book on how to be a tough hand. He had served his apprenticeship on the border with as salty a crew as a man would find. The fact that he was alive at the ripe old age of twenty-five proved his fitness to write the book. He was the only one of the old bunch who could do any writing; the graves of the others were scattered from the Rio to the Dakota badlands.

The summit was above timber line. Now Kim came to the first stunted spruce on the east side of the pass and reined his buckskin off the road. There was a level stretch here just above a sharp pitch where the stage always made a brief stop. He dismounted, shivering a little, for it was cold at this altitude even in August. He rolled a smoke, considering the slowly approaching stage.

This wasn't the sort of job Kim liked. Too many people involved who had no part in the business, and he'd had his doubts from the first that the man he wanted would be on the stage. Besides, Johnny Naylor who was riding shotgun was an unpredictable gent who might decide to be a hero. But when a man was drawing gun wages from a boss like Peg Cody, he didn't question his orders. Not if he liked his job, and Kim liked this job pretty well. There might be a future with Peg and her Clawhammer spread. She was single, pretty, and in need of a man like Kim Logan.

Kim led his horse behind a spine of rock and stepped into the road. The stage rounded a curve below him and came laboring on up the steep grade. Kim eased back around the rock and waited. Minutes later the coach stopped, the driver saying, "You can see for yourself there ain't no trouble. You've been drinking too much coffee. You're getting so damned jumpy you'll be shooting at shadows."

·Kim stepped into view, his .44 palmed. "A little trouble, Butch. Take it easy, Johnny."

The driver cursed. Johnny Naylor shouted, "Logan," in a scared voice; his lips quivered and tightened. Jumpy, all right, and dangerous.

"I told you to take it easy, Johnny," Kim said as if this were a casual thing. "You've got a wife. Butch, you've got three kids and a wife. I'd hate like hell to make some widows and orphans today."

"All right, let's see what he wants, Johnny." The driver hunched forward on the high seat, the tip of his tongue moistening his lips. "But I'm telling you one thing, Logan. The sheriff'll trail you to hellangone, and don't figure on Clawhammer being big enough to save your hide."

Kim had had his look at the passengers. His man was here. He said, "You've got a fellow I want. Yuma, step down."

"Kidnapping," Johnny Naylor cried. "You're loco, Logan. The box is plumb heavy. Why ain't you taking it?"

"I ain't a thief. You oughtta know that, Johnny. And Butch, you don't need to say anything to Ed Lane. I'm saving a man's life. Even our chuckle-headed star toter wouldn't jail a man for that. Yuma, I ain't telling you again. Step down."

There were three passengers: a drummer Kim had seen a few times in Ganado, a fat woman with a cartwheel hat who looked as if she was close to fainting, and a little man with a deeply lined face scoured by wind and sun to a dark brown. The little man would be Yuma Bill. He would be tough if pushed too far, Kim judged, and for a moment it was touch and go.

"And who would you be saving my life from?" the little man demanded.

"Some gents you never heard of," Kim answered, "but I'm saving it all right. Take my word for it."

Still Yuma Bill made no move to get out of the coach. His right hand was not in sight. He asked, "What's this Clawhammer you're talking about?"

Kim grinned. He liked a man who had guts. Not the jumpy ones like Johnny Naylor. To Kim's way of thinking, that wasn't guts. His kind died young. But old Yuma Bill was something else. He figured things before he made a play.

"Clawhammer's my outfit," Kim said. "A woman named Peg Cody runs it."

"Don't let that fool you," Johnny Naylor cried. "She's as tough as Logan."

"Clawhammer," Yuma Bill murmured. "Peg Cody. Them names don't mean a damned thing to me."

"Maybe Brit Bonham does," Kim said.

"Yeah," Yuma agreed, it does." He swung the coach door open and stepped down, a shoe box clutched in his left hand. "Roll 'em, driver. I'll go along with this Logan."

"You're loco..." Johnny Naylor began.

"Shut up," the driver shouted, and kicked off the brake, the silk flowed out and cracked with pistol-sharpness, and as the coach lumbered on over the pass, the fat woman quietly fainted.

Yuma Bill held out his hand. "Things must be doing over

here in this country. Wilder'n hell, Brit wrote."

"Plenty wild," Kim agreed, gripping the outstretched hand. He nodded at the shoe box. "Got your lunch there?"

For an instant the little man's faded blue eyes narrowed as doubt flowed across his face. He said, "Yeah, my lunch."

"Well, throw it away. We'll pick up a bait of grub on the other side of the pass."

"If you don't mind," Yuma said, "I'll hang onto it."

"Sandwiches for Brit Bonham maybe," Kim murmured, and turned toward the rock ledge.

Yuma followed, and when he saw there was only one horse, he asked, "Figgering on me walking?"

"I'll get a horse for you on the other side of the pass. We'll ride double that far. You never know how a job like this is gonna turn out. I didn't want to leave a horse if I had to make a run for it."

The little man nodded. "Now suppose you tell me what I'm heading into."

"Nothing, I hope. I aim to deliver you personally to Brit Bonham at Ganado along with your lunch. Then you'll hear the stage was held up twice today, and you'll thank me for taking you off."

They mounted, Yuma Bill hanging tightly to his shoe box. He remained silent until they were over the pass and swinging southward through the spruce. Then he said, "I knowed Brit right well when he had a bank in Las Animas, and he was never one to get into trouble."

"They've got law in Las Animas," Kim said. "On Pass Creek a man packs his law on his hip. That leaves Brit in bad shape."

"Who's building a fire under him?"

"Ever hear of a gent named Hank Dunning?" Kim asked. "Or the HD outfit?"

"No."

"You will if you hang around these parts. Takes pretty long steps, Hank does."

They rode in silence for a time, dropping fast as they

angled southwest. An hour later the trail curled through a stand of aspens, and Kim pulled up at the edge of slick-rock rim that fell away a sheer hundred feet. The slope directly below was covered with pine, but farther to the west the timber played out. It was a rough country below the pines, sparsely covered by cedars and piñons and broken by ridges reaching finger-like into the valley.

"This rim goes all around the west side of the valley," Kim said, "but you'll get the best look from right here you'll get anywhere along it. That silver ribbon you see winding around down there is Pass Creek. The valley is Pass Creek Valley, and right in the middle you'll see some buildings. That's Ganado, or what's left of it. Used to be a big mining camp, but it's just a cow town now."

Yuma Bill studied the long flat sweep of the valley, made a little hazy now by dust and smoke from some distant forest fire. He asked, "Where's them ranches you were talking about?"

"Clawhammer's on this side, HD's on the other, and both stay on their side of the creek. You can't see the buildings from here."

"A damned big valley for two ranches." Yuma said.

"There's some little outfits scattered aroun the fringe, but they don't cut much ice."

"You say Clawhammer is run by a woman?"

"That's right." Kim swung his horse back into the trail. "We'll get there, come evening."

"I thought you were taking me to Ganado."

"I didn't say when."

"Damn it, Brit wrote like he was in a hurry for..." Yuma Bill stopped, then added, "For me to get there."

"Now maybe he is, but I work for Peg Cody, so I take orders from her. She said to bring you to Clawhammer."

"Why?"

"You'll have to ask her."

Kim felt the sharp pressure of gun muzzle shoved against his spine. "You're taking orders from me," Yuma Bill said flatly. "We're going to Ganado. Savvy?"

"Sure," Kim said, "but we'll take the long way. Now if that don't suit you, go ahead and blow my backbone in two. Then you'll play hell getting to Ganado. Alive, I mean." He turned his head and gave Yuma Bill a grin. "You won't be real popular around that burg. Not with Hank Dunning anyway. I figure he'll have a reception committee waiting when he hears you weren't on the stage for his boys to pick off."

"All right." Yuma replaced his gun. "Maybe you're hoorawing me. Maybe not, but I'll find out."

"One thing I ain't clear on," Kim said. "Your coming to Pass Creek is about as smart as sticking your head into a bear trap. What's it gonna buy you?"

"Not a damned thing," the little man said, "but I'm hoping I can save Brit's hide."

"And get your full of lead."

"I'll take that chance. I'ved owed him something for a long time, and I reckon I'm the only one he could get help from. I couldn't turn him down."

"I'll deliver that shoe box with Brit's sandwiches. You can catch the stage back to Del Norte. Or go on to Durango if you want to.

"I'll see it through to the finish," Yuma said. "In my book a man pays a debt personally."

"My book don't read that way," Kim said.

Yuma Bill let it go at that. The trail followed the rim for half a mile, then swung westward through a break to the pines below. Near noon they reached a small park with a log house and barn and corrals set in the center.

"What's this?" Yuma asked.

"Shorty Avis's place. One of them little outfits I was talking about. This one is here because Peg Cody lets it. Same as all the others on this side of the creek."

They rode toward the cabin, Kim calling, "Rocky."

A girl stepped out, a Winchester held on the ready. She asked, "Who you got there?"

Kim reined up and Yuma Bill slid down. Kim said, "I just met the stage. Yuma, meet Shamrock Avis, and don't be fooled by her size. Don't take much dynamite to blow a man to pieces."

Yuma lifted his hat. "Pleased to meet you, ma'am."

Frowning, the girl pinned dark eyes on the little man as if making a judgment of him. "Glad to know you, mister, but if you call me Shamrock, I'll blow up in your face."

Kim laughed. "You see, Yuma? Poison, that's what she is. Her mother named her Shamrock, but she's got other ideas, so folks call her Rocky."

"My mother, God rest her soul, made one big mistake in her life. That was naming me."

"Where's your pa?" Kim asked.

She gave him a questioning look, then said, "Out."

"Then you can feed a couple of strays. Yuma here has got a lunch, but he's saving it. Danged selfish, I claim."

"Sure, I'll rustle some grub," the girl said, "only I'll have a tough time explaining to Pa where it went to."

Rocky turned into the cabin. Yuma Bill asked softly, "What's this about her dad?"

"He just don't cotton to having anybody around who works for Clawhammer. Plumb proddy, Shorty is, but you can't blame hime. If I was in his boots, I wouldn't want to be living on the fringe of Clawhammer range, neither." Kim motioned to the cabin. "Go on in and get acquainted. I'll put my horse up."

CHAPTER 2
ROCKY AVIS

Kim loitered outside the log barn after he had fed and watered his horse. It was pleasantly warm now, but clouds were rolling up above the Dragon Peaks on the other side of the valley. By midafternoon a storm would strike with a flurry of lightning and booming of thunder and probably a sharp downpour. Then the sky would clear and the freshly washed earth would steam under a hot sun.

Kim had been over most of the West, but this, to his way of thinking, was the most perfect spot he had ever seen. He liked the pines, the tiny-leafed aspens that shivered with each breath of wind, the columbines and mariposa lilies that were blooming now; he liked the wild smell of the high country that seemed to satisfy some inner hunger he had never fully analyzed. And he liked Rocky Avis who was as unspoiled and natural as this country in which she lived.

He moved toward the cabin, thinking of Shorty Avis who, by the grace of Clawhammer, took a precarious living from the wilderness. A little money invested in good stock could make this a profitable spread, but Shorty Avis had no money. If he or his neighbors did spread out, Peg Cody would, for her own protection, start making it rough for them. There was a chance she would anyhow when she quit feuding with Hank Dunning. Clawhammer could use the mesa for summer range.

Rocky was breaking eggs into a frying pan when Kim came into the cabin. Yuma Bill, his shoe box on his lap, was saying, "I just can't figure this business out. Brit Bonham was never one to make trouble for anybody, and it ain't right for him to be having trouble now."

Kim stopped in the doorway, a bony shoulder pressed against the jamb, and took off his hat. He was a tall man with a lean face that was weathered to the color of dark leather. Now he brushed back a stubborn lock of straw-colored hair that fell across his forehead, his blue eyes pinned on the girl's straight back.

An old thought came into his mind now, that Rocky Avis fitted the life she lived. It was rough, even the furniture in the cabin was homemade. Luxuries familiar to Peg Cody in her sprawling ranch house were unknown to Rocky. But somehow Kim had the notion that Rocky would take everything just the way it was if the choice was hers to make.

Rocky slid the frying pan to the front of the stove, stuffed the firebox full of aspen chunks, and turning saw Kim. She frowned as she set plates on the table, and then straightened to face him, slim hips pressed against the edge of the table. "When it comes to trouble," she said, "you can get all the answers from Kim. Trouble is his busines."

Yuma Bill glanced at Kim's face and lowered his gaze to the black-butted .44 holstered low on his thigh. He said, "I figured it was, but I still can't add it all up and get a sensible answer. It's Brit who's having the trouble, ain't it?"

"It adds up," the girl said evenly. "Brit Bonham's having trouble, all right, and so are a lot of other folks. With Kim it's a proposition of having too good a nose. He can smell trouble as far as a hound dog can smell coon."

"It's Brit Bonham I want to know about," the little man said. "What's that got to do with Logan?"

"Everything. It's all tied up into one package. A year ago Kim rode into Clawhammer and told Peg Cody he'd heard she needed a snake stomper. For a hundred dollars a month he'd stomp her snakes for her, and she's been paying him that ever since."

Kim hung his hat on a peg in the wall and dropped into a rawhide bottom chair. "When you get done gabbing about me, you'd better take a look at them eggs, Shamrock. I sure do hate burned eggs."

"You call me Shamrock again," the girl cried furiously, "and you'll get your eggs down the back of your neck." Kim laughed softly as she turned to the stove. "I told you how it was, Yuma. There ain't even a mountain lion in these parts that'll stand up and look her in the eye."

Rocky, still facing the stove, said in the same angry voice, "Look at him, wearing fancy Justins and a Stetson that set him back fifty dollars. Silver spurs. He's even got gold in his teeth. Nobody else can afford stuff like that but Kim Logan."

"What are you getting so heated up for?" Kim asked. "I ain't robbed a bank."

"You're working for Peg Cody. Same thing." Rocky

spooned the eggs into a platter that held a dozen pieces of salt side. She slammed the platter down on the table with a bang. "You wouldn't know how it is, trying to make a living when any minute Peg Cody may take it into her head to run all of us off the mesa and take our places over."

"You're just dreaming things," Kim said mildly. "Peg's never bothered you."

"I'm not dreaming, I'm nightmaring." She pulled a pan of biscuits out of the oven, placed the biscuits on a plate, and set them on the table. "It isn't just Peg that makes me so mad. I know what to expect from a greedy woman. It's you I can't figure out. You've been doing what you call snake stomping all your life. What's it got you besides fancy duds? Nothing."

"I get along," Kim said, his voice still mild.

"Sure, you get along. You could drift out of here tomorrow and put everything you own in your pockets. You haven't got a dollar in the bank. You don't own a cow. Not even a calf. You could come here and work for thirty a month and beans, but no, that would mean chasing cows through the scrub oak, and you're no brush popper. You're...you're just a snake stomper."

She flounced to the stove, picked up the coffeepot and filled their cups, and flounced back to the stove again. "Come on and eat." She dropped into a chair, shoulders sagging as if suddenly tired. "I guess that anywhere we went, there'd be greedy people like Peg Cody and Hank Dunning. It's just that you seem different, Kim."

"Reckon I never thought about it," Kim said.

There was no more talk for a time. Kim and Yuma Bill ate, Kim wondering what had got into the girl. He had never seen her so angry, and apparently over nothing at all. When he was finished, he canted his chair back and rolled a smoke, eyes turning to Rocky's white face. He asked, "What set you off?"

"Nothing much." She got up and filled their coffee cups. "I just got to thinking about Brit Bonham who used his bank to help folks. Little folks like us along with the big ones like

Peg Cody. Now look at the jam he got himself into."

The shoe box had been laying beside Yuma Bill's plate. He picked it up and scooted his chair back. He said "I'm getting tired of being in the dark. What kind of a jam is Brit in?"

"Dunning aims to..." Rocky began.

"I'll tell it," Kim cut in. "He loaned too much money. That's all. Peg borrowed thirty thousand to stock her range. Clawhammer was in debt and pretty well run down when her old man died. Leastwise, that's what I hear. So when she borrowed from Brit, she went whole hog. It's too much, cattle prices being what they are. Looks like she and Brit are going broke together."

"She could save a hundred dollars a month by firing you," Rocky said sharply.

Kim shook his head. "I ain't flattering myself too much, I reckon, when I say she needs me and she knows it. Dunning would start pushing tomorrow if I wasn't around."

"Start pushing," the girl cried. "What do you think he's doing now?"

Kim grinned and winked at her. "He's just warming up to the job."

"You mean you've got Dunning bluffed?" Yuma Bill asked.

"Sort of. You see, he's a scheming sonuvagun who likes a sure thing. Fighting a woman is his size. Long as I'm working for Clawhammer, he ain't got a sure thing."

"He has if Peg doesn't fire Dutch Heinz," Rocky said. "I'd bet my bottom dollar he's sold out to Dunning."

Kim rose. "Let's ride, Yuma."

"You'd sure as hell better." It was Shorty Avis standing in the doorway, a cocked Winchester in his hands. "I told you before you wasn't wanted here. Now git afore I put a round window in your skull."

"Take it easy," Kim said. "You've got no quarrel with me."

"I've got a quarrel with Clawhammer," Avis bellowed. "Git, I said."

He was a tough bantam of a man, this Shorty Avis, with a knobby face and black piercing eyes that were alive with fury. Although Avis had never been friendly, Kim had liked him from the first because he instinctively liked any man who had a hard core of courage. Shorty Avis had it, or he wouldn't be here on the mesa telling Clawhammer men to stay off his land.

"Tell him, Dad," Rocky said quietly. "I was going to, but I hadn't got around to it."

Kim swung to face the girl. "Tell me what?"

"I'll tell you all right," Shorty barked. "You damned betcha I will. Dutch Heinz was up here early this morning. Said we had to get out of the country. Offered me a hundred dollars for this quarter section. Well, I ain't stirring my stumps, Logan. You go tell that woman you work for."

Kim studied Avis a moment, finding this hard to believe. Chores like that fell to him, and Peg had never indicated she wanted to oust the little fry.

"I'll talk to Peg," Kim said finally. "It don't smell right."

"Nothing smells right about Clawhammer." Avis gave him a wicked grin. "But I ain't gonna worry about you. I knowed all the time that Dunning would get you. He will afore sundown. I'm betting on it."

Kim moved toward Avis, warned by the triumph he sensed in the man. He said, "Keep talking, Shorty."

"I'll enjoy talking, and I'll enjoy seeing the finish. I sure as hell won't lose no tears when they plant you."

Kim put on his hat. "You know something, Shorty."

"You bet I know something." Avis backed out of the doorway. "Won't be long till you find out all about it. Now dust."

"What do you know, Dad?" Rocky crossed the room to stand beside Kim, and when her father's lips tightened into a stubborn line, she said with some sharpness, "Kim is taking a friend of Brit Bonham's into Ganado. In case you've forgotten, Brit is the best friend we have on this range."

"Now wait a minute," Kim said. "Have I done anything to

make you think I wasn't your friend?"

"You're taking Peg Cody's orders," Rocky said.

He looked down at the girl's defiant face. "That don't mean I ain't a friend of yours."

"You won't be anybody's friend very long," Avis said. "Dunning sent Phil Martin over here with five HD hands. They're hunting for you now."

It took Kim a moment to fully grasp the significance of Shorty Avis's news. There had been a good deal of sparring between Clawhammer and HD in the year Kim had been in the valley, but not once had a Clawhammer man crossed the creek on HD range, nor had HD riders crossed to the Clawhammer side. Now if Martin, Dunning's ramrod, had come hunting for Kim it must mean that Dunning had decided it was time to wind things up.

"Where are they?" Kim asked.

"Indian Springs the last I saw of 'em."

Kim stepped out of the cabin. "Let me have a horse, Shorty. We can't dodge 'em riding double."

"Thought you had a horse for me," Yuma said angrily.

"I have. At Clawhammer."

"You mean you figured on me riding double all the way to your damned ranch?" Yuma Bill shouted.

Kim swung to face him. "I didn't figure you'd be on that stage. Didn't make sense to me that a stranger would come toting a bunch of dinero into this country just to help out an old coot like Brit Bonham.

"Let him take Blackie, Pa," Rocky said.

Shorty Avis began to swell up. "When I let a Clawhammer man take a horse of mine, I'll be fit for the asylum..."

"You're fit for it if you don't," Rocky cut in. "It's Brit Bonham's friend who needs the horse. Anyhow, if we're able to stay here, it will be because Kim helps us."

"Helps us," Avis howled. "Why, this gun-toting varmint wouldn't help his own grandmother if that Cody woman told him to steal the gold teeth out of her head."

Kim started toward the barn, calling over his shoulder,

"Fetch your sandwiches and come on, Yuma."

"You touch my horse and I'll..." Avis bawled.

"You'll do nothing," Rocky cried.

Kim went on, not looking back, and presently Yuma Bill caught up with him. He said, "I hope that girl runs the roost."

"She does," Kim said.

He threw gear on Shorty Avis's black gelding, tightened the cinches on the buckskin, and swung up. He said, "Let's ride."

Bill mounted, the shoe box gripped under one arm. They left the clearing on the run, Kim lifting a hand to Rocky. He had one glance at Shorty Avis, whose knobby face was filled with a dark and forbidding anger. Kim grinned, knowing Avis would do nothing more than rail at his daughter, for when the chips were down, it was Rocky who called the turn. Then Kim and Yuma Bill were in the aspens, the trail dropping swiftly toward the valley below.

CHAPTER 3
FOXES AND HOUNDS

The trail curled downward in a series of looping switchbacks. Kim kept a fast pace, Yuma Bill following closely. An hour after leaving the Avis place, they reached a stand of pines, and here the trail straightened and ran directly down the slope. It was an old Ute trail that the Avises and their closest neighbors, the Fawcetts, used regularly on their trips to town. Kim had been over it many times. Now he pulled up, motioning for Yuma Bill to do the same. For several minutes he sat listening, the little man's eyes pinned on him.

Indian Springs lay to the right. Probably Phil Martin had stopped Shorty Avis there and asked about Kim. If Avis had known where he was, he would have told the HD man, for Avis wasn't smart enough to see that if Hank Dunning smashed Clawhammer, he would move across the creek and take the entire valley. Then Avis and the rest of the small fry would be worse off than they were now. Peg Cody was greedy as Rocky Avis had said, but she lacked the driving ruthlessness which was so much a part of Hank Dunning.

"How far to Clawhammer?" Yuma Bill asked.

"'Bout three hours from here," Kim said, "if we went straight, but I don't figure we can. Chances are Martin and his bunch is off there somewhere." He motioned toward the southwest. "I'll feel a hell of a lot better if I know exactly where they are."

"You reckon they're after me?"

Kim shook his head. "Me. Dunning will figure his boys got you, so that ain't worrying him, but I've been in his hair ever since I got here. If they can make wolf meat out of me here in the hills, it'll be safer and maybe easier than doing the job in town."

"How would they know where to look?"

"I ride through these hills all the time. Part of my job is seeing that HD men stay on their side of the creek. Phil Martin knows that, so it's just a case of looking until they find me."

"Suppose they get you?"

Kim shrugged. "Then they'll move in. Our hands are with the cattle in the high country. Just Peg and an old man at the ranch. Chances are Dunning will burn the buildings, figuring Peg will sell for any offer he makes."

"Why hell, she wouldn't quit that easy, would she?"

"I ain't sure," Kim said thoughtfully. "She talks pretty tough, but she's never been through a range war. Her old man used to be the big push in the valley, but now the shoe's on the other foot."

"Hasn't she got a crew and a ramrod?"

"She's got a crew, but they ain't a very salty outfit. And Dutch Heinz, he's the ramrod, claims he ain't a fighting man."

He let it go at that. There was no point in telling Yuma Bill his suspicions. He had never been sure of Dutch Heinz and he was less sure now. He found it hard to believe that Peg had sent Heinz to warn Shorty Avis out of the country. On the other hand, it might be Dunning's idea to force the small ranchers into a war against Clawhammer. It would be like Dunning to get someone else to do his fighting for him.

"I don't savvy," Yuma Bill said. "Looks like this valley's big enough for both of 'em."

"Not for them it ain't," Kim s id. "Let's ride."

He pulled off the trail and took a parallel course to it for a time. Phil Martin was a methodical sort of man who would systematically comb the hills, spreading his hands out so that they could cover the most ground. If Avis had not warned him, Kim would have ridden squarely into the HD guns. But now there was a chance he could slip through them.

The ground levelled off and Kim reined up again. He hipped around in the saddle. "Smell anything?"

Yuma nodded. "Dust. They've been through here."

"And they ain't far away." Kim motioned to his left. "Ganado Creek is yonder on the other side of this ridge. The canyon's deeper'n hell. We don't want to get run into it. Come on."

They circled a barrier of rocks and came again into the thick timber, the slope now quite gentle. Ten minutes later they broke out of the pines into a small park. An HD man was riding directly toward them, a burly cowhand named Tonto Miles.

For an instant all three were too stunned by surprise to do anything. Then Miles let out a squall, pulled his gun and fired, the bullet going high and wide. He cracked steel to his horse as Kim threw a slug at him and missed. Then he disappeared into the timber toward the trail.

"They're all around us," Kim said in disgust. "Ran smack into 'em."

Now other shouts sounded from the left. There was the thunder of hoofs swinging in from the trail as Kim put his horse into a run and headed directly across the clearing. Just before he reached the wall of the timber, he looked back. Yuma Bill was ten feet behind him. Four men had reached the far side of the park, Phil Martin in the lead.

Whatever thought Kim had of stopping and making a fight of it left him. He had no idea how Yuma Bill would pan out in a showdown. Even if he was a good man, the odds were still too long.

Kim slanted down grade, hoping to get out of the rough country. If they could reach the flat, there was a chance they could outrun Martin's bunch, but the valley was still a long ways off. Besides, there was no telling how many others there were, or where they were. Shorty Avis had said six, but he might not have seen all of them, and Hank Dunning was not a man to do a half job.

Almost immediately Kim was forced to reverse direction, for two riders came into view directly in front of him. He angled back toward the rim, shaking his head at Yuma Bill's yell, "Thought we wanted to go the other way?"

"Come on." Kim called.

He knew now there was no way to avoid a fight, but if there was to be one, it would be on the battleground he picked. Here the pines were small and scattering. Martin and the three riders with him remained in sight, the distance between them unchanged. The other two had altered their course to parallel Kim's and Yuma Bill's, apparently aiming to block their escape to open country.

A mesa hill loomed ahead, and Yuma Bill bawled, "Damn it, you're letting 'em run us into a bottleneck."

Kim didn't answer. A gun cracked behind them, but the distance was too great and the bullet fell short. They reached the mesa hill and slanted up it, their horses laboring under them, red dust kicked up into a motionless cloud. Another gun roared. This time the bullet came too close for comfort. The climb had slowed Kim and Yuma Bill, and Martin had cut the distance between them.

They topped the crest and Kim waved for Yuma Bill to go on. He reined up, drawing gun. Martin, well ahead of the others, had reached the base of the hill. He looked up, close enough for Kim to see his broad face clearly, the sweeping sand-colored mustache, the crooked nose, even the smudge of red dust across the right cheek.

Martin gave out a frantic yell when he saw Kim's gun sweep down. He jerked his horse to a stop and plunged out of his saddle just as Kim fired. He dived toward a boulder as Kim squeezed off a second shot. Then he was under cover, bellied flat against the ground, and Kim was not sure whether he had scored a hit either time.

The three men following Martin had pulled and were firing, but it was too far for accurate shooting with hand guns. Kim wheeled toward his horse and snaked his Winchester from the boot, thinking that this might be as good a place as any to make a stand. He could keep Martin nailed behind the boulder until dark.

For the moment Kim had forgotten the other two riders who had bobbed up in front of them. Yuma Bill had swung back, yelling, "Come on, you idiot. They'll pot us like two ducks in a puddle."

Then Kim remembered. He looked for the two men, but they had disappeared. A slab of rock ran like an unbroken red wall from the base of the hill to the crest. They must have reined in behind it and were climbing to the top. Probably they wouldn't go that far. They'd dismount and hole up behind the rock slab. Then it would be like Yuma Bill said. The HD men would be forted up while Kim and Yuma Bill were in the open.

Kim whirled back to his horse and shoved the Winchester into the boot. He shouted, "Damn it, I told you to hightail."

"I never went off and left a man in a tight in my life," Yuma Bill shot back. "What the hell do you think I am?"

Kim swung into leather, motioning toward the red rim that inclosed the east side of the valley. "Dust," he called. "We'll make 'em come after us."

The cliff rose sheer above the mesa, a nest of boulders at its base. Kim pointed his horse toward the rocks. Yuma Bill swung in beside him, his angry voice rising above the clatter of hoofs, "You aiming to fly to the top?"

"Save your wind, We'll fort up."

They rode hard, hoofs beating against the rocky ground. When they were out of gun range, Kim pulled his buckskin down and looked back. No one was in sight. They went on, slower now, Yuma Bill eyeing him with sour disapproval. Minutes later they reached the boulders and swung in behind them. There was protection of a sort here, for the cliff formed an overhang so that the horses could be safely left at the base without danger of being seen from the rim.

Stepping down, Kim pulled his Winchester from the boot. "Take the horses back there." He motioned to the cliff. "Keep 'em there."

"Wait a minute, you danged chuckle-headed...," Yuma Bill began.

But Kim didn't wait. He climbed to the top of the largest boulder and dropped flat on its smooth, weather-torn surface, eyes scanning the rocky flat in front of him. Still no one was in sight.

The ridge was about a mile long with a steep drop-off on every side except the east end which butted against the cliff; its surface was covered by small clumps of sagebrush, the smooth gray sweep of the flat broken only occasionally by a wind-gnarled cedar.

Westward beyond the break-off there was another steep slope dropping to the level floor of the valley. Kim could see the valley from this elevation, bright green where the sunlight was upon it, or freckled by islands of shadow. Clouds were boiling up now in a dark forbidding mass from the sullen Dragon Peaks. It would not be more than an hour until the clouds would cover the sky, and the sunlight would be blotted out for a time.

Ganado canyon lay just to the south, an ugly slash that ran from the great peaks of the continental divide to the valley. There its walls disappeared, and the creek which tumbled with white-laced violence from the high altitude slowed its course to make a series of looping meanders across the grass-covered valley.

Kim glanced up at the sky. The storm was moving in. Lightning had begun to flash in weird shifting veins above the Dragons, and thunder was rolling out its deep booming sounds, muted somewhat by distance. Kim brought his gaze back to the sage-carpeted flat. In one way this was a good position. Martin would find a direct attack difficult and costly, for the flat offered no shelter that was adequate for either man or horse.

On the other hand, the surface of this boulder where Kim lay might be a place of death. There was a break in the cliff to Kim's right. If an HD man climbed to the rim, he could look directly down upon the boulder. But right or wrong, Kim had picked his spot, and here the battle would be fought out to a decision.

CHAPTER 4
UNDER THE RIM

The minutes dragged while the sky darkened and the ominous roll of thunder came closer. Then Kim heard the grating sound of boots on the side of the boulder. Turning, he saw that Yuma Bill was climbing toward him.

"Damn it," Kim said in exasperation. "I told you to stay with the horses."

Yuma Bill dropped down beside him. "They'll stay where I left 'em. Now maybe you'd like to tell me why you holed up here."

"Where would you be wanting to go?" Kim flung a hand out toward the flat in front of them. "Out there maybe?"

"We could have kept riding. If they had poked their heads up over the hill, we'd have blowed 'em off their necks."

"About the time we got far enough out there for them two hombres to notch their sights on us, we'd have got our heads blowed off. This was the only place we could go and keep out of their sight unless you wanted to go down into Ganado Canyon which I didn't."

Yuma Bill scowled, gaze swinging toward the lip of the canyon. "Reckon I forgot about that hole in the ground. I figgered on slanting back that way."

Kim jabbed a finger in the direction of the valley. "Clawhammer's off there. Just below where the creek comes out of the canyon. I figured we'd hole up here until dark and then make a run for it."

"How about the rim?" Yuma Bill jerked a thumb at the sullen red cliff behind them.

"That's the joker," Kim admitted. "If Martin's got a mountain goat in his outfit, he'll climb up there and we'll be caught like your two ducks in a puddle."

Yuma Bill rolled a smoke and fired it, his forehe d furrowed. He said, "Logan, you've got all the time in the world, but I haven't. All that means anything to you is the hundred dollars a month you're getting; but I'm in this tight because I want to help a friend who gave me a hand once. Now I'm going to Ganado, and I don't aim to sit here till dark."

"Maybe we ain't so different at that," Kim said. "We both want to save our own hides, and you sure won't do Bonham no good if Martin plugs you and nabs your lunch box."

"You know what's in that box as well as I do." Yuma said sourly. "Brit's letter sounded like he didn't have much time, and here we are, nailed down on top of a damned rock."

"You still want to stay alive, don't you?" Kim demanded.

Yuma Bill glanced at the cliff behind him. "I ain't sure I'm going to."

"Git back with the horses," Kim said irritably. "What do you think I told you to stay there for?"

"Maybe you need some help to stay alive. It's like you said this morning. I'd never get to that damned town if I struck out alone."

Kim's eyes had been searching the flat. He sat up,

Winchester across his lap. "Take a look, friend. Five of 'em."

The HD ride s had come into view where the rock slab levelled out on the flat. They reined up, remaining motionless for a time as they studied the cliff. Kim could not tell whether he and Yuma Bill had been seen or not, but in either case it seemed unlikely that Martin would close in.

"Five," Yuma Bill muttered. "Where's the other one?"

"Chances are he's crawling to the top," Kim answered. "It'll take him an hour or so. By that time we'll be under the overhang."

"Then we can't watch the other five and they'll walk in on us," Yuma said sourly. "I don't like it, Logan."

"I ain't in love with this deal either. What do you want to do, make a run for it?"

Yuma shook his head. "Not with them kind of odds."

They sat in silence, watching Martin and his men who had come on and then stopped just short of decent rifle range. Kim considered taking a few shots to worry them, and decided against it. The only shells he had for the Winchester were those in the magazine, and he'd need those and more before dark.

Kim gave some thought to climbing to the rim so Yuma Bill's back would be protected, and gave it up. The only break in the cliff for a mile or more to either side was a long trough-like slot that furnished precarious footing at best. If the other HD man had already started up, and Kim was sure he had, a climber below him would make a clear target.

There was nothing to do but wait, and Kim was not a man who found waiting easy. Nor did Yuma Bill seem to like it any better. He kept shifting from one part of the boulder to the other, smoking incessantly, eyes on the HD men who had dismo nted and were hunkered in a tight little knot in front of their horses.

"Damn it," Yuma burst out. "Damn it to hell. I'm gonna ride out there and talk to 'em. You said it was you they wanted."

"Go ahead," Kim said. "You'll get halfway there if you're

lucky and their shooting ain't good."

The little man beat a head against the rock. "You haven't told me all of this."

"No," Kim admitted, "but I'll tell you now. Brit Bonham's spread himself so far that folks got to talking. It's my guess Dunning got the talk going, aiming to start a rush on the bank. Bonham ain't got the cash to pay off his depositors, so he'll have to close. He'll call in his loans. That breaks Peg Cody."

"So that's why you were so damned interested in keeping me alive?"

Kim nodded. "Only I don't figure it'll go quite like that. Dunning is a big depositor. If he pulls his money out, Bonham's finished. So somewhere along the line Dunning will make Bonham an offer for Peg's notes, and Bonham will have to sell 'em."

Yuma Bill tapped finger tips against the rock. "If I get my cash to Brit in time, I'll save the bank and while I'm doing that, I save Clawhammer."

"That's the size of it," Kim said. "Bonham told Peg when he was expecting you. Like a damned fool, he told Dunning, too. That's why we figured you'd never get to Ganado alive if I didn't stop the stage, so I stopped it just on the off chance you'd be on it."

"I still don't savvy why you're taking me to hellangone to get me to town," Yuma said sulkily.

"Reckon Peg wants to thank you." Kim grinned. "She's got a right nice way of thanking men who are on her side, but she's hell on the others."

It began to rain, a driving downpour with lightning breaking across the sky in vivid leaping flashes. "Come on," Kim shouted above the rolling thunder. "We've got to keep that lunch box dry, or your sandwiches will sure get damp."

Kim slid off the rock and dived under the overhang. Yuma Bill following. It was dry here, for there was little wind, and the rain was coming straight down in heavy slapping drops.

"Won't last long." Kim leaned his Winchester against the

sandstone cliff, and untied his slicker from behind the saddle. "Stay here. This might be what they've been waiting for."

He stepped back into the rain, this time circling the big boulder instead of climbing to the top. He hunkered in front of it, his back hard against its wet surface so that a man on the rim above would have to lean out from the edge to see him.

The rain had spread a silver curtain across the flat, pelting it with fierce violence and hiding the five HD men who were out there. The summer storms seldom lasted more than a few minutes, but it might be long enough to give Martin the cover he needed.

A Winchester cracked from the rim, the bullet striking the rock and screaming off into space. Kim pressed back against the boulder, the beat of hoofs sweeping in from the sage flat coming clearly to him between the rolls of thunder. They had timed it perfectly, he thought. He was caught between the men riding in and the one on the rim.

He glimpsed them, shrouded by rain. He must have eased forward as he brought the Winchester to his shoulder, for the man on the rim squeezed off another shot, the slug slicing across the edge of the boulder, sending rock splinters flying. Martin and his riders were close enough now, and Kim began firing.

It was poor shooting, for the light was thin and the HD men were low in their saddles and riding fast. Kim missed with his first bullet, tagged Martin with his second, and missed with a third. He wiped his face as a slug from the rim slapped into the ground in front of him. A quick gust of wind swept the rain against him, blinding him for a moment. He squeezed his eyes shut and opened them, shaking his head and swearing.

Martin's men were angling a little now as they opened up with their Colts, bullets peppering the rock around Kim. He pronged back the hammer of his Winchester and squeezed off another shot, knocking an HD rider out of his saddle in a rolling fall.

A scream sounded shrilly through the heavy roar of guns, a human scream of wild, absolute terror. A body thudded into the rocks to Kim's left, but he had no time to see who it was. He was working his Winchester steadily; he heard Yuma Bill cut loose with his Colt. A moment later he saw that the fight had been won. Martin had stopped to help the fallen man up behind him, right arm swinging in a wide signal for retreat.

Yuma Bill was beside Kim saying, "That yahoo on the rim fell off. Sure got busted up."

Another Winchester was cracking from the rim, but the bullets were not slanting down at Kim and Yuma Bill. They were being aimed at the HD riders who were in full retreat across the flat. Kim emptied his rifle at them, puzzled by what had happened. He did not know how much damage he had inflicted on Martin's crew, but it must have been considerable to have knocked the fight out of them as effectively as he had.

Kim rose, glancing at Yuma Bill who was staring after the retreating HD crew. The little man brought his eyes to Kim and wiped the rain from his face, blinking and shaking his head. He asked, "Who's up here?"

"I don't know, but I've got a hunch."

Wheeling, Kim glanced at the broken body of the man who had fallen. He had seen the fellow a few times in Ganado with Phil Martin, but he didn't know his name. Just a gunhandy drifter who had taken Dunning's wages and made a bad bargain. As Kim ran past him to his horse, a thought cut its way through his mind. It could be me lying *there*.

He slipped his Winchester into the boot, and stepping into saddle, brought his buckskin around. He rode out of the shelter of the overhang into the rain. It had slacked off now to a fine mist; the lightning was gone from the sky. The storm had moved on, but the smell of rain was heavy in the air and the red sandstone cliff was wet and bright.

Yuma Bill shouted, "What are you up to?"

"Finding something out," Kim said.

He rode directly away from the cliff until he could see the rim. Rocky Avis was standing there, a slim boyish figure in a man's shirt and trousers, a rifle in her hand. She waved when she saw Kim, calling, "Both of you all right?"

"Nary a scratch," he answered, reining his horse around. "How'd you come to buy into this ruckus?"

"I figured it was a good idea to keep you two alive," she said. "I got up on the rim after you left and watched them give you a run. Then when you forted up down there, I thought you might need a hand, so I rode over. What about that hairpin who went over the edge?"

"Dead."

She shook her head. "I'm sorry."

"What for? He wouldn't have been sorry if he'd plugged me or Yuma Bill in the back."

"I know, but it seems a poor thing to die for. He was leaning over trying to get a bead on you when I saw him. I got up close before he knew I was there. I told him to hook the moon. He jumped and took a step back and over he went."

"Well, you sure did a job for us. It would have been a little rough if they'd kept coming in." He cuffed back his hat. "Rocky, this ain't good. You're into the fight now if they saw who you were."

"We're in the fight anyway. Pa's just too stubborn to see it. You two better get along now."

"We'll have to take the body in."

"Tie him on his horse. I'll have Pa take him to town. You'd better make tracks while you can. They might still give you trouble."

Kim shook his head. "They had a stummickful, but we'll find his horse and leave him here. You hightail home, and get it through Shorty's bonehead that Dunning's the man he'd better be scared of."

"I'll tell him, but he won't believe it. Not after seeing Dutch Heinz this morning."

She waved and disappeared over the lip of the rim. Kim

rode back to Yuma Bill. He said, "It was Rocky Avis. She don't see this business like Shorty does. She trailed us, figuring we might need a hand."

"So a woman saves our lives," the little man said. "I don't like that, Logan."

"I do. It was kind o' touchy there for a minute."

"Most women don't forget what you owe'em," Yuma said bitterly. "I know."

"Rocky's different," Kim said, and rode past Yuma Bill to the break in the cliff.

The dead man's horse had been tied there to a small cedar. Kim led him back to the rocks, saying nothing as they lashed the body across the saddle. Later, riding across the flat steaming now under a hot sun, he glanced at Yuma Bill, wondering what was in the man's mind.

Suddenly Yuma felt Kim's eyes and turned his head. He burst out, "I hope to hell you know what you're doing. If we're too late to save Brit's bank, I'll take it out of your hide."

"I'm in this to earn my hundred dollars a month, you know," Kim said. "Remember?"

"That's got nothing to do with . . ."

"I just got to thinking about what you said. Then I got to asking myself how you got so damned high and mighty that you could preach to me."

Yuma Bill's craggy face softened. "So that's it. Well, I didn't aim to preach. Just seemed like you had things twisted a mite."

"Like what?"

"Like putting your orders above saving Brit Bonham's bank."

"Hell, I'm just doing my job. Strikes me that when a man takes a job, he'd better do it."

"That ain't enough. I'm more'n twice your age, Logan. That's given me twice as much time to think as you've had. Now I ain't saying I ain't done my share of ornery things, but somewhere along the line I've found what pays a man and what don't."

"My job pays me," Kim said, "and pretty damned good."

"No, you're getting short-changed unless you're in love with this Peg Cody. It's like this, Logan. Every man sows some seed, it grows, and it's gonna be harvested whether he does it or someone else does. Now what kind of seed have you sowed?"

"Aw, get a pulpit," Kim said resentfully.

Yuma Bill smiled. "Well, maybe I oughtta, but you started this sermon, and I aim to finish it. It's short and sweet. You get to the last hill. We all do, sooner or later, and I'm a hell of a lot closer to it than you are. You take a look back and you see all them crops you've planted. If you've used the right seed, you go over the range feeling purty damned good about everything. But this other hombre, the one who didn't give a whoop what he planted, why, I reckon he's gonna burn in the hellfire the parsons talk about."

"I suppose you know all about women, too," Kim said. "You seem to know about everything else."

"I know a little all right," Yuma said, bitterness creeping into his voice. "I've always had a little money, and that draws women like honey draws bees." He scratched his nose. "But maybe I had your little Rocky girl all wrong. If she loves you, she won't be holding you in her debt. Some women ain't capable of love. Maybe she is."

"Love me? Why hell, she's just a kid . . ."

"Nineteen or twenty, ain't she? Old enough to be in love. I can't see no other reason for her getting so huffy with you at noon if she wasn't. Or risking her hide to save yours."

Kim let the talk die. It was something he had not thought about before, and he dismissed it as an old man's idle talk. But there was one thing he did know. The last person in the world he wanted to hurt was Rocky Avis.

CHAPTER 5
CLAWHAMMER

The sun tipped down behind the Dragon Peaks and dusk flowed across the valley, the purple twilight giving a sense of weird unreality to it. Darkness moved in, and to the west the Dragons became sharp black points against a pale sky. Then the last trace of light above the horizon died, and the mountains were lost to sight, their lines fading into indistinct blurs.

When Kim and Yuma Bill rode down off the last bench to the valley floor, the darkness was so complete that the distant lights of Ganado gleamed like clustered stars that had dropped from the black sky. They turned toward Clawhammer, following a bend in the bench, and presently the lamp-brightened windows of the big ranch house came into sight.

Ten minutes later they reined up under the ancient cottonwoods that had prompted Peg's father to build his house here. A man called from the corrals, "Who is it?"

A dog bounded toward Kim, barking in short angry yaps. Kim said, "All right, Nero," and when the dog was silent, he called, "It's me, Limpy."

Kim dismounted and waited. The man drifted up out of the darkness, asking, "Any trouble, son?"

"A little," Kim said. "Peg in the house?"

"Yeah, she's there. Just got back from town. Go on in. I'll take care of your horses."

"Come on, Yuma." Kim swung around and crossed the yard, a little soft now from the afternoon rain, and stepped up on the porch. "Scrape the mud off, Yuma. She's hell on a man who totes mud into her house."

"I respect a clean woman," Yuma Bill said, "if she don't make a religion of it."

"She don't." Kim cleaned his boots on the scraper and went in. He called, "Peg." The smell of coffee and frying ham

223

was a fragrance in the house that sharpened the hunger in Kim. He shouted "Peg" a second time, and crossed the living room to the kitchen door, Yuma Bill following, the shoe box under his arm.

Peg Cody turned from the big wood range where she was frying ham, and gave Kim a quick smile, She was tall, almost as tall as Kim and about the same age. Her hair seemed even redder than usual in the lamplight, and her hazel eyes that could reflect a smile or be bright with wild and sudden anger were warm now with pleasure at seeing Kim. She was a temperamental woman with a disposition that swung easily from one extreme to the other, and Kim had learned long ago to walk easy until he read the mood which possessed her at the moment.

"Come in, Kim," Peg said. "I had a hunch you'd be dragging in as hungry as an old bear in the spring, so I fixed a little extra. I just got back from town."

"This is Yuma Bill," Kim said. "Yuma, meet Miss Cody."

"I'm glad to know you," Peg said pleasantly. "I've been worried about both of you all day."

The little man stood with all the height he possessed, hat dangling from one hand, the shoe box under the other arm. He said, his voice cool, "Howdy, ma'am."

She turned back to the stove. "Brit Bonham calls you his friend. The way I see it, that's the finest thing one man can call another."

Yuma Bill nodded, her words thawing him. "Thank you, ma'am. I'm proud to be Brit's friend."

She motioned toward the back door. "Wash up, Kim. Supper's ready."

Kim crossed the kitchen to the back porch, pumped a pan of water, and stepped aside for Yuma Bill to wash. He moved to the end of the porch and looked out across the valley that seemed to stretch on and on into black eternity, and thought of the first time he had seen Peg a year ago. He had ridden in from Ganado on his buckskin, tired and gaunt and looking tough enough to impress the devil himself. He must have impressed Peg, for she had hired him at once with no more recommendation than the toughness of his appearance.

In the year since then he had kept on riding, but with a definite purpose. As soon as he had caught the full picture, he told Peg that there would never be peace in the valley until Hank Dunning was dead. On at least two occasions he had prodded Dunning until he thought the man would go for his gun, but the HD owner had wanted none of it.

Kim had puzzled over it many times. Dunning did not give the appearance of being a coward. Almost everyone in the valley was afraid of him, for he was fast with the bone-handled .45 he wore on his right thigh. Still, he had turned his back and walked off.

Yuma Bill emptied his pan over the railing and said, "Yours, Logan." He dried and drifted back into the kitchen. Kim washed and combed his hair, thinking that in the year he had worked for Clawhammer, he still did not really understand Peg. He had never felt the sting of her tongue, although he had seen her go into towering rages when some of her riders made a mistake or failed to carry out an order. She must have sensed from the first that he was one man who would take nothing from her, and she had treated him accordingly.

Kim did know one thing. Clawhammer meant everything to her. For that reason she had gambled recklessly in borrowing so much money from Bonham. But, perhaps failing to foresee that Bonham's bank might close her out, she had not considered it a gamble. She seldom discussed the ranch business with Kim, and she never asked his advice. Their relationship had been strictly that of employer and employee. Still, she had the power to stir him as she could stir any man who possessed a normal man's desires; she had often gone out of her way to be with him. Yet after a year on Clawhammer, Kim had a feeling that her deepest thoughts and ambitions were secrets known only to herself.

"Break your leg out there?" Peg called.

He went into the kitchen, patting the stubborn cowlick

that never stayed in place. He said, "Yeah, broke my leg."

"Have to shoot you. No room on this spread for a useless horse." She motioned to a chair. "Sit down. I'm so hungry I'm going to start eating whether you two do or not."

It was a good meal of ham, beans, fried potatoes, biscuits, apple butter, and hot black coffee. Kim had often eaten with er when the crew was gone, and he had never had a bad meal at her table. It was one of the many things he liked about her. She could ride a horse with the best; she made a hand when she was needed, but there was this other side to her. She kept the house immaculate, she made her own dresses, and she baked the best chocolate cake he had ever tasted.

"Better fetch your crew in," Kim said, reaching for the ham. "Dunning's fixing to force a fight."

"Then he'll get one."

"And we'd better be ready. I don't like the notion of your being here with just Limpy, and I won't be earning my wages if I sit here keeping the seat of my pants warm."

She frowned, throwing him a sharp glance as if not liking his advice. "I'm not afraid of Dunning, but I am worried about our cows. That's where my boys belong, and that's where they'll stay."

"We had some trouble," Kim said.

She rose and went to the stove for the coffeepot. "Let's hear about it."

Kim told her what had happened, leaving out only the fact that Rocky Avis had bought into the fight. He wished he had told Yuma Bill to hold his tongue about it. Glancing now at the little man, he was relieved to see that he had finished eating. Yuma Bill had canted his chair back against the wall and was busying himself with a cigarette, apparently satisfied to let Kim do the talking.

Peg drank her coffee and put the cup down. "I don't like it, Kim. I don't like it at all, but it doesn't change anything. I've contracted to deliver five hundred head of steers in Durango this fall. I've got to do that. Nothing else is important."

"Your life is," Kim said doggedly.

"My life isn't in danger. We have law here, Kim. You're overlooking that."

"Law?" Kim laughed shortly. "What kind of law does Ed Lane give this valley? He's picked his side, and it ain't ours."

She gave him a close questioning glance. "That's the way it's got to be, Kim. You're all the army I can afford to hire."

Kim rose, suddenly angry. He had no illusions about himself. He was a good man to a certain point, but no man, regardless of how good we was, could fight Hank Dunning's outfit. It was up to every Clawhammer hand from the ramrod, Dutch Heinz, on down to old Limpy.

"I ain't one to tell my boss how to run her business," Kim said sharply, "but I've been through some range wars and I know how they go. Likewise I know about sheriffs like our great Ed Lane. When Dunning's ready to finish us off, Lane will go fishing."

"All right, Kim," she said, her tone matching his. "Don't tell me how to run my business. I hired you to use your gun. Use it."

"I will, damn it." Kim pounded the table with his fist. "I'll use my gun, but I don't cotton to being chased by Martin and five of his boys. Call your hands down and let me take 'em across the creek. I'll finish this in one night, and then you can raise your beef in peace."

Peg was on her feet then, face red with anger. "My boys are cow hands. You're the snake stomper. Now you can either stomp or drift. This is the first time you've smelled powdersmoke, and it looks like you don't care much for the smell."

Wheeling, Kim stalked toward the door. Yuma Bill said quietly, "You're losing a good man, Miss Cody. As good as you'll find."

"Wait, Kim," Peg cried, and ran after him. "I'm sorry. I shouldn't have said that."

Kim turned, glaring at her. "You're damned right you shouldn't have said it. Maybe you don't know it, but you're in a hell of a fight. The only way to win is to get the jump on Dunning and finish him."

"Let me think about it." She put a hand on his arm, a quick impulsive gesture. "It's just that I don't want to force trouble if I can help it I . . . I guess the money I owe Bonham is making me crazy."

"What about Bonham?" Yuma Bill asked. "His bank all right?"

Peg nodded. "There's been no run yet, but you'd better be in town by nine in the morning."

"I aim to." Yuma Bill got to his feet and reached for the shoe box. "I couldn't figure out why Logan wanted to fetch me here first. I still can't, but if Brit's all right, it don't make no difference."

"He's tired, Kim," Peg said. "Take him out to the bunkhouse. Then you come back."

She was suddenly contrite, and that was not like her. She seldom as far as Kim knew, apologized about anything or admitted a mistake, but in her way she was doing both now. A small inviting smile lay in the corners of her mouth; her eyes were half closed as if she were enjoying the anticipation of something which lay ahead.

Kim nodded and turned toward the living room door. He stopped, suddenly tense, hand dropping to gun butt. Someone had ridden up and was crossing the yard, spurs jingling. Kim backed away to the table, and waited there until the man came into the kitchen. It was Dutch Heinz.

Kim glanced briefly at Yuma Bill who had set the shoe box down on the table again. Heinz stood in the doorway, spread-legged. He nodded at Peg, gave Kim a cool stare, and brought his gray eyes to Yuma Bill. He was a stocky man with a wide flat nose, and possessed of an overbearing insolence which never failed to arouse resentment in Kim when he was around the man.

"Who's this?" Heinz asked, motioning to Yuma Bill.

"It's Bonham's friend that we were expecting," Peg said.

"Bonham's friend, eh? So Logan got him off the stage.

Any trouble?"

"A little," Kim said.

Heinz walked toward the table. Yuma Bill threw a questioning glance at Kim and brought his eyes back to Heinz, furrowed face dark with trouble.

"Things don't look good in town, Dutch," Peg said. "There's talk of the bank being shaky."

Heinz said nothing. Kim did not guess what was in the man's mind until he reached the table. Without a word he picked up the shoe box, snapped the cord that was tied around it, and jerking the lid off, upset the box. Bundles of greenbacks fell on the table, more greenbacks than Kim had ever seen in his life before.

Yuma Bill cried out, a wild incoherent sound, and grabbed for his gun. Heinz, expecting that, wheeled and struck him, a brutal blow that sent the little man crashing against the wall. His feet slid out from under him and he sat down, glassy-eyed. Stooping, Heinz pulled Yuma Bill's gun and threw it on the table.

Kim was caught off-guard. It seemed senseless, so senseless that he was momentarily stunned by it. Then a wild rage was in him; he lunged at Heinz, left fist swinging to the man's wide jaw. Heinz went down, falling hard. Peg screamed, "No, stop it," but neither man heard. Heinz rolled, grabbed for his gun, but he was dazed and a little slow. Kim jumped at him, a heel coming down on Heinz's wrist and bringing a yell of pain out of him.

Kim screamed again, "Quit it, you fools."

Kim stepped back. Heinz lifted himself to his hands and feet, and looked up. There was a wildness in his gray eyes, and a driving hatred.

"You've got your gun," Kim said quietly. "Get up and make your play."

But Peg was between them then. "No more of this. You understand? Clawhammer has enough enemies without fighting among ourselves."

"His idea." Heinz got up, feeling of his injured wrist. "It's time we found out who's running this outfit."

"It's past time you found out," Peg cried furiously. "I'm running it, and I tell you I won't have this brawling."

"Then fire him," Heinz bellowed. "He's drawing good wages for nothing."

"I still need him," Peg said, her voice ominously low. "You've got a good job, Dutch. Do you want it or not?"

For a moment Heinz said nothing. He stood with his head dropped forward on his great shoulders, his breath sawing into the quiet. Then he said, "Yeah, I want to keep it, which same you know, but you don't seem to know you're making a hell of a mistake. Your dad wouldn't have made no such mistake."

Peg stepped forward, and for a moment Kim thought she was going to strike Heinz. She said, her voice controlled, "I'm not my dad. Why aren't you with the crew?"

Heinz ignored the question. He motioned toward the money. "Use your head, Peg. Look at that. All the dinero you need to pay off every debt you owe. What the hell difference does it make about Bonham and his bank. This is here for the taking."

Peg glanced at Kim, biting her lower lip and saying nothing. Yuma Bill was on his feet now, a hand raised to his face where Heinz had hit him. He said bitterly, "I suppose I was brought here so you could steal my money. That right, Logan?"

"No," Kim said.

But Heinz had eyes for no one but Peg. "Bonham couldn't trace it. Nobody could. Take it in first thing in the morning and pick up them notes. I'll fix it so nobody will ever see the old man again." He motioned toward Yuma Bill. "And if Logan thinks as much of Clawhammer as you allow, he won't squawk."

For a moment there was silence except for the metallic hammering of a clock on a corner shelf. Kim, too, was watching Peg. For that moment it seemed to him she was being tempted by what Heinz had said.

Then she said, "No. Get back to where you belong, Dutch."

Heinz took a long breath and shook his head as if this was beyond his comprehension. He moved to the door, then turned, cuffing his hat, and gave Kim a straight look. He said, "I'll kill you, Logan. That's a promise."

"Shorty Avis said you'd been up there telling him to get out of the country. That his idea, Peg?"

"Tell him Peg," Heinz said. "Tell him, or I will."

"No, it wasn't my idea," Peg said quickly. "I won't ask you again, Dutch. Get back to the crew."

Heinz's meaty lips fell apart. "Why you..." He stopped as if reading something in Peg's face. Then he said heavily, "All right. Play it your way." Turning, he tramped across the living room and left the house.

Peg said nothing until the beat of hoofs came clearly to them. Then she nodded at Yuma Bill. "I'm sorry this happened, but there's no use apologizing for it now. You go get some sleep. I'll have breakfast for you before sunup. You'll get to town in time before the bank opens. And Kim, you come back in. I want to talk to you.'

CHAPTER 6

A KISS

There was a light in the bunkhouse. The old chore man, Limpy, was pulling off his boots when Kim and Yuma Bill came in. He looked up, started to say something, and closed his mouth when he saw their bleak faces.

"Get your sleep," Kim said curtly. "We'll dust out of here afore sunup."

Yuma Bill, his nerves wound tight, said, "This is a hell of a thing you fetched me into, Logan."

"I know," Kim said, "I know," and left the bunkhouse.

When Kim returned to the house, he saw that Peg had

moved the lamp from the kitchen to the big oak table in the living room. She was not in sight, but the door of her bedroom was ajar, and she called, "Sit down, Kim. I'll just be a minute."

He walked around the room, too restless to sit down. He stood for a moment in front of the picture of Sam Cody, Peg's father. It was covered by glass; its heavy frame with its curlicues did not seem to fit the heavy-featured, boldly arrogant face. Even his eyes were insolent. They glared at Kim from under bushy brows as if resenting Kim's presence in the house.

A pusher, Kim had been told in Ganado, a driver who slammed through to whatever he wanted, and to hell with anybody who was in his way. Dutch Heinz had worked for him, and he had, Kim thought, learned his methods from old Sam. But Peg didn't even look like him. She was different. She had to be. She was fighting for Clawhammer's life, but her ways were not the ways of her father.

Kim did not know Peg had come up behind him until she said, "You think I look like him?"

He turned, catching the rich smell of a French perfume Fred Galt had recently put on the shelf of his Mercantile in Ganado. She had changed from her riding skirt and blouse to a blue dress with a tight-fitting bodice, a dress designed to make a man instantly aware that she was a woman, roundly molded and appealing.

"No," Kim said. "You don't look like him at all."

"Why not?"

He held his answer a moment, letting her see the admiration that was in him. This was the side of her that he liked; he did not like the other side that made her wear straightlined mannish clothes and ride on roundup when she could have hired another hand.

Kim turned, motioning to the picture. "He looks like a tough hand. Kind o' like a bull with his mind made up."

Peg laughed. "He was that way, all right. He drove a herd into the valley a long time ago. It was just after the mining boom was tapering off, and there were a few ranchers along the creek who didn't take to being pushed." She stopped, her eyes thoughtful. "But they got pushed just the same. He was a fighting man, Kim, and a good one."

"There's fighting men and then there's fighting men," he aid. "I don't like anybody who ain't willing to live and let live," he said bluntly. "The ten-cow outfits like Shorty Avis's have a right to make out without somebody pushing 'em out of the country."

She walked away from him and sat down on the leather couch, smoothing her dress over her knees. "I don't see it that way, Kim. If they aren't big enough and tough enough to hold what they've got, they won't last."

"They'll last if they're let alone."

She shook her head. "But they won't be let alone. The world I see all around me is made for big people, so I aim to be big, so big that all the valley will be mine. It's not just money that I want. It's respect if you want to call it that, or prestige, or whatever. I'll have it, Kim. You'll see."

"What about the Avises?"

"I don't really care one way or the other. Right now I don't need the mesa range. Maybe I will tomorrow. If I do, they'll go." She gave him a close look. "Why are you interested in them? Is it the girl?"

He shook his head. "I just cotton to folks who don't run easy."

"Sit down." She patted the leather seat. "I was wondering if I should be jealous."

"No reason for you to be jealous of anybody." He dropped down beside her. "Looks like I'll be drawing my time in a day or two."

"Kim!" She laid a hand over his. "You wouldn't pull out when the ship's sinking, would you?"

"No place for me here. Not if Heinz stays."

"Don't get your neck bowed." She squeezed his hand. "I have some virtues along with my faults. Being loyal is one of them. Dutch was a kid wrangler when Dad came to the valley. He knows the cattle business, and I owe him a job if he wants it. If he doesn't, you're in line."

"Not me," he said quickly. "Not if it means pushing folks like the Avises."

"You aren't being very smart." She drew her hand back. "None of these little outfits are worth us quarreling over. Give them every chance and they'll never be anything but what they are."

"They've got the right to try," he said hotly. "Or just stay like they are if that's the way they want it."

She leaned back, one hand clasping a knee. "Kim, I need you. It's a funny thing how much you've done for me without actually doing anything. Hank Dunning is a lot like Dad was. He goes after what he wants. If you hadn't come, he'd have us backed against the wall by now."

"I've played my string out unless I do something," he said.

"I don't think so."

"I know so. It's smash or get smashed. Tomorrow we save the bank. Dunning won't like it a little bit. He'll move, and that's when you'll need every man you've got."

She closed her eyes. "Kim, listen to me. I'm ambitious. You know that, but you don't know how I've laid awake nights, dreaming about what I'm going to do and thinking about where Dad made his mistakes. A bad winter and low beef prices almost ruined Clawhammer. I suppose it was worry that killed him. Well, I'm not going to make his mistakes, but I'm a woman, so I'll use the weapons the Lord gave a woman."

"What are they?"

She laughed, and bringing her knees up under her chin, she faced him, her eyes bright. "Dutch is one weapon. You're another."

"I ain't so sure about me," he said roughly. "You've got use for me next week. Or next month. By that time Dunning will be dead or you'll be licked. Either way, you won't need me after that."

"I'll always need you, Kim."

She got up and walked across the room, her back to him, her skirt making a tight fit across her hips. She reached the table, and turning, raised her eyes to him. For a moment she stood there, smiling. She ruffled the pages of a mail order catalog that lay in front of her, then pushed it away.

"You believe that, don't you?" she asked in a voice that was close to pleading.

"No. You need somebody. It don't have to be me."

"It's got to be you," she said quickly, "but there are times when I don't understand you. I wake up in the night thinking about you, and then it seems you're almost a stranger."

"I get the same notion about you."

"Oh, you're talking crazy. I've lived in the valley since I was a little kid. I don't have any secrets, Kim."

"You do in your head," he told her.

She came back to the couch and sat down again beside him. "I've told you the only secret I have. It's why I mortgaged everything to Brit Bonham, hoping to put Clawhammer back to where it was before Dad lost so much. It's why I hired you. It's why I do everything I do." She leaned back, hands laced over her knees again, long legs swinging. "I'm going a long ways, Kim, but I have one fear. Maybe I'll be alone when I get there. Then it won't be any fun."

For some reason Kim thought of what Rocky Avis had said that noon about Peg's being a greedy woman, about his being a snake stomper without a dollar in his pocket. That wasn't true, but compared to Peg Cody, he might as well have been broke.

"I don't savvy," he said finally. "Not exactly, but I know one thing. A gunslinger ain't fit to go along to where you're headed."

"Depends on the gunslinger. Why do you think I hired you in the first place?"

"Dunno."

"It's very simple, Kim. You aren't like most of the grub line riders who come through here. I've always prided myself on my knowledge and judgment of men. I didn't make a mistake in you."

He looked at her curiously. "How am I different?"

"I guess it's just that there's more to you. I mean, well, like insisting on taking the crew across the creek to finish Dunning. Most men who had a good thing would follow my orders and be satisf ed."

"I've got my notions about how to do a job," he said.

"I know," she said softly. "You have a good many notions, Kim, strong ones. I can't help wondering where you got them. Tell me about yourself. Who your folks were and where they came from and everything."

"Nothing to tell. I was born in Missouri. Folks moved out to New Mexico and my ma died of smallpox. My dad died a couple of years later. I threw in with a salty bunch when I was sixteen. Been riding ever since till I got here."

"What was your mother like?"

"I don't remember her very well," he said, and let it go at that. It was one thing he would not talk about.

"I don't remember much about my mother, either," she said. "She had red hair like mine, and I do remember the terrific quarrels they had, but you know, Kim, they were terribly in love with each other." She laughed, wrinkling her nose at him. "We'd quarrel, too, wouldn't we?"

She had drawn her legs up under her, and she was leaning toward him, her face quite close to his, red lips lightly pressed. He put his arm around her and drawing her to him, kissed her. In that instant she became a living flame in his arms, her hands reaching up to hold him, her lips passionate and clinging.

Later, when she drew away, her hands came up to his cheeks and caressed them with a touch. "Kim, Kim," she murmured, "you were so slow. I'm getting pretty old, you know. Twenty-three. Almost an old maid."

"You're talking crazy now," he said. "A little encourage-ment would bring any man in the valley walking to you on his knees. Even Hank Dunning, I reckon, if you wanted him."

She straightened, suddenly tense. "Kim, are you out of your mind?"

"Maybe. Kissing you would put any man out of his mind." He rose, looking down at her long slim body, her lips that were smiling again. "I can't ask you to marry me. Not yet."

"Why?" she demanded. "Don't tell me you never thought about it. After a year on Clawhammer . . ."

"I've thought about it all right." He paused, wondering what had happened to him today. This was what he had wanted; what any man would want, a pretty wife and a big spread. But now that the opportunity was here, he could not take it. "Just another one of my notions. Seems like I've got to bring something to you besides my hands and a gun."

She looked at him for a long moment, her face grave, then she shook her head. "Don't make a mistake now, Kim. Our life wouldn't be all sweetness and sunshine, but there would be other things to make up for it."

"Maybe I'm thinking about Dutch Heinz," he said. "Or maybe it's just that I don't want to be Mr. Peg Cody."

He left the house, leaving her staring after him, frowning as if she were deeply troubled. He walked slowly toward the bunkhouse, wondering how big a fool he had been. If he had asked her to marry him, she would have said yes. He was as sure of that as he had ever been sure of anything. But he had not asked her, and the right moment might never come again.

Suddenly Kim was aware of the smell of cigarette; he saw the bright tip of it glowing in the darkness. He reached for his gun and then drew back his hand at once, realizing that an enemy would not give his presence away so carelessly. He said, "Well!"

"Waiting," Yuma Bill said. "Just waiting. I ain't of a mind to trust anybody after what happened tonight."

"Damn it, you can trust me," Kim said angrily. "Are you making out you can't?"

"No, I ain't," the little man said. "I was kind o' dozing after Heinz cracked me, but I got the notion you sort of whittled him down to size."

"Well, why ain't you sleeping?"

"Why, it's just a matter of arithmetic. Anyway I count, you still add up to just one man, so I'll stay awake till this dinero is in Brit's safe."

"It'll be there by nine in the morning."

They walked on toward the bunkhouse. Then Yuma Bill said, "She's playing with you, boy."

Kim gripped the little man's arm. "You damned pussy-footing window peeper. I oughta . . ."

Yuma Bill jerked away, angry. "I ain't no window peeper. I just knew how she'd perform. You think you're gonna marry her, don't you? Sweet as the bottom of the sugar bowl, wasn't she?"

"Yeah, sweet enough," Kim said. "But I dunno about marrying her. Maybe I'll never have another chance."

"Then you'll be lucky. If you let her, she'll use you and drop you when she's done with you. I know because I've been through the mill."

"Women ain't all alike. Just because . . ."

"Her kind are. I can read her brand easy as I could the Clawhammer iron on a steer. She's thinking first, last, and always of Peg Cody, and she'll never change. You'll see."

"You're too damned suspicious," Kim muttered, and went into the bunkhouse.

But he did not sleep for a long time. He lay staring at the dark ceiling, more discontented with himself and his life than he had ever been before. In spite of himself, he mentally compared Rocky Avis, sarcastic and sharp-tongued and at times cruelly honest, with Peg, and it surprised him that Peg was not flattered by the comparison. Still, he understood her as he had never understood her before, and he could not doubt the truth of what she had told him about herself.

CHAPTER 7
THE HOUR OF NINE

They ate breakfast by lamplight, Peg silent and oddly aloof, her shoulders slack with weariness as if she had not slept during the night. Only now and then did her eyes brush Kim's face, and they told him nothing.

When they finished eating. Yuma Bill rose, the shoe box under his arm. He said, "Thank you, ma'am. I hope my coming will be of some help to you as well as Brit."

"You're saving Clawhammer," she said simply. "I'm the one who's doing the thanking."

Kim drank his coffee and got up. "Time to go. I oughtta be back a little after noon. Then I'll stay here unless you change your mind about hitting Dunning before he hits you."

"I'm not changing my mind, Kim," she said wearily, "but there's one thing I want you to do. Feeling against the bank was running pretty high yesterday. Dunning has convinced most people that Bonham's finished and we're to blame becau e the bank loaned us so much."

"That's why he'll be so damned mad when his scheme misses. He'll come high tailing out here with his outfit."

Peg waved his words aside. "I'll take care of him if he comes here. Right now your job is to save the bank. If you take Yuma Bill into town, you'll probably both get killed before the money gets to Bonham, so what I want you to do is to leave Yuma outside of Ganado while you ride in and look things over. He could stay at Salty Smith's cabin, if he don't mind getting a leg talked off."

"I'm supposed to be bullet bait. That it?"

"That's it," she said, "only it'll be Dunning who gets the bullet if I know you."

"Thanks for your confidence in my shooting eye, but Yuma Bill won't want to . . ."

"She's right," Yuma Bill said. "It'd sure be hell to get to

town and then have something happen so Brit didn't get the dinero."

Kim shrugged. "We'll play it that way if you want to, but I ain't sure it's the smart way."

He moved to Peg who stood beside the stove and kissed her, but he found little warmth in her lips. When he stepped back, she gave him a tight smile.

"You see how it is," Peg said. "I threw myself at you last night, and you threw me back."

"It wasn't that way," he said. "It's just that I've got to know you trust my judgment."

"I trust your judgment, but I'm still giving the orders."

"Then you'll always give them," he said angrily, "and I'd still be Mr. Peg Cody."

For a moment they faced each other, their wills clashing, and he sensed it would always be that way with them. Tur ing, he walked out of the house into the growing light. The air was cool and heavy with dampness. It would rain again that day.

Kim and Yuma Bill saddled by the murky light of a lantern, and when they rode past the house, Peg stood silhouetted in the doorway, a tall slight figure, her back very straight. A chill of sudden fear ran down Kim's spine as he thought this might be the last time he would see her. He lifted a hand and she waved back. Then he rode on, the dark sprawling shape of the ranch house falling behind.

They splashed across Ganado Creek, running smoothly here between low banks, and followed the twin ruts of the road toward Ganado. The sun had tipped up over the Continental Divide, its scarlet light touching the Dragon Peaks across the valley. Slowly it climbed higher until it had rolled back the last of the shadows and full daylight was upon them.

Neither spoke for a time. Then Yuma Bill said, "Good grass."

"Cow paradise," Kim said. "Too damned bad anybody has to fight over it."

"Who's to blame?"

Kim shrugged. "I ain't paid to pass judgment, but if I was, I'd say old Sam Cody got his share of it. Peg's trying to hold what he left her."

"You'll find the blood of little men on every range like this," Yuma Bill said somberly. "And sooner or later you'll find the blood of more little men like Shorty Avis on the mesa. I never saw it fail. Greed begets greed. You're on the wrong side, boy."

"There's no right side," Kim said.

They rode in silence again, the level valley sweeping away all around them. Once Kim hipped around in his saddle and looked eastward to the series of benches that rose, step-like, toward the slick-rock rim that swung in a wide circle around the east side of the valley. Somewhere below that rim was Shorty Avis and his handful of cows, living in fear of Dutch Heinz's return.

Kim thought of Rocky Avis and what she had done for him and Yuma Bill the day before. He turned back, glancing at the little man's weathered face as he thought of his words, "You'll find the blood of more little men like Shorty Avis on the mesa." And discontent became a burning bitterness in Kim Logan.

"You hear anybody ride out last night?" Yuma asked suddenly.

"No. I didn't go to sleep for a while, and after I did, I didn't hear nothing. Why?"

"I did."

"You were dreaming, Nobody around but Peg."

Yuma Bill nodded. "That's just what I was thinking."

"But hell, she wouldn't . . ." Kim stopped. The little man was staring at the willow-lined, twisting course of Pass Creek, his leathery face very thoughtful. "Maybe she couldn't sleep and took a ride."

"She don't make a habit of it, does she?"

"No." Shrugging, Kim let it go at that, and pointed to the cluster of buildings ahead of them. "That's Ganado yonder."

Yuma Bill lifted himself in his stirrups, staring at the town. A church spire pointed skyward; a weathered brick building stood to the right of the church. Yuma asked, "What's that brick building?"

"Courthouse. Ganado is half cow town and half ghost town. The mining boom made it, and the old timers figured they'd have the biggest city in Colorado, so they built a courthouse that'd be fit and proper."

"Mines wear out?"

Kim nodded. "Nothing lasts, I reckon."

"Some things do. You just ain't found 'em yet."

"Preaching again," Kim said irritably.

Yuma Bill shook his head. "Just talking." His craggy face softened as a grin worked across his mouth. "I was the same when I was your age, full of sass and vinegar and never thinking past the next glass of whiskey or the next gal I was gonna kiss. Them are the things that don't last."

"What does?"

"No use me telling you. Every man has got to find 'em out for hisself." He swung a hand in a sweeping gesture. "I can't help wondering why you don't get your own outfit. More grass here than two outfits can use. Or if there ain't, go back where Avis is. He's up purty high, but there's plenty of range."

"That would have been a good idea twenty years ago, when a man with a rope and a running iron could get a start, but folks kind o' frown on them antics now."

"You can borrow."

"Where?"

"From the bank."

"And everything I'd make would go to Bonham for interest." Kim shook his head. "I never thought much about it until I got here with ten dollars in my pocket. Then I got to thinking. That started me to saving. First time in my life, but it's mighty slow."

"How much have you got?"

"A little over a thousand."

Yuma Bill nodded, apparently surprised that Kim had saved that much. He said, "Let's swing over to the cabin. I'll wait out here for half an hour or so. If you don't come shagging back, I'll trail along into town."

They could see the cabin now, a low long structure on the east bank of the creek. As they reined toward it, Kim said, "I don't cotton to this idea much, even if it is Peg's."

"Just one reason I do. It's to her interest that we get this dinero to the bank."

Kim said nothing more until they reached the cabin, Kim's eyes searching the willows that crowded the creek. He said, "Looks like Salty's gone. If he ain't in town, he's usually fishing."

"Who is he?"

"An old Civil War vet. Been here for years. Made one of the first strikes and lost everything over a poker table. Now he's living here just waiting to die." Kim stepped down. "I'll see if he's inside."

There was no answer to Kim's knock. He pushed the door open and looked in. The cabin was empty, the smell of it an insult to Kim's nostrils. He stepped out, closing the door. "You can go in if you want to. Smith wouldn't care. Right friendly old cuss when he ain't drunk, but he ain't what you'd call clean. The air's better out here."

"I'd just as soon sit in the willows. Might skip a rock or two across the creek." Yuma Bill glanced at his watch. "Getting along toward nine. You high tail into town and take this box to the bank. Dunning'll be looking for me. He won't figure on you having it."

"I don't like the idea. Damn it, I said I'd deliver you and your . . ."

Yuma Bill made an impatient gesture toward town. "Go on now. There's forty thousand in that box. I'm packing another ten in my money belt. I aimed to give all of it to Brit, but coming across the grass just now, I got a sudden hankering to go into the cattle busines." He winked. "With a hairpin named Kim Logan."

Kim's mouth sagged open. "Why . . . you . . ."

Yuma Bill laughed. "Pull your eyes back inside your head. You dust along. We'll be needing that bank one of these days, you and me."

"You know what we'll be into?" Kim demanded. "We'll be fighting Peg and Dunning both."

"All right. We'll fight 'em. Don't strike me that you're the kind of huckleberry who'd be afraid . . ."

"I ain't. I just didn't figure you'd want to buy a war of your own."

"I've bought one already. So have you. Let's say I want to sow some good seeds. Been a hell of a lot of weeds planted in these parts. Now take this box and move, or hod dang it, you'll be too late."

Shrugging, Kim took the box and stepped into the saddle. "Keep your eyes peeled."

Kim reined his buckskin around and touched him up, leaving the little man sitting his saddle in front of the cabin, his weathered face very thoughtful. As Kim rode away, he wondered what sort of past Yuma Bill had behind him, a past that had molded him into the kind of man who would travel halfway across the state with a fortune in a shoe box, his sole purpose that of repaying an old debt to a banker who had once helped him.

Ganado lay just ahead, false-fronted business buildings crowding Main Street, many of them deserted now, and dwellings, decorated with gingerbread and carved barge-boards and surrounded by picket fences with their carved corner posts. Most of the houses were empty; all were weathered to a dingy gray, their paint long gone, the fences needed repair, and the bulk of the boardwalks were splintered and grown up with weeds. A sort of genteel decay lay upon the town as if it had one eye upon its splendid past, the other closed to the future.

Kim reached the south end of Main Street when Rocky Avis appeared from a livery stable and rode toward him. It was a moment before she saw who he was, and when she did, she brought her horse to a gallop, waving at him to hurry.

When he came alongside her, she cried, "You're mighty slow. Where's Yuma Bill?"

"He's laying low at Smith's cabin till I see how things stack up. I've got his box."

"Then get a move on. It's almost time for Brit to open up, and there's a line waiting."

"Then they're gonna get a surprise. Come on and help me laugh in their faces."

Kim cracked steel to his buckskin and swept on down the street to the bank. He reined up and tied, eyes sweeping the line of grim-faced men. Some were little ranchers from Dunning's side of the valley, the small fry dependent upon HD just as Shorty Avis and his neighbors were dependent upon Clawhammer.

It was the others who brought a quick blaze of temper to Kim, townsmen who had no part in the feud, men who should be supporting Bonham: Doc Frazee, Fred Galt who owned the Mercantile, Luke Haines the barber, and a dozen more. Sheriff Ed Lane was in the line, a bald man who gave Kim a small nod, tongued his quid to the other side of his mouth, and turned his eyes away.

"What the hell you boys doing here?" Kim demanded.

"What does it look like?" Galt asked.

"Waiting for breakfast," Kim jeered. "Why don't you go home and eat?"

Doc Frazee, wearing a Prince Albert that had once been black and now was faded to a sort of dingy green, glared at Kim. "We'll go home when we get our money, and don't think you can stop us. Bonham wouldn't have got in this fix if he hadn't loaned our money to Clawhammer."

"That's right," Luke Haines cried in his shrill voice. "Just 'cause you're a tough hand working for Clawhammer don't mean you can change our minds."

Galt, the first man in the line, looked at his watch. He was a nervous man given to stomach trouble. Now he shoved his watch back into his pocket and began pounding on the door.

"Nine o'clock, Bonham. Open up, damn it. Open up."

Others crowded against Galt, adding their voices to his until the words, "Open up, open up," became a sullen threatening rumble.

Kim could have showed them the money in the box; he could have said there was plenty to pay them and more, but he did neither. This was a selfish, senseless thing, a crime being committed by common men who thought they had their share of ordinary decency. It might have been forgivable in a man like Hank Dunning who pretended to be no better than he was; it was not forgivable in these townsmen.

Drawing his gun, Kim fired a shot over their heads. The faced him, bitter sullen men who had been swept by mob hysteria past the point where they were capable of honest reasoning.

"Do that again, Logan," the sheriff bawled, "and I'll throw you into the jug for disturbing the peace."

"Try it, Ed," Kim invited.

Lane looked away, jaws working steadily on his quid, a politician who had carried the star for ten years because he was a master at bowing to the right man. After Sam Cody had died, Dunning had been the man. It was common gossip on Pass Creek that every HD man had voted five times at the last election.

"What's the matter with you?" Galt demanded. "This ain't none of your put in."

"Now maybe it is," Kim said. "I've got some money in this bank, maybe, more than most of you boys, but I ain't asking for it. I figure the bank's sound."

"I don't," Galt flung back. "I ain't taking any chances."

"Are you trying to bust Bonham?"

"All I want is my dinero," Galt said doggedly.

"And you'll get it because you're first in line," Kim said, "but you don't give a damn about the boys behind you. You're a two-bit, selfish, stingy, money-loving son."

There was a crowding up from the tail of the line, men ramming and elbowing as their bitter voices rose in a menacing roar. Galt threw a quick look behind him, wizened face flooded with sudden fear.

Lane, the fourth man in the line, drew his gun and waved it at the ones behind him. "Order now, boys. Keep your places. Every man will have his turn."

They quieted, and Kim asked, "What time did you get here this morning, Fred?"

"None of your damned business!" the storeman screamed.

A rancher far back in the line said, "He was here at dawn. We had to do chores and ride in after that, so we couldn't get here that soon."

"Logan's just fixed to make trouble, Ed," Luke Haines said bitterly, "Run him in."

But Lane stood motionless, chewing steadily, eyes pinned on something down the street. Kim laughed, a contemptuous sound that ripped the last shred of dignity from the man.

"You poor damned fools," Kim flung at them. "You're doing Dunning's dirty work, and you ain't smart enough to know it." He looked back along the line, watching them stir and shift, boot heels scraping on the broken boards of the walk. He asked, "Where is Dunning?"

"Inside," Doc Frazee said. "Talking to Bonham."

"Listen now, you chuckle-heads," Kim shouted. "This ain't just my fight. Or Clawhammer's. It belongs to all of you. You've bowed and scraped to Dunning until you've forgotten you were men. You'll get your money if you want it, but you don't need it, and when you see that the bank's safe, you'll beg Bonham to take it back."

But they didn't stir. They stared at him defiantly, saying nothing, the men in the back of the line still pressing forward so the the ones in front were jammed hard against the door.

"I want to look at your ugly mugs in about ten minutes," Kim went on. "If you're worth a damn, you'll get down on your knees to Brit Bonham. Then you'll go tell Dunning to crawl under a rock where he belongs."

Without another word, Kim bulled his way through the

line, knocking Luke Haines flat on his face, and stalked round the corner to the back door of the bank. It was locked. He looked through the window, saw Bonham sitting at his desk, head bowed. Dunning sat across from him, hawk-nosed face barren of expression.

Kim tapped on the window. When Bonham turned to look at him, he shouted, "Let me in, Brit. I've got something for you."

Bonham jumped up. Dunning said something that Kim couldn't hear, but Bonham shook his head and running to the door, turned the key and pulled the door open. Kim stepped in, his eyes locking with Dunning's. He said, "Hank, I've waited a long time for this. You're licked."

Dunning rose. He was a tall man, taller even than Kim, and now he seemed to be looking down, very confident. Quite casually he brought a hand to his face and scratched his great beak of a nose. He said, "I reckon not, Logan."

Kim walked to the desk and laid the box down. There, on the scarred walnut, were Peg Cody's notes. Bonham dropped into his swivel chair, faded eyes pinned on Kim's face. He asked hoarsely, "Did you see Yuma Bill?"

"I saw him." Kim slashed the cord that was around the box. "Funny thing, Brit. I've learned more about human nature since I met Yuma Bill than I'd learned in ten years before. It takes a pretty good man to have a friend like him." Kim lifted the lid from the box. "Better open up, Brit. There's a few boys outside who seem to want some cash money this morning."

CHAPTER 8
POWDER FLAME

Bonham cried out, a strained hoarse sound that a man would make who has lost all hope and then, unexpectedly, finds it again. He grabbed the box and ran out of his office into the bank, shouting, "Charlie, open up. We'll pay 'em right down to the last nickel."

Kim backed away from Dunning, hoping that this would be the moment he had long sought when Hank Dunning would go for his gun. Then he saw it was not. Dunning brushed at a lock of rebellious hair, dark eyes probing Kim with cool insolence. Kim had never seen him excited; he had never seen him hurry in anything he did. Now Dunning said, very deliberately, "Still lucky, Logan."

"Yesterday you sent Phil Martin and some of your boys across the creek after me. I reckon that opens the ball, don't it?"

Dunning shook his head. "Not today it don't."

"I don't cotton to the notion of playing coyote to your hounds. Let's finish it."

Again Dunning shook his head. "I never swap smoke with a hired hand." He walked past Kim and went into the street.

For a moment Kim stood staring after the big man until he disappeared around the corner. Then he turned and followed Bonham into the bank.

The teller, old Charlie Bemis, had unlocked the front door, but for a moment he was unable to get it open, so tightly were the men in front jammed against it. When he did, Fred Galt sprawled on his face, jumped up and lunged on across the room to the teller's wicket.

"I'm cleaning out my deposit," Galt yelled. "Every damned cent. You hear, Bonham?"

"I hear quite well, Fred," the banker said, very casually as if this were an ordinary occasion. "You'll get every cent as soon as Charlie looks up your balance."

Galt stood leaning against the counter, his bulging eyes fixed on the piles of currency that were stacked on a table beyond the teller's wicket. The others peered over his shoulder, Doc Frazee and Luke Haines and the rest. The silence was unexpected and strange, the shocked silence of men so stunned they were incapable of speech.

Then Haines let out a shrill squall. "Hell, he's got enough

dinero on that table to buy the Denver mint. Look at it, Fred."

That broke the tension. They stormed forward, trying to get a closer look at this money they had not believed was here, jamming and shoving and cursing. There was no line at all now; the smaller men were pushed back. A rancher cried out in pain, screaming for somebody to get off his corns. The sheriff got an elbow into his stomach that knocked his wind out of him. He reeled away from the others and fell slack against the wall, struggling for breath.

Charlie Bemis called, "Fred's got a balance of $3,298.52."

"Be sure he gets that fifty-two cents," Kim said contemptuously.

"I certainly will." Bonham picked up a wad of greenbacks and counted out Galt's money. "There you are, Fred. Three thousand and two hundred." He dipped into a drawer. "I'll let you have the rest in gold and silver, except for the two pennies."

"Two-penny Galt," Kim jeered.

"Say, that's a good handle for him." A rancher slapped his leg, roaring with laughter. "Two-penny! Yes sir, that sure fits Galt."

Red-faced, Galt scooped up his money and pushed his way through the crowd. "Don't call me that, Rushmore, or I'll cut off your credit."

The rancher thumbed his nose at Galt. "To hell with you. We've needed a new store for a long time in this burg, Two-penny."

"What are you gonna do with that dinero, Two-penny?" Kim demanded. "Gonna lock it up in that cracker box of a safe of yours?"

Galt fled. Doc Frazee was staring at the currency through the teller's window, his bony face thoughtful. He said, "Boys, where'd we get the notion this bank wasn't sound?"

"Dunning," a rancher said. "You know that. He passed the word out that we had to be here today and ask for our money, or we'd have a hell of a hard time hanging on to our spreads."

"Tell 'em, Brit," Kim said. "Go on. Tell 'em so they'll know what caliber Hank Dunning is."

Bonham straightened, the corners of his mouth working. "Peg Cody borrowed thirty thousand from me to restock Clawhammer range. She's got five hundred head of prime steers she aims to sell in Durango this fall. That'll give her enough to pay the interest she owes me and maybe take up a few of the notes. Dunning wanted them notes. He was in my office just now offering me ten thousand for them."

"Why, the damned thieving crook," Luke Haines splutered. "He aimed to bust Clawhammer."

"No doubt about it," Bonham said. "This bank is good. You boys ought to know that. I've got enough cash for ordinary business, but you'd have made me close my doors today if Kim hadn't fetched a chunk of money from a friend of mine who came in on the stage yesterday. Now if any of you want your deposits, you can sure have 'em. Just remember one thing. I don't want your business after today."

Doc Frazee pulled at his goatee, grinning as abashedly as a boy caught at a cookie jar. "Well, Brit, I haven't got a real good place to put my money if I had it. Reckon I'll just leave it here where it'll be safe."

"Me too," Haines cried.

"You boys ought to go take a look at yourselves," Kim said. "I wish I had your pictures right now. They'd be handy to look at if you forget what kind of ears a jackass has got."

Doc Frazee felt of his, grinning shamefacedly. "Pretty damned long, ain't they?" He moved away from the window to where Kim stood b hind the gate at the end of the counter. "Say, you and the HD boys must have had quite a tussle."

"Burned a little powder, all right," Kim said.

"They rode in late yesterday," Frazee said, "wan ing me to patch 'em up and they sure needed it. Tonto Miles was the only one who didn't. Martin's got a busted left arm, and that young Ernie Deal is gonna have a hard time making it. Got a slug in his brisket." Frazee lifted a bushy brow, hesitated, and then asked, "What started it?"

"They jumped us," Kim said shortly.

Frazee did not press the question. Shrugging, he turned away. "Well, Luke, let's go see how your wife's making out. You'll be a father before noon, or I miss my guess."

The medico walked out, Haines trailing behind him. The rest followed, abashed and silent. Bonham rubbed his face with trembling hands and dropped into a chair. "Put the money in the safe, Charlie." He brought his gaze to Kim. "Where'd you leave Yuma?"

"At Smith's cabin. We stayed the night at Clawhammer. When we left this morning, Peg allowed that Dunning might have a trap set up. She said for me to come in and see how things stacked up. Then Yuma got the notion I'd better fetch the box to you. Dunning wouldn't figure on me having it."

"He didn't," Bonham said. "No sir, he didn't. Have any trouble yesterday?"

Kim told him what had happened, adding, "You know, Brit, I've never been one to count on another man to pull my irons out of the fire. I didn't really figure Yuma Bill would be on that stage, but Peg said I'd better find out. Well, he was there all right."

"I gave him a little help once a long time ago. I knew he'd be there unless something happened." The banker rose. "Come on back, Kim."

Bonham walked to his private office, a tired, stoop-shoul-dered old man. He sat down behind his desk, motioning for Kim to take the other chair, and then picking up Peg's notes, stacked them neatly.

"I've been here a long time," Bonham said. "I've seen this town boom and I've seen it rot. I had the first bank here, and the last. I could have been a rich man if I'd used my money like some did, but I always had the notion that I'd live longer and die happier if I mixed a little justice with the banking business." He made a gesture toward the street. "But look what it got me Just let somebody start some talk and they want their money."

"Well, I guess you sowed the right seeds," Kim said, "or Yuma Bill wouldn't have been on that stage."

Bonham started to fill his pipe. He stopped, glancing up at Kim. "Yuma still talking about sowing seeds?"

Kim nodded. "I told him he oughtta get a pulpit."

Bonham dribbled tobacco into his pipe and tamped it down. "No, he don't need a pulpit. You know, there was a time when he was the meanest, orneriest son of Cain who ever toted a gun. Now he's a different man. Call it a miracle if you want to, or just come out and call me a liar, but I seen it happen."

Kim waited, watching the banker light his pipe and blow out great clouds of smoke. There was more to the story, but he saw that Bonham was not of a mind to tell it now. He motioned to the notes. "How close did Dunning come to getting them?"

"Damned close." Bonham chewed on his pipestem, eyes filled with misery. "So close that I'm ashamed of myself. It was that or go bust. After being in the banking business for thirty years, well, I was reaching for any straw I could see."

"It would have finished Peg," Kim said morosely. "I don't savvy it, Brit. Dunning don't strike me as being the kind of a hairpin who'd figure out a sneak deal like this."

Bonham puffed for a moment. Then he said, troubled, "There's something that ain't right, but I can't put my finger on it. Just a feeling I get sometimes. Now old Sam was the sort who kicked everybody out of his way. He didn't have a friend in the valley except old Limpy and Dutch Heinz. When Sam was alive, Dunning behaved. He was afraid of Sam and Sam was a little afraid of him, I reckon. Then after he died, Dunning decided he'd start pushing."

Kim rose. "Well, might as well ride out and tell Yuma that everything's all right."

"I'll ride along." Bonham reached for his hat. "Been a long time since I saw old Yuma."

"Kim." It was Rocky Avis. "Kim, you here?"

"He's talking to Brit," Charlie Bemis told her.

Kim wheeled out of Bonham's office. Rocky stood in front of the teller's window, her face paler than Kim had ever seen it before. He asked, "What's up?"

She pushed open the gate at the end of the counter. He had always thought of her as a steady, capable girl, the kind who belonged to this wild land in which she lived. Now he saw the terror that was in her dark eyes; he sensed that she was close to being hysterical.

"Tonto Miles." She gripped Kim's arms. "He's been in the Belle Union all morning. Now he's out in front talking to Ed Lane. He says he'll kill you the minute you come out of the bank."

A deep satisfaction filled Kim as he considered this. It was Dunning he wanted, not Miles, but a fight with Miles might force Dunning. Kim said, "Tonto can try, Rocky. That's all."

"But Lane says he'll jail both of you if you start anything."

"If we're both alive." Kim shrugged. "But if I know Ed, he's just talking through his hat."

"He's Dunning's man. It's a trap. You can't go out there, Kim."

Bonham had come up. He nodded, saying, "Rocky's right. Up till now you've just been a gnat buzzing in Dunning's ear, but when you knocked the bottom out of his scheme, you fixed it so he's got to get you, come hell or high water."

"I'll bring your horse around to the back," Rocky urged. "You've got to get out of town."

He shook his head, giving her a tight smile. "You've been in this country long enough to know I can't do that."

"No sense getting yourself killed for nothing," Bonham said in exasperation. "Get back to Clawhammer and fetch Heinz and his boys in. You're gonna have a finish fight sooner or later."

"Peg don't see that," Kim said. "She says she hired my gun, and it's time I was earning my pay."

"Why, she knows . . ." Bonham stopped, suddenly thoughtful. "I wonder."

"You wonder what?"

He shook his head. "Nothing. Just wool gathering."

Kim stepped away from Rocky and checked his gun. She moved in front of him, her small chin outthrust. The fear was gone from her now. She was angry, the same quick anger he had seen in her the day before when she had bitterly called him a "snake stomper."

"Kim, do you think Peg Cody is the kind of woman a man should die for?" Rocky demanded.

"Why, I hadn't thought of it just that way."

"Then start thinking. I told you she was a greedy woman."

"Well, we're all a little greedy, I reckon."

"But not like Peg Cody. Kim, you can't go out there and get yourself killed just for her hundred dollars a month."

"It's a little more than that, Rocky."

"No it isn't. Kim, can't you see how it is? There are some things that are worth dying for. I mean, things a man can believe in, but this is . . . is just throwing your life away for nothing."

He shook his head, looking down at her flaming face, and oddly enough, he thought of her as being pretty. Not in the way Peg Cody was. More like the beauty of a mountain storm. He put the thought from him. He said, "I've got a job to do."

"Let him go, Rocky," Bonham said.

Rocky whirled on him. "You men are all alike, but I thought you'd be different. He saved your bank for you . . ."

Kim moved past her, his .44 riding easily in its holster, and walked out of the bank into the sunlight. He stopped for a moment, letting his eyes get used to the glare. He heard Bonham say, "Charlie, get them Winchesters out of the closet." He would have a fair fight, and that was all a man who lived by the gun could ask.

Tonto Miles stood in front of the Belle Union, a burly man who had come to the valley after Kim had. Seeing Kim, he bawled, "I've been looking for you, Logan."

Ed Lane was standing beside Miles. Now he drifted away

and disappeared. Kim moved along the walk until he was clear of the hitch pole, then stepped into the street, hands at his sides. Neither Dunning nor Martin were in sight. There had been other men on the boardwalk. Now they were gone.

Miles stepped off the walk and moved into the street, great head canted forward on massive shoulders. Suddenly, and it was the first time in his life that Kim had ever felt this way, he was tired of fighting.

A few minutes before Dunning had said he never swapped smoke with a hired hand. Kim Logan was that. No more. No less. Here they were, Tonto Miles and Kim Logan, hired hands, both of them, although the hope was in Kim that he was more than that to Peg Cody. Their deaths would settle nothing. Other men would be hired. He thought of the fellow who had fallen off the rim the afternoon before, a man who had made a bad bargain. Then the thoughts fled; this was no time for them if he wanted to live.

Slowly Kim and Tonto Miles moved into the street, tense, watchful. One measured step, then another, boots falling into the street dirt, still soft from yesterday's rain. Overhead the sun was a brilliant searing ball in a clear sky, sucking up moisture from a wet earth, the air heavy with the smell of it. From some vacant lot a bird began to sing, a sweet clear sound that beat against Kim's ears. A thought jarred him. It might be the prelude for his passage into eternity.

They were close, so close that Kim could see the purple veins in Miles' cheeks, the red flecks in his eyes. Then Miles made his draw. Warned by the down drop of the man's right shoulder, the quick flick of lips pulled tight against yellow teeth, Kim drove his right hand toward gun butt and swept it clear of leather. It was swift sure motion without waste, the perfect co-ordination of nerve and muscle that comes to a man only after long and honest practice.

The gun bucked in Kim's hand; powder flame made its brief stab of fire against the sun's glare. The roar of the shot ran along the street, deserted except for these two, the one who died and the one who lived. Then Kim stood alone, staring down at Tonto Miles who lay with his face in the dirt, right hand flung out beside his unfired gun. Then, and again it was a strange new feeling to Kim, a revulsion swept through him, a sort of sickness, and with it was a bitter hatred for Hank Dunning who had caused this.

Men boiled into the street, Doc Frazee in the lead, black bag in hand, the tails of his faded Prince Albert flying behind him. Kim looked back and saw Brit Bonham and Charlie Bemis standing n front of the bank, cocked Winchesters in their hands. Then he crossed the street, moving past the men knotted around Miles' body, and heard Frazee say, "Right through the heart. Never saw no better shooting."

Kim went into the saloon. He said, "Whiskey," hoping it would take the sour taste out of his mouth. On y then was he aware that he still held his gun at his side. He holstered it, eyeing the bartender who shoved a bottle and glass at him with the wariness of a man approaching a coiled rattlesnake. That, too, was grimly familiar. Kim was used to it, but after all these years, he still resented it.

They would remember him, these men who had watched from open doorways and windows with the sadistic pleasure of ancient Romans gathered in the Coliseum, and remembering it, they would be afraid of him. There had been a time when street fights were common occurrences in Ganado, but that had been years ago, and only a few like Doc Frazee and Brit Bonham would remember. There had long been talk of trouble between Clawhammer and the HD, bets had been placed as to when the first blood would be spilled. Now the day had come, and from this hour, Kim Logan would be a marked man.

He took his drink and set the glass back on the polished mahogany. He filled it again and let it stand, staring moodily at the amber liquid. No good. The sourness remained in him. Liquor could not take it from him.

Men came in. The batwings clapped shut, the sibilant sound reached Kim at the bar. He turned his head. Sheriff Ed Lane stood there, tobacco quid bulging one cheek. Johnny

Naylor, the shotgun guard, stood behind him. Both were scared and showed it, Naylor so panicky he was close to bolting. Lane came on until he stood within ten feet of Kim. He said, trying hard to make a tough appearance, "Lay your gun on the bar, Logan. You're under arrest."

CHAPTER 9

JAILED

For a moment Kim said nothing. He did not move. He stood with his left hand on the bar, right at his side within inches of gun butt, staring blankly at Lane as he mentally groped for an explanation. He said finally, "Say that over, Ed."

"You're under arrest," Lane repeated. "Put your gun on the bar and head for the door."

"You can't pull this off," Kim said, "A dozen men saw that fight. You know I couldn't duck it."

"I ain't arresting you for plugging Miles," Lane said, emboldened by Kim's lack of resistance. "It's for stopping the stage yesterday and taking a gent named Yuma Bill off it."

Kim's gaze swung to Johnny Naylor, anger stirring in him. "So you've sold out, too, Johnny. Your caliber is a damned sight smaller than I thought it was."

"I didn't sell out to nobody," Naylor cried. "I just ain't gonna let you get away with stopping the stage and taking a man off at point of a gun. You ain't that big, Logan."

"I didn't take him. He got out when I mentioned Brit Bonham. Remember?"

"Yeah, and you had a gun in your hand. Remember that?"

Kim shrugged. "If I hadn't you'd have drilled me. I had to keep you quiet so I could talk to Yuma."

"You held a gun on us," Naylor said doggedly. "You scared hell out of us. That fat woman fainted. Might have died of heart failure. If we've got any law around here, it won't stand for it."

"We've got law all right," Lane said smugly, "and it don't stand for them kind of shenanigans. Now are you . . ."

"Oh hell! If I hadn't taken Yuma, some of Dunning's outfit would. He'd have been beefed by now and the bank would be busted."

"He wouldn't have been touched," Naylor said with malicious triumph. "We rolled into Ganado without no more trouble."

Doubts struck Kim then. He had not asked if the stage had been stopped again. He had been so sure it would be Dunning's move that he had not questioned it. He said, "You're lying, Johnny."

"I ain't neither. Ask the driver. Or the passengers. The drummer's over at the hotel and that fat woman is Luke Haines' mother-in-law. She was coming to take care of Mrs. Haines. She's in Luke's house now. Go ask her."

"All right," Kim said, "but you still haven't got a charge against me, Ed. We stopped at Rocky Avis' place on our way down and she cooked dinner for us. She'll tell you Yuma wasn't no prisoner. You can't make kidnapping out of it."

"I'm making it kidnapping all right," Lane said doggedly. "I'll ask Rocky, but as long as Johnny sticks to his story, I've got to throw you into the jug."

Ed Lane was a poor excuse for a lawman. Still, Kim could not draw a gun on him. Killing a man like Tonto Miles was one thing; shooting the sheriff was quite another. Kim drew his gun and laid it on the bar. He walked toward the batwings, saying, "I won't be in long, Johnny. Not when Yuma Bill tells his story. Then you'd better get out of my way."

"Take more'n that to get you out of the jug," Naylor said, his terror gone now that Kim's gun was not in holster. "Butch told you Clawhammer wasn't big enough to save your hide."

"We'll see," Kim said, and pushed through the batwings.

Miles' body had been moved and the street was empty. Kim paused, wondering who would go to Clawhammer for him. Peg, he was sure, would arrange for bail and get him out as soon as she heard.

"Keep moving," Lane said. "Try anything and I'll plug you. Just anything."

Kim turned toward the courthouse, resentment smoldering in him. Lane did not need to keep the gun in his back, but it was like the man, now that Kim was unarmed. It gave him his chance to play big; he would relish telling Dunning how he had arrested and disarmed Kim Logan, the man who had killed Tonto Miles.

They moved slowly, Lane two paces behind Kim. They passed Luke Haines' barber shop, Galt's Mercantile, and when they reached Doc Frazee's drugstore, Kim heard running steps on the walk behind him. He turned. It was Rocky Avis and he saw at once that her temper was honed sharp again.

"Ed, what are you up to now?" Rocky demanded.

Lane stepped back so that he could watch both Kim and Rocky. He licked brown-stained lips, eyeing Rocky warily.

"Don't you try none of your tricks, You're a wild cat all right, but my jail can hold wild cats along with gunmen."

Rocky stamped a foot, so angry that for a moment Kim thought she was going to slap Lane. "Why are you arresting him?"

"What's that to you?"

"Plenty. You put out some talk about arresting anybody who got into a gun fight in Ganado, but you can't make it stick and you know it."

"I'll make this stick. He's arrested for kidnapping a feller named Yuma Bill. Now git back…"

"Why you pumpkin-headed fool! Yuma Bill wasn't kidnapped. They stopped at my place and I cooked dinner for them. I saw how it was."

"Johnny Naylor says different. Now git out of the way, Rocky, or so help me, I'll…"

"Johnny Naylor, is it? We'll see about that."

Rocky whirled and started back along the walk. Kim called, "Rocky, wait." She turned back, standing motionless as if poised for flight. "Ride out to Clawhammer and tell Peg what happened. She'll get me out."

Rocky stared at him blankly for a moment before she seemed to understand what he had said. Then she flared, "You don't need your precious Peg. I'll fix this." Again she whirled and this time Kim let her go.

"She ain't so big," Lane said with his usual smugness. "Move along."

The brick courthouse stood at the end of the block, Ganado's chief reminder of the glory that was past. Only the first story was used. The other two were empty, most of their windows knocked out by Ganado's stone-throwing boys. In recent years they had been boarded up, giving the building the same appearance of decay that was typical of the town.

Kim pulled the front door open, said, "Some oil would stop that squeak," and went on down the dark hall to Lane's office, floor boards squealing dismally under his feet. He stood motionless beside the desk while the sherriff threw a cell door back and motioned with his head.

"Ain't had much business lately " Lane locked the door behind Kim. "Time it was picking up. A sheriff oughtta earn his salary, hadn't he?"

"Yeah. Dunning's money."

Lane turned to spit in the direction of the big brass spittoon at the end of his desk. He swung back, wiping a hand across his mouth. "Well now, you go ahead and talk ornery if you want to. Won't make me mad. Won't do you no good, neither."

Kim sat down on the bunk and rolled a smoke, paying no attention to Lane who stood staring at him a little uncertainly, apparently surprised that Kim was taking the arrest so calmly. He asked, "Hungry?"

"No."

Lane dropped Kim's gun into a drawer of his desk. He said, "I'll fetch you a meal from the hotel afore sundown," and walked down the hall, the squeal of the boards coming back to Kim. After that there was silence.

Kim had been in jail a few times, but never more than an hour or so, and never for anything more serious than cracking some local cowboy on the nose during a Saturday night free-for-all. This, he knew, could be serious. He smoked his cigarette down and rolled another, his hatred for Hank Dunning becoming a poison in him.

One thing was clear to Kim. Dunning was a more careful man than he had thought. He had rigged up one trap behind another so that if the first failed, there would be the second and then a third. He had not succeeded in buying Peg's notes, so he had tried to remove Kim by throwing a gunman at him. That had failed, but at least he had Kim in jail, and it was more than probable that he could swing enough influence to secure a conviction. Then he could move on Clawhammer without fear of serious opposition.

Kim thought briefly of Rocky Avis, wondering what she had in mind and having no real hope of her success. He should have aske Lane to send Brit Bonham to see him. Bonham, he was sure, would see that Peg heard what had happened.

Peg would get him out. He had no doubt of that. She needed him. He had every reason to think she loved him. Then he swore softly and rubbed his cigarette out. He had missed a bet last night because of a perverse notion that he had to prove to Peg what he could do before he asked her to marry him. He wouldn't pass up another chance if it came.

He heard steps in the hall, the floor squealed, and Kim got up from the cot and ratt ed the bars. He yelled, "Hey, you out there." There was no answer, but the steps kept coming, the floor boards squeaked just outside the sheriff's office. Then the door opened. Lane came in, red-faced and sullen. Johnny Naylor was behind him, then Rocky Avis and Naylor's wife Della. Naylor looked like a kid who has just been soundly threshed, Rocky was smiling, and Della had the appearance of a tornado with the cork pulled.

Without a word Lane unlocked the cell door and swung it back. He said sourly, "You're free. Naylor changed his story.

Said the stage had already stopped and Yuma Bill got out
'cause he wanted to."

Kim walked out of the cell and crossing to Lane's desk,
opened a drawer and took out his gun. He checked it and
dropped it into holster, guessing that Della was the one who
had pulled it off. She was Rocky's age and her best friend,
coming from one of the small ranches on the mesa. Kim
knew she often visited Rocky, and whenever Rocky stayed in
town overnight, it was always with Della.

"What are you waiting on?" Rocky asked. "You like it in
here?"

Kim grinned. "Can't say I do, but I'm a mite curious."

"I'll settle your curiosity right now," Della said sharply.
"It's going to take some regular Sunday School living from
Johnny to make me forget this. If we can't get along on his
wages..."

"Now Della..." Naylor began.

"Don't Della me," she flung at him. "I wouldn't blame
Kim if he blew your head off, but I've got a hunch I'm saving
your life by telling him what you did. He was sore about your
stopping the stage, Kim. Maybe he had a right to be, but he
didn't have a right to take Dunning's hundred dollars and
swear you into jail. Now he's swearing you out."

"A hundred dollars, was it?" Kim asked softly. "You lie
cheap Johnny."

"I didn't do no lying," Naylor muttered. "You did have a
gun in your fist."

"But you didn't think to tell Ed about it until after Tonto
Miles cashed in. That right?"

"Yeah, it's right," Naylor said sulkily.

"And you knew that Miles was going to make a try for
me?"

Naylor looked at Kim defiantly. "I knew all right. He was
sore 'cause you shot hell out of his bunch below the rim
yesterday. Dunning claims you're fixing to pull this valley
into the damnedest range war the country ever saw If it takes
killing you to stop it..."

"All right," Lane broke in. "No use of this palaver. Vamoose."

Della gripped Kim's arm. "Johnny got you into this, but now he's got you out. Not sore at him now, are you?"

"I can take care of myself," Naylor shouted, his pride outraged. "Del, you'd better stay out..."

"I ain't sore." Kim gave Della a sour grin. "Not much. Anyhow, you're too pretty to be a widow. Come on, Rocky."

They went down the hall, Rocky half running to keep up with Kim's long strides. She said, "I knew Della would fix Johnny. She doesn't like Dunning any more than I do. When Johnny started bragging about the hundred dollars he'd won at poker, Del guessed what had happened and she made him tell her."

"Wouldn't be hard to guess. Johnny's the worst poker player in the valley."

"Del tells him that, but Johnny doesn't think he's so bad. He keeps trying to show her that he's not as hopeless as she thinks he is."

They stepped into the sunlight, Kim taking a deep breath. "You know, Rocky, good air is something you don't put the right price on till you're cooped up in a stinking jail for awhile."

"It's that way with a lot of things, I guess. What are you going to do now?"

"Go back to Clawhammer. Say, did Yuma Bill get into town?"

"Why, I don't know. I haven't seen him."

"Let's take a sashay out to Smith's cabin and see what's holding him up. You'll want to pick up your dad's horse anyhow."

"Kim." The girl gripped his arm. "Look."

He stared down the street, shocked into silence by what he saw. Hank Dunning and Phil Martin were riding into town from the south. Smith's cabin was in that direction. Dunning was leading the black horse that Kim had borrowed from

Shorty Avis for Yuma Bill; a man was lashed belly-down across the saddle.

Kim ran toward them, a terrible fear crowding him. Yuma Bill was dead! He was too far away to recognize the man tied in the saddle; he could not tell at this distance whether the man was dead, but he knew. He should never have left Yuma Bill alone.

· Other men were boiling into the street. Someone shouted, "Another killing." By the time Kim and Rocky reached Galt's Mercantile, Dunning had reined up in the middle of the street, motioning for Martin to stop. Men crowded around them, asking questions, but for a moment Dunning ignored them. Kim shouldered through the crowd, his eyes making certain what had been in his mind. The man tied across the saddle was Yuma Bill and he was dead.

Brit Bonham was beside Kim, shaking his shoulder. "It's Yuma Bill, isn't it? It is Yuma Bill."

Kim backed away, nodding. He put his gaze on Dunning who was staring down at him, black eyes somber and probing. Kim asked, "You killed him, Dunning?"

Fury swelled the big man's chest. He swore, motioning to Ed Lane who had come up behind Kim. "Hear that, Sheriff? This killing thief wants to know if I done it."

"Did you?" Kim asked hoarsely.

"Tell 'em what you saw, Phil," Dunning ordered.

Martin was a sick man. His left arm was in a sling; his broad face was gray, mirroring the suffering that was in him. Now he licked dry lips, right hand clutching the saddle horn as if was an effort to remain upright.

"I was coming into town to have Doc look at my arm," Martin said slowly. "Logan and another hombre was riding in from the southeast. From Clawhammer, I reckon. They stopped at Smith's cabin. They got down and Logan opened the door. He looked in, then he turns around and shoots the other fellow. He grabs the dead man's money belt and lights out for town."

"You've got it easy, Ed," Dunning said. "It ain't often

you've got an eyewitness to a murder."

Kim stood motionless, stunned by Martin's story. He heard the sullen mutter of the crowd, heard Fred Galt shout, "That's why he was so high and mighty about us getting our money out of the bank. He already had his nest feathered."

"It's a lie," Rocky cried. "I met Kim on his way to town this morning..."

"But you didn't see him at Smith's cabin, did you?" Dunning demanded. "You didn't see 'em from the time they stopped at Smith's cabin till Logan left, did you?"

"No, but..."

"All right, Ed," Dunning said. "This girl don't know nothing about it. Phil does because he saw it."

Kim stepped back, hand dropping to gun butt. It was a rigged play, smart and brutal, another trick lined up behind the others that had failed.

"Take it easy, Logan." Lane's gun rammed aginst Kim's back. "That cell you left is empty and waiting." He lifted Kim's .44. "Back you go."

"Hold on," Kim shouted. "Martin's lying just like Rocky said. This man was alive when I left him. If I'd aimed to kill him, I'd have taken the dinero I fetched to the bank, and I'd have kept going."

"No," Dunning said. "You're too smart for that. Bonham told around that he had a friend coming with some money. It's my guess you spent the night at Clawhammer and Peg Cody knew what was in the box, but chances are she didn't know he was toting some more dinero in his money-belt. You could take that and figger you was safe 'cause no one around here knew he had it on him."

"I saw what I saw," Martin said doggedly. "I'll swear to it if this killing son lives long enough to be tried."

"He won't," Galt bawled. "I'll donate the rope myself, and I'll put the loop on his neck."

Lane wheeled on the storekeeper, making a show of anger. "None of that talk, Fred. I never lost a prisoner out of my jail yet, and I ain't starting with Logan."

Bonham had stood like a man struck by paralysis. Only now did he seem to fully grasp what was happening. He gripped Lane's arm. "Listen, Ed. If you used your noggin you'd know that Martin's lying. Logan's been in town since nine this morning. Martin wouldn't have waited all this time to tell what he saw."

"I waited all right," Martin said. "I tried to get to town, bu I couldn't make it. Fainted, I reckon. Fell out of my saddle anyway. Hank found me. I told him what I just told you." He stopped swaying, and pitched headlong to the ground."

"Doc," Dunning called. "Take care of Phil."

Doc Frazee motioned to Galt and Johnny Naylor. "Tote Martin over to my office. Dunning, you take the body to my back room." He reared back, long face dark with anger. "But before you do it, there's one thing I want to say. When I first hit this here camp, it was wilder'n hell, but I never seen nothing like this for framing a man. It's too pat, Dunning, just too damned pat."

Turning, Frazee stalked across the street to his office, the tails of his faded Prince Albert flapping behind him. Lane said, "Move along, Logan."

"Get word to Peg, will you, Brit?" Kim asked, and when Bonham nodded, Kim winked at Rocky. "It's all right. I'll be out again by sundown. Ed's gonna be plumb discouraged locking me up."

Kim paced along the boardwalk to the courthouse, knowing it wasn't all right, not on a murder charge with Fred Galt hating him the way he did, and Dunning willing to oil men's throats with free whiskey in the Belle Union. Nothing more was needed to start a blood lusting mob toward the courthouse. Saner men like Brit Bonham and Doc Frazee would be pushed aside.

Kim reached the courthouse, Lane two paces behind, looking very smug and sure of himself. He asked, "Scared?"

"Some."

"You've got cause to be," Lane said with satisfaction.

The heavy outside door had been propped open. They went in and on down the length of the dark hall, floor boards squeaking dismally under their feet.

"Go right in," Lane said. "I left your cell open."

Kim obeyed, and for the second time that day the cell banged shut behind Kim.

CHAPTER 10
FOUR WALLS

A strange uneasiness suddenly possessed Ed Lane. He dropped Kim's gun into a drawer and paced around the office for a few minutes, chewing nervously on a huge quid of tobacco. Finally he asked, "Anything you want, Logan?"

"No."

"Hungry yet?"

"No."

"Ain't et since breakfast, have you?"

"No."

"I'll go over over to the hotel and have 'em cook you up a good meal. Anything special you want?"

"What are you trying to do, ease your conscience by giving a condemned man his last meal?"

Lane bristled. "You won't get your last meal till after you're legally tried and convicted, which same you will be. And don't say nothing about my conscience. I didn't take an old man off the stage and then plug him right here at the edge of town."

"Been smarter to have plugged him farther out, wouldn't it?"

"It sure would. Looks to me like you ain't as smart as Dunning allows you are."

"How come you didn't arrest Martin and his outfit for jumping me and Yuma Bill yesterday?"

"Nobody made no complaint," Lane said, turning sullen.

"If I'd arrested anybody, it'd be you, jumping 'em like you done."

"So that's the way Martin tells it. How did he account for being on Clawhammer's side of the creek?"

"He didn't. They wasn't breaking no law, just riding like they was."

Lane wheeled and stepped out. The boards squeaked and were still. Silence then, tight and oppressive. Kim sat down on his bunk and rolled a smoke. He fired it and took a long drag, but there seemed to be no taste to it. He ground it out under a boot toe, got up and paced the length of his cell, physically sick. In the few hours he had known Yuma Bill, he had learned to respect him as he had respected few men in his short turbulent life.

Death was not a new thing to Kim. Like most men who live by the gun, the knowledge that death is the natural and inevitable destiny for every human was never fully absent from his mind. But these last hours had changed him as surely as a dam diverts a flowing stream, and it had been Yuma Bill who had done the changing, a Yuma Bill who would have made himself felt in the entire valley if he had lived. Now Kim was haunted by the thought that he was at least partly to blame for the little man's death.

There was another thing, too, that added to his misery. As far back as he could remember, he had wanted to own a ranch, a natural ambition for a man who had been raised in the cattle country. Until he had come to Pass Creek Valley, he had never really planned beyond the next day. As Yuma Bill had said, he had been satisfied to think about a glass of whiskey, a girl to kiss, the transient things which had no lasting qualities.

After he had come to the valley, change had begun to work in him. Here was a country big enough for a dozen ranches, but there were just the two with the threat of war between them. It had been that threat which was largely responsible for keeping other cowmen out and for holding the little outfits back on the poorer graze of the mesa.

Then Yuma Bill had proposed a partnership. It had been there, right at his finger tips, the thing he wanted more than anything else. Now it was snatched away. He was back where he had started from, a hired gun hand with a thousand dollars in the bank, accused of murdering the very man who had promised to turn a dream into reality.

Later, hours later it seemed to Kim, Lane brought Brit Bonham to his cell. The banker was wearing a slicker. He said, "Rain's about here."

Kim had not been aware of the gathering storm. He said, "Won't last long," and watched Lane search Bonham for a gun, saying in a surly voice that he wasn't taking any chances. He drifted back to his desk and stood there, watching, giving Kim and Bonham a chance to talk. It was a courtesy Kim had not expected from him.

"I sent a man to Clawhammer," Bonham said. "He oughtta be back in another hour or so. If Peg's got any sense, she'll send her boys in and yank you out of here before it's too late."

"I won't run," Kim said sharply. "Running convicts a man if nothing else does."

"You can't prove your innocence locked up here," Bonham snapped. "Use your head, boy. Dunning's buying free drinks in the Belle Union right now. He's bent on getting rid of you, and a rope is a cheap way to do the job."

"Must be some men in town who don't figure the way he does," Kim said.

Bonham glanced at the sheriff and brought his eyes back to Kim. "Sure. Me and Doc and Charlie Bemis. Maybe one or two more. Or supposing you stand trial? What chance have you got against Martin's testimony." Bonham shook his head. "We've got to bust you out someway."

Kim gripped the bars. "I've been wondering about a couple of things. Was Dunning in town when me and Tonto Miles tangled?"

"Dunno. I'll find out."

"And what about old Salty Smith?"

"I've been wondering that myself," Bonham said. "I don't think he's been around town today."

"Then he'd be fishing."

Bonham nodded, considering this. "He never fishes downstream. Usually he goes about a mile up the creek and fishes back down. Thick as them willows are, he could have been in sight of his cabin when it happened and seen the whole thing."

"He knows Dunning and Martin," Kim said. "If he saw it, he'd be afraid to talk."

"I'll ride out there. He'll talk to me."

Bonham swung away from the bars. Lane asked, "Done?"

"Yeah, except for one question, Ed. It's a pretty poor stick of a sheriff who don't think of justice first. You ain't gonna be proud of yourself if you hang the wrong man."

"What're you getting at?"

"I've been wondering what you'd do if you had proof that Martin or Dunning shot Yuma Bill?"

Lane snorted. "Hell, I've got proof that Logan done it. That's all I need."

"A good lawman looks a little deeper than what's throwed on top for him to see. It's like Doc said. This thing is too pat."

'Makes sense," Lane said doggedly. "Anyhow, it's up to the jury, not me."

"Maybe it'll never go to a jury."

Lane chewed hard on his quid, face turning red. He burst out, "Damn it, Brit, nobody's gonna take Logan out of here. You hear? Nobody."

"They'll try, and I can't see you being man enough to die bucking a lynch mob. There's another thing you'd better be thinking on. If Kim killed Yuma Bill, he done it before nine this morning. That right?"

"Yeah, but..."

"Doc says he hasn't been dead that long." Bonham turned back to Kim. "Your horse is in the stable. He'll be taken care of." He swung around and went out.

For a long moment Lane stood motionless. Then he muttered, "Aw, hell, Doc couldn't tell," and stomped out after Bonham.

It began to rain in sudden violence much as the storm had come the day before. Kim stood up on his cot and looked out of the one small window. This was the shabbiest and most decayed part of a decaying town. Log cabins scattered haphazardly about, doors half off their hinges, roofs falling in, yards and streets grown high with weeds. Now, for one brief moment, the rain drew a silver curtain across this tawdry scene.

Kim got down, futility weighing heavily upon him. He had always been a man to depend upon himself and his gun, confident of his strength and speed. Now, for the first time that he could remember, he was completely trapped. There was no way out, no way by which he could help himself. There were those who wanted to help him, but if they did, they would risk their lives, and that was something he did not want.

He rolled a cigarette and smoked it, seeing the situation with stark clarity. His one hope lay in old Salty Smith, but in spite of what Bonham had said, the hope at best was a slim one.

At first he had expected help from Peg. Now with the slow minutes dragging by, he realized that Peg could not help him, tha his trust in her was as empty of real value as a pocketful of fool's gold. Even if she was willing to bring her crew down from the high country, Dutch Heinz would refuse to do anything.

Then a new fear clutched Kim. This might have been pulled off by Dunning to lure Clawhammer men away from the cattle and leave them unguarded. He pushed the thought from his mind at once. One thing overshadowed everything else in Peg's mind, the safety of her herd. She would not order her men to leave her cattle whether Kim Logan's neck was stretched or not.

The storm moved on. Thunder was softened by distance;

the only lightning was that along the horizon. Kim knew how it would be outside: a hot clear sun, the heavy damp air, mud squishing under boot heels, the clean smell of a washed steaming earth. Those were things that a free man could see and smell and feel.

A free man! Panicky, he jumped up and pounded the bars; he shouted and kicked, and then realizing what was happening to him, he dropped back on the cot, ashamed. He wasn't licked. A man had a chance as long as he was alive, but no one except Brit Bonham would gamble on that chance. Even Rocky Avis hadn't come to see him. Not that he blamed her. She'd probably taken her father's black horse and headed for home. She'd already done enough for him. More than enough. More than he had any right to expect.

He clenched his fists and spread them and clenched them again. He got up and began pacing the floor, fighting the fear that beat at him. If he had any kind of a chance, he would run. They could think what they wanted to. As Bonham had said, he could not prove his innocence here. He might, if he was free.

Free! The word hammered at his mind like the rhythmical roll of distant drums. Free! Free! Free! Only a free man had strength and will and the capacity to fight. Here he was like a wild horse in a corral. Now he understood how a stallion felt, driven in from the high open mesas to have his great heart broken; he knew why a stallion would fight until he killed himself or broke a leg and had to be killed.

Then, and he was not aware just how or why, the queer feeling of panic began to die. He thought of Peg who had gambled on him for protection just as she had gambled on the future, borrowing every cent she could from Brit Bonham. He thought of Shorty Avis who hated him because he hated and feared Clawhammer, of Rocky who had helped him.

Then, and he felt as if a sharp blade had been driven through him, he thought of Yuma Bill who talked about planting good seeds. Kim had had a lifetime of freedom, but he had taken little of it to think. Now he had time. He sat quietly on his cot, his mind on Yuma Bill, and he realized that he had respected the little man for a very simple reason. Yuma Bill had lived the life he'd talked. There could be no other reason for his coming here to help Brit Bonham. That was what he had meant when he'd said that a man must find the things that lasted. He had found them, Kim Logan never had.

It was close to evening when Ed Lane came with his meal; hot coffee, a thick steak, fried potatoes, and biscuits, the kind of meal Kim would have ordered if he had been in the hotel dining room. He said, "Thanks, Ed."

"Thought you'd be getting a little lank," Lane said. "I told that China boy he'd better do a good job on that steak, or I'd have his pigtail."

Kim understood. Ed Lane knew what to expect tonight; he was not a man to die for an abstract principle called duty. As far as he was concerned, Kim Logan was a dead man swinging from a limb. By bringing this meal, Lane was easing his conscience. Later he would say he had done all he could.

When Kim finished, Lane took the plate, cup, and coffeepot. "Time to put the feed bag on myself," he said, and left the jail.

Silence again after the last board had squealed under Lane's feet, but it did not seem quite so oppressive now. Kim emptied his sack of Durham and smoked the last cigarette. The sun was almost down. He remembered how it was, the Dragon Peaks forming giant saw teeth against the western sky, the vivid sweep of scarlet sunset, shadows darkening the edge of the valley and slowly moving on across it.

The world could be a good place to live, but it was seldom that. There was a right and a wrong side to every human difference, but few sides were completely right or wrong. That was why there was so much trouble in the world, for it was natural that a man who had only a part of the right would think he had all of it.

Hank Dunning could probably make a case for himself.

And old Sam Cody if he were still alive. Even back before that there were the gold seekers chasing the yellow floozy, greedy men too often without conscience. A man could not tell where it had started. Perhaps it had always been that way. Kim only knew he had been a part of it, using his gun and dealing in death for those who could pay.

He felt no pride in his past. He could not change anything he had done. The page was full. He rubbed out his cigarette, feeling none of the panic that had been in him earlier in the afternoon. He realized that these were the thoughts of a man facing death.

The light was very thin when Lane returned with Bonham. Again the lawman searched Bonham for a gun and stepped back so that they could talk.

"I found out a couple of things," Bonham said. "Dunning was in town until after you plugged Tonto Miles. Then he rode south. Mean anything?"

"Not much. How do you figure it?"

"Looks to me like maybe Martin was holding Yuma prisoner out there till Dunning told him what to do. They wanted the dinero Yuma had on him, and they wanted you out of the way without having to dry gulch you which might be a little dangerous for them."

Kim nodded. "Could have been that way all right."

"I was the cause of it," the banker said bitterly. "If I hadn't..."

"None of that," Kim cut in. "I can say the same thing about myself. My mistake was doing what Yuma wanted, but hell, it sounded reasonable. A man just can't foresee things like this."

"I reckon that's the way to look at it," Bonham agreed, "but it's pretty tough just the same."

"Smith?"

"I dunno. I spent half the afternoon on the creek. He might have been fishing. Couldn't tell. The rain probably washed out any sign there was before I got there. The only thing I'm sure of is that he ain't around now."

The last small hope was gone, but it was no more than Kim expected. He asked, "Peg?"

"She got my note," Bonham said heavily, "but I don't know what to expect. She just said 'Thanks,' gave the boy a dollar, and went back into the house."

"I guess that's it."

Kim gripped the bars, knuckles white, and he felt again the empt ness in his middle that made him want to scream and beat at the bars. He thought of men he had seen die with a rope on their necks. He had had a part in some of those hangings. At the time there had seemed to be no doubt of their guilt. Rustling! Horse stealing! Murder! Now he wondered. Most of the men who would have a part in lynching him would have no doubt of his guilt. Johnny Naylor. Luke Haines. Even vindictive Fred Galt. Men who had nothing to gain, small men who lacked the courage it took to stand against the current that Hank Dunning had started.

"Kim." Bonham brought his mouth close to Kim's ear. "You're getting out of here right after dark. You be ready. One minute either way might decide it. Don't waste no time."

"I don't want you..."

"Don't make no difference whether you want it or not. I owe you the same kind of a debt that Yuma owed me. It's the rest of 'em I'm worried about. I'd do it myself, but I need help to pull it off."

Turning, Bonham started across the room. Lane said, "Brit." Bonham made a slow turn to face him. Casually the sheriff opened a desk drawer and laid Kim's gun on the spur-scarred desk. "I made a jackass out of myself this morning just like Logan said. So did Galt and Luke Haines and everybody else who was in the line. We should have knowed the bank was good."

Bonham shifted his weight uncertainly. He said, "You're a little late thinking of that."

"I am for a fact." Lane laid a double-barreled shotgun on

the desk beside Kim's Colt. "What I'm trying to say is that I know you're an honest man. You've done a hell of a lot for the country. Believed in it and stayed here. Even bucked old Sam Cody when he was riding high and handsome. Well, now you're an old man who deserves to die in bed with his boots off."

"I aim to," Bonham said evenly.

Lane gnawed off a chew of tobacco and slipped the plug back into his pocket. "Naw, you don't aim to do no such thing. That whispering with Logan didn't fool nobody. You're fixing to bust him out of here. Now I'd hate to do it like hell, but if you make a try, I'll drill you the same as I would any man."

Bonham threw his stooped shoulders back, trying to gain all the height that he could. he said with dignity, "You'd be doing your duty, Ed," and walked out.

The sheriff dropped into his swivel chair and cocked his legs on his desk, chewing steadily until the hall floor stopped squeaking under Bonham's feet. He said then, "I've been wondering, Logan. That dinero wasn't on you. What'd you do with it?"

"So that's it. I wondered what you was working up to."

Lane straightened and swung his feet to the floor. "I wasn't working up to nothing."

"But you'd make a deal, wouldn't you?"

"I don't savvy," Lane said, his face a mask of innocent guile.

"If I split the dinero you think I stole, you'd shoot wide if Brit tries to break me out of here. That it?"

Lane choked. He got up and spit into the brass spittoon at the end of his desk. "Damn it, I didn't make no such proposition..."

"Yuma Bill had ten thousand dollars in his money belt, Ed. How would you like to have five of that?"

Lane sat down, scratching his bald head. "I'm listening."

"Aw, go to hell," Kim said wearily, and dropped down on his bunk.

"You'll be there afore I will," Lane bawled. "You don't need to think I'm gonna get myself filled with lead to protect a killing son like you. They'll haul you out of here tonight and you'll be dancing on air."

"I ain't surprised," Kim said. "No sir, I ain't surprised. Dunning really bought himself a sheriff when he pinned the star on you."

Lane leaned back in his chair. He said with smug satisfaction, "I got the star, ain't I? That's more'n you're getting from Clawhammer."

CHAPTER 11
ESCAPE

Ed Lane had been in and out of his office all afternoon, apparently convinced that no effort would be made to break Kim out while it was daylight. Now, with darkness upon the town, he stayed at his desk, chewing steadily, eyes almost lidded shut, feet cocked in front of him.

Lying on his bunk, Kim watched the man, lamplight throwing a yellow glare on his shiny head. Kim wanted a cigarette, but his pride would not allow him to ask Lane for the makings.

It seemed very quiet. Kim climbed up on the bunk and looked through the window. The sky was clear now; stars glittered with cold brilliance. The sound of thunder had died, but lightning still played along the eastern horizon above the Continental Divide.

He sat down on his bunk again, impatience winding his nerves tight. Usually a lynch mob gave out its own peculiar sound. Some of the men would be drunk on Dunning's free whiskey. Others, probably Dunning and Fred Galt, would be cold sober. They would be the brains of the mob. There would be no fight, Ed Lane being the man he was. Still, they must think of some device which would make it appear that

Lane had no responsibility for what was to happen.

Bonham would not be intimidated by what Lane had said. He and whoever was with him, Doc Frazee and Charlie Bemis perhaps, would make some kind of a try, but it was a question in Kim's mind which group would reach the jail first. If it came to a fight between them, Bonham was licked. Numbers favored the mob, and some of its members would be HD hands, better fighting men than the few townsmen who would be siding Bonham.

A noise behind the courthouse startled Kim. Horse? He might be imagining it. He rose, yawned and stretched, and stepped up on the cot again. There were three dark blobs out there that might be horses, but he couldn't be sure. At such a time a man's senses are not to be fully trusted, and the starlight was so thin that he might be seeing what he wanted to see and not what was actually out there.

Kim stepped down, saying casually, "Storm blew over."

"The big one ain't." Lane rose. "Too bad about Bonham. Like I said, he's a fine old gent." He picked up the shotgun and sighted down the barrel. "Buckshot sure messes a man up. And don't count on Bonham doing the job. One of Dunning's boys is outside. I ain't playing this alone."

Hot words were on Kim's tongue. He wanted to say that if anything happened to Brit Bonham, Ed Lane would get his, too. But there was no use. Not unless Kim could get out of here with a gun in his hand. Whatever he said now would be an idle threat. He stood with his hands clenching the bars, hating Ed Lane as he had never hated a man before in his life.

The floor boards in the hall squealed. Lane grinned and picked up the shotgun. "Shut your eyes, Logan. This ain't gonna be purty."

Quick steps sounded closer, more boards squealed. Then Kim's eyes widened as surprise shocked him. It was Della Naylor who came in, not Brit Bonham. Lane was even more surprised than Kim. He stood staring at the girl uncertainly, his lips parted. Then he laid the shotgun down and scratched his head.

"You gave me a turn, Della," Lane said. "I figured you was old man Bonham aiming to bust this killing son loose."

Della shook her head. "I'm not Bonham." She wrinkled her pug nose. "Or do I look like him?"

"Hell no." Lane walked around the desk to her. "You're mighty purty, and you can't say that for that old goat."

She laughed. Kim had always liked the sound of her laugh, but now it struck him that there was a false note to it. He demanded, "Why ain't you home with Johnny?"

She looked past Lane at Kim, frowning. "That's a smart question. I'll tell you. First place Johnny isn't home. Second place, I've got an apology to make to Ed."

"Apology?" Lane reached out and patted her hands. "You don't need to make no apology to Ed Lane, not for nothing."

"Get out of here, Della," Kim shouted.

"Well, you'd do well to keep your mouth shut," Della said. "Ed's the kind who appreciates a girl, which is more than I can say about Johnny. Or you, either."

Lane laughed easily. "That's sure true. Leastwise I appreciate you."

"Where's Rocky?" Kim demanded.

"Gone home." Della drew away from Lane and danced across the floor to Kim's cell, her slim back to Lane, hips swaying. "Johnny's in the Belle Union getting drunk. Both cats are away, Ed. No reason the mouse shouldn't play."

"I wouldn't mind playing mouse," Lane said.

Della danced back toward the door, heels making clicking sounds on the floor. "About that apology, Ed. If I'd known Kim had killed that poor old man, I'd never have made Johnny back up on his story. Rocky likes Kim. I just did it because she asked me to."

"Rocky's mistook, too," Lane said. "He's not worth much, Logan ain't."

Della stood in the doorway, scowling at Kim. Then she shrugged. "Well, he'll get what he's got coming. Rocky's the only one who'll be sorry." She started to turn, saying over her shoulder. "You going to be here all night, Ed?"

"I don't figure on it."

Lane took a step toward her, but she moved back into the dark hall, as elusive as a shadow. "Now Ed," she said. "What are you up to?"

"What are you up to coming here?" he demanded.

"To tell you I made a mistake about Kim." She laughed lightly. "And that Johnny isn't home, but that doesn't mean anything to you."

"How do I know you ain't hoorawing me?"

This time Della stood motionless while Lane came up to her. He put his arms around her, the lamplight falling past them, their single shadow darkening the middle of the yellow patch. Della offered her lips, whispering, "I wouldn't fool you, Ed."

Lane kissed her greedily, his attention so closely fixed that he was not aware of Rocky's presence. She slipped out of a dark corner behind him and hit him with the barrel of her gun, an upsweeping blow that brought him to his knees. He had stood too tall for her to do more. He tried to call out, but only a groaning muffled sound came out of him. Rocky jammed a wadded-up bandanna into his mouth and swung the gun again. He went limp and Rocky stepped away and let him fall.

"Good job," Della said, running into Lane's office. "How do you like my acting, Kim?"

"Too good. I wish you hadn't got into this."

Della grabbed Lane's keys from his desk and tried one in the lock of Kim's cell. It failed. A second failed, but the third turned the lock and Della pulled the door open. Rocky had come in and stood watching, trembling under the nervous pressure of the moment.

"Let's lock him up," Della said. "It won't help Ed's reputation any if they find him locked up in your cell. I hope they hang him."

Kim dragged Lane's limp body into the cell and locked the door, wondering how badly he was hurt. Blood trickled in a small scarlet stream across his bald head. He wheeled to the desk, scooped up his gun, and slid it into holster.

"Horses are in back," Rocky said, jerking her head toward the front door. "Here." She pressed a sack of Durham and a package of cigarette papers into his hand. "I thought you'd be smoking all afternoon."

Kim said, "Thanks," and blew out the lamp, bringing total blackness to the room.

Della was halfway down the hall. Rocky gripped Kim's arm. She said, "The front door is propped open but we can't just make a run for it. Pete Delaney's outside. He knows we're in here, so we've got to take care of him."

They moved toward the front door the floor boards squeaking. The hall was a dark tunnel, but apparently Della had reached the steps. She called, "Pete."

"Here." A man drifted up out of the darkness. "Anything wrong?"

"Plenty. Come here and look."

Rocky and Kim were at the end of the hall, the faint light from the street falling through the open doorway. Kim moved close to the wall and remained inside, but Rocky went on to stand beside Della.

"Hurry, Pete," Rocky said with quiet urgency. "The light's out."

The HD man swore. "You don't reckon Bonham got Logan out?"

"It's as black as a tomb in there," Rocky breathed. "We couldn't see. Maybe somebody shot Kim."

"No such luck as that," Delaney growled, and started up the steps. He reached the top one and stopped, suddenly suspicious. "What kind of a trick are you two pulling off? Ed had a light back there a minute ago."

"He hasn't now," Rocky said. "Have you got any matches?"

Rocky and Della were both on the top step, Delaney between them. For a moment he stood motionless, turning his head to look at one and then the other, the only sound that of his breathing.

"Yeah, I've got a match," Delaney said finally, "but I ain't going in there. Maybe you're sweet on Logan, Rocky. Maybe you got him out and when I go in there, he'll burn me down."

"I just want to see him get a square deal," Rocky flared. "I want to know what happened."

"I guess you're afraid of the dark," Della said scornfully. "Give me a match and I'll find out what's wrong."

"I ain't afraid of the dark," Delaney said, "but I'm afraid of Kim Logan, and I ain't the only one. I'm gonna get Dunning."

Delaney swung around to go back down the steps, but before he'd made the full turn, the girls grabbed his arms, Rocky calling, "Kim."

Delaney bawled a surprised oath, and perked his hands free, slamming both girls back against the courthouse wall, but it was something he had not expected, and it took a moment. Before he could lift his gun, Kim was on him.

Kim got his left arm around Delaney's neck and squeezed while he drove his right into the HD man's face. Delaney gurgled and tried to break free, but his frantic threshing accomplished nothing. His back was against Kim's stomach, and the best he could do was to lash backwards with a foot, his heel catching Kim on the shin and sending pain lancing up his leg.

"Bust him," Della urged. "Somebody's coming."

Given time, Kim could have choked him unconscious, but there was no time. Once the alarm was sounded, a dozen men would rush out of the Belle Union and Rocky and Della might get hurt. This was the sort of situation Brit Bonham had foreseen when he had warned Kim to be ready and not to waste time.

Kim pulled Delaney back into the hall, his left arm still hard against the man's throat, then he let go. Delaney, with nothing to support him, went down, his head rapping against the floor. He lay on his back, half-stunned. Kim dropped on him, knees slamming into the man's hard-muscled belly and driving breath out of him. He swung his right fist to Delaney's jaw. When he rose, Delaney lay still.

Wheeling, Kim plunged through the doorway. Rocky and Della were on the ground at the base of the steps, Rocky saying softly, "This way, Kim."

He glimpsed their shadowy figures as they faded toward the corner of the building. A man turning in from the street heard their pounding steps. He yelled, "Dunning," and fired, a wild high shot. Kim ran after the girls, hit a slick spot still wet from the afternoon rain, and fell headlong. He scrambled up as the man threw another shot that went wide, and printed on to the rear of the courthouse as Della swung into saddle.

"I'm going home, Kim," Della called. "Don't get into a fight with 'em. I don't want Johnny hurt." Swinging her horse, she rode away.

"Here." Bonham pressed the reins into Kim's hands. "Rocky's black. Do what she says. She's got it all planned."

Rocky was in the saddle now, calling in a hurry-up tone, "Come on, come on."

Kim stepped up, not liking it. "What'd you get the girls into this for, Brit?"

"Rocky's idea, not mine," Bonham said, and drifted away into the darkness.

Rocky was already riding into the cluster of deserted cabins that lay back of the courthouse, holding her horse down, hoofs dropping into the soft earth with faint sucking sounds. The hoofbeats of Della's running horse came clearly to Kim. She was heading east toward the mesa.

Kim reined in beside Rocky, saying angrily, "I can't let her go alone. They're likely to kill her before they find out who she is."

"Don't be a fool," Rocky said sharply. "She's got the fastest horse in the valley and I think she's the best rider. They'll never catch her. Or if they did, all she'd have to do would be to holler. Johnny'll be with the posse."

Rocky turned into an old shed and dismounted. For a moment Kim sat his saddle, fighting his stubborn pride. Then he stepped down and stood beside Rocky, knowing the girl was right. Della was a good rider. He had often met her crossing the valley to her folk's ranch, or on narrow mountain trails. If he followed, there would be a fight, and the posse would have men in it Kim did not want to kill.

A great clatter had broken out in front of the courthouse. Men shouted; there was some wild shooting. Then Dunning's great voice, "We're losing time. I'll take charge here." A moment later they swept out of town to the east, eight or ten of them, but already Della's hoofbeats had faded. In this vast blanket of darkness there would be little chance of finding her.

Kim gripped Rocky's arm and turned her to face him, but he saw only a pale oval that seemed to be devoid of expression. He asked, "Why did you and Della do this?"

"We've got a fight on our hands," she said. "When you get Peg figured out, you'll lead us. We couldn't let them hang a man we needed."

"I don't think Dutch Heinz meant . . ."

"Oh yes he did. We're not going to run again. Maybe you don't know it, but Dad and Della's father and most of our neighbors were driven out of the valley by Sam Cody. We won't be driven again, Kim. Not by Peg or Dunning or anybody."

He had never heard the whole story of Sam Cody's coming to the valley. He had never asked who had suffered from Cody's pushing tactics because he had not considered it his business. Naturally Peg had not volunteered much information about it. Now he understood Shorty Avis's hatred for everything that belonged to Clawhammer. Avis had classed him with Heinz.

"We'd better ride," Kim said.

For a moment Rocky did not move. Her face still lifted to his as if her eyes were trying to pierce the darkness. She said, "I was pretty young when it happened, so I don't remember much about the trouble, but I've heard Dad say that if they had fought together, they could have licked Cody. It'll be the same again unless somebody can make us work together."

It was the old, time-proved technique of divide and conquer. Kim had seen it used many times. A single large outfit could clear a range of the small spreads by taking them one at a time, but if they had united, the small spreads would have been stronger than their common enemy. To weld a bunch of small cowmen together was always a problem. Kim, knowing the mesa ranchers, doubted that it could be done.

"I'm beholden to you," Kim said at last, "and if it comes to a fight, I'm your man. I don't think it will. Peg's got all she can do to hold Dunning off without bothering you folks."

Turning, Rocky stepped into the saddle. She waited until Kim had swung up. Then she said, "It would be an accident if we ran into them tonight. By sun up we'll be hid out."

"I'm not going to dodge around like a rabbit," Kim said hotly.

"Then go back and sit in jail. If you want your neck stretched, they'll accommodate you.'

"All right," he said.

They threaded their way through the cabins until they reached open country, then swung toward the stage road that crossed the valley. Reaching it, they turned directly east until they came to the side road that led to Clawhammer. Kim reined up, saying, "You go on home and stay out of trouble."

"Where are you going?"

"Clawhammer."

"You don't think you'll get the man who killed Yuma Bill out there, do you?"

"I might."

"Or maybe you think Peg will hide you out."

"I've got to have grub. Only thing to do is to duck the posse till I get my hands on Phil Martin. When I do, he'll sing another tune about what he saw."

She took a ragged breath, her saddle squeaking as she shifted her weight. "Kim, you think we hate Clawhammer so much that we're judging Peg wrong. That it?"

"That's about it. Peg's into trouble up to her neck. Looks

like your bunch and Clawhammer had better throw in together, or Dunning will have the valley."

"I've never told you what I know about Peg because you wouldn't believe me. You'd just say I hated her. I do, but hating her doesn't make me blind. You are."

"I don't go switching around when I take a job," he said hotly. "Sure Peg's greedy just like you say, but that ain't a crime."

"I'll ride along with you," she said. "If you find out she doesn't want anything to do with you now, will you go with me?"

"Sure, but what'll you do if you're guessing wrong on Peg?"

"I'm not," she said.

Rocky turned off the stage road, following the twin ruts that led to Clawhammer. Kim caught up with her, admitting to himself that she might be right about his being blind. It had always been a fault with him, believing in people he wanted to believe in until the evidence was final. Loyalty, he knew, could be a fault as well as a virtue. Peg's faith in Dutch Heinz proved that.

There was a pattern of evil that lay upon the valley, a shadow as dark as this night, evil that had brought about the death of Yuma Bill and had very nearly put a rope on Kim's neck. The trouble was that both evil and good were often disguised as one another.

Now, with the cool night wind on his f ce and the tension of the long afternoon finally lifted, he had time to think about Yuma Bill's death. Dutch Heinz could have been the killer. Peg could have told him that Yuma Bill would be at Smith's cabin. That thought brought him squarely back to Peg. It was what Rocky would have him believe, but he could not.

CHAPTER 12
HALF TRUTH

It was near midnight when Kim and Rocky forded Ganado Creek, water lancing out from their horses' hoofs like curving arrows, faintly silvered by the starlight. The big ranch house sprawled before them, the barn and corrals to their left. The place seemed very quiet; there was no light anywhere around it.

"You can't stay here long, Kim," Rocky said. "When they don't pick up your trail, they'll come here."

"I reckon," Kim agreed.

The dog charged around the corner of the house, barking fiercely. Kim reined up, calling, "Shut up, Nero." He swung down, looping his reins over the hitch pole. The dog jumped around, whining eagerly, and Kim stooped to pet him.

Kim waited a moment, expecting a light to come to life inside the ouse, but there was none. Then old Limpy called out from the darkness, "Who is it?"

"Kim."

"Who's with you?"

"Rocky Avis."

There was a moment of silence. Limpy, Kim was sure, would doubt the girl's presence. Then the old man drifted up, thumbing a match to flame when he was close to Rocky. The tiny light spluttered, briefly showing the girl's small chin and sharp nose and dark eyes filled with cool defiance. Then the match flickered out.

"Didn't believe it, did you, Limpy?" Rocky asked.

"No, I sure didn't," the old man admitted. "What'n hell you doing here?"

"Making company for Kim."

"Maybe I'd better ask what you're doing here, Kim. Thought you was in the calaboose for beefing that hombre you took off the stage."

"Kicked a couple bars loose. Sure didn't get no help from

288

Clawhammer."

"Didn't have no help to give you," Limpy snapped. "If you had some powder to burn, why didn't you burn it on one of Dunning's toughs?"

"You making out I drilled Yuma?"

"Lane had an eyewitness, the way we heard it."

"Phil Martin," Kim said hotly. "You believe him?"

"Maybe," the old man said. "Maybe not. All I know is we don't want a hunted man hiding out on Clawhammer."

"You see," Rocky said quietly. "He's been told what to say."

Kim wheeled and started toward the house. Limpy called, "Come back here. Peg's been asleep for a couple of hours."

"She'll wake up," Kim said, and went on.

"Damn it," Limpy bawled. "You come back here. I've got a Winchester . . ."

"But you won't use it," Rocky said. "I've got a gun, too."

Limpy muttered something and subsided. Kim went into the house and striking a match, lit a lamp. Then he crossed the room to Peg's door and tapped. There was no response. He tapped again, louder. Another moment of silence, then Peg called sleepily, "Who is it?"

"Kim. I've got to talk to you."

"Just a minute. Wait till I get my robe on."

He moved back to the table and stood there, worriedly tapping his fingers on the oak surface. Now that the moment was here, he wondered what he would say. He wouldn't tell her he was riding out of the valley to duck a murder charge. Besides, she still needed him.

He heard her door open and looked up. She was wearing a dark blue robe, the cord tightly tied around her small waist, her hair falling far down her back in a red mass. She came to him with quick eagerness, her hands out. She reached him and put her arms around him, and she clung to him for a moment. Then she tipped her head back, eyes anxiously searching his face.

"I've been worried about you, Kim. Bonham sent word

you were in jail. How did you get out?"

Rocky was wrong about her. That was the first thought which came to him, and he felt the tension leave him. Perhaps, as Rocky said, he was blind to Peg Cody's faults, but regardless of those faults, she had been anxious about him. A man was a fool for trusting a woman only when that woman was not loyal.

He said, "I'm out. That's what counts. I've been doing some worrying myself. You still haven't got anybody here but Limpy. Nothing to keep Dunning from riding in and wiping you out."

"He won't," she said with some impatience. "I keep telling you that. You're the one who's in trouble."

"I won't be soon as I get the truth out of Martin. He's the one who tried to put the rope on my neck. Another one of Dunning's tricks to get at Clawhammer, I reckon."

She stepped back and shook her head. "You won't be any help to Clawhammer if they get the rope on your neck, Kim. You've got to get out of the valley and stay out."

He frowned, eyes searching her face. He could not keep the doubt from nagging his mind. It was a poor kind of loyalty that didn't work two ways.

"I'm not getting out yet," he said roughly. "I've got to buy some time, Peg. That's all I need."

"I can't help you, Kim." She shook her head. "I shouldn't have said that because I know you didn't expect it. You wouldn't want to pull me into trouble with the law."

When he had come here, he had had no intention of staying. More than anything else, he wanted to prove Rocky wrong. Now he said, "You could hide me out."

"Not when you're an outlaw, Kim. I'd like to help you, but the best thing for both of us is for you to put a lot of miles between you and Ganado."

He was still looking at her, trying to see something on her face that wasn't there. Her eyes seemed to hold concern for him, but he could not tell what was behind them. Women, he thought, were natural born actors. Della Naylor had fooled

Ed Lane, and he had a hunch that Peg was fooling him now as effectively as Della had fooled Lane.

He took a deep breath, remembering his dreams he had never fully voiced to anyone. Clawhammer might have been all he had hoped for, his and Peg's, if he could have proved to her she needed him. Not in the way she needed Dutch Heinz, but in the way that one woman needs one particular man, prove it so that she would obey the desires of her heart instead of the logic of her mind.

He thought of Tonto Miles, of facing him in the morning sunlight. It had seemed to him they were the same, two men hired for their guns, yet there had been the hope that he was more to Peg Cody. Now he sensed that he had made the mistake of reaching for something he could never possess. He had found only the shadow, not the substance.

"You want me to run?" he demanded. "Let folks think I killed Yuma?"

"You've got to," she said. "Don't you see? Clawhammer can't protect a man who's wanted by the law."

"Looks like it ought to make some difference who the man is."

She shook her head. "Not when it concerns Clawhammer."

He made one quick step and took her into his arms. He kissed her, letting her know his feelings, trying to put everything into that kiss which he could not put into words. He failed. He realized it at once. There had been something in her last night; desire, a demand, a hunger for him. It was not in her now.

He let her go and stepped back to the table. "I didn't ask you to marry me last night because I wanted you to feel that I could do something for you. I mean, something bigger than just riding around and making a show of my gun and seeing that Dunning stayed on his side of the creek. I did it today. It was something you couldn't have bought for all the dollars in the valley."

"I know," she said cooly. "You saved the bank and Dunning didn't get my notes. But Lane arrested you for murder. That changes everything."

"For a murder I didn't do," he said hotly. "That shouldn't change anything. You're the one who's changing things."

She shook her head. "It's like I said, I threw myself at you and you threw me back. You changed both our lives for us then." She made a quick gesture as if dismissing it forever. "It's a poor kind of woman who has no pride. I have mine, Kim."

"You threw Clawhammer at me, not yourself. Maybe some day you'll find you're a woman, not a ranch." He turned toward the door and swung back before he reached it. "Yuma Bill didn't sleep any last night. He said he heard you ride out before dawn."

Her lips made a tight line; wariness crept into her eyes. "He dreamed it."

"I don't think so. I'm pretty good at forgetting things I don't want to remember, but there's one thing I can't forget. You had the idea for Yuma to stay at Smith's cabin while I rode into town. He was killed at the cabin."

"Go on," she breached. "Say the rest of it."

"I don't need to say it. Heinz wanted to kill Yuma last night for the dinero that was in the shoe box."

"And I said no. Remember?"

"Yeah, I remember. But after that you had time to think it over."

"Go on, Kim. Say it. Say that I killed Yuma Bill."

He stood looking at her, not more than a step away, nagged by a suspicion that had been buried in his mind all through the afternoon. Still, even after all of this, he could not put it in words. "I'll be riding," he said, and turned toward the door.

"Kim." She gripped his arm and turned him to face her. "You know now that the only thing I really love is Clawhammer."

He nodded. "I guess that's plain enough. You're making a mistake, Peg. You'll come out holding the short end of the stick."

"I'll take my chances . . ."

From outside Rocky called, "Kim, they're coming."

Startled, Peg asked, "Who's that?"

"Rocky Avis."

"You mean . . ." Peg shook her head and began to laugh. "Well, I've been a bigger fool than I ever thought I'd be. You've been in love with Shorty Avis's brat all the time. I asked you last night and you lied to me."

He saw anger in her that swiftly swelled to a wild fury. She would believe what she wanted to believe, no more and no less. He said, "Reckon I'm fired."

"You're fired all right. You bet you're fired. If you're smart, you'll keep riding till you're a thousand miles from here, and don't think you can stay and save your friends on the mesa. Clawhammer needs all the range on this side of the creek. All of it. Do you hear?" Her voice rose until it was the scream of an angry shrew. "I'm building an empire, but I don't need your help. Keep riding and take the Avis kid with you."

He had seen her talk to other men like this, but it was the first time she had ever whipped him with her tongue. Her eyes were bright with fury; her face was red and the corners of her mouth were working. There seemed to be no reason for it, then it occurred to him that she wanted no more responsibility for him; she wanted to feel that she owed him nothing.

Rocky called again, more urgently this time, "Kim, they're coming."

He said, "So long, Peg," and wheeling, left the house.

Limpy, still standing beside Rocky's horse, said, "You'd better travel, mister. I'll steer 'em the wrong way. Clawhammer owes you that much."

"Thanks, Limpy." Kim stepped up. "Look out for her, will you?"

"Sure, but there's only so much a man can do for her."

"So long," Kim said.

"This way," Rocky called.

The posse, quite close now, was coming in on the road that Kim and Rocky had followed a few minutes before. Rocky turned south. Kim swung in beside her, surprised, for he had supposed she would want to go home. To do that, she would have had to cross the creek and swing west. Instead she followed the bench that rose to the left, an indistinct wall in the darkness.

They rode slowly, their horses' hoofs making little sound in the soft grass carpet. The racket of the incoming posse died; then Dunning called out in his great voice, "We're looking for Kim Logan. Seen him?"

Kim could not hear what Limpy said. He wondered what Peg would say. When he had left her, she had been furious enough to want to see him lynched. He doubted whether her anger had cooled so that she would cover up for him. They went on, Kim listening. He had expected pursuit, but there was none. Either Peg had lied for him, or Limpy had sent the posse across the creek on a wild goose chase that might take hours before they found that their man had gone the other way.

The lights in the ranch house flowed together and made a tiny pinpoint, then it was lost to sight. Presently Rocky said, "There's a trail here. We'll swing up on the mesa."

They were two, perhaps three miles south of the creek. Kim said, "I don't savvy this. You're putting the canyon between us and your place."

"That's exactly what I aim to do. We're not going to my place. Limpy will tell them who was with you, so they'll hightail up there."

Kim laughed. "Shorty'll sure be surprised."

"He'll be mighty mad," she said worriedly. "I don't know what he'll do."

"He won't like you sashaying around through the hills with me."

"I know he won't. If I ever go home, he'll rawhide me, and maybe get out his shotgun and make you marry me."

"He wouldn't need his shotgun for that."

She didn't say anything then. They climbed to the sage flat above the bench and angled southeast. This was open country, dotted by runty cedars. A slim moon was showing above the peaks to the east; the stars still glittered in cold brilliance from a clear, wind-swept sky.

Rocky reined up and untying her coat from behind her saddle, slipped into it. She said, her voice expressionless, "You know, Kim, I wouldn't care for a marriage that needed a shotgun."

"It wouldn't . . ."

"No, don't say that. You've had Peg in your mind for a long time. I don't know whether you ever really loved her or not. Maybe you were in love with Clawhammer. Either way, it'll take some time to get it out of your system."

He rolled a smoke and lighted it, the flame throwing a brief light upon his wide mouth and square chin. The match flickered out; he broke it between thumb and forefinger, destroying the last spark before he threw it into the grass. He said, "You've got some pretty sorry notions about me, Rocky. I can't figure out why you've gone to so much trouble for me lately."

"Not sorry notions, Kim. It's just that you're two men."

"Never knew I was twins," he jeered.

"I do. I've known it for a long time. There's the man you have been and the man you could be. I keep wondering which one you're finally going to be."

"Makes me quite a mess, don't it?"

"It'll be a mess if you ride out of the country now," she said. "Some day men like you will disappear, but that day hasn't come yet. Maybe it's a good thing. We need you."

"You think the country will be better off if men like me disappear?"

"Yes. I mean, the man you have been. Anyhow, I couldn't blame you if you did ride on."

'I couldn't," he said quietly. "There's plenty here to hold me."

"You mean you wouldn't leave a murder charge?"

"That's part of it."

"What's the rest of it?"

"You ain't ready to hear about it."

"I'm ready to listen when you're ready to tell it."

"Maybe I won't have to tell it."

"You always have to tell a woman," she said.

They went on, directly east now, the flat gradually lifting toward the rim that lay in front of them. Presently they were in the timber, limbs interlacing above them and blotting the starlight. Rocky rode ahead, following the twisting narrow trail in a way that brought increasing admiration for her in Kim's mind.

They stopped at a spring to water their horses, the first gray hint of dawn touching the eastern sky. Rocky said, "Almost there."

"You're riding through this country like you know it."

"I do. I like to ride at night. Pa claims I'm half owl."

They took the trail again, climbing steep pitches, crossing small parks and coming into the timber again, hoofs dropping silently into the thick mat of pine needles that was seldom disturbed except by the swift passage of a deer. They splashed across a small stream and Rocky turned to follow it.

Daylight had moved in around them, but the air was still sharp with the night chill. Another five minutes brought them to a cabin at the end of a long stretch of aspens that made a splash of light green against the darker mass of the pines.

"This is it," Rocky said, and swung down.

She stood there for a moment, one hand holding to the saddle horn, bone-weary. Kim stepped down and came to her, saying, "We should have stopped. You're all in."

"Not quite." She gave a quick smile that was a light on her face. "They'll never find us here. We can sleep for a week."

"Us? Look here, Rocky, I'm not going to let 'em find you with me. You..."

"You'll have a hard time getting rid of me." She motioned to a shed behind the cabin. "Put the horses up. I'll get breakfast." She yawned and rubbed her eyes. "You know, Kim, I don't think a week will be long enough. A month sounds more like it."

She had not brought any food. he wondered what she would find to cook breakfast with, but when he had finished with the horses and went in, aspen chunks were burning in the stove with bright crackling pops, and the cabin was filled with the fragrance of boiling coffee and frying bacon.

"How did you..."

She turned from the stove, brushing at a stray strand of black hair that fell across her forehead. "Magic. I said hocus-pocus. Then I waved my hands and said abracadabra. That was all it took."

"I didn't know you were that smart."

He looked around, his amazement growing. The timber around Pass Creek Valley was full of prospector's cabins, but none that Kim had seen were like this. It was clean and tight with a bunk at one end, the stove at the other, and a small pine table and two benches in the middle. Shelves behind the stove were filled with cans of food.

Rocky motioned to a bucket on the packed dirt floor. "Fetch in some more water, will you, Kim."

When he returned, she had poured the coffee. She said, "This isn't much of a breakfast, but it'll do." She yawned again. "I'm about to fall over in my tracks. I didn't get much sleep the night before, either. By the time I took the body in..."

"Body? You mean you took that hombre in who fell off the cliff?"

She laughed shakily. "My head's kind of fuzzy. I wasn't going to tell you that. I just didn't have time to go home and get Pa. Besides, I wanted to be in town when you and Yuma Bill got there." She dropped down on one of the benches, suddenly defiant. "I wasn't sure Pa would do it. He's awful stubborn sometimes."

He stood looking down at her, more humble than he had ever been before in his life. He had always thought of her as more girl than woman, probably because she was small-bodied, or perhaps because she seemed child-like in so many of her desires. Now he realized that what he had considered childishness was not that at all. She was a product of the life she lived: simple, without pretense or sham, almost brutally honest with herself and others, and filled with a kind of courage that few men could claim.

"If I live a million years," he said, "I'll never be able to pay you ..."

"Sit down," she broke in sharply. "You don't owe me anything, so don't talk that way. The trouble with you is that you've always thought there was nothing you and your gun couldn't do. You're going to find out different."

"I have already," he said and took the bench across the table from her.

CHAPTER 13
PROMISE OF EVIDENCE

It was late afternoon when Kim woke. He had gone to sleep in the shadow of the shed. Now the sun had moved far to the west and was drenching him with its warmth. He got up, and walking to the creek, washed his face. He had a brief glimpse of himself in the unruffled surface of a deep pool and shook his head in disapproval. He needed a shave, his yellow hair was matted and overlong, and his gaunt face seemed more gaunt than ever.

"You look pretty damn tough, fella," he said aloud.

He hunkered beside the stream in the shade of a pine and rolled a smoke. Constant riding had honed his long body down to skin and hard muscle and bone; never-ending vigilance had cut lines around his eyes that made him look years older than what he was. Now, and it seemed as if it was the first time in months, he felt no need for vigilance. He was at peace. The impending violence which had long threatened the valley would still be like a stream running in full flood, but at this moment it seemed so remote that it could be shoved into the outer fringe of thought.

A jay flew by, a flash of vivid blue. Overhead a woodpecker was working on a tree with jack-hammer violence. Below him a foot-long trout flashed across the pool like a black knifing shadow. it struck Kim then that he had been too busy trying to keep alive in a world of trouble to notice things like this. This was another world, Rocky's world. She had shared its strength and honesty; it had made her what she was.

It was strange, he thought, how he had lived in country like this most of his life, yet actually he had not known it at all. He had merely passed through it. He flipped his cigarette stub into the creek and lay back staring at the clean sky.

There was no wind, just the quiet steady downpouring of the sun's rays. Here were the smells of a moist earth and pine needles and wild flowers, all flowing together into one common mountain smell. Here were sounds, the squawking of the jay, the rhythmical clattering of the woodpecker, the creek song as it dropped over a rock ledge above the pool, sounds that fell togethe as naturally as those from a trained orchestra, and paradoxically, did not mar the great silence.

He did not know that Rocky had come up behind him until she asked, "Sleeping?"

He jumped and rolled and grabbed for his gun, the natural react on of a man who has long lived with danger. Then he lay motionless, staring up at her and feeling foolish. He started to tell her to never sneak up on him like that again, but he caught himself in time. She hadn't sneaked up on him. It was her natural way of moving.

"No. Dreaming, I guess. How'd you sleep?"

"I didn't. I just died."

He sat up, feeling of his stubbly chin. "I took a look at myself while ago. Sure handsome."

"You look natural." She dropped down beside him. "I didn't tell you this morning, but I think Brit will be along, so

I might as well. This is his cabin."

He reached for the makings. "Comes out to fish, I suppose."

"No. He thinks this is still mining country. He's got a prospect hole across the creek." She motioned toward it. "Over behind that brush. He tells folks in town that he comes up here to fish, but it's really to dig."

"How did you know about his cabin?"

"I stumbled onto it during a storm. Brit was here. He swore me to secrecy. Made me promise that I'd make all my children be hard-rock miners if I ever told anybody, but that promise won't apply to you. He knew I was bringing you out here."

"Sure be awful, having your children turn out to be hard-rock miners."

She laughed. "It would for a fact. I like it on top of the ground."

"So that's why there was grub."

She nodded. "He keeps enough here to last two or three weeks. He was snowed in once."

"Funny a banker would get the notion he was a prospector."

"Not so funny. Doc Frazee's the same way. They'd like to see Ganado come back and the only way they know to bring it back is to have another mining boom." She lay on the bank, her slim body curled so that the hem of her riding skirt worked up to her knees. She didn't notice; her eyes were on the pool, her tanned face eagerly alert. "Kim, there's enough trout down there for supper. Want me to get Brit's pole for you?"

"I wouldn't know what to do with a fish if he reached up and hollered for me to pull him out."

She rolled over, tugging at her skirt. "You mean you've never gone fishing?"

"Not since I was a kid. Been too busy "

For no reason that Kim could see, she was suddenly angry. "Too busy! Hell's bells, if all you've done was to ride around stomping snakes, you'd better start fishing."

He had smoked his cigarette down and thrown the stub into the creek. Automatically he reached for paper and tobacco and rolled another, sensing the same scorn that had been in her when he had stopped with Yuma Bill and she had talked about him being a snake stomper. He said nothing until he lighted his cigarette. She was sitting up, sharp little chin resting on her knees, dark eyes staring morosely at the big pine across the creek.

"Ever figure you might have me wrong?" he said.

"No. I don't, either. There's a place for fighting and a place for work, but you don't know anything about the work. Just the fighting."

He grinned, the cigarette dangling from one corner of his mouth, the blue smoke curling up lazily before his lean face. "Maybe I'm a better snake stomper than a brush popper, but I've done a little staring at the rear of a cow, too. I helped drive a Texas herd plumb to Dakota. Surprised?"

"I sure am," she said skeptically. "I didn't think you'd ever take a chance on ruining your gun hand with a rope or a branding iron."

"Here's another surprise. I've got a thousand dollars in Bonham's bank. Saved it since I got here. Had a notion I'd like to own a little outfit. Up by your place, maybe. Anyhow, I thought I'd keep on working for Peg as long as I could so I'd have a stake when I started."

"You might try poker," she jeered.

"Naw, I'm about as bad a player as Johnny Naylor. That's why I was broke when I got here." He tossed a rock into the creek and watched the ripples spread across the pool. "Just before I left Yuma Bill yesterday morning, he said something about throwing in with me and buying a ranch here in the valley."

She stared at him for a long moment, lips parted as she thought about what he had said. "When he was murdered, you lost your chance."

"Any chance except what I make myself. A man don't buy

many cows and calves with a thousand dollars."

"Well, I am surprised," Rocky said. "It's the other side of you I was talking about."

He grinned wryly, "I've done some thinking but not much talking. I did a lot more thinking after I met Yuma Bill. Seems like I can't forget the hombre who fell off the rim. And Tonto Miles. Sooner or later I'll get the same." He threw his cigarette away in a sudden violent gesture. "A man can't help dying alone, but it's sure hell to live alone."

"I know," she breathed. "I know." She stiffened and was silent, head cocked. Then she said, "Somebody's coming up the trail. Must be Brit. I'll get supper. You cut some wood."

She jumped up and ran into the cabin. Kim sat motionless for a moment, listening, but he heard nothing. he go up, shaking his head. Compared to most of the men he had ridden with, his ears were good, but Rocky made him feel like a greenhorn.

There was a pile of dry aspen in one corner of the shed; an ax leaned against the log wall. He began to chop, watching the trail below the cabin, and presently Brit Bonham appeared. Kim carried an armload of wood into the cabin and when he came out, Bonham had dismounted in front.

"Well, I see you outran 'em," Bonham said. "Figured you would. Don't reckon nobody in the country knows these hills like Rocky does unless it's Della."

Kim told him what had happened, and asked, "Dunning get back to town?"

Bonham shook his head. "Hadn't got back when I left. Kind o' worries me. Dunning sure don't like failures, and so far that's all he's had. Can't do no damage, though, I guess."

"He can play hell with Clawhammer."

Bonham's brows lifted. "Thought you said Peg fired you."

"She did, but I still don't cotton to the notion of Dunning moving across the creek."

"Well, Peg's old Sam Cody's daughter, and I reckon he taught her how to take care of herself. Catch any fish?"

"No."

"Then you've been wasting your day. Take care of my mare. I'll çatch our supper."

By the time Kim had finished staking out the mare and cut another armload of wood, Bonham had pulled three pan-sized trout out of the pool. He cleaned and brought them in, saying "Can't understand a man not fishing when he's got a chance. Good for your soul, Kim."

Rocky looked up from setting the table. "He's never had time to learn, Brit."

"Time," Bonham snorted. "Say, when a man hasn't got time to learn too fish, he's almighty busy. Want me to fry 'em, Rocky?"

"Go ahead," she said.

It was a silent meal, a sudden impatience in Kim at this inactivity. Finishing his coffee, he rose and walked to the door. The sun was down now, and the timber had blotted up most of the thinning light. Rocky had lighted a lamp, and Kim's shadow made a long dark splotch in the rectangle of lamplight spilling out through the doorway.

He rolled a smoke, thinking of what had to be done. He couldn't stay here, and as things stood now, he couldn't go back to Ganado. Still, if Phil Martin was in town, that was where Kim must go. Martin had placed the murder charge against him, so Martin was the one who could clear him.

Without turning, Kim asked, "Martin still in Ganado?"

"Yeah. Doc's keeping him. Seems like he should have gone to bed instead of sashaying around. Now he's a purty sick man."

"Brit, did you know that Yuma Bill was going into the cattle business here?" Rocky asked. "He was planning on taking Kim in as a partner."

"Well, I ain't surprised." Bonham said. "He sold out most of his holdings around Las Animas. I figured he'd stay hereabouts, and if he'd lived, he couldn't have kept his fingers off a ranch."

"What's going to happen to that money Kim brought to you?" Rocky asked.

"Well, that's something I've been asking myself," Bonham said somberly. "Yuma getting beefed sure put things into a mess. I doubt that he left a will, and he didn't have a single living relative. I know that."

"Then he'd want you to have it, you and Kim, wouldn't he?"

"I guess he would."

"Then why don't you use it to buy a big herd and let Kim have his ranch?"

Kim walked back to the table. "She's trying to make a working man out of me."

"It's what you want, isn't it?" Rocky demanded.

"I told you it was, but taking a dead man's money don't seem the right way to get it."

"Maybe marrying a redhead with a ranch would be?" Rocky flared.

"Maybe."

"It'd be right enough, Kim," Bonham said slowly. "As soon as I see the bank ain't gonna need it, I wouldn't be against doing something like that, only..."

He paused, turning his eyes from Rocky to Kim and back to the girl, his face thoughtful. Rocky asked, "Only what?"

"I ain't sure." Bonham got up and walked to the stove. He stood with his back to it, craggy face mirroring the uncertainty that gripped him. "I just ain't sure. You see, Rocky, me and Doc Frazee and Charlie Bemis, well, we're old. Our string's about wound up. The trouble is that the other bunch are young men. Johnny Naylor and Luke Haines and Fred Galt ain't what you'd call real solid."

"Say the rest of it, Brit," Kim said tonelessly. "I'm a fiddlefoot who's likely to be dragging out of here tomorrow."

"Well, damn it, you are," Bonham said, "and there ain't nobody else who can put the brake on Dunning. Or Peg, neither, if she gets some of old Sam's ideas."

"She's already got them. Brit, you're forgetting one thing." Rocky leaned forward. "My people."

Bonham gestured impatiently. "And you're forgetting that

when Sam Cody made a few faces at 'em, they tucked their tails and lined out for the mesa, your dad included. Old Sam moved in. The east side of the valley is Clawhammer range whether you like it or not. Now that money is a kind of trust, you might say, and I've got to decide what to do with it along the line of what Yuma Bill would want."

"Like planting the right seed," Kim said.

Bonham gave him a defiant glance. "I don't know if you're trying to hooraw me or not, but that's exactly what I mean. He kind o' stole that money in the first place. Then he got a change of heart, but there wasn't no way to give it back, so he was bent on doing some good with it."

"Wouldn't it be good to bring peace to the valley?" Rocky asked.

Bonham shook his head. "You can't turn the clock back, Rocky, and I ain't sure putting Kim on a ranch would stop Dunning or Peg."

"He's done pretty well so far," Rocky said.

"Just a skirmish. The big fight's still ahead, and I doubt that we've got enough on our side to win it."

"I'm going back to Ganado," Kim said, "and I'll get a different story out of Martin."

"Doc Frazee's working on Martin already." Bonham came back to the table. "Kim, where would you have gone if you'd been Salty Smith?"

"Wouldn't be north. No place to go. Wouldn't be west 'cause that'd take him past Dunning's spread. He'd have a rough trip getting across the line into New Mexico if he went south. So I reckon he'd head for the pass and go to Del Norte."

Pleased, Bonham laughed. "That's the way everybody but Smith would figure. Not old Salty, though. He'd ask himself what folks would expect him to do, then he'd cross 'em up. He headed south, but he didn't try getting across the line. He's in Sky City."

"He couldn't hide in a dinky burg like that. Dunning's sure to find him."

"That's what I figure. If he does, he'll shut Smith's mouth for good, but Smith thinks he's safe. Fatty York runs the hotel and he's a friend of Smith's."

"How do you know Salty's there?"

Bonham laughed again, proud of himself. "I kind o' tricked Fatty. Soon as the posse left Ganado I sent a man to Sky City. You see, Smith never kept much money on him. Drank it up as fast as his pension came in, so I talked him into putting ten dollars in the bank every month for burial money. Kind of proud, Smith is. He didn't want charity, so he's been depositing the ten dollars and drinking up the rest. Well, I sent a note to Fatty York along with a hundred dollars, telling him it was Smith's burial money but to use it to take care of him. York took it. That means Smith's there, or York wouldn't have touched it."

"I'd better go see Smith." Kim picked up his hat. "Dunning might make the same guess you did."

' Wouldn't surprise me if he had a man down there already," Bonham said. "I thought you'd want to see what you could do with Smith. If you're gonna get yourself cleared, it'll be Smith or Martin who does it."

Kim moved to the door, then turned back, smiling a little as he pinned his eyes on Rocky's grave face. "Thanks for everything, Shamrock."

She rose and walked to him, worried but not angry as she usually was when he called her by her name. She said in a low desperate voice, "You can't go, Kim. Not yet."

"I've got to. You helped me buy some time. That's what I needed."

"You haven't bought enough. ou might as well have stayed in Ganado."

"No. We had a ride and some fun. I'm just sorry you had to risk your neck to save mine."

She tilted her head back so that she could see his face. She said, "Kim, I wanted to be with you long enough so you'd trust me and know I'm not lying to you."

"I've been with you that long," he said quickly.

She put her hands on his arms, gripping them tightly. "Then believe this. Peg and Dunning aren't fighting. She's in love with him."

There was nothing she could have said that would have shocked him more than that, and he let his face show it. He said, "You're mistaken. You must be."

"No. I know what I'm talking about. I've spied on them. I'm not ashamed of it, either. I wouldn't spy on anyone else, but I did them. Della has, too. We've seen him kiss her. I tell you they're working together."

"What do you think, Brit?" Kim asked.

"Hard to believe," the banker said, "but it explains some things I've wondered about. Dunning's done a lot of talking about busting Clawhammer, but he ain't done much busting."

"But what would it get them?"

"I couldn't say," Bonham said slowly. "On the face of it there don't seem to much sense to talk about fighting while they're kissing each other on the side."

"You don't believe me, do you, Kim?" Rocky cried. "You think I'm lying because I hate Peg."

"I just think you're wrong."

"All right," she breathed. "Believe anything you want to, but don't go back to Clawhammer. Promise me you won't."

"I can't make a promise like that."

"Kim, you owe me your life," she whispered, her hands still clutching his arms, her knuckles white. "Kim, Kim, don't throw it away. If you go back to Clawhammer, you'll never get away alive."

"I'm beholden to you," he said stiffly, "but I can't bind myself by promises. Not even to you."

He pulled his arms away from her hands and turning, left the cabin. Minutes later he rode down the creek, and as he passed the open door, he saw that Rocky was sitting at the table, her head on her arms. He went on down slope, an aching emptiness in him. He had talked lightly about not needing a shotgun to marry her, too lightly. Now he knew he loved her.

His thoughts had been muddied up, living close to Peg as he had for a year and thinking he loved her. It had been cheap and he was ashamed. Peg had her way of appealing to a man; he would never forget the way she had kissed him, but that kiss had not been prompted by love. Nor could he believe she loved Dunning. It did not seem important either way.

One thought lay in his mind like a smoldering coal. Rocky did not understand why he had refused to make the promise she had asked; she would be thinking he was still in love with Peg. So he had built a wall between him and Rocky, and it might be impossible to break through to her again, to regain the intimacy that had briefly been theirs. He rode on down the twisting trail, and the night was very dark around him.

CHAPTER 14

SKY CITY

Twice Kim lost the trail, and both times it took several minutes to find it again. Then the black mass of the timber was behind him, and he was on the flat with its sagebrush and scattered cedars. He angled southwest, leaving the trail that he and Rocky had followed the night before.

It had not rained that day at Bonham's cabin, but it had rained here, and the aire was damp and tangy with sage smell. The sky was still overcast, and along the southern horizon lightning played with quick slashing thrusts that threw a weird light upon a dark earth and fled and came again.

Kim rode by instinct, for there were no stars to guide him. At times he wondered if he was going in the direction he wanted to, for in this pitch blackness a man could easily make a half circle and reverse himself. He thought with grim humor that the lights of Ganado might suddenly appear in front of him and he would discover that he was going north instead of south.

He reached the bench and let his buckskin have his head. The animal picked his way down the steep pitch, sliding a little in he mud, for apparently the rain had been heavy here. Then he was on the level grassy floor of the valley, and he came, near midnight, to a stream.

Kim reined up, listening, but there was no sound except that of some furtive night animal scurrying among the willows and the distant call of a coyote from a high point on the rim to the east. Kim had not expected to run into Dunning and the posse. Distance itself made it unlikely. They would not be in this end of the valley anyhow if they had gone to Shorty Avis' place. They would still be north of Ganado Canyon. But long experience at this game, both as the hunter and the hunted, had developed a caution in him so he sat his saddle for serveral minutes, head turned to catch any sound that might drift in from the level floor of the valley.

He was certain now that he was where he wanted to be. Judging from the size of the stream, this was Pass Creek. It ran almost due south. Somewhere to the north Ganado Creek flowed into Pass Creek. There was no meandering about it here, for the tilt of the land was greater than north of town. At this place the stream moved with a steady chatter that would, a few miles to the south, become a sullen roar as it churned between the high walls of the canyon before turning west where it would eventually meet the Colorado.

Kim rode downstream, found a break in the willows, and forded the creek. Again he turned south, following the old road that now had little travel, but at one time had known a steady stream of stage-coaches moving between Sky City and Ganado.

Presently the creek dropped below the road that was now a narrow shelf carved out of the canyon wall. A solitary light showed ahead. He reined up again and listened, but he heard nothing except the steady hammering of the creek as it spewed in white-foamed fury around the huge boulders in its bed. He reined on, slowly, for he had reached Sky City.

It was a strange town, the canyon dropping away on one side, a sheer sandstone wall rising above it on the other, clinging here on a shelf that was barely wide enough for the buildings and the single street that ran in front of them. Kim had been here only once before, but he remembered it well, for Sky City was a town that, once seen, could not be easily forgotten. He pictured it now, the weathered false fronts of the deserted buildings, the long string of cabins with their windows and doors gone and their roofs falling in.

Fatty York's hotel was the only building still in use. He had a small store, a post office, and a bar along with a dining room and the few rooms on the second floor that he rented. Ed Lane made it a rule to stay out of Sky City. It was no place for a sheriff, particularly a careful one like Lane. There were still a few prospectors who haunted the high country to the south and came in twice a year to buy supplies, but the bulk of Fatty York's business was with the toughs who had beaten a posse out of New Mexico.

Kim tied in front of the hotel. There was another horse at the end of the hitch pole. Kim moved toward it, keeping off the boardwalk that was three steps above the street level. He stopped before he reached a patch of light falling into the street from the hotel windows and stood studying the horse.

It was possible that the animal belonged to a man on the dodge who had just got in, but that seemed unlikely. If that was the case, the horse would probably have been put away in York's stable down the street. It was Kim's guess that someone planned to ride out soon, possibly an HD man looking for Salty Smith.

From where Kim stood in the fringe of light he could look into the hotel lobby. Fatty York seemed to be dozing behind the desk, his bald head shiny in the lamplight. No one else was in sight. The bar and dining room were on the other side of the lobby, the interior dark.

Kim stepped up on the walk and went in. York stirred and

opened his eyes. He blinked owlishly for a moment and rubbed his face, then got up and shook his head as if to clear the cobwebs from his mind. He said, "Howdy, Logan. Ain't you off your reservation?"

"Came down to look at the scenery," Kim said.

York laughed, making a show of his amusement. "Scenery, is it? Well, boy, we've got that. Maybe I should advertise."

York was a tall man, but because of his great width, he gave the impression of being shorter than he was. He wore a dark bushy mustache that made a sharp contrast with the pale skin of his face. Kim had no idea how far the man could be trusted. Bonham considered him honest, but Kim was always skeptical of those who made their living from the owl-hoot fringe of society.

"Advertising wouldn't do your business no good, would it?" Kim asked.

York laughed again, taking no offense at what Kim said, "It wouldn't for a fact. I do purty well, but a man oughtta do well, living in this hell hole." He picked up a half-chewed cigar from the desk and put it into his mouth. "Sky City, a population one human being and five thousand ghosts. Funny thing, how fellers like me and Brit Bonham up there in Ganado hang on, hoping the old camps will come back and knowing damned well they never will. Oughtta have our heads examined."

Kim made a quick study of the lobby while York talked. The store and post office were on one side, the door shut and probably locked at this time of night. On the opposite side of the lobby the door into the bar was open, a thin finger of light falling into it from the lamp on the desk. An open stairway to York's left led to the rooms upstairs. The chances were that the man who owned the other horse was not far away. He might have gone upstairs, or he might be in the bar, listening.

Casually Kim made a slow turn so that he faced the bar door, right hand at his side, left dropped casually on the desk. He asked, "How's business?"

York laughed as if everything Kim said was funny. "It

ain't good, Logan. Too peaceful south of the line. What this country needs is a good bank robbery."

"I don't reckon you'd be interested in keeping a man who's wanted in Colorado?"

"Why, I might." York scratched his blob of a nose, watery eyes fixed on Kim. "I just might for a price. No price, no keep. You savvy that?"

"Sure. I've got the price all right, and I don't reckon Ed Lane's likely to be poking his nose down here. He don't want it shot off, Ed don't." Kim leaned against the desk, his mouth close to York's ear. He whispered, "I want to see Salty."

There was no change of expression on York's droopy-cheeked face. "I reckon that's right. Ed sure is a careful gent." He took the cigar out of his mouth, and said in a whisper that barely reached Kim's ears. "Pat Monroney's in the bar."

Kim nodded. He was not surprised. Monroney was one of Dunning's gun hands who had come to the valley within the last year, the kind who was fitted for this sort of job. Kim knew him slightly, but even a nodding acquaintance with the man was enough to peg him as a backshooting killer. He would murder old Salty Smith as casually as he would shoot the head off a prairie dog.

"I don't cotton much to the notion of going on across the line," Kim said. "I like it on this side, but damn it, Ganado ain't real healthy for me."

York's big laugh boomed out again, "I heard about that. Well, you'll be as safe here as if you was in church. Good grub three times a day, plenty of whiskey, and damned fine bed. Fifty dollars a day."

"Fair enough," Kim said. "Let's have a drink on it. Then I'll see how good that bed of yours is. Been riding so long I wore calluses on my saddle."

"Now that's a hell of a place to get calluses." This time York didn't laugh. He put the cigar back into his mouth and chewed on it. Then he said, "Maybe you'd better go on up and start trying the bed. We'll have the drink in the morning."

Monroney appeared in the doorway. "I'll drink with Logan, Fatty. We'll drink to Salty Smith."

York picked up the lamp and waddled into the bar. "All right, if that's what you want, only it's a hell of a thing to drink at this time of night."

Monroney stepped back into the bar. As Kim followed York through the door, Monroney gave him a wink. "Fatty figgers we ain't good pay. Stingy, that's what he is. Fifty dollars a day is standard rate in this boar's nest. I've had some friends who holed up here. It ain't right. They knock a bank over, take all the risks, and then they have to give what they've made to this keg of lard who don't do nothing but rustle grub and hand out a bottle of Valley Tan now and then."

"Don't be so damned smart, friend," York growled sullenly, "Ain't no law making you stay here."

"I ain't staying long." Monroney picked up the bottle and glasses that York had set on the bar and moved to the table. "Sit down, Logan."

Kim followed, wondering about this. Monroney was a knot-headed man with a scarred face and a pair of beady eyes set too close together astride a beaky nose. He was the one man in Dunning's outfit that Kim regarded with high contempt. If it had been Tonto Miles or Phil Martin, he would have come out of the bar with his gun smoking, but that would have entailed some danger, and Monroney was the sort who avoided danger if he could. It was Kim's guess that he had some kind of a trick up his sleeve that he considered foolproof, or he would have remained under cover.

Monroney poured the drinks and shoved one glass across the table. Kim sat down across the table from him, watching Monroney's hands. He said, "So we're drinking to Salty Smith."

"That's right." Monroney's thin l ps held what was meant to be a genial smile. "You know, Logan, you fooled us, which same includes Dunning. We figgered you was just bluff, making all that big talk about Clawhammer hanging onto every foot of range that old Sam had claimed. Well, we know different. Tonto found out how good you are with a six."

Monroney had his drink and put the empty glass down. "I kind o' liked Tonto, but the way I hear it, he had his chance. Well, you see how it is. Talk don't really hurt nothing, but it's different now. If you was smart, you'd get across the line."

Kim waited, saying nothing, waiting for the move that he knew Monroney planned to make. This was like the man, talking with cool confidence, very casually, all the time hoping that Kim's nerves were knotting. There was a moment of silence, broken only by York's heavy breathing from where he stood behind the bar.

Then Monroney, still casual, poured another drink and lifted the glass to his mouth, right hand dropping below the table top. Kim came up out of his chair like a thin spring uncoiling. He heaved the table over on Monroney, his glass and bottle spilling to the floor, and backed away, drawing his .44.

The HD man, not expecting this, fell sideways and rolled and came up with his gun. Kim fired, getting Monroney in the chest. Monroney's shot was a split second slow and went wide. Kim let go with another shot, smashing Monroney's gun arm.

That was all. Monroney lay flat on his back, staring up at Kim and cursing him in a low, wicked tone, the knowledge of death haunting his beady eyes. York came across the room, still breathing hard. He said, "You ain't smart, Monroney. Not half as smart as you allowed."

"A man's smart if he makes it." Monroney's left hand gripped his shirt front. His fingers straightened and he raised his hand and looked at the blood. "He ain't smart if he don't make it. So I ain't smart."

Then, with the last strength that was in him, he grabbed the gun that lay beside him and lifted it. Kim took one quick step and kicked the gun out of Monroney's hand, sending it clattering across the floor. Monroney fell back, eyes glazed, blood showing on his lips. He took one hard, sawing breath, then he was still.

"First time I was ever glad to see a man die," York said. "He was fixing to drill you under the table when he took that drink."

"I know," Kim said.

"He got the drop on me," York said bitterly. "I ain't much good with a gun. Don't have to be. The boys all figger they'll need me some day. If Monroney had drilled me, one of 'em would have got him. He should have known that."

Kim moved toward the lobby, saying, "Come on. I want to see Salty."

York picked up the lamp and tromped through the door. He set the lamp on the desk and faced Kim, chewing fiercely on a cigar. He asked, "What do you want with him?"

"He's gonna answer a question."

"Look, Logan. Salty's a friend of mine." York motioned with a wide inclusive gesture. "I've always been too fat to be good for anything. I mean, like punching cows or working in a mine. Well, I didn't have much money when I came here. Salty took a liking to me and staked me to this. Now I'm returning the favor. I'm protecting him. Savvy?"

"I didn't come here to hurt him," Kim said quietly. "It's the other way around. As long as Dunning's riding high around here, Salty's in a tight. If I can keep my neck out of a rope long enough, I'll get Dunning. Then Salty can go back home."

Still York hesitated. He said finally, "It ain't that simple. Not to me. I dunno what's going on up the valley, but I do know you're with Clawhammer. Why don't you go back and do your fighting where you oughtta?"

"They want me for murder," Kim answered. "I can't do no fighting till I clean that up. Salty can do it for me."

"How do you figger Salty knows anything?"

"He wouldn't be here if he didn't know who killed Yuma

Bill."

Sweat broke out across the fat man's face. He kept chewing on his cigar, and time ran on until the seconds piled up into a minute. Kim, sensing the agony of uncertainty that was in the man, said patiently, "I told you I wasn't here to hurt the old man, York. I aim to do him a favor as well as myself."

"All right," York said. "I'll go get him, but if you lay a hand on him, I'll black your name from here to hell."

York took the lamp and started up the stairs, the steps creaking under his great weight. Kim followed. York called back over his shoulder, "Stay there. I told you I'd get him."

"I'll tag along."

York turned, holding the lamp high, its light falling across Kim's dark, stubble-covered face. "My word goes around here. Savvy?"

"You could get him out while I waited."

"Damn it, I . . ."

"Ever feel a rope on your neck?" Kim asked.

"No."

"I've got one waiting for me in Ganado if I let Salty get away from me. Now go on."

York turned and went on. Reaching the hall, he moved along it in his lumbering walk to the back room. He tapped on the door, calling, "Salty."

"What's wrong?" the old man quavered.

York pushed the door open and went in. "Nothing now, Salty. Everything's all right." He set the lamp on the bureau and turned to face Smith. "There was plenty wrong while ago. Monroney was here. He was aiming to make me tell him where you was, but Logan came in and drilled him."

Kim stood in the doorway, looking at Smith who was eyeing him in abject fear. He cried out, "Go away, Logan. I don't know nothing."

"Logan ain't here to hurt you, Salty," York said, "but Monroney would have if Logan hadn't got him. You owe him something, so you'd best tell him what he wants to know."

Smith looked down at the floor. "I don't know nothing."

"You know who killed Yuma Bill," Kim said. "Dunning wants to hang me for it."

Smith's gnarled hands fisted. He sat on the edge of the bed, a dirty bearded old man smelling of stale sweat and cheap whiskey. Kim, seeing him this way, found it hard to believe that he had once been a wealthy man and one of the town fathers of Ganado.

"I don't know nothing," Smith said, still staring at the floor.

"You want to go back home," York urged. "Only way to fix it so you can is to tell Logan."

"He won't fix nothing," Smith shrilled. "Logan's a Clawhammer man. He'll kill me. Monroney didn't have nothing against me."

"You're wrong, Salty," York said patiently. "I'm your friend. You've got to believe me when I tell you that Monroney would have killed me and you both. He's the one who wanted to shut your mouth."

Kim crossed the room and sat down beside Smith. "Phil Martin claims I did it. You and me know different. I'm not working for Clawhammer any more. That makes a hell of a lot of difference, Salty."

"You're lying."

"No, Peg fired me. Sometimes a man don't know who his friends are. Bonham helped bust me out of jail. Bonham's your friend, too."

"A good friend," Smith whispered. "It's you I don't know about. I figgered you'd kill me if I talked."

"No," Kim said with the patience he would have used with a child, "it's Dunning's bunch that want to kill you. I've got to clear myself. Then I can help you."

Smith turned bloodshot eyes to York. "I'd like to go home, Fatty. I'd like to go home."

"Tell him," York urged. 'It ain't like we figgered, or Monroney wouldn't have come here tonight."

"All right, I'll tell him." Smith's hands gripped his knees. He leaned forward, shoulders sagging. "I was fishing. See? I wasn't paying no attention to anything. I was just above my cabin a piece. I had a bite and I was trying to get that trout out from under a willow when I heard a shot. I looked up. One feller was on the ground. This other feller had a smoking gun in his hand. He stooped down and yanked off the dead man's money belt."

"Who was it?" Kim asked.

Smith drew back, suspicion clouding his mind again. "You're Clawhammer. I don't trust you."

"I'm not working for Clawhammer," Kim told him again, "but it wouldn't make any difference if I was. You see, Monroney wouldn't have been here to shut your mouth if it had been a Clawhammer man who killed Yuma Bill."

"But I saw what I saw," Smith shouted. "It was Clawhammer, I tell you. It was..." He turned his eyes to York. "Get me a drink, Fatty. Seems like I can't remember nothing."

"No drink," Kim said, impatience crowding him. "Not till he answers my question."

"It . . ." Smith got up. "It was . . ." He backed across the room, watching Kim with worried uncertainty. Then he blurted. "It was Dutch Heinz."

Kim forgot to breathe. He had the same feeling that he'd had when Rocky had told him Peg was in love with Dunning. It didn't seem possible that Dutch Heinz had killed Yuma Bill, not with Dunning and Martin trying to protect the killer. Then he remembered other things: Heinz wanting to rob Yuma Bill that night in Peg's kitchen, of Peg's pressing need for money, Yuma Bill's saying he had heard someone ride out of the yard that night. Kim still didn't have all the threads, but he had enough to form the pattern. Dunning and Heinz and Peg were together.

"Surprised?" York asked.

"Plenty."

Kim got up from the bed, watching Salty Smith who had

backed against the wall and was staring at him with the soul-deep fear of a man who thinks he may still be murdered.

"What are you gonna do?" York asked.

"Can't let Smith go back," Kim said thoughtfully. "Too dangerous. You'll have to keep him for a while. Till you get word that Dunning's finished. Then he can go home. you fetch that bottle and bring up a pen and paper. Salty's gonna write out a statement of what he saw, and I'll shove it down Ed Lane's throat."

"The way I heard it, Martin claimed you..."

"You heard right," Kim said, "but now that I know who did beef Yuma Bill, Martin's gonna change his story." Kim jerked his head at the door. "Go get that bottle. Salty deserves it."

CHAPTER 15
THE TORCH

It was mid-morning when Kim reached Ganado. He was sleepy and hungry and more tired than he had ever been before in his life. Still, food and sleep must wait. He had no way of knowing where the posse was, but by this time every member would be worn to a frazzle if it had kept on the move.

The question in Kim's mind was whether the posse ad returned to town. Ed Lane had probably caught up with Dunning and the others. The trick would be to get him and Phil Martin together. If Kim could do that, he was reasonably sure he could clear himself.

Avoiding the business block, Kim rode into town on a side street that, like most of Ganado's streets, was flanked by deserted houses. If he was seen, there was no indication of it. The entire town seemed as empty of life as the empty buildings facing the street.

Ed Lane lived in a white house one block east of the

courthouse. Kim turned into an alley and came to the rear of the sheriff's place. The only sign of life was the column of smoke rising from the chimney. Dismounting, Kim led his buckskin into Lane's barn and left him in the second stall so he would not be seen by anyone casually passing the sheriff's house. Lane's horse was in the first stall, and judging from his appearance, he had been ridden long and hard.

Kim walked up the path to the back door, hoping that Lane would be inside. He knocked, and Lane's housekeeper opened the door. Without waiting for an invitation, Kim shoved past her into the house.

"I want to see Lane," Kim said.

The woman began to swell up. She said in a strident voice, "You can't force your way into a house like this. Ed will arrest you for breaking and entering. Now get out before I call him."

"I've already entered, and I'll sure break something if I don't see Ed. Where is he?"

The woman backed away toward the stove, apparently recognizing him, for she was afraid. "You're... you're Kim Logan, ain't you?"

"That's right. Where's Lane?"

"You're wanted for murder. Now you've come here to kill . . ."

"Shut up. I'm not going to hurt you. Or Ed if he behaves, but I don't figure on standing here all morning asking you where he is."

"He's asleep. He just got in a little while ago."

"Looks like he'll be waking up pronto. Which room?"

She kept backing away from Kim until she stood with her back pressed against the sink. Now she put her hands behind her and gripped it. "Don't you come no closer. Don't you lay a hand on me."

The woman was a middle-aged blonde, as dumpy as a filled wool sack. Kim said mildly, "You're exaggerating your talents, ma'am. Ed's the one I want. Now unless you want him hurt, you stay right there, peaceful like."

He stepped into the living room. One door opened into the parlor; the door on the other side of the room was closed. Kim opened it and looked in. He had guessed right. It was Lane's bedroom. He lay crosswise on the bed in the manner of a man who had fallen there and gone to sleep at once, too tired to move. He had not even bothered to undress. Only his coat, Stetson, and gun belt were on the chair beside the bed.

Kim pulled the chair back so Lane could not reach his gun. Then he put up the blind and the morning sunshine cut squarely across the sheriff's face.

"Time to get up and start the day, Ed," Kim said, shaking Lane.

The sheriff turned over, gave a great gurgling snore, the corners of his mouth working, and kept on sleeping. Kim shook him again, this time with considerable violence, and Lane reared up, eyes blinking in the sunlight.

"No sense sleeping all day, Ed," Kim said. "Time to get up."

Recognition struck Lane then, and his eyes became bright with fear. His face and the front of his shiny bald head turned white; he gave out a hoarse yelp and rolled to the side of his bed, both hands reaching out in a wild grab for his gun. The chair wasn't where he had left it, and because there was nothing to sustain him, he fell out of bed, hitting the floor with a great clatter and shaking a picture on the wall above him.

"Now what do you know about that?" Kim stood with one foot on a chair rung, a hand dropped on the gun belt dangling over the back. "Somebody moved that chair. Ain't that a hell of a note?"

Lane sat up, rubbed his eyes and shook his head. He blurted, "What do you want?"

"Heard you was looking for me, so I came in. Funny thing, Ed. You don't seem real pleased about it."

"Sure, sure. You're showing sense now. Too bad Bonham didn't show as much when he helped bust you out. I'll have him and that Della Naylor keeping you company behind bars afore the day's over."

Lane got to his feet and started toward the chair. He stopped abruptly when Kim held up a hand. "You don't need your cutter. I've got a surprise for you. I didn't plug Yuma Bill."

"You've said that before, but a jury..."

"We don't even need a jury." Kim pulled a folded piece of paper from his coat pocket and held it up for Lane to see, then replaced it. "I've got a statement signed by an eyewitness. You know, Ed, it's gonna be real dangerous, bringing in that hombre that beefed Yuma Bill."

"I won't have to go very far," Lane flung at him. "Not with you standing right here, and I'll have Bonham..."

"Did you see Bonham help me out of jail?"

"Hell, somebody slugged me when Della..."

Lane stopped, red-faced. Kim laughed. "You sure made a fool out of yourself. What do you think Johnny's gonna do when you tell folks you got slugged when you was kissing his wife?" Kim shook his head. "You'd better keep mum. Ed, you do what I want you to and I'll keep still about you and Del. I'll be saving your life, you know. Johnny sure is a jealous hombre."

"All right. What do you want?"

"We'll take a walk to Doc's place and see Phil Martin. I've got a notion he'll change his yarn."

For a moment Lane stood there, blinking idiotically, wanting no part of this, but unable to find a way out. He said sourly, "Gimme my coat. I need a chaw of tobacco."

Kim tossed the coat to Lane who slipped into it, took a plug of tobacco out of his pocket, and gnawed off a mouthful. He said thickly, "Gimme my gun belt. I'd look naked without it."

Kim lifted the gun from holster and removed the shells, then handed the belt and gun to Lane. "You had your fun pushing me down the street the other day. Now I'll have some. Don't load that iron. Walk out ahead of me and keep going till we get to Doc's drugstore."

Lane swore bitterly, but he obeyed. As he crossed the living room, his housekeeper called, "What's he doing to you, Ed?"

"Nothing. We've got some business to attend to."

When they were outside, Kim said, "I thought the posse rode off and left you."

"I caught up with 'em at Clawhammer. I figgered you'd go there."

"Where's Dunning and his outfit?"

"They stopped at Clawhammer. Sleeping, I reckon. We couldn't find you, so Dunning stayed there and the rest of us came back to town. Johnny had to go out on the stage and Luke Haines allowed he'd better get back to see how his wife was."

"Ain't it funny Dunning would stop at Clawhammer?"

"Looked funny to me," Lane admitted, "but they was all in. Needed sleep, Dunning said."

They walked in silence then, Kim thinking that this was further proof of what Rocky had said about Peg and Dunning. They turned into the drugstore. Doc Frazee stood behind the counter, looking tired and sleepy, and even surprise at seeing Kim did not change the expression on his bony face.

"Well, Ed, I see you caught your man," Frazee said. "Shall we hang him this morning, or wait till Dunning gets back to town?"

Lane glowered, saying nothing. Kim said, "Got anything for a sour disposition, Doc?"

"Sure, but you can get it cheaper in the Belle Union."

"Come on," Lane said irritably. "Get on with the business."

"How's Martin?" Kim asked.

"Purty sick. I've been up and down all night with him. The damned fool should have stayed in bed, but no, he figured he was so tough he didn't need to do what he was told."

"I want to see him," Kim said. "He's gonna tell who beefed Yuma Bill. I've got a statement from Salty Smith, so I figured if Martin's story jibes with Smith's, even Lane will get it through his noggin that I ain't the man he wants."

Frazee stood motionless for a moment, stroking his goatee. He said finally, "Let me handle this, Kim. I've got a scheme I've been waiting to use till Ed was here to listen."

The medico led the way to his office in the back of the store building. He went into a side room, motioning for Kim and Lane to wait.

"How do you feel, Phil?" Frazee asked.

"You know damned well," Martin groaned. "I'm burning up."

"They tell me hell's hot, too. I reckon you'll be finding out before long, but it might ease your conscience if you'd tell me who drilled Yuma Bill."

"I'm sick," Martin grunted, "but I ain't sick enough to admit I'm a liar."

Frazee put a hand on Martin's forehead and jer ed it away. "I could fry an egg right there, Phil. I'll stir up something to take your fever down."

Frazee poured water into a glass, dropped a spoonful of white powder into it, and stirred lustily. He stepped back to the cot. "Here, Phil. Drink this."

Frazee got a hand behind Martin's head and tilted it up so the man could drink. Martin emptied the glass and Frazee stepped back, grinning. He said, "Phil, there's times when a sawbones has to stick his nose into business that ain't rightfully his. That's just what I done. Logan didn't beef that hombre. You know who did. Now the way I see it, that makes you guilty of murder if Logan hangs, but there ain't no court hereabouts that'll see justice done. So I took care of it myself."

"What're you driving at?"

"I executed you. That was poison you just drank. Tasted awful, didn't it? In about a minute you'll feel a tingling in your fingers and toes. Then it'll be in your hands and feet. Pretty soon it'll go up into your arms and legs. When it hits your heart, wham, you're dead.

"You're lying."

"Think so? Well, all I've got to say is that I wish I had Hank Dunning here so I could lie to him the same way."

Martin must have believed him then, for he cried out, "Do something, damn it. You just can't stand there and let me die."

"Getting into your legs, ain't it? It'll be up in your arms. First they tingle, then they'll get stiff. Pretty soon..."

Martin lifted himself on his one good arm, yelling, "Shut up, damn you, and do something."

"You'll make your fever worse, carrying on thataway." Frazee said reprovingly. He took a bottle down from a shelf and filled a small glass with amber liquid. "This is the antidote, Phil. I aim to get the truth out of you or kill you. Tell me who drilled Yuma Bill and you get the antidote."

"Go to hell," Martin breathed, and fell back on the cot.

"Well sir, I didn't think you were that big a fool," Frazee said contemptuously. "You're lying to get rid of Logan, and you're doing it because Dunning told you to. Now ain't that a fine thing to die for?"

"Go to hell," Martin said again.

"You're the one going to hell. My conscience won't hurt me for sending you there. I'm trying to save an innocent man's life. Do you think that what Dunning told you to do is enough to kill yourself for? Getting it in your legs and arms now, ain't you? When it hits your heart..."

"All right," Martin screamed. "It was Heinz."

"Now that's better. Here's your..."

"Wait a minute," Kim called from the door. "Did Dutch get the money?"

"Sure, Sure. Hank and that Cody woman rigged it. She said he'd have all the dinero in a shoe box. Forty thousand. Said the old gent was gonna keep the dinero while you rode into town, but you crossed 'em up when you took the box. Dutch couldn't find it, so he figured the old man had the dinero on him. That's how he found the money belt. Now gimme that stuff, Doc."

"Here you are." Frazee said.

Martin hoisted himself up on his good arm and drained the glass. "Whiskey," he yelled. "Nothing but your damned cheap whiskey." He threw the glass against the wall. "You lying son! When I get out of here, I'll..."

"Cool down, boy," Frazee said. "That's no way to act after my saving your life. Whiskey is a good antidote for a lot of things. Look at all the fellers who use it."

Frazee walked out, leaving Martin staring after him, uncertain whether he had been tricked or not. The medico shut the door, winking at Kim. "If properly used, bicarbonate of soda and imagination can do more to change men's lives than all the pills a doctor can roll."

Kim handed Smith's statement to Frazee. "You know Salty Smith's handwriting, Doc?"

"Sure. Nobody could forge that old fool's scrawling. Not even a barnyard hen." He glanced at the paper and nodding, handed it to Lane. "It tallies, Ed."

Lane studied the paper a moment and then glanced up at Kim. "Where is Smith?"

"He's safe. You go get Dutch. Salty'll be here to testify at his trial."

"Where is he?" Lane asked again.

"I wouldn't trust you as far as I could throw you by the hair on your head," Kim said bluntly. "If Smith was dead, Martin could go back on his story, so I'll do all I can to keep Smith alive."

Lane wheeled toward the door. Frazee called, "Ed." Lane made a slow turn to face the medico and stood glowering at him. Frazee said, "Ed, you're a tinhorn politician. We all know that, but if you haven't got the guts it takes to go after Dutch Heinz, you'd better turn your star in."

"I don't get it," Lane shouted. "I tell you I don't get it. Heinz has been with Clawhammer ever since Sam Cody drove into the valley. It don't make sense that Dunning would protect him and try to hang Logan."

"I'm not working for Clawhammer," Kim said in a low

tone. "That's the difference."

"I still don't savvy."

"You don't need to savvy. Are you going after Heinz?"

Lane stood in the doorway, trembling, sweat breaking through the pores of his skin. "I'll go look for him," he muttered.

"You'd better find him," Frazee said. "Things are changing around here. For the better, too. A few more funerals will just about clean things up."

Again Lane turned and this time Frazee let him go. When he had left the drugstore, Kim said, "He's a dead man if he goes after Heinz."

"Or a man without a job if he don't," Frazee said. "He can't make up his mind which way to jump."

Kim walked to the door and leaned against the jamb, shoulders slack. He yawned and rubbed his face. "Guess I'll get some breakfast and sleep till Christmas." He yawned again. "Thanks, Doc. I'm so damned near all in I ain't got it through my noggin that I don't have to keep ducking the law."

"No need to thank me, Kim." Frazee's bony face was very grave. "You know, the other morning when I was standing in front of the bank, I wasn't much different from Fred Galt and Luke Haines. Kind o' felt that the country had gone to the dogs and I didn't give a damn. Then you fetched in that dinero and well, things began looking different."

"Yuma Bill was the one who made things look different," Kim said.

"To you," Frazee agreed. "It's like a chain. But it was some different with me. I'd been rotting inside for years. I'd seen this country boom and I'd seen it die. I've seen a few honest folks and a lot of crooked ones. Why, if I could collect all the money I've got coming, I'd be a rich man. I've got enough, though. The thing was I got to talking to Brit, about what the country used to be like. We want to see it come back and I think it will. Trouble is, it ain't good for folks to live with ghosts. A lot of us have been gripped by the dead hand of the past till we've been paralyzed."

"It ain't the dead hand of the past that's been bothering me," Kim said, and left the medico's office.

He had flapjacks at the Chinaman's, and taking his horse out of Lane's barn, rode to the livery stable. It was a grim sort of joke, he thought, that he had cheated the lynch mob by riding out of town on Shorty Avis's black, for Shorty hated him with only a little less bitterness than Hank Dunning did. He told the stableman to keep the gelding until Shorty or Rocky came for him, stopped to talk to his buckskin, and left the stable.

Kim went to the bank. What Doc Frazee had said about being gripped by the dead hand of the past had given him an idea. Charlie Bemis froze behind the teller's wicket when he saw Kim. He blurted, "You loco, Kim? The posse just got back this morning. They'll . . ."

"No they won't. I'm gonna laugh in Fred Galt's face soon as I get some sleep. Brit back yet?"

Bemis nodded. "He's in his office. Lane . . ."

"He don't want me," Kim said, and stepping through the gate at the end of the counter, walked on back to Bonham's office.

Kim knocked, and opened the door at the banker's "Come in." He said, "Don't get excited, Brit. The law don't want me. Charlie had himself a conniption when I came in."

Bonham had started to get up, his face paling when he saw who it was. Then he dropped back into his chair, his body going slack, and it seemed to Kim that his shoulders were more stooped than ever.

"Let's hear the yarn afore I die of heart failure," Bonham said, filling his pipe, eyes dropping to his tobacco pouch.

Kim told him what had happened, then asked, "What about Rocky?"

"She lit out for home. Mighty worried about you, too. You'd best ride out there as soon as you get some sleep."

"I aim to." Kim canted his chair back against the wall and rolled a smoke. "What do you want most, Brit?"

Bonham lit his pipe, blinking as the smoke rolled up around his face. He took the pipestem out of his mouth. "Now that's a hell of a question."

"Sure is," Kim agreed. "Maybe it's because I'm so sleepy that my head's spinning, but I think I've got an idea. Strikes me that some of you old timers, you and Doc for instance, want to see this country come back before you go over the range."

Bonham pulled on his pipe a moment. He said, "That's right, but who's gonna bring it back? I've got a little claim up there back of my cabin, but it ain't gonna be no bonanza. Same with Doc."

"Mines come and go, Brit. Trouble with you and Doc is that you saw this country when it had its boom, so you figure that another strike is the only way to bring it back. You're wrong, Brit. The grass will always be here."

Bonham gestured impatiently. "We've had cows in this valley ever since Sam Cody brought his herd in. Before that even, but it didn't bring no big prosperity."

"And I'll tell you why. Clawhammer and HD are both big outfits. It's the little fry who'll bring the country back, fellows like Shorty Avis that Sam Cody ran off the creek. If this range was handled right, there'd be enough grass for fifty outfits. Think about that, Brit. It means business for everybody, more'n you'd ever have with two big spreads and a few dinky ones on the mesa."

Bonham shook his head. "There's a gent named Hank Dunning . . ."

"Won't be long." Kim's face was bone-hard. "I'll attend to Dunning, and I'll attend to Heinz if Lane don't."

Bonham puffed for a moment in silence. Then he said, "You've been a fool for luck, although I've always claimed that it takes a real good man to have good luck. Anyhow, you might pull it off, but no matter what happens to Dunning, there's still Peg."

"You've got her notes."

"Yeah, and it won't hurt my conscience to close her out

after what's happened." Bonham studied his pipe, eyes almost lidded shut. "But I had the notion you were in love with Peg."

Kim's face reddened. "Rub it in. I guess Rocky called it right. I was in love with Clawhammer, not Peg. Anyhow, I'm seeing it straight now. It's Rocky I'm in love with, and I'll prove it to her if I stay here a million years."

"Might take that long. It's my guess that Rocky's gonna be hard to convince."

"I'll do it if it takes that million years. Now you've got forty thousand dollars you don't know what to do with. My idea is for you to loan it out to the little fry. Let 'em start in the valley again. If we don't have talk of a range war, there'll be others who'll move in."

Bonham leaned back, puffing steadily on his pipe, eyes on the ceiling. "You're dreaming, boy, just dreaming, and there's a lot to be done before what you're talking about can be anything but dreams."

"We'll do 'em."

"Kim," Bonham said slowly, "there's one thing I can't get out of my mind. You've been a fiddle-footed drifter. How do I know you've changed?"

Kim got up. "You don't. Go ahead and keep Yuma's money in your safe till it rots, but I'm betting on one thing. When you go over the range, Yuma will be standing beside St. Peter and he'll blackball you before you get through the pearly gates."

Kim swung around and would have stalked out if Bonham hadn't said, "That might happen. I'll make you a deal. Interested?"

"Maybe," Kim answered, turning back.

"A lot of things can change a man," Bonham said, "but a woman's one of the best. That's how it was with Yuma. Like I told you, he was mighty damned ornery once. Bought a big grant in New Mexico and sold land to settlers that wasn't no good for farming. They failed and moved on and the land went back to him. Then he sold it over again. He piled up a lot of money, then he fell in love with one of them farmer's girls, and she made him into the Yuma Bill you knew. By that time he couldn't give the money back to the fellers he'd taken it from, so he came up to the Arkansas Valley and since then he's done his damnedest to help other people with that money."

Bonham rose and kicked back his chair. "Kim, what you've said is right in line with what Yuma Bill would want done with his money. You see, even after his wife died, he went right on like he had been. If you'd marry Peg, you wouldn't be no different than when you rode into the valley, but if it's Rocky you marry, you'll be different. I'll gamble on that."

"What's your deal?" Kim asked in a dry brittle tone.

"The day you marry Rocky, I'll loan that forty thousand dollars."

"You've made a deal," Kim said, and left the bank.

He was angry, as angry as he could be at a man who had helped save his life, but as he crossed the street to the hotel, he found that he could not remain angry at Brit Bonham. The banker had always been the little rancher's friend; he was Rocky's friend. If his and Bonham's positions had been reversed and he was looking at Kim Logan's record, he would have figured on the future exactly as the banker had.

Kim took a room and climbed the stairs, thinking of Rocky. Without her, his future would be little different from his past. It was, he knew now, not the kind of future he wanted. He pulled off his coat and gun belt, tossed his Stetson on the bureau, and fell across the bed. His last thought was of Rocky and how she had changed so many things in the last few days.

It was dark when Kim woke. His door was open and a thin pencil of light from the bracket lamp in the hall fell half across his room. He wasn't sure, in that first moment of sleep-fogged consciousness, what had wakened him, but he thought someone was shaking him and talking to him. He turned toward the wall, hoping he was dreaming.

No dream. It came again, a slender hand on his shoulder shaking him with nagging insistence. A woman's voice beat against his sleep-numbed brain, "Wake up, Kim. Wake up."

He sat up, knuckling his eyes and shaking his head. Then he saw it was Della Naylor. He yawned and mumbled, "Howdy, Del. Thought you was a dream."

"And I thought you were dead. Are you awake enough to listen?"

"Sure," Kim said, suddenly conscious of the urgency that was in her voice. "What's wrong?"

"Everything, Kim. The Avis place was burned last night and Shorty Avis was beaten up. Doc's on his way out there now, but I'm afraid he's too late."

CHAPTER 16
FAITH AND DOUBT

Kim swung his feet to the floor, his brain as numb as if he had been struck on the head. This was a nig tmare. It had to be. When he had cleared himself of Yuma Bill's murder he had thought that the immediate problem had been taken care of. He had never been a man to do a job that belonged to the law. Arresting Dutch Heinz was the sheriff's responsibility, and that, Kim had supposed, was the only other chore which needed to be done at once.

Now, staring at Della's face, pinched with worry, he knew that the worst fears of the mesa ranchers would soon be re lized, that this blow at Shorty Avis was meant as an example if what would happen to the rest if they didn't get out of the country.

Kim rose and buckled on his gun belt. He asked "Who did it?"

"We don't know. Shorty's been unconscious. Rocky stopped at our place after she left Bonham's cabin. Then she went home and found her dad. Everything they own is gone except their cattle."

"They'll lose their beef, too," Kim said somberly, "unless something happens to change Dunning's mind."

Kim put on his hat and coat and turned to the door. Della cried out, "Kim."

He swung back to face her. "What?"

"Rocky doesn't know I'm here. I mean, well, it was my idea. I came to get Doc and he told me you'd found out about Heinz. I got to wondering what you'd do. There's nothing to hold you in the valley now that you've lost your job with Clawhammer."

It was natural enough for her to think that. Probably her father, Abe Fawcett, and the rest of the mesa ranchers would think the same thing. He was a gunslinger, they'd say, and when he lost his job, he'd ride on. A year ago he would have done exactly that. He might have a week ago. But as Doc Frazee said, the events of the last few days formed a chain going back to Yuma Bill who had owed a debt to Brit Bonham. When Kim had delivered the money, Bonham had owed him. Now it was Kim who owed a debt to Della Naylor and Rocky Avis. That would have been enough to make him stay even if he had not loved Rocky.

"I've got another job to do," Kim said. "I aim to hang around awhile."

She came toward him, the faint light from the hall touching her troubled face. He had never supposed she had a serious thought in her rattle-brained head. When she had married Johnny Naylor, folks said they were two of a kind, reckless and wild, and they belonged together.

But Della had changed just as everything on this range was changing, for people and their relationships were distorted by the gods of evil that had been loosed upon the valley when Hank Dunning and Peg Cody had opened Pandora's box. Now Kim wondered whether Della and Johnny did belong together. She had grown up and Johnny had lagged behind.

"There's another thing, Kim," Della said. "Yesterday Heinz saw every rancher on the east mesa. He's giving us till sunset tomorrow to get out."

"He gave Shorty a warning like that the other day."

She nodded. "Sam Cody drove us out of the valley, and Heinz thinks he can drive us off the mesa just as easy. He said that if we wanted to sell, to be in town tomorrow afternoon and Peg would buy our land and cattle. If we didn't, we wouldn't get anything."

Kim turned toward the door again, saying, "Come on."

She followed him along the hall and down the stairs, and as they crossed the lobby, he asked, "Where's your horse?"

"In front of the drugstore."

"Ride over to the stable."

"Where are we going?"

He was on the boardwalk in front of the hotel when she asked that. He wheeled to face her. "That's the craziest question I ever heard. We're going up on the mesa and we'll get your neighbors together. If they want to run, there's nothing on God's earth anybody can do for 'em, but if they want to fight, we'll show Dutch Heinz a thing or two."

"They won't run, Kim," she said with grim certainty. "They've had one meeting. That was the night after Shorty had his warning. They saw that this was coming."

"Then we'll fight."

"It's not as simple as that, Kim. Try to understand. Rocky and I believe in you. So does Frazee and Brit Bonham. But Dad and the rest don't know all that's happened. To them you're still Peg Cody's snake stomper."

"Then we'll have to do some arguing," he said, and went on to the stable.

They took the stage road out of own, keeping a steady, ground-eating pace, and saying nothing. They passed the Clawhammer road and within the hour reached the road that led to Indian Springs. It was little more than a trail and was seldom used except by Shorty Avis and Abe Fawcett who followed it when they came to town. Beyond their places it climbed to the top of the slick-rock rim through a narrow break and ran on through the aspens and spruce to where it joined the stage road just west of the pass. Kim had followed the upper end of this road when he had brought Yuma Bill to the Avis place.

The bulk of the mesa ranchers lived north of the stage road, for that part of the mesa had the best grass, and it was natural that they would go there when Sam Cody had driven them out of the valley. This sudden and violent move on Heinz's part must have been supported by Dunning.

It was Kim's guess that Dunning and his tough crew had been with Heinz when Shorty Avis was beaten and his buildings burned. There could be but one answer. Kim's thoughts came back to the same place they had been many times since Rocky had told him that Peg and Dunning were in love. At least they had thrown in together and were planning a big expansion of their herds. Only a frantic need for more summer range would explain a raid like this.

The country south of Ganado Canyon was not used by any of the ranchers, for it was poor graze all the way to the New Mexico line where it became a maze of impenetrable gorges. As it stood now, Clawhammer was obliged to seek summer range in the high country between the mesa and the divide where the season was comparatively short. In the past it had been sufficient because Clawhammer beef had been held in the valley most of the year, but the valley grass would not be enough if the Clawhammer herd was doubled.

It seemed incredible, but it must be this way. The much talked about fight between Clawhammer and HD had been faked, a smoke screen to hide Peg's and Dunning's real intent. A few shots had been fired across the creek; there had been a good deal of maneuvering when the two outfits had hit Ganado the same day. Supposedly Kim's reputation had held Dunning back, but all the time Peg had known Dunning would not make a serious attack. That was why she had been so sure she would be safe when she stayed at home with no one to protect her but old Limpy.

At last logic forced Kim to the conclusion that his pride had kept him from reaching before. He had been a tool, a small but essential cog in Peg's scheming. It was the reason she had hired him; it was the reason she had paid him the high wages she had.

There were still some facts that Kim did not have and he needed them to bring the muddled pattern out clearly, but this much he could no longer doubt. She had told him she was ambitious; she aimed to be big, so big that the valley would be hers. She had said that when she needed the mesa, the little ranchers would go. Her time of need, he thought, grimly, must have come very quickly after his talk with her the night he had brought Yuma Bill to Clawhammer.

Apparently Yuma's coming had forced Peg and Dunning into the open. They had planned to steal his money. That was why Phil Martin and his men had crossed the creek. It was why Peg told Heinz that Yuma Bill would be at Smith's cabin with the money. There it was, as plain and brutal a pattern of robbery and murder as Kim had ever seen. A man could not have fooled him, but Peg had for the simple reason that he had wanted to believe in her.

One thing still bothered Kim. Doubling the Clawhammer and HD herds would take money. The ten thousand Dutch Heinz had stolen from Yuma Bill would not be enough. They must hold another trump card they had not played, or they wouldn't have started pushing the mesa ranchers so soon as they had.

It was after midnight when Kim and Della reached the bench. They climbed the steep pitch to the mesa and pulled up to blow their horses. Kim asked, "If you knew the law didn't want me and you thought there was nothing here to hold me, how come you bothered to wake me up?"

"I had to be sure," she answered. "Rocky and me invested quite a bit in you. I guess Rocky had her own reasons, but mine were pretty simple. I just figured that when the chips were down, you'd have to be on our side."

"I won't be much help if your bunch won't trust me."

"That worried me more than anything else." Leather squeaked as Della shifted her weight. "There's something else, too. Take me. I know what folks have said. I'm as wild as a March wind and reckless and a little crazy. Johnny's the same, so the old gossips say we'll have the meanest kids in the country." She laughed softly. "Well, maybe we will. Right now I'm awful mad at Johnny, but I'll get over it. When he gets back from his stage run, we'll have a fight and I'll call him terrible names, but after that we'll make up and it will be wonderful. I love him, Kim. No matter what he does, I'll still love him. Don't ask me to explain why. I guess it's just the way a woman's heart works, and you can't explain that."

They rode on across the mesa, through the sage and the scattered black dots that were the wind-shaped cedars, and Kim's thoughts were as dark as the night that pressed down around them. Della had been talking about her heart, but she had been really trying to tell him about Rocky's.

Rocky must have loved him for a long time. When he had needed help, she had been there. Kim Logan was not a praying man, but he prayed now, riding through the night with the wind on his face and cold brilliant stars above him prayed that the knowledge of his love for Rocky had not come too late.

They reached the pines, climbing steadily now, not far north of the tableland where Kim and Yuma Bill had fought Phil Martin and his bunch. Then, with dawn not more than an hour away, they reached Abe Fawcett's place, windows bright with lamplight.

"Keep your temper, Kim," Della said, "no matter what happens. Maybe I made a mistake bringing you. I mean, Dad and Ma and the rest of them up here have been afraid of Clawhammer so long they're going to be hard to convince about you."

"I know," he said, "but that ain't worrying me as much as the time. It's gonna take all day to get 'em together."

"Dad started north when I left for town," she told him. "They'll be at the Avis clearing a little before sunup."

As they reined up in front of the house, the front door opened and Della's mother stood there, a rifle in her hands.

She called, "Who is it?"

"Me," Della answered. "Kim Logan's with me."

"Logan!" Mrs. Fawcett came down the path, Winchester held on the ready. "You get out of here. Shorty Avis is lying in my bed right now looking like he's going over the range, and you've got the brass . . ."

"It wasn't Kim that done it," Della cut in. "Don't talk like that. He's on our side."

"Our side," Mrs. Fawcett cried out in rage. "Maybe he can pull the wool over your eyes, but he don't fool me. Not a little bit. Now you get out of here, Logan, and . . ."

"Then I'll go, too," Della said quietly. "So will Rocky. Doc here?"

"He's working on Shorty now. Don't get me sidetracked. Della. We don't need this double-crossing gunslinger. If he's on our side, which I doubt, he'll want pay and we haven't got it to give him. I don't trust a man who fights for money, and I wouldn't trust Kim Logan anyhow."

"You don't understand, Ma. There's been a lot that's happened the last few days. Everything's changed. Doc will tell you that."

Mrs. Fawcett sniffed. "Everything's changed, has it? I'm too old to swallow that. Nothing changes. You slap some paint on a tiger and you make him look different, but the stripes are still there. Same with a skunk."

Kim did not know Mrs. Fawcett as well as he knew Della and her father. Looking down at the woman now, he could not make out the expression on her face. It was just a pale blob topping a wide body, but her hostility was a tangible pressure laid against him. Della had said all she could, and Kim had a feeling that it would take very little to make Mrs. Fawcett fly into an insane rage and start shooting. If she did, no one on the mesa but Rocky and her own daughter would condemn her.

He had to work on her pride. It was the only weapon he could use, the same weapon he must use later when he faced Abe Fawcett and the rest of the mesa ranchers. He said evenly, "A skunk has his way of fighting, ma'am. But you take a band of sheep now. They're different. They just run."

He heard her gasp as if he'd knocked the wind out of her. She would give ground or she'd shoot. Pride was one of the few things these people had left. The younger ones like Rocky and Della did not remember, but the older ones, men and women both, would remember and they would be ashamed. Fear would be in them again when the time came that they must make the decision to fight or run, and all the tough talk in the world could not hide it.

Then he knew he had won, for she said harshly, "I suppose you think a skunk can protect sheep?"

"He can if he makes enough stink," he said.

Stepping down, Kim walked past Mrs. Fawcett and went into the house. A moment before she had been capable o shooting him in the back, but he was not afraid of that now. He heard the hum of talk between Della and her mother, then he was in the house and the sound of talk died.

The Fawcett house was a rambling, two-storey structure built of logs, the most pretentious place on the mesa. The front room took up half of the lower floor. At one end an open stairway led to the bedrooms overhead; a cavernous stone fireplace occupied almost all of the other end. It was an in hospitable room, its furniture homemade and crude, the rough plank floor bare. Kim had never been here before, but now in this one quick glance, he had the feeling that the Fawcetts had hoped to hold a little of their past glory by building this huge house.

The kitchen formed one back quarter of the first floor, a bedroom the other quarter. The bedroom door was ajar, and Kim pushed it open and went in. Rocky stood at one side of the bed, Doc Frazee on the other. Shorty Avis lay motionless between them, a faded quilt pulled up under his chin. His head was bandaged, and his face was a mass of cuts and bruises.

Rocky turned, giving Kim a tired smile. Frazee rose and snapped his bag shut. "Nothing more I can do. He may come out of it. Can't tell yet. Just keep him quiet."

Frazee walked out. Kim crossed the room to stand beside Rocky, and looked down at Shorty's battered face. Shorty Avis was the one man on the mesa who would have stood and fought. That, Kim knew, was the reason he had been picked.

"I'm sorry," Kim said, realizing how utterly inadequate the words were.

He put an arm around Rocky. She turned and buried herr face against his shirt. For a moment she stood that way, crying softly. It was the first time he had seen her break down, the first sign of weakness he had ever seen in her. She regained control of herself almost at once. She wiped a sleeve across her eyes and looked up at him, trying to smile.

"I didn't tell Della to let you know," she said, "but I'm glad she did. Thanks for coming. '

' No need to thank me," he said.

He looked at Shorty's battered face, a slow anger beginning to burn in him. He had always considered himself a tough man, but this was too much. The way he saw it, a man under any circumstances had the right to a fair fight. They had not given Shorty Avis that, or any part of it.

"You see why I hate Peg Cody," Rocky breathed. "We knew this would happen after Dutch Heinz brought us that warning, but we didn't think it would be this soon."

He let the silence run on for a moment, making no effort to defend Peg. He said then, "If it hadn't been for me, you'd have been there."

"I've thought of that, Kim, but it wouldn't have made any difference. I couldn't have stopped them, and it might have been worse."

"I'm afraid it would," he said. "I'll square this, Rocky. That's a promise."

"Squaring it won't save Dad."

"It may save some others."

She moved away from him, her shoulders slack as if all the weariness and worry and fear that had crowded her for so long had finally caught up with her. "I know, Kim. It's got to be finished. We'll run or we'll fight, and if we fight, more men will die. It's wrong, it's all wrong."

"You said something about when the country grows up, men like me will disappear. I don't think so, Rocky. There'll always be things like this."

"Not if the law is strong," she whispered. "This wouldn't have happened if Ed Lane was a different man than he is."

Kim nodded, knowing it was true. He had seen this same drama played out time after time. Different names, different scenes, but essentially the same grim drama of strength bullying weakness. When law was only an ideal, a theory, people like Hank Dunning and Peg Cody, consumed by the fires of greed and ambition, could not be controlled, but the right kind of man wearing the star could make law something more than a theory.

It had always been that way; it always would be. The fault went back of Ed Lane, even back of Hank Dunning and Peg, back to the complacency of the people who permitted Lane's election. Brit Bonham and Doc Frazee as well as Fred Galt. And Kim Logan. He had not been here when Lane had been elected, but he had been in other places where the same thing had been done, and he had stood by, watching, and doing nothing.

"We'll get a different man," he said. "Now you'd better get some rest. You can't do anything for Shorty by standing here. It's out of your hands."

"Out of my hands," she breathed. "Yes, I guess it is."

She blew out the lamp and left the room, Kim following. Rocky went on into the kitchen. Doc Frazee had laid his black bag on the pine table in the middle of the room and had dropped into a rocking chair. Kim drew another chair up beside him and sat down, asking, "How bad is he, Doc?"

"Pretty damned bad," Frazee said gloomily. "Busted ribs. Concussion. A face that'll never look the same again." He shook his head. "They must have knocked him down and booted hell out of him. Pretty brave outfit, that bunch."

"I wouldn't call them that," Kim said.

Frazee gave him a straight look. "What are you going to do?"

"Why should I do anything?" Kim motioned toward the kitchen. Talk flowed through the open door. Mrs. Fawcett's voice rising above the girls, her tone bitter and accusing. "Della's ma don't believe I will."

Frazee stroked his goatee, bony face grave. He said finally, "I'll tell you. Some of us have our bets down on you, me and Brit and Rocky. Della, too, or she wouldn't have brought you out here. You gonna welsh on them bets?"

"I didn't make the bets," Kim said.

"Well, we made 'em for you. It adds up to the same thing."

"Looks to me like a thankless job. About like pulling a drowning man out of the river. He'll fight you like hell while you're saving him."

"Yeah, I know," Frazee said gloomily. "Same thing with me. Cuss me because I dose 'em with medicine that don't taste good, but I keep on dosing 'em. Don't ask me why. I just do it."

Della came out of the kitchen. She said, "Breakfast is ready."

They ate by lamplight, Mrs. Fawcett plodding between the table and the big range to fill coffee cups or bring more biscuits and bacon. When they were done, a faint gray light had crept across the eastern sky.

Della said, "Time to ride, Kim. I'm going with you, but Rocky's staying with her pa."

Kim rose, nodding. Mrs. Fawcett stood with her back to the stove, a wide-hipped, shapeless woman, the mark of the hard years on her face and hands, on a body that might once have been as slim and attractive as her daughter's.

"Don't you get into none of the fighting, Della," Mrs. Fawcett said. "You come back here when the palaver's finished." Then she looked directly at Kim, doubt clouding her broad face. "We'll see how much stink a skunk can make, mister, and maybe you'll find out what a bunch of sheep can do."

"Then Hank Dunning and Dutch Heinz will be surprised," Kim said.

For just a moment Kim stood looking at Rocky, filling his eyes with the young vibrant beauty of her face. Then he wheeled and followed Della out of the house.

CHAPTER 17
BALL OF SAND

It was full daylight when Kim and Della reached the clearing that only a few hours before had held the Avis buildings. Now there was nothing but the gray piles of ashes where the cabin and barn and other buildings had been. The cabin's chimney was still standing, a grim monument that would be here long after the ashes were scattered.

Kim had not wanted Della to come with him, but he new that if he went alone, he would never convince the mesa ranchers of his intentions. Now, riding across the clearing, he saw that Della's presence was even more necessary than he had first thought.

Six men were hunkered in the yard, idly talking and smoking. The instant Kim was recognized, they stood up, hands dropping to gun butts. They began backing toward their horses, wary eyes on Kim. They would have started shooting before he'd ridden half the width of the clearing if Della had not been with him.

Della and Kim reined up ten paces from the men, Della smiling as if this were a pleasant social gathering. She motioned toward Kim, saying, "Boys, you know Kim Logan, don't you?"

"I'm sorry I do," one of them said. "What the hell you doing here, Logan?"

"I'm throwing in with you," Kim said, "You could use another gun."

They scowled, finding his words mentally indigestible. He

stepped down, gave Della a hand, and swung away from the group. There would be enough explaining to do when the rest got here. He made a wide circle around the yard, leaving Della to talk to her neighbors. Presently two others rode in, and after ten minutes had passed, Abe Fawcette arrived with Clay Mackey. That was all. Kim joined the group then, standing beside Della and facing the others.

There was no talk for a time. Della had apparently said all that she could, and it hadn't been enough. They eyed him a moment, anger stirring in them. Then Fawcett said, "I've always had quite a bit of faith in Della's judgment in things like this, Logan, but I'm damned if I do this time. She says you want to throw in with us. Why?"

Kim stood motionless, his back held stiffly straight, probing blue eyes making a cool study of these men. Fawcett was as near a leader as there was among them. Big-chested and paunchy, Abe Fawcett had a pair of steel gray eyes and silver hair that gave him a sort of dignity, but his appearance would have been more impressive if he had not worn a sweeping mustache that added a faintly comical touch to a face that otherwise was quite severe.

Most of these men were, like Fawcett and Shorty Avis, middle-aged or older. Only two were young, sons who had stayed with their fathers. Most of the boys had drifted out of the country, knowing they weren't needed at home and that there was little chance of finding work in Ganado. The only possible jobs were with HD and Clawhammer. None of them wanted those jobs except Clay Mackey's three boys who were riding for Clawhammer.

"Well?" Fawcett prodded.

"I'll tell you why," Kim said, bringing his eyes t the big man. "We're on the same side. I can use some help and you can use another gun, so we'd be smart to team up."

Little Joe Scanlon, at the end of the line, shook his head. "It wouldn't be smart, mister. It'd be plain stupid. You've been riding around talking tough for Clawhammer. Been a year now. We've got no reason to think you've changed." He motioned around the clearing. "It's my guess you had a hand in this."

"You're guessing wrong, Joe," Kim said mildly. "A lot's happened the las three or four days. Everything's turned inside out. No use taking time to tell all of it, but there's two things you need to know. I couldn't have been here because Ed Lane had me in the jug on a murder that Phil Martin and Hank Dunning rigged. After I got out I was too busy keeping my neck out of a rope to be in on a torch party. The second thing is that Peg Cody fired me."

They were silent a moment, weighing his words in their minds. Then Fawcett said, "I ain't satisfied. You could pull us into a trap and get our heads shot off. We know you'd been warned to stay off Shorty's property." He motioned toward the chimney. "Might be your way of getting square with Shorty."

Kim shoved his thumbs into his belt, eyes moving along the line of hostile faces. "I'll tell you something else which I hadn't aimed to, but it's what makes the difference in me. I love Rocky."

They might have cursed him for wanting one of their women. Or laughed at him. They did neither. Instead they shifted uneasily, toes digging into the dirt, and he saw at once that he had said the one right thing.

Clay Mackey demanded, "You fixing to marry her and live up here?"

"I haven't asked her," Kim answered, "but I will if I'm alive when this is settled. If I live and Rocky will have me, we'll stay in the valley, but not here on the mesa. I don't think you boys will either. You'll be back on the creek where you belong."

Fawcett blew out a great breath, fat jowls trembling. "What kind of a damned fairy tale are you getting off?"

Kim smiled. "No fairy tale, Abe. Let me ask you a question. Why did you round these boys up?"

"Hell, you can see for yourself. I had a look at Shorty when Rocky fetched him in. I...why, damn it, Logan, I wanted the boys to see what Clawhammer will do if we don't stop 'em."

"How do you aim to stop Clawhammer?"

"Well, I...I thought we'd figure out something this morning."

Again Kim swung his gaze along the line of faces, not so hostile now, faces weathered by wind and sun, faces of men who wanted nothing but the right to live in peace and deeply frightened because they knew there was no peace for them.

"Then you need me," Kim said. "I know what to do."

Again they shifted uneasily, wanting his help but still uncertain about him. It was Della who said, "Don't stand there like a bunch of ninnies. Go on. Tell him we'll work with him."

"We could use some help," Fawcett said reluctantly, "but even if you're on the level, Logan, your gun won't make the difference. Dunning's outfit is at Clawhammer. We just ain't tough enough to lick 'em, and that's the truth."

"So you'll run again like you ran once before when Sam Cody kicked you off the creek," Kim said with biting contempt. "You don't really think you can win if you hang and rattle. You're wrong, Abe. I say you can."

"I reckon we'll go along with you," Joe Scanlon said. "Trouble is we allowed you'd be the one who did Peg Cody's pushing."

"Not me," Kim said. "Like everybody else, I figured she was scrapping with Dunning, but it don't look that way now. Anyhow, it's Dunning and Dutch Heinz who'll do the pushing, and they can be licked."

Kim hunkered in the dirt and picking up a stick, sketched a map of the valley. "My notion is to divide the valley. If others come in, we'll make room for 'em. As long as we can, anyhow. What I'm saying is that this can be a good cattle country for all of us. A lot of folks can make a living here without fighting and without making hogs out of ourselves."

He drew several lines across his map. "I ain't trying to tell you how to divide the valley, but it might work like this.

Fawcett here." He made an F. "Scanlon here." He went on down the line, following the east side of the creek, filling in initials until he was finished. "It means buying good bulls and more cows. Putting up buildings and corrals. Going off and leaving what you've done here." He rose, facing them, and added, "Remember one thing. If you'd knocked Sam Cody's ears down a long time ago, you wouldn't be up here." He pointed at his map. "You'd be down here."

"Damn it to hell," Fawcett burst out. "This is worse than a fairy tale. We're trying to think of some way to save our homes, not move back to the creek and give Peg Cody a real excuse to wipe us out."

"You mean you wouldn't go back to the creek, Abe?" Kim asked. "That's funny. They tell me you used to be quite a cowman."

Fawcett got red in the face; his fat jowls were trembling again. He tried to say something and failed. Then Joe Scanlon said, "Even if we did move in on Clawhammer and made it stick, this would take money. We couldn't swing it, Logan."

"Brit Bonham's got money to loan," Kim said, "I talked to him about it yesterday. I claim that a lot of little outfits will bring more prosperity to this country than two big ones. Brit will gamble, providing you boys will gamble your lives."

"We've got till sunset," Clay Mackey said worriedly.

"Maybe not that long. I'm guessing, but I figure Peg will leave her crew with the herd. It's Dunning's bunch we'll have to fight. Near as I can read the sign, there was nine or ten men here yesterday. That tallies with what Dunning's got." Kim pinned his eyes on Mackey. "If Peg was pulling her crew in, your boys would have been home before this, wouldn't they?"

"That's right," Mackey said, "if they knew what was up."

"I know the way Peg thinks," Kim went on. "It'll be cattle first and fight second. We lick Dunning and our troubles are over."

"Not if we're moving back on the creek." Scanlon pointed

at the map. "That's Clawhammer range you're giving away."

"Clawhammer's done," Kim said. "Peg don't know it, but that's the way it is, providing we finish Dunning. The bank will close Peg out."

Fawcett shook his head doubtfully. "Don't make sense to me. Bonham won't close her out."

"He will. You'll see."

Fawcett swung o face his neighbors. "I wanted you boys to see this. Maybe it's Dunning or maybe it's Clawhammer, or both. Whichever way it is, you see what you're up against. Now we'd best get home. We'll keep our eyes open and..."

"No," Kim said.

Fawcett wheeled to face him. "You ain't giving the orders."

"I am if I'm with you in this ruckus."

"He said he knew what to do," Scanlon said.

"All right," Fawcett muttered reluctantly. "If you've got a plan, let's hear it."

"Fighting's an old game to me," Kim said, "but a blind man could se it's new to you. If you go back to your homes, you're licked. Dunning will knock you off one at a time. The only chance you've got is to stick together and take the fight to them. If you want your women safe, let Della fetch 'em to her place."

"There wouldn't be nobody there to fight..." Fawcett began.

"I've got a hunch your women will put up quite a scrap. Now I'll tell you what I want you to do. Give me half an hour's start. Then you light out for Clawhammer, but don't go on down. Leave your horses on the bench, back a piece so they won't be seen from the house. Then you wait there. Keep watching. About noon or later Dunning and his boys will ride out. Let 'em get close before you give it to 'em. Surprise has won more fights than hot lead, and they'll sure be surprised."

"We'll be leaving our homes wide open," Scanlon objected.

"They'll be wide open if you all go home and figure on fighting by yourselves. That's what they'll expect. Dunning knows you boys ran once when Sam Cody wanted your places. He'll figure on your running again."

They looked at each other, bitter men, shamed by their past record, held here now only by their pride. Watching them, Kim could not be sure what the end would be. Welding them into a fighting unit was about as difficult as making a ball of dry sand.

"All right," Clay Mackey said at last. "We'll be there."

Kim mounted his horse.

"Where are you going?" Fawcett demanded.

"To Clawhammer."

"You can't, Kim," Della cried. "They'll kill you."

"Maybe," Kim agreed, "but I'm figuring on surprise being on my side. Anyhow, there's a thing or two I need to know."

"And something they'll need to know," Scanlon shouted. "You can tell 'em where we'll be."

"I could." Kim turned to his buckskin and stepped up. He sat his saddle, eyes searching their faces, worried and uncertain. He said, "I may need some help if it don't go like I figure."

"If Rocky was here, she wouldn't let you do this," Della said.

Leaning down, he said in a low tone, "I've never told Rocky I love her. If I don't see her again, I'd like for her to know." Reining his horse around, he rode across the clearing and into the timber.

CHAPTER 18
IN THE LION'S MOUTH

It was well toward noon when Kim reached the bench above Clawhammer and looked down upon the big house and barns and maze of corrals. Sam Cody had built well, certain of his future and equally certain that he had trained Peg to run the ranch as efficiently as he had. But there are always two uncertain factors over which a cowman has little control, weather and the price of beef. They had combined to beat bigger men than Sam Cody, and they had beaten him.

The early trouble in the valley was ancient history. Kim had never heard the whole story, but he knew enough. History never fully died; fingers of the past continually reach into the future, and it was that way with Clawhammer. Peg had inherited Sam Cody's ambition and lax ethics, so she was using the same ruthless, pushing tactics he had used.

Kim, sitting his saddle at the edge of the bench, found the same questions prodding his mind that had been there for hours. How much had Peg ever really counted on him? Had she turned fully to Dutch Heinz? Had she gone to Dunning or had Dunning come to her? That was the difference between her and her father. She was forced to look to men to help carry out her plans, Sam had needed no one.

Still, the answers to these questions were not important, not when Kim thought of Yuma Bill, of Shorty Avis and the ashes that had been his and Rocky's home. If the chance came, Kim would kill Hank Dunning as quickly as he would kill any wild animal that needed killing. He would do the same to Dutch Heinz. But it was different with Peg. In that way her woman's weakness was her strength. He could not beat her down with his fists; he could not draw a gun on her. Even the law would not touch her unless the evidence against her was conclusive. So far it was not.

Kim rode down off the bench and crossed the creek. He could not make a definite plan of action until he saw the shape of things. There were those who would have said he was crazy for coming in like this, but it seemed worth the risk. Regardless of the part Peg had in the trouble, Hank Dunning was the hub around which it revolved. If Dunning was dead, trouble would disintegrate like a whirling wheel coming apart, and a dozen lives would be saved. It was a gamble, Kim Logan's life balanced against those that might be saved.

There was a knot of men in front of the barn. Dunning's riders, Kim saw as he came up, but Dunning wasn't with them. They were covertly watching Kim while appearing to be idling there. Limpy was not in sight. Neither was Dutch Heinz.

It was as peaceful a scene as a man would find, too peaceful, and Kim was warned by the very innocence of it. He reined up and dismounted, keeping the buckskin between him and the men by the barn. While he tied, his eyes swept the yard. Apparently no one else was around. He stepped away from the hitch pole and deliberately rolled a smoke, standing so that Dunning's men could see him.

The thing was wrong. It was too casual, so casual that it must have been carefully planned to appear this way. Kim felt a chill ravel down his spine as he considered the two things he could do. He could walk straight toward Dunning's crew with his gun in his hand, or he could ignore them and go into the house. Dunning was probably inside, and because Dunning was the man he wanted, he chose the house. It was too late to back out now. He had to play it through.

He fired his cigarette and flipped the match away, then turned up the path to the house. The front door was open. No one was in sight in the big living room. He stepped up on the porch, throwing a quick glance at the men in front of the barn. They were openly watching him now, tense. He went on across the porch, hand on gun butt. If he read the sign right, this was trouble.

Kim stepped through the door. He had no chance to pull his gun. Dutch Heinz was waiting for him, back pressed against the wall. He slammed into Kim, big fist battering him in the stomach. It was treacherous and unexpected, a brutal blow that slammed wind out of him and sent him reeling back through the door. He had a brief glimpse of Peg and Dunning behind Heinz; he heard a yell from the men at the barn and the pound of boots as they ran toward the house.

Heinz had a slow stubborn mind, the sort that never

forgave an old injury. Now the need to square accounts with Kim made a driving maniac out of him. He hammered Kim with one fist and then the other, in the stomach, on the chest, on the head. Kim had been caught off balance and kept that way; he had no chance to swing an effective fist. He backed across the porch, trying to block Heinz's blows, to hold long enough to gain the initiative, but it was like trying to dam a stream in high flood.

Kim fell backward off the porch. He landed on his back and yanked his gun clear of leather. Heinz was poised on the edge of the porch, instinctively planning to jump on him, but he held himself there, teetering and swearing in a tough wicked voice. Kim lay motionless, gun tilted up to cover Heinz, while he fought to drag breath into aching lungs.

Dunning's men were there then, but they didn't close in, for the first move would have brought death to Heinz. Slowly Kim came to his feet. He said, "You've got an iron, Dutch. I'm putting mine back. Then we'll settle this."

Heinz shook his head. "Not me. I heard about Tonto Miles." He motioned to Dunning's men. "You're done, Logan. Too many of us. What'n hell did you ride in here for?"

"I didn't expect this." Kim backed away now so that he could watch Heinz and Dunning's crew. "I thought you'd be out of the country. Ed Lane's looking for you."

Heinz laughed jeeringly. "Not now he ain't. He was out here this morning, but he decided he didn't want to be sheriff no more. He's halfway to Del Norte by now."

"He resigned?"

"Resigned? Hell, he quit. We don't have no sheriff at all now, not any."

Dunning had crossed the porch to stand beside Heinz, towering above him, his black hair rebellious and uncombed. A smile touched the corners of his long-lipped mouth; his dark eyes seemed entirely lacking in expression. Somehow Dunning was able to clothe himself with a sort of arrogant dignity. It was that dignity which had given him the reputation he had in the valley.

"Why are you here, Logan?" Dunning asked.

"Natural enough for me to be here," Kim answered. "But it ain't for you. Or maybe you're taking Clawhammer over."

Dunning shrugged. "Now maybe I am. Or put it the other way. Clawhammer's taking HD over. I want to know why you're here."

"I want to see Peg."

Dunning jerked his head at the door. "Put your gun up. She's inside."

"I'll keep my gun in my fist. I'm not giving my back to your wolf pack."

"Drop your gun, Kim," Peg called. "You'll have a chance to see me, but not with a gun in your hand."

She was behind him. She must have gone out through the back door and come around the house. He made a slow turn; he saw the Winchester in her hands. He had no doubt she would use it, for she was very close now to the thing she had been working for.

"Looks like your pot," Kim said, and shoved his gun into holster.

That was when Heinz came off the porch in a headlong rush. Kim whirled and sidestepped and swung a fist to Heinz's face as he charged by. Then the roof fell on Kim. Dunning's crew swarmed over him and he went down. He struck out, squirmed and kicked, tried to roll, to break free, to get space in which to fight, but there were too many. They smothered him by sheer weight, but even then, with consciousness almost battered out of him, he heard Peg's voice, "Quit it. That's enough. Damn you, I said it was enough."

Kim lay on his back, winded and hurt, staring up at men who seemed to be ten feet tall. They had backed away, and Peg was standing over Kim, her cocked Winchester held on the ready. "Hank, maybe it was a good thing this happened. Now get this through your head. Marrying me won't make any difference about one thing. I'm giving the orders on

Clawhammer and I'll keep on giving them."

"You're forgetting Chuck Dale," Dunning said in a low bitter voice. "He's the boy I lost off the rim the day Logan brought Yuma Bill here. You're forgetting Tonto Miles and Pat Monroney. And you're forgetting you said Logan was just a drifter you could get rid of any time you wanted to. He's blocked everything we've tried from the minute he took Yuma Bill off the stage, and I aim to stop it."

"I'm not going to stand here and let your boys kick him to death," Peg snapped. "Not after I told him he'd have a chance to see me."

"He's been damned hard to kill," Dunning said in the same bitter tone. "We'd best do the job while we've got his fangs pulled."

"He'll wait," Peg said. "Your boys have got a job to do. Get them started on it."

"Not time yet," Dunning said.

For a moment they stood facing each other, straight-backed and proud, their wills clashing. Then Dunning broke under the force of Peg's stare, and turning, motioned his men back to the barn.

Heinz remained by the steps, great shoulders hunched forward in the ape-like posture that was characteristic of him. He said, "You've made some mistakes before, Peg, but saving this hombre's hide is the biggest one. You're soft."

"Soft?" Peg shook her head. "Not me, Dutch. I just think a little farther than you do. Kim may be some good to us alive, but he's no good to anybody if he's dead." She prodded Kim with a toe. "Get up. I'm locking you in the storeroom."

Kim got to his feet, reeling a little as he wiped a sleeve across his battered face. Peg pulled his gun. He stood staring at her, his vision clearing. She was wearing riding clothes; her red hair was carelessly pinned on the back of her head, and her hazel eyes that he had so often seen filled with good humor were sharp and calculating.

Turning, Kim walked past the glowering Heinz and into

the house. He went on through the kitchen and into the storeroom behind it, stumbling occasionally, for he was still groggy from the beating he had taken. He dropped down on a sack of sugar and held his head, a steady pain flashing across his temples.

Peg stood in the doorway a moment, looking at h m. She said, "I wish you hadn't come here, Kim, I wish you hadn't." She stepped back and, closing the door, twisted the turnpin. There had been a note of sincere regret in her voice as if she had been talking to a man condemned to death.

CHAPTER 19
ALL BETS ARE DOWN

Kim Logan had never been one to doubt his own destiny, but there were doubts in his mind now. He was in a tighter spot than when Ed Lane had locked him up in the Ganado jail. He'd had a few friends in town, but here he had none.

He walked around the room that was filled with the composite food smells of Clawhammer's supplies. Sam Cody must have planned it for a jail. There were only two windows, both high and one so small that a grown man could not have escaped through either of them. The door was at the other end of the room. Kim had often noticed it when there had been no thought in his mind that some day he would be held behind it, and he had wondered why a mere storeroom needed a door so thick and so solidly hinged.

Kim put a shoulder against the door and pushed. There was no give to it. He stepped away and slammed against it and bounced back. No use. Tactics like that would get him nothing but a sprained shoulder. Kim, always a realist, had no illusions about his position. It was practically hopeless. He didn't know why Peg had saved his life, but he was sure of one thing. Sooner or later Dunning and Heinz would wear her down, and they'd have their way with him.

It must have been close to an hour after Kim had been locked in the storeroom that the door swung open. Limpy came in with a plate of food and a steaming cup of coffee. Peg stood behind him in the doorway with her Winchester. She said, "I'm going to town this afternoon and I didn't want you to get hungry."

Limpy set the plate and cup down on a box of condensed milk. He said, "You sure played hell coming back, L gan. Why didn't you have sense enough to stay away?"

"I didn't figure Peg meant it when she said I was fired," Kim answered.

Peg waited until Limpy left the storeroom. Then she said, "Don't try to jump me. Hank and Dutch want to see you dead. I don't."

"Maybe you mean you don't want the job of beefing me. You can always hire somebody to do dirty jobs like that."

Two spots of red showed on her cheeks, but she held her temper. "No, I don't mean that. I don't want you killed, but I don't know what to do with you." She made a gesture with a hand as if begging him to believe her. "I've done some things I'm ashamed of because I've been a little crazy with my dreams about Clawhammer, but I haven't knowingly been guilty of murder. Please believe that."

"Maybe you think Yuma Bill died of measles."

"No. Dutch shot him, but not because I ordered it. I told him to take the money, but like a fool, he didn't wear a mask. so he killed the old man to shut his mouth."

Peg was silent a moment while she watched Kim eat. Then she asked, "Why did you really come here?"

"To get Dunning. That's what you hired me for."

"What made you think you'd find him here?"

"Rocky said you and him were working together. She says you're in love with him."

' You don't believe that," she flared.

"I'm wondering."

"Clawhammer's the only thing I love. You ought to know that by now."

"So you're marrying Dunning because you love Clawhammer. Now that makes a lot of sense."

"Of course it does. After I marry Hank there won't be any HD. Just Clawhammer range on both sides of the creek."

"Think you can run Dunning?"

"Of course. I never saw a man I couldn't run. Except you." She shook her head. "Kim, I'm sorry the way it's gone between us, but I gave you every chance that night and ou wouldn't take it."

"You'd already promised Dunning, hadn't you?"

She shrugged. "A promise doesn't mean much to me. I aimed to buy the best husband for Clawhammer I could get. I thought for a while you'd be the one, but that night I found out you had too many fool notions about the mesa ranchers."

"Clawhammer's got along without the mesa range."

"It won't. Not with the plans I have. Anyhow, you're too soft. Or maybe it was because you're in love with Rocky Avis. Anyhow, I found out you wouldn't do."

"No, I reckon I wouldn't, but nobody ever said I was soft before. Looks to me like you've got some pretty big schemes cooked up for Clawhammer, or you wouldn't want the mesa range so bad."

She nodded, letting him see the satisfaction that was in her. "I have. I'm not patient, Kim, and I won't grow old waiting to do what I want to do. Clawhammer will be the biggest outfit in the state. Maybe in the nation. I'll have the valley and the mesa and the high range to boot. All mine just like I told you that night."

"The little fry won't run, Peg. You're spreading too far. You've fixed it so you've got to win or you're finished."

She laughed scornfully. "I will win, and you're loco about the little fry. They'll run all right. Dad's mistake was in not chasing them across the divide when he moved them off the creek."

"You're wrong, Peg. Why can't you hang onto what you've got and be satisfied?"

"I wasn't born to be satisfied. I know people, so I don't have the slightest doubt about the way this will go. When a man has run once he'll run again. That's why I'm going to town this afternoon. They'll be there to sell to me."

"You gave the order to bust Shorty Avis up?"

She nodded. "I had to show them what would happen if they had any notion of fighting. Before I'm done, I'll have the little fry off the other side of the valley, too."

Kim finished his meal, thinking he had heard the truth from Peg at last. She was a greedy fool reaching for everything when most people would have been satisfied with what she had. She had been carried away by the magnificence of her dreams, she was counting on Hank Dunning and Dutch Heinz, and in the end she would destroy herself.

"Funny thing," he said. "I guess I know you better than anyone in the valley."

She laughed lightly. "Of course you do. I still wish you were on my side, but it's too late now." Her face turned grave then. "You're like the rest of them, Kim, a sucker for a kiss, but you insist on still being a man, and that's the reason I knew I couldn't manage you." She motioned toward the rear wall. "Step back and I'll get your plate and cup. I've got to ride."

He moved back, asking. "Why did you hire me in the first place and put out this fake war talk?"

"Money. That's the whole answer. I wanted a lot of money to stock Clawhammer range, so I borrowed thirty thousand from Bonham. I got his sympathy by telling him Dunning would push me off the range if I didn't hold it. Of course I didn't want him or anyone else to know that Dunning was going to work up a rush on his bank so we could buy my notes back. It would have worked if you hadn't delivered Yuma Bill's money."

Peg picked up Kim's plate and cup and moved back to the door, smiling ruefully. "As for hiring you, I had to make some show of protecting myself against Hank. You rode in just when I was looking for a tough hand and you looked like one. At the time I didn't realize you really were a tough hand." She stood there a moment looking at him, frowning. "Maybe I'll figure out what to do with you while I'm gone. I just wish you'd ridden off like I told you to."

He said nothing while she moved out of the storeroom, her Winchester covering him until the door swung shut. It was clear enough now. Bonham had fallen into Peg's trap when he'd loaned her the thirty thousand, and the fake war had accomplished exactly what Peg had wanted it to. She was a woman pretending to hold out against a ruthless neighbor, and because she was a woman, she had succeeded in winning sympathy, something old Sam Cody had never done. In her way she was a genius, a great actress hiding her real ambition from Brit Bonham and Doc Frazee and the rest of the townsmen.

Thirty thousand dollars for ten! That was how her deal with Bonham had meant to work. Dunning had been in Bonham's office that morning trying to buy Peg's notes and Bonham had come very close to making the deal. Kim laughed, a sour laugh, for it was a sour kind of joke, this sympathy they'd had for Peg while she had been planning a neat profit of twenty thousand.

It hadn't worked, but still Peg was talking about having the biggest outfit in the state or even in the nation. Wild talk, the crazy talk of a woman consumed by her ambition. Crazy or not, she was coldly logical. It meant, then, that she had another idea to make quick money, a lot of money, for her grandiose plans would not include any penny-ante business.

A sense of futility touched Kim. This thing still had to be fought to its final irrevocable end. Dunning and Dutch Heinz had to die, and Peg would have to leave the valley, but here he was, a prisoner without any kind of a weapon. The chances were good that while Peg was gone, Heinz would come in and shoot him.

Thinking about it now, Kim realized that for all of Peg's expressed love for Clawhammer and her wild dreams about it, there was a real difference between her and Dutch Heinz and Dunning. She had a soft spot whether she would admit it or not. Heinz and Dunning did not. She had saved his life today. By that one act she had showed that the gulf between her and these men she thought she was using was wide and deep.

There was no sense in sitting here and waiting for Heinz to come in and finish him. He began searching the room for some kind of a weapon, any kind that would give him a chance. There was nothing. Not even an ax handle. Then, in desperation, he kicked a flour barrel apart, coughing as a white cloud swirled up around his head. He picked up a stave, balanced it in his hand, and shook his head. A sorry weapon, but the best he could find.

He walked to the door, shoved some boxes out of the corner, and moved into it, putting his back against the wall. Somebody would come after him, probably Heinz, and if he didn't see Kim, it would be natural enough to step inside. The barrel stave, brought down in a sharp blow across a man's wrist, would make him drop a gun. Then Kim would have a chance, for the blow would be painful and there would p obably be a moment of shocked surprise that would give Kim an opportunity to beat him to the dropped gun.

The big house must have been deserted, for no sound came from it as the minutes dragged by. Then another hope came to Kim. Perhaps Dunning and Heinz had ridden out. They might not return until after Peg did. Still, it was a thin hope. She had saved his life once; it was doubtful if she could do it again.

Suddenly Kim was aware of gunfire. He ran to a window and looked out, but he could not see anyone. The shooting came from the north, and he could see nothing but the bench which lay directly behind the house. He turned back to the door, anxiety growing in him. He guessed what had happened. The mesa ranchers had waited on the other side of the creek, and when Dunning and his bunch had left Clawhammer, they'd ridden into an unexpected fight.

The firing grew closer. Then Kim heard steps on the

kitchen floor. He drew back into his corner, raising the stave. The door was pulled open, and Limpy called, "Logan! Logan! Where the hell are you?"

Kim's hands tightened on the stave, nerves tense, but Limpy did not come in He remained in the kitchen just outside the door, and he cried out again, his voice frantic. "Logan, here's your gun. No sense hiding this way. I don't like Dunning's bunch no better than you do."

Kim didn't understand, but this was no time to wonder why Limpy was doing this. The shooting was close now, almost in front of the house. Kim lunged through the door, slamming Limpy down and knocking the gun out of his hand.

"What'd you do that for?" the old man yelled. "Hell, I was just trying to help..."

Kim scooped up the gun. "I didn't know whether you were alone or not."

"Nobody else around here who'd give you a hand," Limpy cried. "I can see through that damned horse thief of a Dunning if Peg can't. I kept telling her she had no business letting him come around here. She can't make no silk purse out of a sow's ear. She should have taken a shotgun to Dunning the first time . . ."

But Kim wasn't waiting to hear the old man. He checked the gun and ran out of the kitchen and through the living room and on to the porch. The fight was directly in front of the house. It was the last thing Kim expected. The mesa ranchers had got the jump on Dunning's riders and had chased them back across the creek.

For a moment here seemed to be no pattern to the fight. The yard was filled with milling horses, smoke made a swirling fog over them, guns roared, and men shouted and bawled out wild oaths and cried shrilly in agony. Kim stepped down off the porch, thinking that this would be the end, one way or the other, that it could be fought out to a final bloody end here in Clawhammer's yard.

Dutch Heinz's great voice bawled out an order above the

uproar "Inside. Inside." Kim saw Heinz come off his horse and plunge toward the house, some of Dunning's crew following.

Then Heinz saw Kim and he stopped flat-footed, a strangled involuntary cry coming out of him. Kim sensed the fear that was in the man; he had this one quick look at the wide-jawed face. Heinz had his gun in his hand. He came on now, lifting his .45 and throwing a shot at Kim that came too late, for Kim had laced a bullet into his great chest.

Heinz rocked forward and fell, hands flung out, and lay still. Kim stepped over him and went on. He felt the sting of a slug gouging flesh away from a rib; he fired again and knocked another man off his feet. Limpy, on the porch behind Kim, let go with a shotgun, the load of buckshot blowing a huge hole in a man's stomach.

It was enough. Caught between Kim's and Limpy's fire on one side and that of the mesa ranchers' on the other, the rest of Dunning's outfit threw up their hands. Kim called out, "Hold it. Hold it."

There were four of them still on their feet, two wounded and two untouched by bullets but badly scared and having all desire for fighting knocked out of them. Kim kept them covered until Abe Fawcett tramped up, his neighbors strung out behind him, some bleeding from bullet wounds and all filled with the glow of complete and unexpected victory.

"Where's Dunning?" Kim demanded.

Fawcett stopped, surprised as if he had not thought of Dunning, and stared at the dead men on the ground. He said, "Why, I never saw Dunning. Maybe he wasn't with 'em."

"He wasn't," Joe Scanlon said. "I'll swear to it, Logan, Heinz was running the outfit. They rode right into us. Didn't figure we were within ten miles of here. It was like you said. Surprise was worth a couple of cannons. We knocked hell out of 'em with the first volley. They lit out for here and we got on their tails as soon as we could hit leather."

Kim motioned to Fawcett. "Take these hombres inside. Patch 'em. Looks like some of your boys need a little patching, too." He swung to face Limpy. "Where's Dunning?"

Limpy threw a scared look at the mesa men. "Kim, you tell these hombres I helped you. Tell 'em I didn't like Dunning and Heinz, neither."

"All right, all right," Kim said hurriedly. "Hear that, Abe? Limpy's on our side. Treat him right."

"You bet," Fawcett said. "I seen what he done with that scatter-gun."

"Where's Dunning?" Kim as ed again.

But Limpy was not to be hurried. "What about Peg? This ain't her fault. It was Dunning's and Heinz's."

"I want to know where Dunning is." Kim shouted in exasperation. "What's the matter with you?"

Limpy gripped his shotgun with white-knuckled hands, harried eyes swinging around the half circle of men in front of him. "He's in town. Rode in with Peg. I want to know about her. I promised Sam the day he died that I'd look out for her. I tried to keep her out of this, but she was too damned stubborn to listen. You can't hang a woman. What about her, Kim?"

"She's got to leave the valley," Kim said. "If she don't try to make more trouble, she won't be hurt. That's the only promise I can make."

Limpy licked dry lips, trembling now as he pinned his gaze on Kim. "Dunning aimed to show up in town and tell folks that him and Peg had buried the hatchet. No more trouble. Then about dusk he was gonna leave. These fellers was supposed to run everybody off the mesa this afternoon and they'd swear Dunning was with 'em all night. Then after dark he was going back to town to rob the bank. He was gonna take all the cash and get Peg's notes."

Then it wasn't over. It wouldn't be over until Hank Dunning was dead. Kim put a hand to his side where the bullet had raked a rib. He threw his hand away and stared lankly at the blood, trying to think what was to be done.

Scanlon shouted, "Let's go get Dunning and hang him."

"I'll get him," Kim said. "I'll send Doc out. Take care of

your wounded. I'll fetch Heinz's body with me so Dunning will see how it is. You can bring the rest in later."

"You'll need help," Scanlon said.

Kim shook his head. "No. This is my job. I'll do it. Alone."

CHAPTER 20
DUST TO DUST

It was late afternoon when Kim reached the fringe of cabins that surrounded Ganado. He was leading Heinz's horse, the dead man lashed face-down across the saddle. All the way in from Clawmhammer he had thought about Peg. She had saved his life today. He would probably never know exactly what her motive had been, but regardless of motive, the fact that she had saved his life could not be questioned. Whatever she had done and planned to do, he owed a debt to her.

Before Kim had left Clawhammer, Limpy had drawn him aside, saying, "Peg just couldn't look ahead. That was her whole trouble. She ain't bad. She was just mixed up about what she could make men do. Dunning wanted to marry her all right, but then there wouldn't have been no Clawhammer. Just HD. Heinz knew that, but Dunning was paying him on the side, unbeknownst to Peg. All them shenanigans like busting Bonham and getting Peg's notes cheap was Dunning's ideas. If Sam had lived, he'd have busted Dunning sooner or later, but after Sam cashed in, Dunning set to work on Peg, telling her how they'd have the biggest outfit in the valley, chase the little fellers out and put more cows on this range than there is in the state of Texas. She took it all in, bait, hook, and sinker."

Limpy had gripped Kim's arm then. "I tell you she ain't bad, boy. Young and foolish and full of big wild ideas. That's all. She just didn't see all the misery she was bringing on the valley. Take care of her, will you?"

There was nothing for Kim to say except to repeat, "She'll have to leave the valley. She won't be hurt if she does."

"Then I'll go with her," Limpy said. "Tell her that."

Now, with Ganado before him, Kim did not know what to say to Peg, or what he could make her do. His thoughts were on her rather than Dunning, for there was no doubt of Dunning's part in this trouble but there was of Peg's. She was stubborn and she was proud, and she would not easily give up the fine dreams that had been hers.

He remembered his talk with her the night he had brought Yuma Bill to Clawhammer. She had said she'd stayed awake at nights, dreaming about what she was going to do and thinking of the mistakes her father had made. She wouldn't make them; she would use the weapons the Lord gave a woman. That had been her mistake. Now, thinking about her and about old Sam Cody, it struck Kim that it was Sam who was really to blame for what Peg had done. He had died, plagued by a sense of failure, and Peg, possessed of the same big plans that had been in her father's mind, had been driven by an obsession to carry those plans to fulfillment.

Kim rode down Main Street, watching for Dunning and Peg, and seeing neither of them. He reined up and dismounted. Someone saw him and raised a cry, Kim waited while men crowded around him, Bonham and Doc Frazee and Johnny Naylor and half a dozen more, all throwing questions at him.

Kim handed Bonham a heavy money belt. "I reckon that's Yuma Bill's. I took it off Heinz." He told them what had happened. Then he sensed that something was wrong and stopped talking.

Bonham said softly, "There's Dunning."

Men spilled away as Kim made a slow turn. Dunning stood in front of the hotel, bare-headed, black hair freshly trimmed and slicked down. Peg was behind him in the lobby, staring through a window, and at this distance Kim could not see the expression that was on her face. But there was no mistaking Dunning's.

The HD owner must have been surprised to see Kim; he must have been more surprised when he saw Heinz's body. But there was more than surprise on his eagle-beaked face. There was a cold and bitter hatred for this man whom he had regarded too lightly. His long lips were pulled so tightly against his teeth that they made a thin bitter line; he still wore his cloak of arrogant dignity, but the air of cool assurance that was usually a part of him was gone. Kim thought, *He can't duck a fight now and he knows it.*

Kim stood motionless a few feet in front of the horse that carried Heinz's body, the slanting sunlight hard upon him, his shadow a long dark streak at his side. He was remembering Tonto Miles and his own thoughts when he had fought Miles. He had been forced to kill the man to get at Dunning. Now the moment was here.

The seconds ticked by; the town was very quiet, waiting. Still Dunning stood there, tall, his hawk-nosed face mirroring the cold rage that gripped him. Then Kim laid his voice against the man, "Your string's wound up, Dunning. The mesa bunch was waiting for your outfit and shot hell out of 'em."

Dunning stepped down off the walk, hand within inches of gun butt, black eyes on Kim as he took two deliberate steps. There was a chance for him even at this time if he could outdraw Kim, for the valley people had long been in the habit of obeying him, and such a habit would be hard to break as long as he could beat down those who had the courage to stand against him.

Two deliberate steps. That was all, then his hand moved toward gun butt, very fast, and the barrel was clear of leather and coming up. Two shots rolled out together, the reports hammering against the false front of Ganado's Main Street, hammered out and were thrown back, and faded. Two shots, no more. Kim stood motionless, smoke curling up from the muzzle of his .44, and waited until Dunning's knees gave and he spilled forward and the slanting sunlight fell across his back.

Someone yelled from the front of the drugstore, a high yell that was almost a scream. Another gun sounded from the boardwalk behind Kim and to his right. He whirled, his .44 coming up. Then he lowered it. It was Johnny Naylor who had fired. He held his Colt in front of him, eyes fixed on the drugstore. Kim, turning to look, saw Phil Martin, clad only in his underwear, fall forward out of the doorway. Then Kim knew what had happened. Martin, dog-like in his devotion, had made this futile effort to square accounts for Hank Dunning.

"Thanks, Johnny," Kim said. "I didn't expect that from you."

Naylor gave him a tight grin. "Della's been currying me with her tongue ever since the stage got in. You're all right, Logan. She pounded that into me."

Kim slipped his gun into holster and walked across the street to the hotel. He stepped into the lobby. Peg stood motionless at the window. She said without turning, "Looks like I put my money on the wrong man."

"The wrong man," he said, and walked to her. "Now you're finished."

"You haven't touched Clawhammer," she said.

"Bonham will do that. The biggest mistake you made was to think that because a man ran once he'd run again." He told her what had happened at Clawhammer, and added, "You've got one chance to get out of here with a little money in your pocket. Go see Brit. Sell for anything he'll give you. Otherwise he'll close you out and you'll have nothing."

"I'm remembering you saved my life this morning, Peg. I'd like to do more for you, but I can't. You'll have to leave the valley."

Dunning's and Heinz's bodies had been moved from the street, but men still stood in little groups talking about what had happened. She made a slow turn from the window and looked at Kim, her face softening. She asked, "Why do you want to help me?"

"I told you," he answered. "You saved my life."

"That all?"

There was more, much more, but he had no words to tell her about this fault of his, this loyalty to Clawhammer that had been as misplaced as her faith in Dutch Heinz had been. But it was not a question of loyalty now. If she stayed, there would be more trouble. There had been enough.

He said, "That's all. You haven't got a friend in the valley but Limpy. He said to tell you he'll go with you."

"Not a friend in the valley," she said as if talking to herself. "I'm Sam Cody's girl. I guess that's the whole trouble. He never tried to make friends. I have, but now there's just Limpy." She put her hands behind her back, fingers laced together, eyes pinned on his lean face. "You've been right about a lot of things, Kim, and I've been wrong. I guess you're right about this. I'll see Bonham and I'll ride out of the valley with Limpy."

If she felt any grief over Dunning's and Heinz's deaths, she gave no indication of it. She moved past him and left the hotel, her shoulders square, her back very straight, her face rigid, hiding any emotion that was in her.

Kim could not hate her, even when he thought of Yuma Bill. She had gambled everything that was important to her. She was to be pitied. It was a word he had never thought he would apply to Peg Cody. He knew that she was not escaping her punishment; she would never be free from the hell of her thoughts, the regret that came from failure.

Kim waited until Peg disappeared into the bank, then he walked to the drugstore. Doc Frazee stood in front with Luke Haines and Fred Galt. Kim said, "There's some men at Clawhammer who need you."

"I'll go out right away," Frazee said.

"Peg will be out for her things. Tell Fawcett and the rest of 'em that she's leaving the valley."

"I'll tell 'em." Frazee cleared his throat. "I've been waiting to talk to you before I went out there, Kim. Maybe you heard that Ed Lane had a stomachful of being sheriff and lit a shuck out of the country. How would you like the star?"

"I never packed a star in my life," Kim said.

"We ain't worried about how you'll make out," Frazee said quickly, and even Fred Galt nodded agreement. "We need a good man, now that we've got a new deal for the valley."

"Let me think about it, Doc," Kim said. "Right now I've got a ride to make."

Frazee grinned and winked. "Sure. And Shorty's gonna be all right. He came around before I left Fawcett's."

Turning, Kim strode to his horse and mounted, glad to hear that Shorty Avis would make it, for he had been afraid that Avis had been too badly injured to live. He rode out of town to the east, suddenly filled with a driving urgency to see Rocky, and his thoughts were filled with the things he must say to her.

Hours later he reached the Fawcett place. The door was open; he saw Rocky's slim figure in the rectangle of light and he forgot the words he had planned to say.

She ran to him, crying, "Kim, Kim," and he came down off his horse in a quick swinging motion and opened his arms to her. She was in them then, saying again, "Kim, Kim," and he knew what Yuma Bill had meant when he had said there were some things which lasted and a man had to find them for himself.

She drew back, and looked up at him, her hands cupped against his cheeks, and he remembered some of the things he had planned to say. "I love you," he said. "I never knew what love was before, but I've learned from you."

"I knew how I felt about you," she said simply, "and I kept hoping that sometime you'd feel the same way about me."

"But I was twins. You were loving the man you wanted me to be."

She laughed softly. "I was loving the man you were, the real Kim Logan. You just had to find out for yourself. When you came back, I knew you'd found out."

"I reckon you'd call that faith," he said. "You were right

about something else, too. About me being a snake stomper and not a brush popper. I kept telling myself I wanted a ranch, but seems like it's kind of hard to get away from stomping snakes. They asked me to sheriff, but if you. . ."

"No, Kim. It's what you want, isn't it?"

"Yes, but..."

"Then it's what I want."

He held her close against him, loving her and wanting her to know it. His drifting years were behind him, the years which had belonged to the old fiddle-footed Kim Logan that Brit Bonham had not entirely trusted, a Kim Logan who had known only the transient values of life. The past was a turned page; the future was a clean white one ready to be written upon. They would write upon it together, Kim Logan and Rocky Avis.

THERE WAS A SEASON — T.V. OLSEN

Winner Of The Golden Spur Award

A sprawling and magnificent novel, full of the sweeping grandeur and unforgettable beauty of the unconquered American continent—a remarkable story of glorious victories and tragic defeats, of perilous adventures and bloody battles to win the land.

Lt. Jefferson Davis has visions of greatness, but between him and a brilliant future lies the brutal Black Hawk War. In an incredible journey across the frontier, the young officer faces off against enemies known and unknown...tracking a cunning war chief who is making a merciless grab for power...fighting vicious diseases that decimate his troops before Indian arrows can cut them down...and struggling against incredible odds to return to the valiant woman he left behind. Guts, sweat, and grit are all Davis and his soldiers have in their favor. If that isn't enough, they'll wind up little more than dead legends.

__3652-5 $4.99 US/$5.99 CAN

ARROW IN THE SUN
T. V. OLSEN

Bestselling Author Of *Red Is The River*

The wagon train has only two survivors, the young soldier Honus Gant and beautiful, willful Cresta Lee. And they both know that the legendary Cheyenne chieftain Spotted Wolf will not rest until he catches them.

Gant is no one's idea of a hero—he is the first to admit that. He made a mistake joining the cavalry, and he's counting the days until he is a civilian and back east where he belongs. He doesn't want to protect Cresta Lee. He doesn't even like her. In fact, he's come to hate her guts.

The trouble is, Cresta is no ordinary girl. Once she was an Indian captive. Once she was Spotted Wolf's wife. Gant knows what will happen to Cresta if the bloodthirsty warrior captures her again, and he can't let that happen—even if it means risking his life to save her.

—3948-6 $4.50 US/$5.50 CAN

GLORIETA PASS

GORDON D. SHIRREFFS

Quint Kershaw—legendary mountain man, fighter, and lover—is called from the comforts of the land he loves to battle for the Union under Kit Carson. His mission is to help preserve New Mexico from the Confederate onslaught in a tempestuous time that will test the passions of both men and women.

His sons, David and Fransisco, turn deadly rivals for the love of a shrewd and beautiful woman. His daughter, Guadelupe, yearns deeply for the one man she can never have. And Quint himself once again comes face-to-face with golden-haired Jean Calhoun, the woman he has never gotten out of his mind, now suddenly available and as ravishing as ever.

—3777-7 $4.50 US/$5.50 CAN

Dorchester Publishing Co., Inc.
65 Commerce Road
Stamford, CT 06902

THE MANHUNTER GORDON D. SHIRREFFS

2 ACTION-PACKED WESTERNS IN ONE RIP-ROARIN' VOLUME!

"Written by the hand of a master!" —*New York Times*

The Apache Hunter. Lee Kershaw is out for the bounty on Yanozha, the ruthless Apache. But the brave is laying his own ambush—and soon Kershaw is being hunted by the deadliest enemy of all.
And in the same action-packed volume....
The Marauders. When Kershaw is hired to track down a shipment of stolen weapons, the trail leads to a bloodthirsty colonel carving his own empire out of Mexico. In his battle against the mad soldier, Kershaw will need all his strength and cunning—or the courage to die like a man.
__3872-2 **(two rip-roaring Westerns in one volume)** $4.99 US/$6.99 CAN

Bowman's Kid. With a silver button as his only clue, Lee Kershaw sets out to track down a boy abducted almost twenty years earlier by the Mescalero Indians. Kershaw has been warned to watch his back, but he hasn't earned his reputation as a gunman for nothing.
And in the same rip-roarin' volume....
Renegade's Trail. Kershaw has never met his match in the Arizona desert—until he is pitted against his ex-partner, the Apache Queho, in the world's most dangerous game: man hunting man.
__3850-1 **(two complete Westerns in one volume)** $4.99 US/$6.99 CAN

Dorchester Publishing Co., Inc.
65 Commerce Road
Stamford, CT 06902

Please add $1.75 for shipping and handling for the first book and $.50 for each book thereafter. NY, NYC, PA and CT residents, please add appropriate sales tax. No cash, stamps, or C.O.D.s. All orders shipped within 6 weeks via postal service book rate. Canadian orders require $2.00 extra postage and must be paid in U.S. dollars through a U.S. banking facility.

Name _____
Address _____
City _____ State _____ Zip _____
I have enclosed $_____ in payment for the checked book(s).
Payment <u>must</u> accompany all orders. ☐ Please send a free catalog.